The Sen...

By

Tory Richards

Editor: Alisha Corsi

Cover Design: Self Pub Book Covers.com/RavenandBlack

'Author's note: All characters depicted in this work of fiction are 18 years of age or older.'

Table of Contents

Chapter 1

R^{uby}

Shit! It was starting to rain. Usually I didn't mind the rain, but I hated driving in it. I pulled over into the right-hand lane and dropped my speed. That was the cause of half the accidents that occurred in the rain, people didn't know enough to slow down. They just continued on, ten miles over the speed limit, as if the roads hadn't turned to black ice, squinting through their windows that had fogged up so much that they couldn't see clearly.

I couldn't afford to have an accident. Or, rather, my old station wagon couldn't afford it. The old Ford doubled as my home. I knew that was pitiful, but that was my life, and I was okay with it. What I was looking for I wasn't sure. I just drove from small town to small town, working odd jobs until I'd saved up enough money to move on again. Living out of my car was a necessity, and a comfort that I was used to. Maybe someday I'd find a place that I wanted to stay, where I could put down roots and become a member of society. Right now that thought sounded good, considering the rain that was pelting down on my car in a way that would peel more of the paint off.

Did I miss anything? Not really. I had everything that I needed to get by. I was content with my life, moving around, making an occasional friend that opened their home to me for a home cooked meal and a chance to feel like I belonged. Soon it would be a year since I'd been on the road, and my next stop would be (I squinted at the sign ahead) Daytona Beach.

I smiled. Would I make it?

As the pelting rain slowed to a steady drizzle, I could just make out the turn-off. I could also see that there was an old truck parked at an odd angle on the shoulder of the highway. Figuring that someone must have run out of gas or broken down, and had probably walked the rest of the way to Daytona, I was about to keep

1

on driving by when I saw an old man sitting in the driver's seat. Not one to ignore someone who might need help, especially the elderly, I pulled over.

I turned off my car and glanced in the rearview mirror, finding that the back window was too fogged up to see anything more than the shadowy outline of the truck behind me. Grabbing my keys, I slipped them into the front pocket of my jeans as I made my way back to the rusty truck. By the time I reached his window I was soaked.

I smiled as he rolled down his window. "Hi, are you okay?" I guessed his age to be around seventy-five. His long, grey hair was pulled back into a long braid that reminded me of Willie Nelson.

"Hi there, cutie. Damned truck stopped running," he grumbled. "You know how to work on engines?"

I couldn't help it, I laughed. "Afraid not, but I can drive you somewhere to get help," I offered.

He shook his head. "Naw, been broke down before. It'll start in a little while."

"How long have you been here?"

"What time is it?"

Oh, God. I shook my head with a shrug.

"Guess about, oh, a couple of hours, maybe."

I could tell that he was guessing, and I looked him over to make sure he was okay. I'd already taken in the smell of cigarettes on him, but other than that his clothes appeared a little wrinkled, but clean. The t-shirt he was wearing revealed that his arms and neck was covered in tattoos that seemed to be faded. Some had lost their shape, too, as gravity wasn't kind to the aging body.

"Are you hungry or thirsty?" I questioned, wondering how long he'd really been stranded there. "I have some water and half a sandwich left over from lunch. You're welcome to them."

His smile grew, deepening the lines of age on his face. "That'd be real nice, cutie."

I turned and walked back to my car and retrieved an unopened bottle of water and my leftover tuna sandwich from the cooler on the back seat. On impulse, I also grabbed an apple. The rain began coming down even harder, but I was already as wet as I could get. My long hair was plastered to me, my cropped top was clinging to my breasts, my jeans were soaked, and my feet were making a squishy sound in my sneakers. A truck honked at me on the way by, and I had a feeling it was in response to my wet t-shirt, which I was sure made it obvious that I wasn't wearing a bra.

"Here you go." I handed him the water and food. "My name is Ruby."

"I'm Pops," he smiled, cramming half of the sandwich into his mouth with one bite.

Pops? Seemed like an odd name to me. "Is someone coming for you?"

He nodded. "My boy is on his way," he said around a full mouth. "Will ya keep me company till they get here?"

They? He must have more than one son on the way. "Sure, I don't mind." I leaned against the truck as we fell into a silence while he finished eating. As fast as the rain had come it suddenly stopped, leaving behind a steamy, humid heat. Before I knew it, Pops was opening his door and getting out.

"Thank you, cutie. That hit the spot." He slammed his door shut. "Wouldn't happen to have anything stronger than water, would ya?"

"You mean like soda?" I grinned. He made a face that told me that he meant something even stronger than that. "Sorry, no." I pulled the bulk of my hair forward and began to squeeze the water out of it.

I heard the distant sound of what I thought was thunder, until it grew closer and I realized that it was actually the rumble of motorcycles coming our way. I expected them to ride on past us, but when they slowed and pulled up behind Pops' truck I straightened nervously. They weren't just weekend bikers, I could tell that immediately by the way they were dressed and the air of danger that they exuded. The six men belonged to an honest to goodness motorcycle club, and their worn, leather cuts were decked out in colorful patches and name tags.

They looked serious, and mean as hell. As I watched them climb off their large bikes and slowly approach us, I added big and handsome to their description. I glanced at Pops, looking for a sign that he knew these bikers. If he didn't, I was going back to my car to retrieve my baseball bat out of the back seat. He just smiled and gave me a wink.

What was I worried about, anyway? We were on a busy public highway. I took a deep breath, smiled, and said in my usual, cheery tone, "Hi, boys."

I couldn't tell where their eyes were focused, since they were all wearing dark sunglasses. The man who appeared to be the leader, the hunk wearing the president's patch, came to a stop a couple of feet away from us. I began to feel self-conscious of my clinging, wet clothes, especially when I felt my nipples turn hard against my thin tee. I crossed my arms, but the quirk of the man's lips told me that it hadn't been fast enough.

Jerk!

"You pickin' up strays now, Pops?"

Ohmygod! The deep, gravelly tone of his voice was sexy as hell, and it did something quirky to my core. The man wasn't too bad on the eyes, either. He was taller than most, his sun-tanned skin pulled taut over his super hot muscles. He oozed dominance, and the clunky silver rings on his fingers screamed that they were his backup.

"'Bout damn time you got here," Pops grumbled, pushing away from his truck. "And be nice to cutie, here, she stopped to help, and fed me, too."

"Cutie?"

Now I knew that his eyes were full on me, and I could tell by the tilt of his head that he was looking me up and down, as if he had the right to. I didn't like his intimidation tactics, even if his presence was having an unexpected affect on my lady bits, something I'm sure he was accustomed to when it came to the opposite sex. The devil in me prompted me to lower my arms and slap my hands on my curvy hips in a move that I knew was challenging. A big mistake, I knew, when his sexy mouth turned up at both corners.

"Looks like a drowned rat to me." The bikers behind him laughed.

"Flattery will get you nowhere," I responded sarcastically, meeting what I thought were his eyes. I turned my attention back to Pops, putting my hand on his thin shoulder. "Now that your boy is here, I'll be on my way. It was nice meeting you." I glanced back at the group of bikers. "Goodbye, boys." I gave them a wave, eager to be on my way.

"Baby—" The sound of his growly voice made me stop in my tracks to look back at him. "You call me a boy again, and I'll be only too happy to show you that I'm a man."

My jaw dropped for a second before I recovered the wherewithal to snap it shut again. I didn't think. I never did, reacting first, as I usually did. I gave him a big wink, knowing that my ill-timed sense of humor was going to land me in trouble some day. "I suppose you'd like to think that you're man enough to try." I turned back around with a feel-good smile, feeling as if I'd put the cocky, too sexy biker in his place.

Loud guffaws sounded out, and Pops sputtered loudly. "She got you good!" His uncontrolled laughter turned into uncontrolled hacking, and for a moment I was worried that he wasn't going to catch his breath. "Girl's...got...balls."

"Can it, old man."

Gee, what a way to talk to his dad. I opened my car door, thankful for the vinyl seats as I slid my wet butt over them, and nearly screamed when the biker wedged his body between the door and me so that I couldn't close it. *How had he moved so fast?* I glanced up at him with a nervous laugh. "You scared the hell out of me!" I glanced back. Two of his friends were looking at the truck's engine while the others waited on their motorcycles. "You're not here to show me the difference between a boy and a man, are you?" I joked.

His laugh was deep and caused a shiver of awareness to travel down my spine. The man was just too sexy! "Naw, maybe some other time," he teased back. "Just want to thank you for helping Pops." His gaze went to my back seat and beyond, and I knew what he was seeing. "You living out of your car?" he frowned.

"Yeah," I nodded, still smiling. "I've been on the road for a while, and it's cheaper than getting a hotel room every night."

I knew that I didn't owe him an explanation, but it just slipped out unconsciously. Besides, my life was laid out right there for all to see. My back seat held everything that I owned, and behind that was my bedroom, complete with air mattress, blankets, and pillows.

"Not very safe," he commented with a deeper frown.

My smile grew bigger. "Been doing it for almost a year, and nothing's happened yet."

He released a deep breath, seeming to think hard about something. "Where are you heading next?"

I pointed to the road sign. "Daytona."

He dug for something in his back pocket and pulled out a business card. "Take this. You run into any trouble you call, okay?"

I quickly read it over, surprised that a biker would have a business card. It was for a garage. "I'm not planning on being here for very long."

"I don't care. For however long you're here, you're under my protection. You helped Pops, and I won't forget that."

I'd never had someone offer to take care of me, and I wasn't sure how to react. "I didn't really do anything other than offer him a drink and half of my sandwich."

He just stared at me long and hard before saying in a no-nonsense tone, "Call."

He started to turn around. "But, wait, you don't even know my name."

He kept walking. "Yeah I do, baby, it's Trouble."

I watched him in my side mirror, taking in the sexy way he filled out his faded jeans, before shrugging to myself and putting his card in the glove box, certain that I wouldn't need it.

Chapter 2

Tanner

I wasn't expecting Trouble to call. She seemed too independent and resilient to ask anyone for help, and that was just my opinion after knowing her for all of five minutes. The fact that she'd stopped to help Pops told me that she was confident in her ability to take care of herself. As far as I was concerned, she was too fucking trusting. A lone woman, a damned pretty one at that, didn't stop on the side of a highway to help an old tatted-up coot without putting herself at risk. Christ, she didn't know any of us, and yet she hadn't flinched with fear after we'd arrived. Most people became visibly shaken and cautious when facing a group of bikers dressed like us in cuts and patches.

That's why she was trouble. She hadn't shown an inkling of self-preservation around us, which told me that she didn't have much experience with MCs. Well, she couldn't have chosen a place that was more inundated with biker clubs and nomads than Daytona Beach. The year-round warm weather and easy access to the ocean was a magnet for bikers, and with Daytona Beach Bike Week approaching, she was going to be educated in the culture, whether she wanted to be or not.

I didn't like the thought of her, or any woman, living out of their car. It was too fucking dangerous. But she wasn't my concern. I had more pressing matters to worry about.

"Wow, cute as hell."

Mike thought every woman was cute, but this time I couldn't agree with him more. I didn't bother looking at him because I already knew what his crooked, smug grin looked like. "Yeah."

"Nice rack," he said.

Her wet tee had already given me an idea of what her large tits and those sweet little nipples would look like naked.

"Round ass," he continued.

My palms itched with the thought of being filled by those fleshy curves.

"Long legs."

Long enough to wrap around my waist while I was fucking her hard.

"I'd tap that in a heartbeat," Mike finally admitted. "Wrap that long, black hair around my wrist

and bury my dick inside her so deep she'd be gagging."

I knew he'd try, because he was a man-whore. I swung back to Rod and William. The hood was up on the truck, and they were both bent over the engine. Pops was standing next to them, giving them advice, a cigarette dangling out of the corner of his mouth. I frowned. It seemed like his truck breaking down was an everyday occurrence, and he refused to get a new one. "What's up this time?"

William's head came up. "Same fucking shit as usual," he grumbled. "The whole damned engine is about shot. Don't know how this piece of shit is still running."

Fitting for an ancient-as-hell truck. "Can you jury-rig it to get him home?" William nodded and went back to what he was doing. Pops and I locked eyes, but I kept quiet in the face of his stubbornness. We'd already had one too many heated conversations about him getting new wheels, but he was adamant that this was going to be his last truck and that it would last him until he went to meet his maker.

The old man was stubborn as hell, and angry, too. I couldn't blame him for that. He'd been a founding member of an outlaw MC back some forty years ago, but age and health issues had forced him to step down into a menial position in the club. It had been hard going from road captain, to VP, to taking over the books, and then being reduced to ordering consultant, which had been made up just so that he would have something to do. He'd spent years at the table as an officer, and in the thick of things on runs with his brothers, just for it to all end up at a desk. There was no fucking excitement in that, and eventually he'd retired.

We were all heading toward the same fate. It was just a matter of time. There were always going to be changes. Christ, in the fifteen years I'd been a member of the Sentinels I'd gone from prospect, to soldier, to enforcer, and now president. We were a small MC, twelve members only, but we were made up of vets who'd seen and experienced war. We knew how to carry out strategic missions for the good of our town and the club. Each one of us brought a different expertise to the table, and that made us a force to be reckoned with.

Our main goal was to take care of our town, as was the other Sentinel chapters that had popped up throughout the U.S. We weren't one-percenters, but other than not having the diamond patch, there wasn't much difference between us and them. Our reputation spoke for itself. Not many messed with us. We lived by our own rules, obeyed the laws, and kept any shit that we were involved with legal. Well, mostly legal.

Sometimes we were forced to take illegal measures to get the job done. The fact that none of us had been in prison yet was thanks to luck and pushing a little extra cash where it needed to go. For the most part we worked on the side of law enforcement, but a generous donation helped them to turn a blind eye when our type of support didn't exactly go by the books.

"Start the engine, Pops," I heard William say. I watched the old coot slide in behind the wheel and turn the key in the ignition. After a couple of tries and pumping the gas, the engine coughed and turned over.

"See?" Pops shot me a satisfied smirk. "Nothin' wrong with this ole truck. It'll be around a lot longer than I will."

I released a deep breath, running my hand over the bottom half of my mouth. I could hear the light snorts of my brothers, but they were smart in keeping any comments to themselves. They knew my frustration with Pops, and they knew that the time was coming sooner rather than later when I'd have to put my foot down and make some drastic changes. None of them wanted to be in my boots.

"See ya at home!" Pops shouted out the window as he pulled onto the highway and gunned his sputtering engine.

I shook my head, making the mistake of meeting Sid's gaze as I headed toward my bike. I could tell that he was about to say something, and I held up my hand. "Don't say it, I know," I grumbled.

He shrugged. "I feel for ya, brother, I really do."

"Yeah, well, you're lucky that your mom is still living." I swung my leg over the seat of my bike. "She keeps your old man home." Sid's parents were about ten years younger than Pops, and were retired doctors living in the Appalachian Mountains.

"Maybe it's time," Rod advised. I knew exactly what he was referring to.

"Yeah, brother. You know we love pops, but–" Gabe cut himself off, shrugging.

No one wanted to say the words that would gut me, because in the end it would gut Pops, too. You didn't retire an ex hard-core biker to an old folk's home, a place where people dropped off their aging parents because they couldn't deal with them anymore. Pops had always told me those places were where the old went to die, stating he'd rather eat a bullet than sit in a rocking chair all day, wrapped up in a blanket and drooling on himself.

No, no way in hell was I going to even consider putting him in a place like that. "Not gonna happen," I said firmly, kicking my bike to life. I revved up and took off toward the clubhouse bar, where I'd meet up with the rest of the crew.

Exiting off the highway onto A1A I traveled about three miles until the bar came into view. It had been a restaurant at one time, so there was plenty of parking. I'd had it renovated into a bar, designating a separate room for pool, and keeping a couple of rooms in the back for an office and storage. Since the place didn't open for business until later in the afternoon, we had the privacy we needed to conduct club meetings in the morning.

Later, when the hang a-rounds showed up, and they always did, we used the alley out back to relieve tension with them. It wasn't very classy, but none of us wanted to bring the women home, for obvious reasons. It was hard kicking a woman out of your bed and house after she'd spent the night giving it up, not to mention the drama that was connected with a woman's emotions once she'd convinced herself that she was special to you. I couldn't stand a clinging, whining woman.

Sid and Mark were the only two club members that had old ladies. The rest of us took care of our physical needs with the hang a-rounds that frequented the bar.

We didn't have clubhouse whores, or sweet butts, as they were known by some of the larger

biker clubs. We weren't that kind of club. Besides, we didn't want the hassle, expense, or the drama that that kind of situation could bring. My brothers and I owned legit businesses in and around the Daytona area, and because of that the twelve of us were pretty well-off financially. I owned a garage, and the bar, After Hours, which doubled as our clubhouse.

The parking lot was already filling up when we arrived. Weekends were wild in Daytona, a combination of bikers, tourists, and locals who knew where to go for a good time. There was nothing fancy about the bar. The atmosphere was dimly lit, the music loud, and we provided entertainment in the way of a couple of busty pole dancers. People didn't go there to sit around and be bored. The three waitresses were also eye-candy, and the two bartenders doubled as bouncers, and there was almost always a brother in the house to make sure that everything ran smoothly.

I opened the door to the haze of blue smoke and the sounds of Led Zeppelin. My gaze took in the whole scene in one quick glance. Jasmine was gyrating on the pole, naked, with the exception of two tiny pieces of fabric that amounted to a bikini. Bob was behind the bar working on an order that Anne, one of the waitresses, was waiting on. By the time the door closed behind us, my eyes had become adjusted to the dim atmosphere.

"Shit!" Gabe said beneath his breath behind me. I gave him a questioning look over my shoulder. "She's here." He nodded in the direction that he wanted me to look.

A woman sitting at a table with her friends was smiling from ear to ear and waving excitedly in our direction. Since her gaze was focused on something behind me, I knew that her enthusiasm was meant for Gabe. I chuckled without sympathy. I'd warned him that she was going to be trouble.

"Good luck, brother." I pivoted to the bar, thirsty for a beer. I had my own problems. I'd had a shit day at the garage. Parts we'd been waiting on hadn't arrived, which put the owner of an old corvette in a bad mood and threatening to take his business elsewhere. Then one of the boys had gotten hurt by slipping on some grease he'd spilled and been too fucking lazy to clean up. Finally, the call from Pops that he'd broken down again.

Breaking down on the side of the road was no big deal for most folks, but Pops was as old as dirt and not in the best health. The fact was that he shouldn't be driving at all, and him being on the road was a disaster waiting to happen. Being alone was going to do him in if I didn't do something about it, and soon. His argument that I lived with him didn't hold water. I was gone most of the day, some evenings, and on the weekends. The MC took up any time I had left after a day working at my garage.

I was able to grab a few hours a week at the bar with my brothers, or getting my rocks off to relieve some stress. I wanted to relieve a little stress now, thanks to the memory of the hot little number who'd stopped to help Pops. Christ, I'd like to tap that. There'd been something fresh and innocent about her, and I bet that she was a firecracker in bed. It didn't sit well with me that she was living out of her car, but that was out of my hands.

Besides, I had to deal with what I was going to do with Pops. I wasn't out to save the world, and thinking about pussy wasn't going to solve my fucking problem.

A high-pitched squeal drew my attention to a table in time to see Gabe's little girlfriend jump into his arms and wrap her legs around him. I shook my head and took up my usual stool at the bar. He was good and screwed.

And not in a good way.

Chapter 3

R^{uby} I pulled into an empty spot beside the diner, turned off my car, and sat back in my seat. The place looked like one of those little mom and pop places, where the food was cheap but usually decent. The parking lot was almost empty, and I was able to see enough through the fogged up windows to make out that the inside of the restaurant appeared the same. It looked like there was just one waitress and someone else behind the counter cooking. It didn't look promising for a job, but I opened my car door and got out anyway.

Waitressing was about the only thing I knew how to do. I could clean rooms and bartend, as long as no one wanted a fancy cocktail. Anyone could pour beer on tap, but I preferred to stay away from bars. When men got drunk they got grabby and mean. Besides, the tip money I made waitressing wasn't bad. I was able to save up fast and then move on to my next adventure. Not staying in any one place for too long worked out good for me, and I didn't have to worry about Billy catching up to me.

Since I was still wet from my stop on the road, there was no reason to straighten my clothes or run my fingers through my hair to try and look more presentable. I looked like a drowned rat, exactly as the biker had said. I could only hope that the person I spoke to about a job would be understanding, and not too picky. Normally, I'd wait a day or two before looking for work, but an unexpected tire purchase had drained my meager savings down to my last ten dollars.

When I opened the door a blast of cool air hit me all at once, making me that much more aware of my damp clothes. Halfway to the counter I had goose bumps spreading over my arms. I managed a smile when the man, who I assumed was a short order cook, looked my way. As I came up to the counter he met me on the other side.

"Can I help you?" His smile showed a row of slightly uneven teeth. I gauged him to be around fifty. He was just a couple of inches taller than me, thin for a cook, I thought, but his expression and the warm look in his brown eyes seemed welcoming. His graying hair was cut short, military style.

"I guess I don't look hungry," I joked.

"You look like someone who needs warming up," he surprised me by saying. "And who's
looking for a job."

"Yes on both counts." I rubbed my hands up and down my arms. "Got wet helping someone broken down on the road."

"How about some hot coffee?"

"I'd love it." I sat down on one of the stools. "You wouldn't happen to be looking for another waitress, would you?"

He shook his head while pouring the coffee. "Afraid not. What you see now is rush hour."

I took a quick survey of the room. Only four tables were filled with a total of eight customers, not too good, considering that there were around thirty tables and it was lunchtime.

"Stop exaggerating, Tom," the waitress said with a downturn of her very red lips. She walked over and joined us, handing him her empty coffee pot. "We get busy at breakfast and dinner time, lunch and weekends not so much."

"Well, I might be exaggerating but the truth is we're not hiring right now."

I tried to keep the smile on my face, fixing my coffee the way I liked it while I thought about my options. Daytona seemed to be a busy place, and I knew that there were other restaurants I could try. I hadn't really expected to land a job at the first place I looked.

"Hon." I glanced up at the waitress while stirring my coffee. "I know what you're thinking, but you'll spend a lot of time looking before you find a job here. Daytona Beach Bike Week starts

16

tomorrow, and the folks who live here grabbed up any available jobs already. You'll do better to wait until it's over."

"How long does it last?"

"A week, but some bikers come early, and some leave late."

I sighed. I could make ten dollars last a week, but it would be tough. "I need a job like yesterday," I admitted with a wry grin.

"You like your coffee with sugar and cream?" Tom asked with a humorous look in his tired-looking eyes.

I laughed. "That's my one weakness, I like sweets." I took a cautious sip. I'd added so much cream that it was already lukewarm.

"Wait a minute!" Tom said, as if a light bulb had just gone off in his head. He gave his waitress a look that said that he was surprised that she hadn't already thought of it first. "There is one job you might have a shot at."

The waitress, guessing at what he'd been thinking, began to shake her head. The look on her face gave me the impression that whatever Tom had in mind, she didn't think that it was a good idea. This made me suspect that it wasn't any kind of job I'd want in the first place. "I'm not a dancer, so poles are out," I smiled. "And I'm not going to take my clothes off, so stripping is out. I will work at a bar if I have to, though putting up with drunken, handsy guys isn't my favorite thing."

Tom burst out with laughter. "It's not that kind of job, honey."

"But—"

He gave the woman an aggravated look. "Let the girl make up her own mind, Sunny. She looks old enough." He gave me a wink.

Sunny shrugged and spun around. "Hope this doesn't turn into an 'I told you so' moment later on," she said as she walked away.

Her comment almost sounded like a threat. Still smiling, I met the amusement in Tom's brown eyes. "Not sure I like the sound of that, Tom."

He waved Sunny off, even though she couldn't see it. "Sunny is a worrier, and you're about her daughter's age so she's naturally protective." He noticed my cup was almost empty and topped it off.

I released a deep breath. "Beggars can't be choosers." I added more sugar to my coffee, but he hadn't left enough room for the amount of creamer I usually poured in. "So, what is this job?" I was almost afraid to ask.

"It's not that bad. Do you know how to clean and cook?"

I thought about my cooking skills. Martha Stewart I wasn't, but I lied anyway. "Sure, what woman doesn't have those talents?"

My answer seemed to please him. "Have any qualms about taking care of an old man?"

I crossed my arms and raised a brow. Apparently my body language didn't worry him, so I finally asked, "Depends on what you mean by taking care of him. I won't have to bathe him or wipe his butt, will I?"

He laughed so loud that the customers glanced our way. "Nothing like that. He can still get around okay on his own, but he's getting up there in age. His sister wants someone to stay with him during the day so he won't be alone, do some light housekeeping and cooking for him so he won't get into, a-uh, trouble. You'd also have to drive him places."

All of that sounded doable to me, and I began to get excited at the prospect of having found a job so quickly. "Do you think this job is still available?" I asked eagerly. I could totally take care of an old man. It sounded like a companionship position, and what was hard about that? As my mind raced I noticed Tom writing something down on a napkin.

He handed the napkin to me when he was done. "Here's the address, it's a large one-story place right outside of town, painted white with grey trim. Located on the beach. Once you pass the After

Hours Bar it's down the road a ways on the left. Go there and discuss it with Marge, she can tell you more about it".

I glanced down at the address and phone number. "Marge is the sister?" He nodded. "I'll call them right away. Thank you! This is so nice of you!" God, if this panned out it could be the perfect job. I might still have to sleep in my car, but it sounded like food might be involved, since I'd be cooking, and that would save me money. "Do you have a phone I can borrow?"

The man was actually blushing. "Better if you just go down there. They don't always hear the phone anyway." He grabbed a Styrofoam cup and poured the remainder of my coffee into it.

"Okay, I will." I took the cup and jumped off the stool. "Thanks. I might be back for dinner."

I'd never been a companion before. In fact, I'd never even babysat a child, and I didn't have any family. I'd been in and out of foster care for most of my life, and right on the cusp of turning eighteen, I'd run away. My step-brother, who was actually my foster brother, had begun to get weird with me, so I'd skipped out of there. I'd thought that would be the end of it, but two months later Billy had hunted me down. That's when I'd begun to realize that his fascination with me bordered on being unhealthy and dangerous.

My survival instincts had made me pretend that I'd been happy to see him when he'd shown up but as soon as the opportunity presented itself I'd packed up my meager belongings that I had at the hostel I'd been staying at, and had run again. Four years later, I still didn't know if Billy was looking for me, and I didn't care. He wasn't the reason I kept moving. I loved my life on the road, exploring new places and meeting new people.

Now, as I drove to my prospective job sight, I wondered why did a certain sexy biker's face flashed before my eyes. I'd probably never see him again, which was a good thing, because if I spent too much time in his presence I would probably say or do something stupid.

Had I stayed with him any longer than I had, I likely would have jumped his bones right there on the side of the road, in front of his biker friends and Pops. The thought of is made me shiver. Yes, it was probably a good thing that we would never see each other again.

He was a complication that I didn't need.

Chapter 4

Tanner

I leaned my head back against the brick wall and closed my eyes, releasing a long breath. The woman knew how to give head, but when I closed my eyes it wasn't the brown-eyed blonde whose lips were wrapped around my dick right now that I saw. No, it was *hers,* with her long, black hair and blue eyes, and that killer body. No matter how hard I tried to wipe her image out of my head, *she* was the one sucking my dick. *She* was the one pulling an orgasm from me. I hadn't intended on getting with anyone tonight, but thinking about her had given me a hard-on that wouldn't quit, and I'd made eye contact with the first woman and motioned to the back door.

Sheila, Shelly—Christ, I couldn't remember her name—was really working her mouth. She was like a fucking vacuum, taking me in deep, but not deep enough. I grabbed her by the hair and forced her to take me deeper, until I was hitting the back of her throat. She gagged, but I didn't give a fuck. I needed to come, and she'd known the score when she'd followed me out back. It wasn't the first time she'd sucked my dick, and it probably wouldn't be the last.

We were in the narrow alley between the bar and an adult store. I was glad it was dark, because it aided in keeping the illusion alive of having the woman that I really wanted on her knees before me. I tried not to think about all the times the alley had been used for the very same thing we were doing now, how much DNA was spattered over the brick walls, but it was a hard fact that if there was an alley between a bar and an adult store it was going to be used for fucking.

Ten minutes and I still hadn't come. My balls felt as if they were about to explode. Sheila or Shelly used her hands to caress the part of my dick that she couldn't swallow, her fingertips toying with my testicles, but I couldn't seem to cross the line. And fuck, I was so close! I thrust my hips, picturing Trouble, because that's what she

21

was, picturing what she would look like naked, with her large tits and dark nipples, and her pretty little bush. Would she be bare down there?

Christ, what did it matter? All that mattered would be her tight, wet pussy and how it swallowed my dick, how her pretty blue eyes would grow large with pleasure while I pounded into her without mercy. I let out a loud groan and thrust deep, spilling my seed down the woman's convulsing throat. She wasn't fast enough to swallow it all, they never were, and as I emptied my balls some of my cum leaked out of the corners of her mouth.

I panted heavily, staying inside her warm mouth until I grew soft. The woman made a mewing sound that drew my gaze down to her. She made a show of licking my limp flesh clean, staring up at me with a satisfied look. With a grunt I pulled away from her and did up my pants, frowning at the wetness around the zipper.

"Are you ever going to fuck me again, Tanner?" she asked from her position at my feet.

I could still feel my heart hammering. I wasn't going to lie to her, because the truth was that I never fucked a woman more than once. "You know my rule." Besides, we both knew that she'd still be available for the occasional blow job. Her next words proved it.

"Tomorrow night? Same time, same place?" she smiled, licking her lips.

I shrugged. "Maybe. If I'm not busy."

With an exaggerated pout she ran her hands up my chest and leaned in for a kiss. I turned my head, because I didn't do that shit, either, especially when the woman had just had her lips around my dick. I had to feel something for a woman to kiss her. Christ, I couldn't remember the last time I'd felt something deep for a woman. Maybe not since Olive, and that had been, what, three years ago?

The back door opened, and Gabe stepped out. His brows rose with surprise when he saw me. He reached inside his jacket for his cigarettes and lit one up, amusement glittering in his eyes while he watched Sheila or Shelly walk through the door into the bar. "Well, at least one of us got something tonight," he said after blowing out a stream of smoke.

"What happened to your happy squealer?"

"I had to break her heart. Told her it wasn't happening. That I never fucked a woman more than once."

I laughed out loud at that. "That seems to be our club motto. Did you at least offer to be her friend?" I was joking.

He snorted. "Fuck, no. They don't want friendship, bro. Women think they've got you by the balls if you fuck them more than once. They think they're all special and want commitment. I'm too young to settle down. I like different pussy too much."

Too young to settle down? What was the age for that, anyway? Most of us were in our early thirties, some of us nearing forty, too old to be worried about looking out for that special someone to settle down with and start a family. Maybe that was the problem. We were set in our own ways and had been running solo for too long. Settling down wasn't even on my radar. I was content with my life the way it was.

The door opened again, and this time Sid and Mark came out.

"Having a party without us?" Mark joked.

"I'm gonna take off before Lonnie locks me out of the house for good." Sid and Lonnie had been together for a year, and things seemed to be working out for them. She worked as a paralegal downtown. Her goal was to become a lawyer, and her knowledge had come in handy in a few situations.

"Why are you taking off?" Gabe asked Mark, grinding his cigarette butt beneath his boot.

"I've got jury duty in the morning, remember?" We all laughed, he gave us the finger, and walked off.

"Think they'll pick him to be on a jury?"

"There's no reason why they shouldn't," I replied. "We're all upstanding citizens."

It was the truth. We may not have looked like it, but our club was on the right side of the law most of the time. There were clubs out there who thought they had something to prove by messing with us, but we didn't go looking for trouble, it usually found us. Daytona may have been inundated with biker clubs, but most of them were MC's like ours, people who liked the freedom of doing things their own way and following their own rules. That didn't mean that we were all bad men. The Sentinels wasn't on anyone's radar as far as we knew, and more times than not we helped the law. As far as I was concerned, we'd served our country in a way that wasn't much different from policing our town.

"We going back inside?" I asked Gabe, who'd just smoked his second cigarette. Hmm, that was interesting. Gabe didn't usually smoke like that unless something was bothering him. Could it be that he wasn't as over his little gal as he thought he was? Far be it from me to say anything. Gabe was a huge mother fucker with a lethal right hook.

"Naw. You can if you want, but I'm ready for some shut-eye."

All of a sudden sleep sounded good. I'd had a few beers, and had gotten a nice blow job to relieve some of the stress. Before I knew it I was walking with Gabe toward our bikes. I noticed Mike and William's bikes were still there.

We said our goodnights and spun out of the parking lot. It was while I was driving home that my thoughts drifted to Pops. I never really knew what I'd be walking in to. On a good night, he'd be asleep when I got home.

On a bad night, anything could happen. He could fall asleep with a smoke in his hand, set the place on fire, and fall down the fucking porch steps like he had a few months back. He'd been lucky he hadn't broken anything. We lived on the beach, so I suppose the sand had cushioned his landing. Then there was the time he'd gone for a ride on his old Harley. He'd come home okay, but I'd nearly had a stroke until he had. That night I'd taken a hammer to his fuel tank, and as far as he knew we were still waiting on the replacement to come in.

I loved the old man, but worry over him was causing me a lot of stress and sleepless nights. There was a solution out there, I just didn't know what that looked like. Hell, I was the president of the Sentinels and I didn't know what to do with one old man. I knew what not to do with him, and that was to put him in an old folk's home. That would kill him quicker than anything would.

I wouldn't do that to him.

The house was dark when I pulled into the drive. It was a quiet night, and I could hear the noise of the surf behind the house. Many nights I'd gone to sleep with my sliding glass door open, letting the peaceful sound soothe the unrest simmering in my blood.

I didn't turn on any lights when I opened the front door and entered the house. I knew where everything was. The layout of the furniture hadn't changed in years. I closed and locked the door behind me and made my way down the hall to check on Pops. I grinned, hearing his loud snores before I even reached his doorway. I closed his door and pivoted to go to my room at the opposite end of the house, thankful by the time I reached it that the distance muted the thunderous sounds coming from Pops' room.

I stripped, went to the connecting bathroom and took a piss, and then crawled into bed with a heavy sigh. As soon as my head hit the pillow Trouble's beautiful face came to my mind. Jesus, what the fuck was it about her that wouldn't leave me alone? I'd only seen her for five minutes. I was starting to get angry about my reaction to her. I'd never let a woman get to me like this before. She was a stranger, for fucks sake! I punched my pillow and closed my eyes, determined to go to sleep.

TORY RICHARDS

Tomorrow was another day.

Chapter 5

R^{uby} I knew I was heading in the right direction when the After Hours Bar came into view. That it was a biker's bar was obvious. There were rows of motorcycles lined up filling the parking lot. The building looked rustic with rough, wood siding that reminded me of washed up drift wood. Either the windows had been blacked out, or the lighting inside was very dim. Someone opened the door just as I was level with it, and I could clearly hear music and the sound of laughter filter out from inside. It brought a smile to my face, because I was all about having fun. I might have to check it out sometime.

It soon became apparent that I was leaving the lights and noise of the town behind as I traveled the busy coastal road. I slowed down when the numbers of the sparsely spaced residents revealed that I was nearing the address that I was looking for. Since most of the houses were tucked in behind lush trees and shrubbery, I assumed that I'd be taking a long driveway once I made a turn. I hoped that no one appeared in the opposite direction, because it was clearly a one way road. At the end of the drive the road opened up to reveal the one-story house with a detached garage.

I parked my car, turned it off, and just stared at the home. Tom hadn't been kidding when he'd said that it was a big house. The three-car garage was bigger than any place I'd ever lived in growing up. I glanced back down at the napkin in my hand to make sure that I had the right address. I looked back at the huge house. It didn't look like anyone was home, and I was starting to worry about my appearance. I looked a wreck. This looked like the kind of place that would expect someone who was applying for a job to look a little more professional.

As I sat there trying to decide what to do a light came on, and then the front door opened. *Ohmygod!* I pushed open my door with a big smile of surprise. "Pops! Is that you?" I made my way toward him.

"You stalking an old man, honey?" There was surprise and humor in his craggy old voice. "How long you been waitin' out here? I was out back having a smoke."

"I just got here." I stopped in front of him, trying not to smile at the crumbs of food in his beard.

"What ya here for?"

It suddenly dawned on me that Pops was the old man needing a companion. "Well," I was a little hesitant, because something warned me that he wasn't going to appreciate my reason for being there, "I'm supposed to talk to Marge?" Part of me was hoping that Tom had given me the incorrect address after all. I didn't want to see Pops' grin disappear.

Like it was doing now.

"Goddamn that sister of mine!" he hollered angrily, and I expected him to stomp his foot like a five-year-old. "She won't leave well enough alone!" His face turned red. "I don't need no fucking baby-sitter!"

I stood back in the face of his outrage. He looked mad enough to spit. "Wow, Pops, that's the bedroom word," I smiled, trying to diffuse the moment with a little humor.

He began to sputter, his face turning redder, and I had a moment of fear that he might give himself a heart attack or something. "That's not why I want to speak to her," I said, thinking fast. "And I can tell that you don't need a baby-sitter." I smiled and waited, trying to think of what else I could come up with that would calm him down. "I'm, uh, here to talk to Marge about, uh, about a place to stay." Yeah, that sounded reasonable.

He narrowed his gaze on me for a long time, long enough for me to feel my ears burning from the lie I'd told. I could tell that he wasn't ready to believe me, that he was working it out in his head. I kept the smile glued to my face, praying that Marge didn't live in a tiny little studio apartment. In spite of that, in my mind I derived what I thought was a plausible story, in case I was forced to continue on with the lie.

"A place to stay?" he grumbled skeptically, tugging on the end of his beard.

I nodded eagerly. "Yeah. I, uh, I'm broke. And until Bike Week is over there aren't any jobs, so, uh, someone mentioned something about people taking in borders for the extra cash—"

"You said you were broke."

He was quick. "Yeah, but I plan to work, and, uh, I was hoping Marge would let me pay up later." His expression told me that he was thinking deep about what I was saying. "I was probably just given the wrong address anyway."

He raised a bushy brow. "Who gave it to ya?"

"Tom, down at some restaurant I stopped at."

Pops shook his head. "Yeah. Tom down at the corner diner. He's a friend."

"He and Sunny are nice people. Just trying to help me. Well, I'm sorry for disturbing you." I began to back up. "I can always sleep in my car for a week or two. Nothing dangerous about that." I turned around to leave, crossing my fingers that he'd stop me.

"Wait a sec, cutie." I swung back around in time to see him scratching his head. "I wouldn't put it past Marge to take in strays for a spell. She's kind like that, always trying to save the world."

"Is she here?" I asked hopefully.

He shook his head. "Naw, she has her own place closer to town. Tom must have got mixed up giving you my address instead of hers. Why don't you come in and we can talk."

"I don't want to be a bother."

"Nonsense! I'm here alone most of the time. Can use the company." He turned, and I followed him inside.

I noticed his prominent limp as he moved, but then my gaze moved on to take in the rest of the house. Pops turned on lights as we walked in, and it was clear that he, or someone in his family, had money. Though the huge living room was decorated like a bachelor pad, it was tastefully done in big, bulky, leather furniture, a huge TV took up one whole wall, and a pool table was nestled in a corner. I marveled at the wall of glass that spread across the back from one end of the room to the other. It was dark out now, but I was sure that during the day the window provided a beautiful view of the ocean.

"Nice place."

Pops sat down in one of the recliners that looked soft, comfortable, and slightly worn. "Belongs to my son." He motioned to the couch across from him. "Sit down, honey, take a load off."

I didn't take offense to his 'take a load off' comment. It was just an expression, I knew that he was not referencing my curves, which no amount of exercising diminished. I'd long ago accepted that I was a little too busty, but that it went well with the curve of my hips and my generous butt. I was happy with my twenty-two-year-old-self. I sat down where he'd indicated, praying that my slightly damp clothes didn't ruin the leather.

"You wanted to talk?" I reminded him, smiling.

He frowned. "I don't like the thought of you sleeping in your car," he began in a serious tone. "A lot of shit happens during Bike Week, and a pretty, young thing like you would be bait for the assholes out there."

"I'm sure it's not that bad."

He waved me off with a low growl. "You don't know, and I can't let you leave here knowing you aren't protected. I owe you one."

"I can always call Marge," I said.

"Naw!" he snapped, shaking his head. "I know her. She's ain't lookin' to rent out space, she's lookin' to hire me a babysitter. I ain't down with that. But—"A conniving grin came over his weathered face and his aging eyes lit up like tiny little Christmas bulbs. "I been thinking, with you here she'll get off my ass about being alone."

I laughed softly, secretly proud of myself that by stretching the truth a little I had ensured that Marge was going to get her way of having someone stay with Pops. Okay, maybe it was a little white lie I'd told, but the way I looked at it, no harm, no foul, right? All I had to do was get to Marge and explain what had happened. Pops was jumping for joy that he'd one-upped his sister.

"You did all this thinking from the front door to your chair?" I joked, settling back into the soft cushions of the couch.

"Yep!" His chuckle sounded positively evil. "This'll show my meddling sister what's what."

"So, ah, what's my weekly rent?" It suddenly dawned on me that I'd be paying Pops to take care of him instead of the other way around, only he wouldn't know that I was taking care of him. And if Marge ended up paying me to stay with him, I'd be turning around and giving it right to Pops. What a mess!

He waved me off with a gesture I was beginning to recognize. "Nothin'!" he replied firmly. "Do some cooking, a little house work, and we'll call it even."

Again with the cooking. I would just have to wing it and stick with things that I knew how to cook. Unfortunately, that wasn't much. I was pretty good at cooking instant oatmeal, spaghetti—because who couldn't cook spaghetti—and eggs. Hopefully Pops had a cookbook I could use.

"What about your son? You said this was his place. Will he be okay with our arrangement?"

"He won't care, he's hardly here. Besides, he likes a home cooked meal as much as the rest of us."

I winced, but kept the smile on my face. "Well, if you're sure." I stood up, deciding it was time to leave, wondering where I'd be able to park my car for the night and not be disturbed. For some reason, the biker bar came to mind. "When would you like me to start?"

"What about right now?" Pops surprised me by saying. "You can spend the night in a real bed."

God, that sounded tempting, but I hesitated. It was getting late and I wanted to try and get in touch with Marge before I moved in. Just as soon as I got a chance I'd call the phone number on the napkin Tom had given me and cross my fingers that it was the right one. I didn't like the lie between me and Pops, even if it was for his own good. Marge might overlook it, because in the end it would get her what she wanted.

As I opened my mouth to suggest that I begin the next day, and I looked into the quiet, almost pleading excitement in Pops' eyes, it dawned on me then that he was really a lonely, old man. And he wasn't well. I didn't need to know what he had to see that whatever it was, it was beating him down. For the first time I noticed how unnaturally gray his skin looked, how thin his frame was. He was practically swimming in the old jeans and tee he was wearing.

My heart constricted with empathy, and I realized that I couldn't do it, that I couldn't just walk away from him tonight. Whatever happened tomorrow happened. If his family tossed me out for my deception I'd deal with it like I dealt with everything else life threw my way. But if my staying tonight gave an old man a little peace, I'd do it.

"If you insist. And I have to admit, the thought of a real bed is too tempting to turn down."

He slapped his knee and got up. "Good!" he said, grinning widely. "Come with me and I'll show you to the guest room." I followed behind him as we headed toward a hallway. "Has its own bathroom, so you'll have plenty of privacy, and all the other bedrooms are located at the opposite end of the house."

THE SENTINELS

Once he showed me the room I went out to the car to get my things. I didn't have much, and I didn't bring much inside in case things didn't work out. Then Pops had me pull my car into one of the stalls in the three-car garage.

He was so sure that I was going to stay.

I wasn't so sure.

Chapter 6

Tanner

I woke up at about five o'clock in the morning to the unfamiliar sound of someone moving around in the guest bedroom. I lay there for a minute, waiting to see if I heard it again, and had just about convinced myself that I'd imagined it when I heard it again. It must have been Pops, but what was he doing in the guest room? He had his own room at the other side of the house where most of the bedrooms were located. When he'd moved in and I'd discovered how loud he snored I'd moved my bedroom to the den. Who the hell used a den these days? It had just been an empty room to me.

There it was again. Now it was the sound of footsteps walking down the hallway toward the main living room. When I heard a thump and then a low curse, I yanked back the covers and jumped from my bed. Now I knew it wasn't Pops, because he would have been swearing like a drunken sailor. Someone else was in the house.

Just as I stepped out into the hallway I saw a shadow disappear around the corner leading toward the living room. I sprinted to the end of the hallway, peeked around the edge, and lunged just as the person walked into the kitchen. I grabbed them, registering the small, soft body as I pushed the person up against the fridge with an arm across their chest. A tiny squeak emitted from them, their arms came up, and then I felt long nails digging into my arm.

"Who the fuck are you, and what the fuck are you doing in my house?" I growled closer to their face. My gut told me that I had a woman up against the fridge, and I loosened my hold enough so she could answer me.

"Ssshh! You'll wake Pops!" came a harsh whisper, her warm breath hitting me in the face. There wasn't an ounce of fear in her tone.

What the fuck? "Who the hell are you?" I wasn't quite ready to accept that just because she knew Pops she was supposed to be there, especially since she'd been wandering around the house early in the morning when it was still dark out.

"My name is Ruby, and it's, uh, kind of a long story why I'm here," she explained in a low tone.

There was fucking humor in her tone. Not something I'd expect from someone I had pinned and helpless. "I have time, suppose you tell me."

She laughed softly. Fucking laughed. And something about it tugged at a not so distant memory, but I was damned if I could place it. "Do you think we can go somewhere more private to talk?"

Releasing a heavy breath, I clenched my hand into the material covering her shoulder and pulled her away from the fridge. "This had better be good," I snarled, losing patience.

"Oh, it is," she assured me with confidence, her light-hearted tone telling me that she wasn't afraid of her situation in the least.

I pulled her down the hallway and into my bedroom. I slammed the door behind us and flipped on the light switch. The last person I'd expected to see was standing there in front of me with a soft smile on her pretty face and amusement swimming in her blue eyes. On the road she'd had her hair pulled back, but now it was loose and wild, looking as if someone had been running their hands through it all night. I let my eyes drop down her body, which was draped in a sleep tee that stopped about mid-thigh. She had gorgeous legs.

I wondered if she was wearing anything underneath. Yeah, my mind went there.

I kept my expression indifferent because the fact was that she was still in my house without my knowledge. I knew that she was a wanderer, and I wondered if she made a living scamming old folks with some sad story to get inside their homes and then rob them? Pops wasn't the typical old man, he was tough as nails, and he had smarts, but he might buckle with someone who'd stopped to help him on the side of the road, a pretty little thing who knew what to say and do to get what she wanted.

I crossed my arms, the unwelcome thoughts that were drifting through my head making me angry. "I'm waiting," I barked.

I watched pretty blue eyes move over me, steeling myself not to be affected, because I was naked. I slept naked, and I wasn't about to apologize for it. The slightest tint of color filled her cheeks, and she cleared her throat. "Don't you think you should put something on first?" Her smile never wavered.

I tilted my head and growled, "Don't change the subject. I want to know what you're doing here. And if I find out that you're working on some kind of scam, you won't like the consequences."

"A scam? No, it's nothing like that." Her nervous laugh didn't convince me. "I'm here legitimately." I just stared at her. "It's really kind of complicated, but here goes . . ."

The whole time she was telling me her story I tried to focus on her words and not the full, pouty lips they were spilling from. A couple of times she tugged her bottom lip into her mouth, the sight of her teeth biting down at the corner and then slowly releasing the flesh caused my dick to jerk. Now wasn't the time to get a hard-on. I'd had enough experience with women to know that once a man let on that he wanted her, she thought she had him figured out. Ruby was sexy as hell, and with my bed just inches away I couldn't help but think about what she would feel like under me.

Naked and hungry.

I quickly pushed the thought aside, listening to the soft lilt of her voice as she began her story at Tom's Diner, the mix-up with Marge, and how she'd come to be here. It sounded plausible but hell, she could have been a consummate actress, too. Scammers were good at convincing the other person that they were on the up and up. I wanted to believe her. After all, she had stopped to help Pops on the side of the road, but for all I knew that could have been part of her MO.

Shit, I was beginning to think like the fucking cops. I would have laughed if this hadn't been serious. Once Ruby completed her story she crossed her arms. I wished she hadn't fucking done that, because it stretched the material of her tee over her big tits, revealing that her nipples were as hard as little stones. My dick took notice, betraying me with the first twinges of movement that told me that I was getting hard. Christ.

She was too damned sexy, and I'd wanted her from the instant I'd seen her.

Her cheeks were on fire, which meant that she'd probably noticed. I couldn't help the smirk. Our gazes clung, and I realized that she was waiting for me to react to what she'd told me. "I'm supposed to believe that?" I already half did, because how else would she know about my aunt?

"It's the truth, I swear." She made a show of crossing her heart. "I tried calling Marge before going to bed, but there was no answer. I wanted to let her know how I came to be here."

"My aunt took off for Rhode Island a couple of days ago to visit with an old friend."

"Oh. Well, she didn't answer her cell." She kept her eyes anywhere above my waist.

"Aunt Marge doesn't own a cell."

Her expression looked surprised. "Oh." She began to fidget.

God, she was cute, and my damned dick was still growing. I wanted to fuck her. Suddenly nothing mattered more than getting my dick inside her sweet pussy. I wanted to pound her into the mattress. But I knew I wouldn't, especially if her story was true, and she was there to take care of Pops. My one-fuck only rule would go right out the window if she was living under the same roof with me. There'd be no way to ignore the temptation if her pretty ass was sleeping in the room next to mine.

"Do you want me to, uh, leave?"

"No. Not yet, anyway. I want you right here where I can keep an eye on you until I can check out your story."

Her laughter caught me by surprise. "You can't make me stay if I don't want to."

My brows shot up at that. "You think not?" I responded to her challenge. I took a step in her direction. She took a step back, but her smile remained in place. "You should never challenge a man who has the upper hand," I said, fighting my own grin. "You don't know me from Adam, Trouble." My dick bobbed in front of me, showing no signs of deflating as long as we were in close proximity of Ruby.

That comment worried her. I could tell from the flicker of apprehension in her eyes. Then she swallowed hard. "You should put on some clothes," she said nervously.

Interesting. "Why? Does nudity bother you?" I took another step forward.

She took another one back. "No, no. I have nothing against nudity."

"Well, what then? Does the fact I have a hard-on for you bother you?"

"It's for me? I thought that maybe you had to, uh, pee. It is morning."

I burst out laughing. "Believe me, Trouble, when I get a hard-on it's not because I need to pee."

"Oh, uh, so you, uh, get random hard-ons?" Realizing that she'd come up against something she reached behind her, turning slightly so she could see what it was.

"I get hard-ons when there's a woman around that I want." Her eyes rounded at that. "But don't worry. You're safe. I don't fuck hired help, and even if I did, it would only be once." I stopped walking. If

I were any closer I'd be pushing her down onto my bed. And if *that* happened...

"Wow, you don't mince words." In spite of everything, the woman still had a smile on her face. Maybe it was a nervous reaction that she couldn't control.

I grinned. "I don't ever mince words." So why the hell was I standing there having this inane conversation with her in the first place? It wasn't like it was going somewhere. I would have liked nothing better than to kiss the smile off her lips, but I wanted more than a taste. "Go back to your room."

She glanced back at the bed, and I could see it in her eyes, the excitement and her arousal. She wanted me, too. She wanted my big dick. I wasn't vain, but I knew that my dick was bigger than most—ten inches when I was at my hardest, my girth bigger than what her little hand would be able to encompass. Thinking about sinking into her tight little hole made it bob some more, as if it were reaching out to her.

Fuck, if I didn't get Ruby out of my room soon I was going to say to hell with it, grab her, and fuck her. "I think you'd better leave." My voice was low, hoarse from the arousal thrumming through my blood. The tip of my bulbous head was already leaking with pre-cum, and I hadn't even kissed her yet.

I didn't miss the disappointment in her eyes. She scooted out around me and I didn't move until I heard her open and close the door behind her. I let out a harsh breath, relaxing. That had been close! I took my dick in my hand and gave it a few tugs. Fuck, it wouldn't take much to make me come, but I didn't want my fucking hand.

I thought about the woman in the next room. Maybe it would be best if her story turned out to be nothing but a big lie. Then I could fuck her out of my system and turn her loose without a backward glance. But if her story was true...

I was screwed.

Chapter 7

R^{uby}

Ohmygod! I couldn't remember wanting to jump someone's bones like I wanted to jump his, and I didn't even know what his name was yet! I'd all but come out and asked him, and I thought I'd done a pretty good job of giving him the 'take me, big boy, I'm all yours' eyes. He'd wanted me. I mean his big—and by big, I mean *huge*—cock had practically waved me over. Had I read the situation all wrong? Crap! Maybe he had a girlfriend or something. I'd never considered that.

The unwelcome thought that he might have a girlfriend pissed me off. How dare he get a hard-on for another woman! But in the next instant I was thinking about, oh what a hard-on he'd had. I didn't have much to compare it to—okay, nothing really. Yes, I still had my v-card. It was hard to believe, but I'd never met anyone that I'd wanted to give it up to. Until now. And he thought I was out to scam Pops.

For some reason that brought a tear to my eye. I wasn't a crier, I never got depressed. Life was too short and unpredictable to let it get me down. I loved my life, as unusual as it seemed to some folks. Oh, I figured that one day I'd meet someone and settle down, once I stopped traveling around the country. I wiped the tear away almost angrily because I loved life and I refused to be sad. Damn that man, that biker, for doubting my motives.

I thought that it might be better if I just left. But then I thought about Pops, and the look he'd got in his eyes the first time I'd been about to leave. He needed me. Deep down I knew that he did. He was just too old and set in his ways to admit that he needed someone around to help him when he needed it. Maybe he was just a little bit lonely, too. Surely his son realized that? Or was he blind to what the elderly needed? Well, if his son wanted to believe that I was a scammer I couldn't change that. He'd figure out that I was telling him the truth once he talked to Marge and everything became clear.

I hoped. I didn't want him thinking bad thoughts about me. I wanted him to fuck me. I giggled at that thought, rinsing the shampoo out of my hair. It had been a couple of days since my last shower, and I took advantage of it, scrubbing, shaving, and shampooing everything that needed it. When I was done I slipped into a pair of clean underwear, shorts, and a dark blue tank that matched the color of my eyes. I left my hair down while it dried and made my way out to the kitchen.

I figured I would make breakfast for Pops. Someone had already beaten me to making coffee. I eagerly opened cupboards until I located the cups, withdrew one, and poured myself a little. I was able to find sugar and milk, and once I had it just right I took a sip and almost spit it out in the sink. Ohmygod! It was strong! No amount of milk or sugar would make it drinkable. If I'd been a man it would have put hair on my chest.

Pops' son came around the corner, looking like the biker God that he was. "Making yourself at home already?"

I refused to let him ruin my morning. "Good morning," I said in a cherry tone. "So this is what you look like in clothes. Not bad." I let my gaze roam up and down his leather-clad body, skipping over the part of him that had been on my mind since returning to my room earlier. The man was beyond handsome, if you liked big and rugged. I wondered how tall he was. At least six-foot-five I'd bet.

"Cute," he said, pouring himself a cup of coffee. I was about to warn him about the strength of it, but then realized that he might have been the one who'd made it, and if he hadn't, then surely he was aware of how bad it would taste anyway. He took a sip, winced, but forced it down. "I guess Pops beat you to making the coffee."

"I don't know what you mean, it tastes fine to me." I took a sip under his watchful gaze, swallowed the bitter brew with a blissful moan. That had been a mistake, if the smoldering look in his eyes was any indication. He was staring so hard at my breasts that it was a miracle my nipples didn't catch fire. I smiled. Look all you want, baby. "Hey, what's your name anyway?"

"Tanner."

"Well, Tanner, I'm going to make Pops some breakfast. Do you want any?" I started to open cabinet doors as I looked for the pots.

"Pops doesn't eat breakfast."

"Well he does now." I still grabbed a small skillet, stood up, and met Tanner's skeptical look. "Want some eggs?"

Humor took over his rugged features. "I'll pass. Good luck getting him to eat them." He forced down another drink of his coffee. "Unless you lace them with beer."

I stared at him for a second. Was he serious? "Can you do that?" As soon as the words left my mouth I could have screamed. If that didn't tell him that I didn't know what I was doing nothing would.

He almost snorted out his mouthful of coffee. "Better stick with milk."

"I knew that," I said, just making it worse by defending myself. I took a step to the fridge before realizing that Tanner was blocking my way. My gaze traveled up a long way to meet the amusement in his dark eyes. "Want to move, big boy?" I knew it was a mistake as soon as I'd said it.

Tanner moved, slowly, placing his coffee cup down on the nearest surface and then turning leisurely back to me. "What did I warn you about the last time that you referred to me as a boy?"

I swallowed with difficulty, unable to take my gaze off his. Should I play stupid? I decided he'd probably see right through me. "Something about, uh, showing me the difference between boys and, uh, men?" I felt my heart rate pick up. I hadn't intentionally brought up the earlier exchange, but now that I had, I was almost breathless with anticipation.

Would he kiss me? Throw me on the countertop and have his way with me? The predatory gleam in his eyes turned me on, and I felt a coil of heat unfold in my core, and felt the wet heat between my legs. "You're not going to spank me, are you?" I teased, knowing that I was fanning the fire.

Tanner stopped abruptly, as if he'd come up against an invisible wall, and then I watched a purely evil-in-a-panty-melting-way grin quirk those full, sexy lips upward. "Now, that's an interesting thought," he grumbled in a low, tiger-like tone. "I was just going to throw you up against the wall and kiss you speechless."

Oh! I puckered my lips into a pout of disappointment. Both retaliations sounded good as retribution. "Do I get to choose?"

Before I knew it he was walking me backwards against the wall. I caught my breath at the impact of the wall and his hard body at the same time. Powerful arms came up on either side of me, hands flat against the wall, entrapping me in the most delicious way. I swallowed, meeting Tanner's fierce, narrowed gaze, which flickered back and forth between my eyes and my trembling mouth.

"No," he said simply, firmly, before closing the distance between us and slamming his mouth down onto mine.

Wildfire was the first thing that came to my mind as his lips met mine, something raw and untamed hammered through my blood the second we touched. In a flash we both lost control. It wasn't just about a kiss. No, that word was too simple to place on the vital, mind-blowing something that was happening between us. The man knew how to kiss, and he used his mouth to claim more than just my lips. He was taking me, body and soul, and I was a willing submissive. I opened my mouth and took him inside, moaning low as more warmth flooded between my legs.

His low, primal growl echoed through the kitchen as he thrust his tongue against mine in a rough, demanding way. His body crushed me against the wall in a way that made me very much aware of our physical differences, which was funny, considering that we fit together like a puzzle. My softness conformed to his hardness, and God he was hard. There was no disguising the hard ridge of his cock grinding against me, causing more liquid heat to rush through my blood at just the thought of what his impressive size would feel like inside me.

Fucking me into sweet oblivion.

I wanted to protest when he pulled back and our eyes locked. We were both breathing hard. Tanner's face was taut with arousal, nostrils flaring and fire in his eyes, and I knew that he was seeing a similar reaction on my face. He wanted me as much as I wanted him, and yet he held back. I could feel him pulling away before he actually did it.

"Fuck," he whispered sharply against my lips.

Yes, I thought, *fuck me,* but I knew that's not what he'd meant. I flinched when he struck the wall beside my head with a fisted hand that revealed frustration. I resisted the urge to look and see if he'd put a hole in the plaster.

"Not going to happen." His tone sounded so flat, so final, as if he'd made up his mind about something and was going to stick to it no matter what.

There were a lot of things I could think of to say to dissolve the suddenly uncomfortable situation, but I didn't believe that he'd find my usual ploys funny. Besides, I had the feeling that Tanner was talking to himself. I could still feel his cock against my lower belly, throbbing like a trapped beast wanting to get free. I thrust against it instinctively, wishing I hadn't because it ruined the moment between us. With dread I watched the haze of desire in his eyes fade to total clearness of where we were and what we'd been doing.

He stepped away from me, shook his head as if he was confused about something, and then ran his hands through his hair. It was on the tip of my tongue to ask Tanner what wasn't going to happen, but my instincts told me that I already knew. Why push the knife in any deeper by having him say the words I didn't want to hear? I'd never wanted a man as fast and as hard as I wanted him, heck, I'd never wanted to go all the way with anyone else before. But the emotions coursing through me now left me feeling vulnerable and rejected because he didn't want me back with the same intensity.

I hated being confused over my feelings. I'd always prided myself on being independent, on knowing what I wanted in life. Being attracted to a man had never entered into it, and I knew that if I let myself feel anything serious for Tanner that it would be that much harder to leave when the time came. And it would come, because leaving is what I was good at. I suddenly had the urge to just walk out and leave now, this very minute, before it was too late.

But then I asked myself, would it be so very bad to settle down?

"Not going to happen," I said, repeating his earlier words. I forced a smile on my face and moved away from the wall, showing an indifference that cost me a little bit of my sanity. "I better get Pops' breakfast done before it's lunch time." I went about preparing the eggs as if I hadn't just had the best kiss of my life. I added a little milk and some cheese that I'd found into the eggs. Cheese made everything taste better. I realized that I was humming, trying to pretend that everything was normal. I never hummed, which probably explained why I was out of tune. "Sure you don't want any?" I turned, only to find that I was suddenly alone.

Oh. I hadn't even heard Tanner leave.

With a sigh I turned back to the eggs, scolding myself for letting the kiss get to me, when it obviously hadn't affected him.

Not.

Going.

To.

Happen.

Chapter 8

Tanner

What the fuck had I done? Tasted heaven, that's what, and now I wanted more, because Ruby's soft mouth was just the right combination of fucking hell and heaven on earth. I was screwed. I should have never touched her, much less kissed her. Now I wanted a helluva lot more.

I wanted all of her.

Feeling those hard little nipples roll against my chest, swallowing her sounds of pleasure, sensing how fucking receptive she had been to letting me fuck her right there in the kitchen had all but worn down my defenses to not let things go too far. When she'd thrust against my dick I'd almost come, and giving her that kind of control would never do. The woman had got to me, too damned fast and too fucking hard, and my gut warned me that if I gave in to what my dick wanted that my one-time-only fuck rule would go right out the window.

Ruby wasn't a woman you only fucked once.

Holy hell! I'd gotten out of there fast, as if the place had been on fire. It may as well have been, because I sure as hell was hot. My dick was still hard, just thinking about having Ruby naked and beneath me. Hell, I could have had her there in the kitchen, against the wall or on the counter. She'd been an eager, hot little firecracker.

Trouble.

I'd known it from the start. I needed to get in touch with my aunt to find out if there was any truth to Ruby's story. I half-hoped that she'd been lying through her perfect teeth so that I could toss her ass out. Yeah, like that was going to solve the problem of wanting to get into her pants. My dick wasn't going to be happy until he had his way.

Well, that was just too fucking bad.

I rode toward the bar to meet with my brothers. It was a morning ritual that we would get together to bullshit while sitting around the table drinking coffee. Whoever got there first made a pot that wasn't much better than Pops' strong brew. No one from the bar would be around until the afternoon, so privacy wasn't an issue. We'd be long gone by then.

As I pulled into the lot, I noted that it looked like I was the last one to make it there. I yanked the door open to find all eleven of my brothers there. They'd pulled two tables together, coffee cups in front of them. Someone had brought donuts, and as Heath, Sully, and Skipper turned my way I burst out laughing. Hard-core bikers and fierce protectors of society? Not today.

"Morning," I greeted, walking toward them. "Ya'll look like little old ladies with your coffee and powdered donuts all over your faces."

"Hey, don't knock it till you try it," Sully said, licking his lips. "Sweeter than pussy."

"But not as satisfying," Rod added, wiping his mouth. "Want one?"

"Donut or pussy?" I glared at Gabe in response to his quip. "Whoa! Someone got up on the wrong side of the bed." His laughter, which I didn't appreciate, was contagious as some of the others joined in.

"Maybe someone is still thinking about a certain cute little someone else who we met on the side of the road yesterday."

I reached for the coffee pot in the center of the table and poured some into the empty mug beside it. "It gets worse." I filled my cup to the rim. "That certain cute little someone else is in my house serving up breakfast to Pops right about now."

Skipper snorted with disbelief. "What? You serious, man?" I just nodded, pressing my lips tight. "You move fast."

I shook my head. "She's the one who moved fast. Sprouted some story about being there to help Pops out and keep him company." I

48

took a cautious sip of my coffee. "Said my aunt was looking to hire him a companion and she got the number from Tom." I chuckled in spite of myself. "Only thing is, she somehow twisted it around so that Pops thinks her being there is his idea." Snorts went around the table.

"What does Marge say?" Gabe questioned while reaching for a donut.

I shrugged. "Haven't talked to her yet." This made me wonder why I hadn't called her first thing.

"What are you gonna do if she's lying?"

I made eye contact with Mike, who was the more serious brother in the club. This could have been due to the fact that he owned a private investigation agency. What was I going to do? Put her across my knee and paddle the hell out of her bottom before sending her on her way? That thought had my dick jerking. Fuck, I had to stop that shit.

Again I shrugged. "Probably just toss her out and tell her to leave town."

Rod laughed, and then drained his cup. "Bike Week starts today. I can picture her getting into all kinds of trouble."

"Speaking of Bike Week—" I decided it was time to get off the subject of my pretty little house mouse, "this is our town. You go down to Main Street, you don't go without backup. Less likely to be trouble that way."

I wasn't worried that my brothers couldn't take care of themselves. We were all big and strong, kept ourselves in shape, and as ex-military we knew how to fight using our words or our fists. We had the reputation of being the kind of MC who kept to ourselves, kept peace in our town, and dealt fairly with pricks who thought we were weak because of it and tried to engage us. The respect of other clubs was there, and those we weren't friends with just left us alone. Only once in a while were we challenged.

"You think that's really going to scare Wicked and his crew if they show up?"

"Yeah, he's been threatening to pound our MC into the ground."

I grinned back at Heath and Pete because they were grinning. No one thought the Kings MC was any real threat. Wicked may have had the numbers, but his crew were a bunch of inept fuckers playing dress up. They weren't locals, but they were close enough to be pests when they wanted to be, and they didn't have the skills that we had. They didn't know enough to keep their asses in Sanford. Sooner or later they were going to piss us off enough and we'd have to put them in their place.

"I doubt we'll have to deal with them. If they're stupid enough to show up during a week when Daytona is inundated with the real deal, they'll become someone else's problem to deal with."

"So what say we all head down to Main Street now and check things out?" Rod leaned back in his chair and crossed his arms. The youngest in the club, his boyish good looks belied the fact that he'd been a sniper in the army and had the most kills of any of us. Not something to brag about, it was just a hard fact. He still had nightmares over it.

Most of us did.

"I'm game. Has anyone checked in on our businesses to make sure they're all covered?" As a whole, the club owned a tattoo shop, gym, and a strip club. Individually, I owned After Hours and a garage, Rod owned a gun shop and shooting range, William and Gabe owned a fishing charter boat, and Sid owned a couple of Tiki bars right on the beach. The rest of our brothers were content to earn a living off their military pensions and a generous cut from club profits once a month.

"All's good."

I took Skipper's word for it, scooted my chair back, and got up. "Let's go, then."

THE SENTINELS

It was the first day of Bike Week. Bikers from all over the country had been pouring into Daytona for days, and I knew that shit was going to be busy and dangerous. We'd never made it through Bike Week without fights and fatalities. Hopefully our presence, along with the presence of some of the other clubs who subscribed to the same philosophies, kept tempers calm and fights at a minimum. That didn't mean that there wouldn't be a lot of drinking, partying, and fucking going on.

That was all par for the course.

Chapter 9

R^{uby}
    I watched Pops clean his plate and then scoot back his chair. He gave me a wink. "That was real good, honey."

I smiled back at him, giving myself credit because I knew that I made good eggs. I'd had to go in search of him when they were cooked and on his plate, finally finding him puttering on a bike in the garage. When I'd told him that I'd made him breakfast he'd informed me that he never ate breakfast. I stood silent for a minute, watching him checking this and that, muttering beneath his breath, before realizing that he had no intention of coming inside to eat.

Injecting the slightest hurt into my voice that I could, I'd said, "Fine, I'll just throw the eggs away." A well-timed sniffle drew his attention to me and I whipped around so that he couldn't see that it was all a ruse.

"Wait a minute, honey." I made a show of wiping my eyes before looking over my shoulder at him. It took him a while for him to get to his feet. "Come to think of it, I'm hungry this morning. I'll eat your damned eggs."

I gave him a trembling smile and turned back to continue to the house. That was one for me! And I realized that the small victory made me feel good inside. I was willing to bet that Pops didn't eat breakfast because there was no one around to fix it for him, which was why I'd made up a plate for myself. I began to realize that Pops was strong-willed and set in his ways. Well, so was I.

"I hope you don't mind my eating with you." I sat next to the plate with the smaller serving.

"Course not," he snapped, and then, realizing the sharpness of his tone, he gave me a grin. "Can't remember the last time I ate breakfast with someone. Once in a while Marge comes over, but she tries to make me eat fuckin' oatmeal and prunes shit. This looks real good."

"So, what were you doing on that motorcycle?" I questioned after swallowing my first bite of eggs. Pops was digging into his with relish, his face lowered to his plate as he shoveled them in.

His gaze shot up to me. "Just puttering around," he said around a full mouth. "Waiting on a part, can't ride when it won't run."

"That's your bike?" I asked with surprise. He just nodded. I couldn't believe that at his age he was still riding a motorcycle. I couldn't believe Tanner would let him. "Why not just take the truck?"

He scoffed loudly. "You're not a biker, you wouldn't understand. We avoid cages like the plague."

I assumed that by "cages" he meant his truck, but I asked him anyway. "Cages?"

"Vehicles. See? You don't understand." He began to cough but quickly brought it under control. "Bikers like the freedom of being on the road in the open air, the thrill of going full throttle with nothing but a powerful bike between our legs. The ladies like it." He winked, and then flew into a coughing fit that turned his face beet red and left him gasping for breath. Concerned, I got up to pound him on his back, but he waved me back. Whatever was in his chest sounded thick and unhealthy.

"Are you okay?" I wondered if Tanner had been privy to one of Pops' coughing fits. I knew that many smokers coughed a lot, but this seemed like it might be something more. Could he possibly have pneumonia?

Eventually he pulled himself together. "I'm good, honey. Wipe that concern off your pretty face." He stood up. "Gotta get myself down to Main Street."

"What's on Main Street?" I rose to my feet too, prepared to go with him. "Do you mind if I tag along?" I smiled enticingly.

"Well," his weathered expression suddenly turned cynical. "It's not really a place for someone like you, cutie." Someone like me? "This is Bike Week and the action down on Main Street gets kind of rough and rowdy sometimes."

That's right! I'd recalled someone mentioning that it was Daytona Beach Bike Week. I quickly stacked our empty plates and headed for the sink. "It sounds like fun, and I can handle rough and rowdy." I set our plates down into the sink. "Do I need to change?" I turned back to Pops, who was standing halfway between me and the door. He looked so ready to run off and leave me that I had to hold back a smile.

"You look fine, honey, but—"

"Good, let's go," I said, before he had a chance to finish that comment. It was clear that Pops didn't want me to go. "I can't believe I'm going to see what Bike Week is all about." I ignored his open-mouthed look of surprise, wrapped my arm around his, and pulled him from the kitchen. "I can drive—"

"Hell no, you ain't drivin'," he grumbled. "No way I'm gonna show up there in front of all my old friends with you driving."

"Fine." I smiled victoriously and walked around the truck to the passenger side. "You drive."

Pops was muttering beneath his breath when he opened the door and climbed inside the truck. I just turned the other way and hid my grin. It was clear that in order to get what I wanted I was going to have to either turn weepy eyes on him or just assert myself, depending on the situation. The ultimate goal was to keep him company and out of trouble, and I had no qualms about using what God had given me in the way of feminine wiles.

Pops' muttering turned into loud cursing when it took him several tries to start the old truck. Once the engine remained running he floored the gas pedal, giving the engine a couple of good revs. I wrinkled up my nose at the strong smell of gas, seeing the blue toxic fumes drifting up from the exhaust out of the corner of my eye.

I coughed. Pops gave me a grin and backed up. When he pulled out onto the main road I reached for the seat belt, only to find that there wasn't one. A horn sounded behind us, and I realized that he'd cut someone off. The next thing I knew, Pops was giving them the finger. I giggled softly, glad that the sound of the rattling truck concealed it. I didn't want to encourage him, even though I doubted Pops needed much help in that area. He didn't have a problem saying and doing exactly what he wanted.

Main Street wasn't far once we got into town. I was amazed at all the bikes that I saw on the road. Had they been present the day before? I hadn't noticed. Some bikers were riding solo, while others traveled in tight groups. More often than not there was a woman sitting on the back, and there seemed to be just as many riding their own bikes. It was clear from the start that there was a vast difference in the types of riders and bikes that were present.

I'd never given it much thought before. Most of the bikes that I saw were what I considered regular motorcycles, black and non-descript, though some had beautiful art work on the gas tanks and logos that revealed that they were part of a club. Those riders were dressed differently and carried themselves with a certain air of superiority, as if they were invincible and untouchable. It reminded me of Tanner and his friends. I wondered if he was there, somewhere in the crowd.

Other bikes were very sleek and fancy, customized extravagantly in ways that I'd never imagined possible. I saw one with horns where the handle bars were supposed to be, another that looked like a spacey, futuristic machine, whose design hid the tires, and another resembled a fire-breathing dragon. Some were new, others vintage. There were fancy bikes on three wheels that I'd never seen before. A lot of them were covered with bright, fancy art work, and I could tell that they were all super expensive. They were the kind of bikes that you might see at a show, but not necessarily riding down the street.

"Oh, I get it!" I finally said, turning toward Pops as I had an epiphany. "This is a bike show, right?"

He chuckled, slowing down when he spotted a parking spot in front of a vendor selling tees. "Not exactly, honey." He pulled into the spot and cut the engine. "Bike Week is for everybody and anybody. It's where bikers come to show off, sell shit, reconnect with other clubs." He hesitated after opening his door, turning back to me. "There'll be a lot of MCs out there, some friendly and some not. So you stay close to me."

I couldn't contain my grin at Pops' protective attitude. I jumped from the truck and had no sooner slammed the door shut than I heard a wolf whistle.

"Hey, sweetheart! What's a pretty ripe thing like you doing with an old fuck like him?" Male laughter followed the man's remark. "His dick's probably all shriveled up like a sausage link."

I glared at the man, wishing that I could think of something to say to embarrass him in front of his smirking friends. Pops came around the truck, passed me, and kept right on going in the direction of the man. Panic raced through me as I feared that he would get hurt confronting them. They were dressed all in black, tattoos running up and down their arms, and some had them on their necks. One of the men had piercings and gages in his ear lobes.

"Watch your mouth, asshole!" Pops yelled out, no fear at all in his scratchy voice. "You think she'd rather have your diseased little willy?"

Oh, God! I could feel my heart rate pick up speed. It would be a miracle if the man didn't kill Pops, and on my first day as his companion! I rushed to catch up with him, wondering what I could do to diffuse the situation. "Pops," I grabbed his arm. He tried to shake me off. I made eye contact with the other man, who looked to be around sixty, but a tough sixty. "I'm sure your, uh, diseased little willy isn't all that bad." I offered a smile, and for a second Pops and I struggled.

The other man and his friends threw back their heads and laughed. "What the fuck, old man? Since when do you need a little girl to protect your hairy ass?"

Pops pulled free and before I knew it the two men were nose to nose. "Who's got a hairy ass?" Pops gritted into the man's cold, expressionless eyes.

There was a distinct growl. "You do old man. A hairy ass and a sausage link for a dick."

Oh, God. I glanced around for help, but we may as well have been alone on the street. The vendor was busy selling her tees to customers and ignoring us completely. The crowd moving around us was oblivious, too, though some did give us a curious look.

"Please don't hurt him," I finally said in a loud voice so that they could hear me. Both men slowly turned their heads, pinned me with their narrowed, beady-like eyes, and then burst out laughing. The next thing I knew they were greeting each other in a hearty man hug.

"You old fuck, how ya been, Tork?"

"Good and you?"

Tork's friends were all smiling at me, and one gave me a friendly wink. "Sorry if we scared ya, darlin'," said the man who'd winked at me, "but it was sure funny seeing a little thing like you step in like a mother bear protecting her cub. You family?"

I shook my head with a weak smile of relief on my face.

"Yeah, she's family," Pops contradicted my non-verbal response. "So hands off."

I looked at him with confusion, but Tork was the one who provided an explanation. "It's for your protection, sweetie." My protection? Yeah, that clarified everything. "Pops and I go way back. I'm Tork, this here is Red, Jimmy, Todd, and Tower." I knew why

Tower was called Tower, he was way taller than anyone else around him. Each man nodded as Tork introduced them.

"I'm Ruby. Nice to meet you all."

"You feel like going for a drink or is it too early in the morning for you?" Tork asked Pops, keeping a friendly hand on Pops' thin shoulder. In comparison Tork was built like a tank.

"Never too early for a drink." Pops turned with Tork and began walking down the sidewalk. "Come on, cutie." He didn't have to worry, I was already walking behind them, and behind me were Red, Jimmy, Todd, and Tower.

I suddenly felt tiny in the midst of the men surrounding me. As we walked I took in my surroundings, marveling at the beautiful bikes parked along the road, all backed into place at a slant. Main Street had businesses up one side of the street and down the other, the sidewalks were almost impassable with people mulling about, drinking, smoking, and talking. Some, the creepier ones, just stood watching, as if they were waiting for something to happen. I wondered how many might be undercover cops.

"You still with us, cutie?" Pops asked without looking back to see if I was.

"Don't worry, Pops," said the winker. I thought his name was Jimmy. "I'll keep my eye on her." He smiled down at me, and there was no disguising the look of interest in his eyes.

I smiled back. He wasn't a bad looking man, at least he had all of his teeth. I'd noticed when they smiled that two of his friends were missing a couple. I gauged his age to be around mine, twenty-two, yet the way that he carried himself, observant and alert, made him seem older. He was a few inches taller than me, and it was obvious that he worked out.

We'd reached Evil Eye Saloon. Tork opened the door and motioned us all inside. It was dark, and I stood motionless for a second, letting my eyes adjust. The room was fairly alive with music and laughter, the clinking of bottles and glasses could heard over that, and I couldn't help but wonder how people could start drinking so early in the day. The atmosphere inside made it feel like it was nighttime, though. The windows were heavily tinted, and the only lighting was the neon signs and low-watt lights hanging around the room.

"Feel like dancing, sweetheart?"

I watched Pops, Tork, and the others continue to walk up to the bar. Before I had a chance to say yay or nay I found myself being pulled by the hand onto the dance floor. Laughing, I started to turn around to face Jimmy, but he put his hands on my hips and kept me facing away from him. "Your name is Jimmy, right?" I loved to dance and began to move my hips.

"Yep." He kept his hands on my hips, controlling the movement of my body, and the next thing I knew his body was flush with mine. "So, how are you family to Pops?" He leaned down to my ear and spoke loud enough so that I could hear him.

I thought about it for a minute. I doubted Pops would be happy with his friends knowing that he had a babysitter. Of course, he didn't know that either, but he would figure it out in time. Besides, I didn't feel like talking. I wanted to lose myself in the music that was blasting through the room. I didn't get a chance to dance very often. "It's too complicated." I hoped he'd be content with that. After a moment, the hands at my hips pulled me more firmly against Jimmy's body.

I didn't question it, after all, we were dancing. Soon I was losing myself to the sensual throb pounding through the room, letting it pour through my blood and warm it. I began to sway and twist slowly against Jimmy. I closed my eyes and tilted my head back, raising my arms slowly over my head. Jimmy's hands smoothed up my arms and back down again, his actions feeling more intimate than they probably should have. As he gripped my hips again he jerked me snug against his lower body, and that's when I felt his hard-on against my butt.

My eyes flew open, landing directly on Tanner's narrowed, angry gaze.

I smiled.

He didn't.

Chapter 10

Tanner

The first thing I saw when I opened the door to Evil Eye was a sexy little thing in shorts and a tight tank doing the bump and grind against the man behind her. My gaze traveled upward to her eyes. Fuck me. I came to a standstill the instant I realized that I was looking at Ruby. She smiled invitingly, turning that lush mouth upwards at the corners until they reached the sparkle of excitement in her eyes. She moved her head from side to side so that her hair was flying around her, arms high in the air above her head, reminding me of Kim Basinger's sexy dance scene in the movie *No Mercy*. Ruby was just as drop-dead gorgeous, and she was nothing but trouble.

I felt my brothers come in behind me. They continued further into the room, heading straight for the bar. One of them muttered something on his way by but I paid him no mind. I couldn't take my eyes off Ruby and her flushed loveliness. It was obvious that she loved dancing, the way she gave herself up to the music as if it were calling to something primitive inside her. She rotated her full hips with enough hip action to turn my dick, along with every other man's in the room, hard. Her tits were snug against the tank that hugged them, showing that her nipples were stimulated little peaks against the thin material. Her movements revealed that she was barely aware of the man behind her. She was dancing for herself and her apparent love for music. That was the only thing keeping me from losing my shit.

That and the fact that I had no claim over her.

If I made a scene by yanking her away from Jimmy, I'd show everyone in there what I was feeling, and that wasn't going to happen. Everyone who knew me knew about my one-time-only rule. They knew I wasn't looking for a woman to spend my life with. I liked my single life. I didn't have to worry about anyone waiting at home for me, I could fuck any woman I wanted. If that made me sound like a prick, I didn't give a shit. At least I was honest about my intentions, and there wasn't a woman out there that I'd been with that hadn't known the score before I'd fucked her.

The next time our gazes met, her eyes filled with a teasing light that promised that she'd fulfill my hottest fantasies. Hell, I'd already guessed that from the steamy kiss we'd shared in the kitchen earlier. But I wasn't going down that road. Any time that I'd ever wanted a woman too fast and too hard, I'd avoided her like the plague, because it usually meant there was something about her that got to me on more than just a physical level. The trouble was, I couldn't remember ever wanting a woman like I wanted Ruby, with an intensity that could ruin her. It could ruin *me* along the way.

Nope, wasn't fucking happening. I could find someone else to fuck and walk away from. Hell, any number of women in the place would do, like the bleached blonde at the bar who was giving me the eye. My gaze moved over the red dress she'd been poured into, appreciating the exposed skin from the strategically placed cutouts. Her tongue came out and slowly ran over the length of her upper lip, the smoky look in her heavily made up eyes an open invitation. I pictured her long legs wrapped around my hips, the fuck-me stilettos digging into my ass as I pounded into her. I grinned and gave her a wink, ignoring that my dick wanted someone younger and more innocent.

I took a deep breath and searched the room until I found Pops at the bar. I should have known that he would have come down here first thing. He had been a hard-core biker back in the day, and he'd been a nomad before that, until he'd met my mom and settled down with one MC. He'd been well into his sixties by the time age caught up to him, forcing him to retire. A hard life full of heavy smoking and drinking had taken a toll, and right then he looked every bit and more of his seventy-seven years. But Pops refused to listen to his aging body and slower reflexes.

I forced a smile I was far from feeling as I watched Jimmy's hand wander up Ruby's ribcage. Fuck, I didn't want to kill him, but the thought did enter my head. His wandering hands stopped right beneath her tits, and I knew that if I stayed there another second I'd lose my shit and make a scene. Her eyes were glued to mine, the exhilaration in them dimming slightly with what? Hurt? Disappointment? Had she expected me to sweep her away from Jimmy and claim her for myself?

Clenching my jaw, I forced myself to walk around them and head toward the bar. I needed a drink, and the knowing looks that I got from some of my brothers as they watched me approach pissed me the hell off. They only thought they knew what was going through my mind, and God help the one who was stupid enough to make a comment. I went straight to Tork.

"Hey, brother, when did you get into town?" We hugged briefly.

"Last night," he said, glancing past me to where Ruby and Jimmy were on the dance floor. "Brought my kid with me this time."

"So I see." I didn't add that I was going to kill him if he didn't keep his fucking hands to himself. I turned to Pops. "You think that's a good idea, Pops, bringing Ruby down here?"

"She insisted, what was I supposed to do? Especially after she made me breakfast." He looked at the dance floor. "'Sides, she's okay. Just having fun."

Yeah, fun. A couple of my brothers scoffed, not afraid to meet my eyes. Gabe was the only one with the guts to say, "They're practically fucking." I clenched my hand, refusing to look back to where Ruby and Jimmy were dancing. Gabe saw it, his fucking smile growing wider.

"Beer!" I ordered the bar tender. "Fuck that, make it whiskey." I needed something stronger to get through the next few minutes.

"Somethin' bothering you, boy?" Pops knew that I was a beer man and only ordered the strong stuff when something was eating at me.

"Maybe it's *someone* that's bothering him," Tork laughed, as if reading my mind. "You gonna beat my boy for touching your woman?"

Fuck. So they'd all witnessed my stupidity upon first entering the bar. As soon as the whiskey was set down I grabbed it up and threw it back, feeling the burn go all the way down to my gut. I slammed the glass down onto the bar. "Let's be clear—" I made eye contact with the lot of them. "She's trouble, and she's not my woman. She can dance with, and fuck, anyone she wants." I couldn't believe the shit that was falling out of my mouth.

Something in Mike's eyes and the way that he looked past me told me that someone had walked up behind me. I turned, meeting Ruby's eyes. Fuck! It was clear by her expression that she'd heard me. What wasn't clear to me was *why* it had affected her. Christ, we weren't even involved, so it wasn't as if it mattered. Still, I felt like a bastard. Then she did the unexpected. She smiled.

"I'm so glad that I have your permission to do whatever the hell I want, Tanner." She chose that moment to grab Jimmy's arm and pull him closer to her side.

Damn, she looked hot, standing there all flushed from dancing, her hair a wild mess that I wanted to bury my fingers in, and, goddamnit, her nipples were still hard as sin. Jimmy stood there with a big stupid grin on his face that gave me an itch to knock his teeth out. Out of the corner of my eye I saw a movement and realized that Tork had taken a step closer to me, obviously worried that I might do something. He didn't need to worry.

"You think because I let you kiss me this morning that I'm after your cock? You have no claim over me, and I have none over you. I give you the same permission to dance with, and fuck, whoever you want." She gave Jimmy a wink before returning her gaze to me. "You're the last one here I'm interested in, so get over yourself."

Christ, she'd just announced to the whole fucking room that she was unclaimed. It suddenly grew quiet, a warning in itself, but I was focusing on the sound of the words "cock" and "fuck" coming from her pretty mouth. They turned my dick hard as fucking stone, but I was too angry to appreciate it. No one, especially a woman who technically worked for me, if her story turned out to be true, got away with that shit. I clenched my teeth until my jaw hurt. You could cut the silence surrounding us with a knife, because everyone knew my temper and reputation for dealing out punishment when someone went too far.

My brothers all seemed to have lost their tongues. Rod, Gabe, and Skipper turned around on their stools to face the bar. A few others averted their eyes to something else in the bar. They'd never heard a woman talk to me like that, not one who had ever gotten away with it, and if they weren't scared at what my reaction would be, they were at least smart enough not to get involved. I was the fucking president of the Sentinels, and the only thing saving Ruby right then was that I knew that she had no idea what she'd started with her smart mouth.

My brothers knew. Pops' eyes shifted around the room and his thin old body stiffened, either in fear for Ruby or anticipation of what I was going to do next. Tork had probably realized that the threat was off of Jimmy now, because he relaxed next to me. I knew that I had to do something because it was expected of me. As I locked eyes with her, it dawned on me that she realized her mistake, yet the look in her eyes still held a fucking challenge. She wasn't afraid of me, and that was her mistake.

I turned my narrow-eyed look onto Jimmy. It didn't take more than a couple of seconds for him to get my silent message to take his hands off Ruby and step away. He didn't like it, though. His expression was set, but I knew that he wouldn't interfere. He knew the rules, and he wouldn't question me, and if he did, the only way he'd get away with it was if he staked a claim. He wouldn't, because he was a newly patched-in member in his daddy's MC and still high on the adrenaline and excitement of fucking their club girls.

"This is the only pass you're going to get from me." Her jaw dropped. Those pretty blue eyes rounding with disbelief, and then her mouth tightened and I knew that she was about to explode. "Watch your mouth."

"Watch my mouth?" She slammed her hands on her hips, bringing attention to the curvy shape of them. It also brought attention to her perfect tits straining against her tee. "Are you kidding me?" In spite of her outraged attitude, there was humor swimming in her eyes, as if she couldn't help herself. "I'm not a child, Tanner. You can't speak to me like one. I've been nothing but nice to you."

"She did let you kiss her," Sid reminded me in a tone I didn't appreciate, and I suddenly wished that I hadn't said anything about it at our meeting. I glared at him, but it did nothing to wipe the grin off his face.

"You owe me an apology," Ruby said smugly, tilting her chin obstinately.

God, the whole damned thing was getting out of hand. My brothers were chuckling not at my anger, but because she was standing there as if she were untouchable and not taunting the president of an MC. She was about to get a fast and brutal education on how we handled shit. Or, more accurately, how I handled a bothersome female who invited trouble. If we were another MC she would have found herself in a much worse situation, the kind she couldn't talk her way out of. That scared the shit out of me.

"You know you gotta do it." The subtle warning came from Pops.

Yeah, he didn't need to remind me. I was just as aware of the other members of MCs that were present and silently watching, waiting to see what I was going to do. Some were hard-core and though the Sentinels had a fierce reputation, we didn't necessarily follow the same rules with our women and how we dealt with them. The fact that Ruby had advertised that she was unclaimed was the real issue, and I could already sense my next move would either be to protect her, or would put her in harms way.

"Do what?" Ruby asked after a few tense minutes. "Wash my mouth out with soap? Spank me?" She laughed, still ignorant of the situation that was brewing.

She didn't see what was coming. I reached for her, wrapping my hand around her upper arm, my fingers brushing the side of her soft tits. "I think you need a fucking attitude adjustment, and a spanking sounds like a good idea." I pulled her with me toward the back door.

"What do you think you're doing?" she rushed out, trying to dig in her heels. She tugged her arm and then gasped when she couldn't break free. "Ouch! You bully!" she struggled some more but I kept on walking. "Is anyone going to help me?"

That brought a grin to my face. I didn't look back, but I could imagine that she did, making eye contact with my brothers and Pops, in the hopes that one of them would step in and save her. I hit the back door open with the palm of my hand, yanked her through it and outside before releasing her. We faced off like warriors. Ruby didn't look so sure of herself, now. Her tits were heaving, she was red-faced, and the color in her eyes reminded me of blue ice, they were so cutting.

"You're crazy!" she said, rubbing her arm where I'd grabbed her. "I don't know what just happened in there, but—"

"And you're dangerous," I shot back through my teeth. "You know nothing about MCs and what they're capable of. If I hadn't dragged your ass out here to teach you a lesson, you can bet that open season would have been called on your ass."

Her eyes grew round at that. "Teach me a lesson?" she scoffed. "I didn't do anything wrong. I was having fun until you said what you said and pissed me off."

"And you couldn't wait to announce to the whole fucking room that you didn't belong to anyone," I snarled. There'd been at least thirty bikers in the bar, and they'd been all ears at her exclamation.

"Belong to anyone?" I wasn't prepared for her snort of laughter. "As in 'claimed' or 'owned' by a man?" she laughed again. "Ohmygod! What century are we in? Do you realize how demeaning that sounds, how archaic?"

"Being claimed by a man in an MC doesn't mean the same thing as it does in the real world." I clenched my teeth. I had to remind myself that Ruby didn't know anything about MC culture, and maybe in a different part of the world it wouldn't matter as much, but right then she was at the worst place for exposing her ignorance. "It's an honor for a woman when she's claimed in an MC. She gets respect and protection from all the members. It shows that she's not just there for pussy."

"That's just wrong," she said, her cheeks coloring for a different reason this time. "So are you saying that as long as I'm not claimed that I could be in danger?"

I released a heavy breath and ran my hand through my hair. "I'm saying don't go around looking for trouble by announcing that you're a free woman who likes to have fun. Tone the attitude down." I could tell that she didn't like that. "Look, MCs from all over the country have come here for Bike Week. Most come for fun, but some are hard-core clubs who've come to drink, party, and fuck, and you can bet there'll be some fighting. A lone woman with a smart mouth is exactly what they'll be looking for to have a good time."

"Maybe I should just avoid Main Street," she said with mild disgust, and I thought in response, *Maybe she should just leave Daytona*. "So is this my lesson?"

"No." I backed her up against the wall that divided One Eye Saloon from the next business, suspecting that we had an audience of on-lookers watching from inside the bar. "This is." I buried my hand in her hair and slammed my mouth down on hers.

Chapter 11

R^{uby}

I automatically opened my mouth to protest, which did nothing but allow Tanner the chance to slip his tongue into mine and send shivers of desire down my spine, even while his possession was punishing and angry. The violence behind it turned me on, and after that nothing else mattered but my raging hormones. I melded into his strength, totally shameless and accepting of his burning possession.

My libido had never gone from zero to ten so fast.

The first touch of his tongue to mine caused a river of wildfire to surge through my blood, hotter than anything I'd ever experienced before, hotter than lava. My taste buds exploded with his wet heat and the mild delicious taste of coffee and something else I couldn't define. I was sandwiched between his hard body and the brick wall at my back, and he was harder, all over. I moaned weakly as arousal exploded inside me, welcoming his hard-core attack with movements of my own.

He thought he was teaching me a lesson. We'd see about that. He seemed to be enjoying what he was doing so much. Maybe it was all for show, so that his friends would think that he was in control, putting me in my place by acting all alpha on me until he had me swooning and drooling and properly tamed. Is that how the men in his MC world handled women when they thought they needed handling? Possess her in public while turning her into a melting pool of quivering nerves?

Two could play at that game, and I vowed before it was over that Tanner would be questioning the outcome of *his* little lesson. If nothing else, I was good at kissing, and I brazenly welcomed his mouth devouring mine. Yes, devouring, because that's what his kiss felt like to me, but in the best possible way. I was literally melting from the inside out from the feelings that were coursing through me. My blood was on fire. His tongue was fucking mine; there was no other word for it, plundering and ravishing every corner of my mouth, behind my teeth, under my tongue, the roof of my mouth. My tongue fought back vigorously, and I moved my mouth into his rough possession, demanding more, but it was when we gradually slowed and I took his bottom lip between my teeth that he shuddered and groaned deeply.

I smiled inwardly like the Cheshire Cat, but didn't give up my well-earned prize. I knew that I wasn't hurting him, it was a move that had suddenly just come to me. I'd kissed other men and had never wanted to bite them, so I wasn't sure where the urge to do it now had come from. I released his lip, soothing the spot with the tip of my tongue. Tanner's breathing hitched, and then he jerked back with a look of surprise in his eyes, as if he'd just figured something out. Our gazes locked for a hot minute.

"Oh, fuck, no," he rasped, a sexy grin moving across his face. I blinked up at him innocently. "Trouble." I caught my breath as he leaned into me until I could feel the hard ridge of his cock against my lower stomach. For the second time I noticed that he wasn't a small man. I moaned and shut my eyes, savoring the delicious feel of Tanner wanting me. At least his cock did. I thrust against the long length of him, found out how good it felt against my pussy, and thrust back again. "Don't tempt me," he snarled between his teeth.

"To what?" I asked innocently, feigning ignorance. "I thought you were teaching me a lesson." I couldn't keep the smile off my face. I knew that he was turned-on, but it was easier for me to hide.

Tanner shook his head and exhaled. "You're playing with fire. I have no qualms about fucking you right here up against this wall, in public."

Ohmygod! My eyes widened with disbelief at that news, while I couldn't help but be even more turned on by it. The image of

Tanner fucking me against the very wall he had me pinned to was so arousingly inappropriate and naughty that it tickled my clit. I didn't wonder *if* he'd fucked in public before, I wondered how many times he'd done it. I felt heat creep up into my cheeks and I hoped that Tanner blamed the added color on embarrassment and not what his confession had done to me. "But you won't," I said smartly and with confidence.

I knew instantly that I'd said the wrong thing. Baiting Tanner was like dangling raw meat in front of a hungry tiger and daring him to take it.

"I never turn down a challenge," he groused, pinning my arms above my head against the warm brick.

No way! I glanced around us with panic, and quickly tried to back pedal. "What I mean is—"

"I don't give a fuck what you meant."

I opened my mouth to protest but his slanted over mine again, and I knew immediately that this kiss was different. It was meant as a distraction, but nothing could distract me from where his hand was moving. While I was held helpless against the wall by one large hand, Tanner's other hand went to the snap and zipper at my shorts. Realizing what he was doing, or *un*doing, I arched in an effort to push him off me. Surely he wasn't serious about fucking me in public? What had I unleashed? I moved my head in an effort to break our kiss, but he followed my movements with ruthless accuracy. I was unsure why I was moaning, inundated with panic, fear, and worst of all, a burning desire.

After he deftly undid the snap and lowered the zipper, Tanner's hand went to my waist. I thought he'd had a change of heart until he gave my waist a squeeze and then smoothed his hand back to the opening of my shorts. I knew what he'd find if he dared go inside. I was so wet that I could feel it soaking my panties. My clit was throbbing to the point that I realized I could come without much manipulation. I was wiggling to get away, and managed to pull my arms away from the wall.

Tanner tore his mouth from mine but remained in my space. His expression was taut, the black of his eyes glittering like polished onyx. One hand encircling both my wrists, he slammed my hands back against the wall. I gasped, my gaze captured by his. I could feel my heart beating wildly in my chest, my nipples were so hard that they ached, and the yearning in my core overwhelmed my common sense. A shiver traveled down my spine when his fingers moved over the exposed skin of my belly where my shorts had parted. I shivered when his fingertips lightly danced over my skin.

I shook my head. "You're insane!" I whispered sharply, unable to turn my eyes away from the fire in his.

"Maybe, but if I teach you anything before we go back inside, it will be to watch your mouth around bikers."

His fingers inched lower. I sucked in my breath, so damned turned on that he could have done anything he wanted to do to me right there and then, and I wouldn't have complained.

"You're so turned on right now you don't know what you're feeling."

I reminded myself of how I'd come to be in this situation in the first place. "Okay, I'll be good," I rushed out in a desperate tone, gasping again when his fingers began to wiggle beneath my panties. "I promise!" My breath caught.

Tanner's grin was cooked and sexy as hell. "Too late, baby."

"It's never too late," I countered, swallowing hard when the cool touch of his finger reached the top of my pelvic bone where the seam to my pussy began. My belly quivered. More heat and wetness soaked my panties.

He shook his head, moving closer, all but covering my body with his. "I want to feel you where it counts." He licked his lips. "You wet for me?" I sucked my bottom lip into my mouth and sank my teeth down into it, shaking my head. The next instant Tanner's index finger was sliding into my slit right over my pulsing clit. A low chuckle vibrated through his body. "Liar. You're so fucking wet it's like dipping my finger into honey." He flicked my clit.

I was lost. I laid my head back, closed my eyes, and opened my mouth to suck in air. I couldn't even pretend that what he was doing to me was against my will. Instinctively, my body arched toward his hand, silently begging for him to continue. If Tanner followed through, this would be my first orgasm at the hands of a man. I knew what it would feel like, I'd given myself plenty, yet there was something so basic and primal for a man to be touching me there.

I wasn't worried that someone would see us. He was so close to me that his huge body had to be hiding most of mine. His fingers were exploring, running through my cream, caressing my swollen labia, tapping my clit and making me jump. God, it felt so good! My little button was so hard and sensitive. In no time I felt the tell-tale swell deep inside me that indicated that I was going to orgasm. When Tanner stopped manipulating my swollen clit I almost cried out with disappointment. I'd been so close that my hips were still moving as if he were still touching me.

My eyes flew open, looking directly into his. His callused hand was suddenly cupping my whole mound, while he buried two thick fingers into me, placing his thumb on my clit. Too much, too soon. My body couldn't take it as pleasure overwhelmed my senses. My knees grew weak, my thighs trembled. I was breathing heavily, almost hyperventilating.

"Come for me, baby." I shook my head vigorously, determined not to give him that victory no matter how fucking good it felt. Everything on Tanner's handsome face revealed that he was just as turned on as I was. His tanned skin was taut over his jaw, and I could tell that he was clenching his teeth. His nostrils were flaring with his deep breaths. His eyes were smoldering, granite pools of fierce need, yet I was the only one benefiting from what he was doing.

His fingers began moving more rapidly, going deeper, curling inside me and brushing something new, something I'd never discovered. The thumb on my clit was merciless. My whole body was trembling. I began to whimper, tears filled my eyes, and I began to wonder if it was possible to have a heart attack while having an orgasm. The thrusting of my hips worked Tanner's fingers as if I were riding his cock.

"Tanner—" I began to panic when I realized that I was going to come, and it wasn't going to be a soft and quiet release. He released my wrists and my arms fell like heavy weights around his shoulders until I was clinging to his neck in weak abandon. "I—"

"It's okay," he muttered against my ear, giving my lobe a not-so-gentle tug, his breathing ragged. "I've got you, baby. Let go. I want to feel your cream coating my fingers."

I did. I buried my face against his shoulder when my orgasm hit, and the only thing keeping from screaming out my release for the whole world to hear were my teeth biting down on him. His hiss barely registered as I climaxed hard. I felt my cream coat the fingers he kept buried deep inside me while I convulsed uncontrollably in his arms. I was panting, my breasts crushed against his solid chest, his erection grinding against me and prolonging my release. If he hadn't been holding me up I would have crumbled to the ground.

As my breathing calmed and my heart rate returned to normal, I let myself relax like a wet dishrag against Tanner's hard frame. I was afraid to separate from him, afraid that we'd drawn a crowd in spite of being in the back of a business. As awareness set in, I realized that his fingers were still inside me. As if sensing my thoughts, he slowly pulled them out. A whimper escaped me before I could prevent it.

"Jesus Christ, you came like a fucking firecracker." I heard the husky timbre of his voice over my head.

The wonder in Tanner's voice revealed that he may not have been used to women who came so hard and intense. What was I supposed to say? That it had never happened like that before? That he was my first man? That it was the first time, and that it probably wouldn't be like that next time? I wasn't about to admit that I'd only ever had an orgasm by my own fingers. God, how pitiful would that sound?

I finally found my voice. "Are you done molesting me?" His chest shook with silent laughter. The occasional tremor shook my body, and I was afraid of what I'd see on his face when he stepped away.

"I could make you eat those words," he threatened mildly.

I shook my head. I wouldn't survive it. "No, thank you, and could you please take your hand out of my pants?"

The way Tanner removed his hand drew a long moan from me. It was slow, and he made sure to run his wet fingers over my sensitive clit on the way out. I stepped away first, raising my gaze to his eyes, which were filled with humor. He knew exactly what he'd been doing. "You're evil," I said jokingly. My eyes took in something on his shoulder, rounding with surprise and a bit of worry.

"What?" Tanner questioned, his eyes narrowing.

"Nothing," I said quickly, looking away with guilt. There was no way I was going to tell him that my teeth marks were visible in the leather of his cut. I couldn't believe that I'd bitten him that hard. Hopefully in time they would fade away. Remembering that my shorts were still gaping open, I reached down to take care of it. "Is my lesson over?"

He snorted. "This one, and if you're smart, you won't put yourself in a position where I'll need to teach you another one." I tried to glare at him, but it was hard to be mad at a man who'd just given me the most intense orgasm I'd ever had. "I mean it, Ruby. This isn't a game. The men around here are dangerous and don't play around. They take what they want, including women."

I could tell that Tanner was being serious. He seemed genuinely worried about my safety, and in spite of everything, I couldn't just ignore it. I knew telling him that I'd been on my own for a long time and had been taking care of myself wouldn't placate him in any way. He was one of the men he was talking about, and he'd just proven how easily he could take what he wanted. So what if he hadn't gotten anything out of my orgasm?

And then, as if he'd known what was going through my mind, he raised his fingers to his mouth and sucked them clean. I couldn't pull my eyes from the dark arousal gleaming in his, watching his mouth close around those digits as he tasted my cream. Lust slammed through me so intensely that I sucked in my breath.

"Taste good?" *Ohmygod!* I wasn't sure what had made me ask that. I felt my ears catch fire as embarrassment enveloped me like a heavy cape. I wanted to run away.

Tanner's grin moved over his face slowly as he pulled his wet fingers from his mouth, and I swear my panties melted from the heated promise in his eyes. "Next time I'll let you have a taste."

Next time?

I swallowed hard.

I spun on my heel and went back inside the bar.

Chapter 12

Tanner

Whew! I watched Ruby's sweet little ass disappear inside One Eye's, re-arranging my dick as she went. It was damned uncomfortable confined the way it was in my pants, hard as fuck behind the zipper, and so damned hungry for pussy that I could probably give it a few rubs and get off. The trouble was that I wanted to lose myself in her hot, little cunt. She'd been so eager and responsive when I'd been fingering her, almost as if it had been a new experience for her and she couldn't believe how good it had felt.

I didn't believe that for a second.

"Hey, man."

I turned, surprised to see an old friend walk around the brick barrier from the road side. "Rebel, man." We shook hands and pulled each other in for a man hug. "How you been, brother?" His dusty, fatigued condition revealed that he'd probably just arrived after days on the open road from wherever he had come from. We'd grown up in the same neighborhood and gone to the same schools, but had gone our separate ways once we'd been old enough to be on our own. I'd joined the service, he'd patched into Dark Menace. I hadn't seen him in about two years. He usually came around during Bike Week.

"Good," he said, his rugged, tanned expression not giving anything away. Neither did his sharp, blue eyes. He'd always been good at hiding his emotions. "Just got into town. Was riding by when I saw you."

I raised a brow at that. "You saw?" I chuckled. Shit, I hadn't even heard his bike, or anything else, when I'd had my fingers buried inside Ruby's sweetly responding pussy.

"Pretty girl." There was the slightest quirk on his mouth.

"Nothing but trouble," I quickly said. "She just got into town, too."

He snorted. "You work as fast as I remember, brother."

"Why don't you come inside for a drink? Pops and my brothers are here." I could sense his hesitation. Rebel was a loner, and it appeared that hadn't changed. Something had happened to him a few years ago, something bad but nothing he'd talk about it, and I hadn't pressed him. The rumors had circulated, though, and if they were even close to being true he'd gone through some seriously dark shit, the kind of stuff you didn't recover from. Maybe that was why he'd spent so much time in Last Hope lately, trying to fight the demons out that had claimed his soul.

"Maybe some other time, man, when I have more time. I'm looking for someone."

"You working a job?" He nodded. "Who you looking for, maybe we can help."

He shook his head. "Thanks for the offer, but this is something I've got to do on my own. It's personal."

Personal. I raised my brows at that because he'd said it was a job. Then I saw it in his eyes, whatever demons struggling to get out were right there, ripping him apart inside. I knew all about that shit. I felt for him because I couldn't help him work through it. "Well, give me a name, maybe I'll recognize it."

"Doubt it, brother. She's someone from my past and not from around here. Been looking for her for a long time. She moves around a lot."

I immediately thought about Ruby, but he'd got a look at her so I knew that it wasn't her. I scrutinized the dead look in Rebel's eyes, wondering. An unpleasant thought came across my mind, one I didn't want to think about, but I asked him anyway. "Hope you're not intending to hurt this woman."

His eyes hardened, and so did his expression. A tic appeared in his jaw before he took a breath and admitted, "Already hurt her."

The regret in his tone was obvious. "I need to find her and set things right, before it eats me up alive."

Christ, I didn't want to think about what he'd done, but it sounded bad. I nodded, waiting to see if he'd say more.

He released a deep breath, as if coming to a decision. "Ginger, that's her name. That's all I know."

"Hell, man, might as well be looking for a needle in a haystack."

Rebel nodded. "Yeah, I'm finding that out."

"What's she look like? You know Bike Week is a chic magnet. There will be a lot of strangers in town."

He nodded. "That's why I'm here," he admitted, and then his gaze moved on to something behind me, turning into an unblinking stare that told me that he was being haunted by something from his past. "She's a pretty girl. Fuck, change that, she's gorgeous. Brown hair down to her waist, brown eyes, skin the color of peaches." He snorted at himself, and met my eyes. "Ripe body. About five-five."

"How old?"

He thought for a minute. "Hell, she'd be about twenty-two, twenty-three now."

"Anything stand out that I can look for?"

He grinned. "Yeah, but you won't see it. She has a butterfly tat right about here." He pointed to a spot that would be the top of her pelvic bone. "And she has a tiny scar here." His finger moved to the corner of his left eye. I nodded. "You know how to get in touch with me if you see her."

"Yep. You sure you won't come in for that drink?" I was suddenly eager to get back inside to see what kind of trouble Ruby was getting in to. Judging from the noise filtering outside through the back door, the bar had filled up and was sounding rowdy.

He shook his head. "See ya around, man."

"Yeah, take care." We shook hands and I watched Rebel walk past his bike and around the building toward the front. I hoped that he found what he was looking for, because my gut told me that she was the key to bringing him back to the living.

I reached for the doorknob and opened the door to find a chaotic scene inside. That was nothing out of the norm for a biker's bar during Bike Week. The place was packed despite the fact that it was still early. The music was loud, forcing the occupants to shout over it to be heard. The sound of laughter and glasses clanking together added to the noise. The bar was overcrowded, some people had squeezed in between the stools, and most of the tables were taken.

My gaze went to where I'd left Pops and my brothers. My brothers were still there, but when I didn't see Ruby I searched the room, specifically the dance area, and didn't see her there either. Then it occurred to me that I hadn't seen Pops. I began to make my way over to my brothers when I felt a hand on my arm. I halted and glanced down into the inviting baby-blues of the attractive blonde in the red dress.

I could tell immediately that she was wearing colored contacts. Once I got a closer look at her I could see that she wasn't a natural blonde either, and she'd had a boob job. Jesus, I hated that fake shit. Why did women have to mess with what God had given them? I was tit man but hell, I wanted soft and pliable in my hands. Glancing down at the flesh that was exposed above her low-cut dress, hers appeared to be too large, too perfectly round.

"Hi, baby. How about we have a drink together?" Her hand smoothed up over my chest.

I returned her smile. "Sorry, doll. Not now. Take a rain check?" I could see the disappointment in her eyes before she masked it quickly with another smile.

"You sure, handsome?" Her hand moved slowly down my abs, and I wondered if she'd stop at my belt or be brave enough to continue to where my dick was tucked behind my zipper. "I could make it worth your while." She did that tongue tracing her upper lip thing again.

I grasped her wrist to keep her from going any further. If I'd had time, and I wasn't worried about what kind of trouble Ruby might be getting into with Pops, I may have taken her out back for a quickie. She looked like she could take a hard pounding. But I wasn't hard anymore. Between Ruby coming back inside and my conversation with Rebel, the urge had gone away.

"You make it hard for a man to say no, doll, but I'm going to have to decline your offer for another time." This time the disappointment remained in her eyes. She must have realized that she wasn't going to get her way. "I'll be around. Maybe next time."

I gently pulled away and stepped around her, meeting the amusement in Mike's eyes as I headed in his direction, my eyes still looking for Ruby and Pops. Tork and his crew had also disappeared, and I clenched my teeth, remembering the interest I'd seen in his kid's eyes when they were on Ruby. Mike was shaking his head with disbelief when I reached where he was sitting.

"I can't believe you turned down an easy piece of pussy," he said, taking a sip of his beer.

I ignored him. "Where the hell did Pops and Ruby go?"

He shrugged.

"They took off with Tork and his boys," Ace said, overhearing my question to Mike. Ace was the oldest of us at forty-three. He was built like a professional wrestler, big and strong as an ox, his face scarred from a helicopter crash he'd survived when he'd been deployed. He'd nearly lost his right leg, too, but the doctors had managed to save it, leaving him with a slight limp. "Heard something about them lookin' for some old friends."

"You worried about your pretty houseguest?" Gabe grinned. "She looked well taken care of."

His words reminded me that I still needed to call my aunt. "Hell, no. I think that little gal is capable of taking care of herself, but she's trouble, and I don't want Pops getting hurt."

"She's the good kind of trouble," Mark said, right before he took a hit off his beer. "If I didn't have Judith..." He let the rest of his sentence trail off.

"Then it's a good thing you have Judith. I don't want any of you getting involved, or even *thinking* of getting involved with Ruby. She's not going to be here for long, and I don't want to have to listen to any of you whining about letting the best pussy you've ever had get away."

Skipper leaned away from the bar enough to make eye-contact with me. "Sounds like someone wants to eliminate the competition."

Grinning, I snorted, "Competition? You may want to wipe the donut powder off your face first, brother." Laughter followed, and I looked at the brother who'd laughed the loudest. "What are you laughing about, Sully? Looked at your face lately?" His smile quickly disappeared, and he snapped his head back to look into the mirror behind the bartender, narrowing his eyes. Then he reached up and wiped the corner of his mouth off. I got a good chuckle at his reaction, and then said, "Just remember what I said." I turned and headed for the door.

"Where you going?" Heath wanted to know.

"To look for Pops," I said out loud. *And Trouble.*

Chapter 13

R uby

    I was amazed at the amount of people that had shown up for Bike Week and the endless activity going on around us as we made our way slowly down the sidewalk. It was obvious that the men I was with were more interested in looking at the people surrounding us than pausing to check out any of the souvenirs being sold. There were a lot of grunts and chin lifts of acknowledgement between them and others, but nothing verbal was exchanged. I quickly learned that their brief, blunt exchange was the norm for bikers.

I couldn't help but notice the women wandering around, the ones who weren't with someone. They were very obvious in what they were looking for, but if a man wasn't decked out in some kind of biker gear and giving off that bad boy vibe he went ignored. I grinned at some of the exchanges that I saw, until one of the men looked at me with raised brows and a question in his eye. I turned my head quickly. I didn't want him or any other man to think that I was interested. The other women were provocative, dressed in revealing clothing and making lewd comments that revealed that they were ready and willing. I was not one of them.

We passed other bars along the way, and plenty of places selling t-shirts and other souvenirs. Apparently, it wasn't unusual for temporary venues to pop up during Bike Week, as Jimmy explained to me. Daytona Beach Bike Week brought in a lot of revenue, and everyone wanted a piece of the pie. There were signs everywhere advertising concerts and events that were coming up, things like wet t-shirt and bikini contests, karaoke night, and a booty shaking dance contest. And there was a coleslaw wrestling match at a place called The Cabbage Patch.

I laughed.

"What's so funny?" Jimmy wanted to know.

"I can't picture any of you guys wrestling in coleslaw."

Jimmy threw back his head and laughed out loud, drawing looks from Pops and his brothers, before leaning in close and whispering into my ear, "The men don't fight in it, baby, the women do."

"Sounds gross to me. Why would they do that?"

This time he just chuckled. "The same reason they do the wet t-shirt and bikini contests, and everything else. To entertain us men. They fight in bikinis, and if we get lucky they lose their tops."

Oh. I rolled my eyes and made a face, trying to imagine being covered in wet cabbage. "You guys probably think that's sexy, right?"

"Damn right!" he agreed enthusiastically. He looked down at me. "You should think about entering in some of the contests going down this week. I'd vote for ya."

"Oh, yeah?" I hit his arm playfully. "Let me guess, the wet t-shirt contest?"

He shrugged with humor in his eyes. "That would be a good one, yeah, and there's also pole dancing, the bike wash-"

"Oh, I see where this is going," I said with amusement. "Are there any contests that don't include getting wet?"

Jimmy grinned and averted his gaze. "What's wrong with getting wet? It's hot as hell right now."

He wasn't kidding. The heat was stifling. Several times I'd lifted the heavy hair off the back of my neck to try and cool off. The contest Jimmy had mentioned didn't interest me until I saw the sign that said that the winner got a hundred dollars. That was a lot of money to me, and I couldn't remember the last time I'd had that much at one time. As the next sign came into view I studied it closer, searching for the place and time. The first wet t-shirt contest was scheduled for the following night at seven o'clock. There was a large glossy showing five well-endowed women wearing tiny pink shorts and wet t-shirts clinging to their breasts. Hmmm, I wasn't sure I had it in me to strut myself on a stage knowing that every man there was focused on my boobs.

I wondered if there was money involved with the bike wash as we continued to walk. The street on both sides was lined with motorcycles, all backed up to the curb. There were plenty of bikers, male and female, walking around, some in clusters, and some riding down Main Street in a kind of parade atmosphere. The ones dressed in leather, dark sunglasses, and bandannas looked like bad asses to me, and I was able to identify the clubs by the leather vests, or cuts, as Pops had corrected me earlier, were wearing. He warned me to stay away from anyone wearing a cut until I checked with him first.

I thought that was funny, considering that I was supposed to be the one looking out for him. But I had to admit that it felt good, having someone who was worried about me. My grandmother had been the last one who'd cared anything about me, but since her death I'd been on my own, even when I'd been living in foster care. That situation had taught me that the only reason so-called good folks took in foster children was for the money, and for the extra help around the house. It hadn't been totally bad, though. At least I'd had a roof over my head, had been fed, and had clothes.

We were nearing the end of the street where we either had to cross over or turn around and walk back the way we'd come. If we'd continued straight we would have crossed at the intersection and continued toward the beach. I hadn't had a chance yet to walk down to the surf and planned on rectifying that as soon as the opportunity presented itself.

"How ya doin' back there, cutie?" We'd just stepped off the curb and were halfway across the street when Pops shouted the question without turning around.

"I'm okay, Pops. Just taking it all in."

I watched Tork lean close to Pops and they exchanged words, but I was too far back to hear what they were saying. Then Pops said, "If ya want to head to the beach for a while that's okay with me. We can meet up somewhere later."

"No, I'm good." He wasn't getting rid of me that easy, if that's what he was trying to do.

"Jimmy."

The next thing I knew Jimmy was taking me by the arm and drawing me away from the group. "What-what are you doing? What's going on?" I looked back to see Pops and his friends continue in the opposite direction from us. I tried to pull away. "Jimmy?"

"Relax, baby." I glanced up to see a muscle twitching in his jaw and an expression that made him look years older than I imagined he was. Where had the smiling, fun-going man I'd danced with earlier gone to? The eyes looking down at me now were serious and slightly cold. "They have some business to take care of."

I didn't care. My concern was for Pops. "What kind of business?" I wanted to know, still trying to break free. I tried not to let panic set in. "Where are you taking me?"

"Nowhere, darlin'. We're just going this way and they're going that way."

His strides were so wide that I had trouble keeping up. I frowned. "Well, maybe I want to go that way!" I tried again to pull free, but his hand was clamped around my upper arm like a shackle. I glanced back to see Pops and his friends mingling with another group of bikers. Their expressions revealed that it may not have been a friendly conversation. "I don't like this, Jimmy. What is going on?" I was getting scared for Pops.

With a resigned sigh he pulled me off the sidewalk and pushed me into a restaurant. "Let's get something to eat. We'll talk inside." I glanced over my shoulder back to where Pops and the two groups of bikers were. "He'll be okay," Jimmy insisted.

There was a podium at the front of the restaurant with a sign stating 'wait to be seated,' but Jimmy ignored it and pulled me to a table away from the others. He pushed me down into a chair and took the one opposite me. He met my eyes and released another sigh. "They have business to take care of."

I crossed my arms. "Yeah, you already said that."

He smiled. "You don't know anything about bikers clubs, do you?"

"Not really," I admitted. "Though I'm learning fast." I was learning through observation. "If anything happens to Pops..." I couldn't finish because I didn't know what I'd do if something happened to him.

"Why you so worried about that old man?" Jimmy asked, motioning over one of the waitresses. She came up behind me so I could not see her, but I sure could smell her. She'd apparently bathed in perfume before coming to work. "Could you bring us two beers, sweetheart?" When he was done eyeing the waitress as she walked off, he returned his gaze to me. "I've known Pops all my life, he can take care of himself."

Now I was the one releasing a heavy sigh. "You said it yourself, Pops is an old man. And he's not in the best of health." I hesitated, wondering if I should admit the truth to him.

"What else?"

He seemed to know that I was holding back. Could I tell him that Pops' family had hired someone to be his companion? To make sure that he didn't do anything dangerous, took his medication on time, and kept him company so that he didn't get bored and go looking for trouble? I hadn't been told the detailed specifics yet, but I supposed that those were the reasons I'd been hired.

But I couldn't do it, and I decided to let Pops keep his dignity. "I want to know why I couldn't be present for this 'business' they had to take care of." The waitress returned with our beers, placing one in front of each of us. She smiled down at Jimmy and he gave her a wink, once again watching her walk away. I rolled my eyes. "Really?"

How did the waitress know that we weren't together? I was sure that my expression was saying what my mouth wasn't.

He shrugged good naturedly and reached for his beer. "I like women," he said unnecessarily.

"So do I," I countered, not realizing how he'd take it.

"Really?" His tone revealed that my admission was the next best thing from chocolate.

I snorted. "I like all people," I clarified. "So get that look off your face. You're not going to see any girl-on-girl interaction." Now he was the one snorting. "So, answer my question." He took a sip of his beer, and I wondered if it were for liquid courage or if he was just stalling.

He crossed his arms and leaned back in his chair. "The business they had was verbal and not for your ears. Tork asked me to keep you busy until it's done."

"Tork? You call your dad Tork?" I took a sip of my beer.

"When it comes to the club and any business concerning the club, yes."

"Boy, you guys are serious about your motorcycle clubs, aren't you?" I didn't expect Jimmy to respond to my observation. "So, are you guys like, hard-core clubs?"

He seemed to think about his answer before responding, "We're not weekend warriors, if that's what you mean. We live, eat, and breathe our club. A lot of hard-core clubs do. It's a whole different culture, one you might have a hard time understanding and accepting."

I thought about that for a minute, taking another sip of my beer. "So educate me, Jimmy. After everything I've seen here today, I'm curious now."

The waitress chose that moment to come over to us. "You ready to order, honey?" She was looking directly at Jimmy.

"The lady first," he said, indicating me.

He may have been young, but he was a gentlemen. "I haven't even looked at a menu yet, but I'm guessing that you have hamburgers?" She nodded. "I'll have a cheeseburger with lettuce and tomato, no onion, please."

"And I'll have the same with an order of fries," he said, not waiting for her to stop writing down my order. The girl nodded and turned to walk away.

"How long have you been in your dad's club?"

"I was born into the club. My dad became president before I was even thought of. My uncle was VP until he retired."

"You retire from a club?"

Jimmy shook his head and leaned forward. "Depends on the club. Look, it's a complex subject. Why don't you just Google what you want to know? It will be easier for you and won't leave me with a headache."

"Sounds like you're trying to avoid the topic. What are you hiding?"

Amusement gleamed in his eyes. "Everything." That answer surprised me into a chuckle. "MCs are tight, and we keep shit close to the chest. We don't like civilians like you knowing our business. The club is like one big family, and we take care of our own. Any trouble comes our way, we deal with it our own way, too."

Well, that was clear enough, and a little ominous. I didn't have access to a TV and didn't spend money on newspapers, so I guess you could say that I was naïve in some things. Once in a while I'd come across a newspaper left on a city bus bench, or on a table in a diner, but not often enough to keep up with world events, much less anything else. But I had an active imagination and could guess at how a hard-core MC operated outside the boundaries of the law.

It made me wonder about the Sentinels, but they didn't appear to be in the same caliber as the clubs that Jimmy was talking about. They looked just as dangerous and they certainly dressed the part, but I didn't get the uncomfortable feeling from them that I got from some of the others I'd come across today. I knew that I was stereotyping, but I couldn't help it. I'd seen a few good-looking men, but just as many with long, stringy hair, piercings and tattoos, gruff demeanors, and dirty looks that were kind of scary compared to Tanner's smoking hot looks in leather.

Jimmy wasn't bad either, but he was young, and my girly parts didn't like him as much as they did Tanner. I didn't want to think about the earth-shaking, mind-blowing orgasm he'd given me

earlier, but it was hard not to with wet panties. The man had magic fingers. I'd never felt that same intensity when I'd played with myself.

The waitress returned with our food, setting it down in front of us. "Either of you need anything else?"

"No, thank you."

"Not right now." Jimmy wasted no time in digging into his fries. Just as he was cramming a couple into his mouth, his cell went off. He lifted enough to dig it out of his back pocket and put it to his ear. "Yeah?" His expression gave nothing away. "Okay. Soon as we're done eating."

I waited until he put his phone down. "Are they done with business?" I teased, picking up my cheeseburger.

He nodded. "Yep. Soon as we finish we'll meet them."

Silence followed after that as we both focused on our meal. The hamburger was good, and I reached across the table a couple of times to steal a French fry from Jimmy. He just smiled silently and kept eating.

Chapter 14

Tanner

I ended the call and slipped my phone into my back pocket. My conversation with Aunt Marge had been interesting. She hadn't known anything about Ruby, but she had confirmed that she'd mentioned wanting to hire a companion for Pops to several of her cronies, and they in turn must have gossiped their way through Daytona. So it appeared that Ruby's story held some merit. Tom from Tom's Diner had backed up her story of how she'd ended up at my house. I figured out the rest of it by going over Ruby's story in my mind.

It had been a complicated mess that just happened to work out for the best, and solved the problem of what I was going to do with Pops, at least temporarily. Mike was going to run a background check on her as soon as I got the information he needed to start it. Christ, I didn't even know her last name. She and I were going to have a serious talk, just as soon as I could find her. For all I knew she could be wanted and on the run for something and I needed to know who Pops had let into my home.

I made a half-assed effort to find her by walking up and down Main Street, but ended up stopping and chatting with friends I'd run into, men that I hadn't seen in a while and who usually only came into town during Bike Week. After a while I gave up, knowing where she'd be at the end of the day. I could have called Pops, but I didn't want to make him suspicious. Aunt Marge and I both agreed that letting him believe that he was helping out a homeless girl by giving her a place to stay was to our benefit. We both knew he'd blow a fuse if he found out the truth.

I noticed some of the clubs weren't wearing their colors, which was typical during Bike Week when the clubs in question didn't want trouble, or didn't want to be easily identified by the undercover cops that patrolled the event in order to keep the peace. Then there were the clubs that didn't give a fuck, or were too stupid to keep a low profile, the ones that thought they were too big and tough, and were looking for trouble. Bike Week drew in MCs from all over the country and it was supposed to be kept friendly, but some clubs just couldn't put their hatred of one another at bay for a solid week

That's why all twelve of us were going to be a strong presence on Main Street during the next few days. We did wear our colors because this was our town and everyone knew what to expect from us. We didn't take shit from anyone, and most of the time we were avoided by a large margin because it was a fact that we took care of our town and its residents. Anyone that was stupid enough to get out of line knew that we wouldn't hesitate to take them down, and if they were alive at the end of it they usually ended up in jail. The Sentinels had a good relationship with local law enforcement, and we'd worked hard to achieve it.

As I sauntered casually through the crowd, two bikers turned the corner and rode down the center of the street. I knew that they were from the Kings MC even before they rode past and I saw their identifying cuts. Wicked was a fool for letting them wear their colors, because it was a rare club that didn't have a gripe against them for something stupid they'd done in the past. They were known to start trouble, liked to fight for little or no reason, and thought they were untouchable.

I shook my head with disgust, as a bad feeling settled into my gut. I glanced across the street and made eye contact with William and Sully. I motioned them toward the riders, getting further and further away to make sure they saw them. They glanced down the road and then back at me, acknowledging with subtle nods. Later we'd discuss what we were going to do about the Kings. We didn't want them in our town on a good day, much less during Bike Week.

The fact that two of them had just ridden by meant that there would be more of them somewhere close.

"Hey, brother!"

I turned toward the sharp tone to see two of Tork's brothers, Red and Tower. My gaze shifted around, looking for the others, but I didn't see them. "Where's the rest?"

They both laughed, but it was Tower who spoke. "You really give a shit, or you worried about your woman?"

"I'm worried about Pops, and she's not my woman," I responded briskly.

Red shrugged, but had the good sense to get serious. "Tork and Pops are talking shit with Hairy down at the station, Jimmy and Ruby took off for the Cabbage Patch for the kick-off party-"

"The kick-off party was yesterday," I snarled, not liking that news.

Red looked to Tower as if he could add something different, but the tall man just shrugged. "Well, I heard Cabbage Patch mentioned," Red continued after I'd interrupted him. "And Todd's busy screwing the brains out of some waitress he met taking a smoke break."

I saw red the instant I heard where Jimmy had taken Ruby. The Cabbage Patch was a biker's bar out in the middle of fucking nowhere, made famous for their coleslaw wrestling. Right next door was Crackleberry Campground. Both places would be packed to the gills with all kinds of activity and entertainment for the folks attending Bike Week. There wasn't a thing wrong with any of that, hell, I was looking forward to going there myself, but I didn't like the thought of Ruby there with a young Casanova trying to get into her pants.

I knew that's exactly what Jimmy was after. She hadn't seen it because she'd been facing the door, but I'd seen the lust in his eyes when they'd been dancing. If I hadn't entered the bar when I had, he would have had his hands all over her.

"So, what's the plan?" I asked, knowing that there had to be one. Tork liked to keep his brothers close when they were away from home and would have told them to meet up somewhere.

"Tork said to meet him at The Crab Shack at six." The Crab Shack was a pier restaurant.

I nodded, wondering what Tork and Pops had to talk to Hairy about. Hairy was typically found at the swap meet at the flea market during Bike Week. He swapped and sold bikes, and was a used parts vendor. His inventory was extensive, and if you needed it, he'd find it, no matter how old the bike or how rare a part was. Just about every biker knew him, and because of that he sometimes found himself in precarious positions. Rival clubs tried to use him as a link for information to other clubs. Pops' bike may have been out of commission, but I had a hunch that

Tork was the one to worry about.

I decided to head down to the station and find them for my own peace of mind. Tork was like an uncle to me, but it wouldn't be the first time that he'd involved Pops in a situation that resulted in backlash. You couldn't teach an old dog new tricks, and that's exactly what they were, two old timers who'd been engrained into hard-core MCs for most of their lives, and didn't know how to live any other way. Pops knew his health was holding him back, but he got involved in shit whenever the opportunity presented itself.

I decided not to lose my cool until I knew for sure what was going on. I reached the station, which had been an old garage back in the thirties, and stopped to look around. Holy shit, there were a lot of people there, and it looked like a band was setting up to play.

"Well, well, well, look who just showed up."

I didn't recognize the voice, but I sure as shit recognized the face, especially after she'd had her mouth wrapped around my dick the night before. She moved in front of me, so close that her body rubbed up against mine in what I knew was a deliberate move.

"Hi, baby."

She wet her lips, reminding me how good they'd felt on my dick, and making me temporarily forget why I was there.

"I didn't expect to see you again so soon."

I grinned down into her smiling, seductive face. "Sorry, sweetheart, but I'm looking for someone."

"And you've just found her," she teased, wetting her ruby-red lips with the tip of her tongue and running her hand up my abs.

Ruby.

Why the fuck had her pretty face suddenly popped up inside my head? I recalled what she'd looked like the last time I'd seen her, looking so soft and inviting after I'd just made her come so fucking hard on my fingers. I gave my head a brisk shake to wipe the memory away and tried to focus my attention on the woman in front of me whose name I still couldn't remember.

Her tits were all but popping out of the bikini-like top of her sundress, which stopped about mid-thigh. Her blonde hair looked messy, as if someone had beaten me to it and had been running their hands through it. Come to think of it, her lipstick did look a little smudged. When she leaned in as if to kiss me I leaned back out of her reach. There was no telling where her mouth had been.

"I forgot, you don't like to kiss either," she said with hard disappointment. "But you'll let me kiss your cock." It was then that I smelled the booze on her breath.

She'd said it a little too loudly, and several heads turned. I ignored them, pinning a hard gaze on her until she looked away with unease. "I told you from the start how it would be, and you seemed okay with it. If you can't accept that it won't go any further then walk away. Otherwise be happy with what I can give you." I reached up and took her chin in my hand, squeezing hard enough to make sure she understood. "You're not the only woman. Do you understand?"

"Yes."

I couldn't see her eyes behind the dark sunglasses she was wearing, but the slight trembling of her mouth revealed that she may be on the verge of tears. I finally remembered her name was Shelly. We'd fucked once, a few weeks ago, and she'd given me a few blowjobs since then. "Good. Now I've got to find someone. I might be around the bar later tonight, okay?" I made sure to say it in a tone that wasn't a firm commitment. She nodded slowly. "I'll buy you a drink and we'll see where we go from there."

Hell, as I walked away I began to wonder if I was going to have to start limiting the women to one blowjob, too. I wasn't afraid of getting attached, but women seemed to connect their hearts to their pussies, and in their minds if you went back for seconds then you must want them. I'd gone out of my way to make sure every woman knew the score before things heated up. That may have made me a prick, but let no one say that I'd led them on in the bedroom. It just wasn't going to happen.

I spied Pops, Tork, and Hairy sitting at one of the open-aired bars. The three appeared to be deep in conversation, their heads were bent close as they talked. I had to wonder if they were worried about being overheard while they were here and not somewhere more private. I prayed like hell that they weren't trying to involve Pops in something, and breathed a sigh of relief when suddenly all three of them were throwing back their heads and laughing at something one of them had said.

By the time I reached where they were sitting the laughing had stopped, but their expressions still revealed that they'd found something funny.

"Hey, son," Pops said upon noticing me.

"Pops."

"You lookin' for me?" Pops asked.

I shook my head. "Just walking around." I made eye contact with Hairy and Tork. "You brothers aren't trying to get Pops into trouble, are you?"

"Naw, we wouldn't do that," Hairy grinned around a mouth full of gold teeth. "Just catching up on old times."

"Thought you'd be at the flea market. You didn't set up this year?" The pretty bartender looked at me expectantly. "I'll have a Budweiser."

"Oh, yeah. I got a big booth this year. Found some vintage bikes to sell. Got my nephew running it right now."

"Vintage bikes, huh, you wouldn't happen to have a forty-eight Harley Davidson EL Panhead, would you?" I took the beer the bartender handed me over the bar.

"That was my first love," Pops said, telling me something that I already knew. He was the reason that I was interested in obtaining one.

"Don't have one but now I know you're interested in one I'll be on the lookout."

I gave Hairy a sharp nod, taking a few sips of my beer. My thoughts drifted to the Cabbage Patch and what Jimmy and Ruby could possibly be doing. There would be a huge crowd there, but where there was a will there was a way, and I knew from experience that if you wanted to find a quiet spot for a quick fuck you could. I didn't know why the thought of them fucking bothered me so much. Maybe it had to do with my wanting a taste of her myself.

I finished my beer and crushed the can before tossing it into the trash. Tork was staring at something off to the side of us, so naturally I turned to see who or what it was. I stiffened on spotting the same two Kings that I'd seen earlier riding down Main Street. And this time they weren't alone. Four others were with them, and their attitude spoke volumes. They were there to cause trouble. I exchanged glances with Tork as I reached for my phone. He reached for his at the same time.

I phoned my VP.

"Yeah, brother, what's up?" Gabe asked.

"Put a call out to the others and get your asses down here to the station. Kings just showed up and I want to stop trouble before it begins."

"Will do." He disconnected the call before I could.

"Tower, Red, and Todd are on their way," Tork said, slipping his phone into his back pocket. He'd had run-ins with the Kings before and hated them as much as we did.

I was suddenly glad that Ruby wasn't there and I only had Pops to worry about. If trouble broke out he'd want to be right in the middle of it. He refused to believe that he was past his prime, that he was a thin, frail, old man who'd passed his golden years and was heading toward the wrong side of the grave. One solid punch could end him, well before the cigarettes that he loved. I chanced a glance at him, thankful to see that he was busy talking to Hairy.

A slight commotion drew my gaze back toward the Kings. Wicked had just joined his crew, loud and obnoxious as ever. His cocky attitude fueled his brothers to act the same way. I scowled, shaking my head, and then swore beneath my breath.

Ruby and Jimmy had just come up behind them.

Chapter 15

R^{uby} Still full from lunch, I was glad that we were walking it off. Jimmy had wanted to head out to a place called the Cabbage Patch, but I'd declined. I didn't think leaving the area completely was a good idea, considering that I was supposed to be keeping company with Pops. Of course, I didn't explain that to Jimmy. It was none of his business, and truthfully, I wasn't even sure how to. The whole situation was complex.

Our plans to meet up with Pops and Tork after lunch had changed with another phone call from Tork. Apparently there was someone with Tork that Pops had wanted to see about his bike, so they were headed to the station. So we'd spent the rest of the afternoon walking around, stopping now and then to talk with acquaintances Jimmy had met up with, and checking out some of the souvenirs. The new plan was to meet up at the Crab Shack at six for dinner.

I didn't like the idea of being away from Pops for so long, but what could I do? Every time I mentioned to Jimmy that we should join up with them he'd brush me off and change the subject. After a while I'd given up.

"You like that one?"

I'd been looking through a bin of discounted tees, slightly surprised that it was the first day of Bike Week and there were already discounted items to be had, when a brightly colored tank had caught my eye. I was holding it up, examining the graphic. "Yeah, it's cool," I replied. The price tag revealed that it was only six dollars, but it was six dollars of the last ten I had in my pocket. I really couldn't afford it. I moved to put it back. No sooner had I dropped it on top of the stack of others than Jimmy snatched it up over my head.

"I'll get it for you," he said with a smile.

"Jimmy, no, I can't let you do that." I tried to snatch it out of his hand, a little embarrassed because I felt like he'd guessed why I was putting it back.

He chuckled, holding the garment up where I couldn't reach it. "I want to. It's only six bucks."

"But you paid for lunch, too."

"So?" he laughed, holding my gaze. "It's the least I can do for you after you've been stuck with me all day."

He was teasing, and it was clear that he didn't care about the money. I wondered if I'd ever have the luxury to afford food and new clothes in the same day. I was careful how I spent my money, always asking myself if I needed an item or did I just want it before spending. Food and gas for my car always took priority over anything else. I wanted to protest harder, but the look in Jimmy's eyes said that I wouldn't win.

"This doesn't mean that we're going steady or anything, does it?" I joked.

"Don't give me any ideas," he responded as we headed for the register. "Maybe you'll let me take you to the Cabbage Patch before I leave at the end of the week."

I smiled, not committing myself. For all I knew I wouldn't be around by the end of the week. "Thank you," I said when he turned and handed the bag to me after paying for it. "And I've had a really nice day. I don't feel as though I was 'stuck' with you."

"This is Main Street Station," Jimmy explained, even though the sign on the front of the building clearly stated that. "It used to be a gas station as far back as the nineteen-thirties when it was owned by the founder of stock car racing, Bill France. There used to be racing on the beach back then, and these are the original pumps."

I nodded, wondering how far 'back then' was, slightly amused that Jimmy was giving me a history lesson, though I wasn't sure how accurate he was. The pumps were the glossy colors of yellow, red, and black, the logos on the front reading 'American Gas,' except for the black pump that read 'Amoco'. They appeared well-preserved.

It seemed to be a happening place. It looked like a band was setting up on stage to perform, and people were mulling around, some were crammed at the bars drinking. I immediately spotted Pops and raised my hand to wave at him and get his attention. "Pops!" Hearing his name, he glanced up and began looking around for the source. He hadn't seen me yet. "Over here, Pops!" Smiling, I waved again, and began to make my way over to him.

What I didn't see was the group of bikers directly in front of me, particularly the one that I then abruptly bumped in to. He stumbled forward and then spun around with a snarl on his face, at the same time that I felt Jimmy's hand wrap around my upper arm.

"What the fuck!" the biker swore. His friends also turned around.

"I'm so sorry!" I began, wondering why Jimmy was trying to pull me back. "I wasn't watching where I was going." I was forced to stumble back a step when Jimmy persisted.

The man's eyes shifted to look at Jimmy, and then back at me, his expression slowly turning into a humorless grin that raised the hair at the back of my neck. In an instant I recognized that I could be in trouble, or at the very least that Jimmy could be, as they began to spread out and surround us. The man I'd run into was looking at me in a predatory way that left me feeling slightly dirty. *Violated* was probably a better word. His beady little eyes undressed me.

"Hey, darlin', if you wanted to get my attention all you had to do was grab *this*." 'This' was his crotch, as his hand had dropped down to clutch his cock area. My eyes grew big. He laughed. "Yeah, that's the same reaction I get from all the chicks."

He thought I was impressed? I laughed in the face of his cockiness. "Don't flatter yourself. There's barely a bump there."

Jimmy groaned low behind me. "Time to go," he said in a firm tone.

I took a step in the direction that he pushed me, only to come up short when the man stepped to the side and cut me off. It was a deliberate move, and his stance was threatening. Jimmy quickly pulled me behind him. "We don't want any trouble, Wicked."

Wicked? Who named their child Wicked?

"That your bitch?" he asked Jimmy. His angry eyes cut to me when I peeked around Jimmy.

He wasn't so cocky now, in fact his face was flushed with anger and he looked ready to fight. His friends began to crowd in around us, but what unnerved me even more was the way that some of the people had shuffled away, as if sensing a fight was coming and wanting no part of it.

"Is this your bitch?" Wicked asked again in a harsh tone.

"Wicked, man-"

"Shut the fuck up!" he hissed at one of his friends, who sounded as if he'd been trying to warn him of something.

"Is she your bitch?" he persisted in an unfriendly tone, and I wondered how many times he'd ask the same question.

Jimmy stiffened slightly, his only reaction to the situation. "No." He nodded sharply at something behind Wicked. "She's with them."

Them? I peeked around Jimmy and beyond Wicked to see Tanner, Tork, and Tork's club coming to a stop directly behind. Wicked turned around and took note of the others, but he didn't back down. If anything he looked excited with anticipation. His friends, on the other hand, looked slightly nervous, but didn't seem to be in a hurry to abandon their leader.

I met Tanner's hard eyes, relieved that he'd shown up when he had. He cut an imposing figure, a head taller than the others, his muscular arms flexing at his sides, his hands fisting. Flashes of black ice shot between Wicked and me, his tight expression showing no hint of what he could be thinking. I smiled and gave him a finger wave, not fully understanding the severity of the situation.

"You got good taste in pussy," Wicked said, directing his remark to Tanner. "But you need to teach her to watch her mouth, or I'll put it to good use."

"What a pig!" I screeched, his meaning not lost on me. I moved to go around Jimmy but his arm shot out, stopping me. "Your mother must be so proud of you!" I struggled against Jimmy's arm to get to Wicked, I was so disgusted.

Wicked laughed along with his friends.

"Ruby." I halted, meeting the dead calm in Tanner's eyes, his rugged face set like stone. "Go wait at the bar with Pops." I opened my mouth. "Now." His cold, unbending tone sent a chill down my spine, and I knew better than to question him. Jimmy lowered his arm and I stepped forward, making sure to stay as far away from Wicked as I could. It put me in closer proximity to his friends, but they didn't bother me.

I walked to the bar without trouble, smiling at Pops and hoping to ease the concern on his wrinkled face. He directed me to an empty stool between him and another man. "Shit's about to hit the fan, cutie," he said close to my ear. "Don't worry if I have to go give them a helping hand."

I didn't know how to respond to that, praying that it didn't come to that. Seeing some of Tanner's club members show up brought immense relief that the tense situation wouldn't erupt into something more. Our side, if you could call it that, had more numbers, and cut far more imposing figures than Wicked and his friends. I couldn't hear what was being said, but it was clear that Tanner and Wicked were the ones doing all the talking, and it definitely wasn't a friendly chat. After a few nerve-racking moments, Wicked motioned for his men to follow him as he stomped away.

He must have realized that he and his club couldn't win against the caliber of men staring him down.

However, I didn't miss his crude goodbye to me. He made a V with two of his fingers, placed them against his mouth, and thrust his tongue through it rapidly several times. I may have been a virgin, but I knew exactly what that meant.

"Why, you fuckin' punk!" Pops swore loudly, apparently catching what Wicked had done. He left his stool and made a dash right for Wicked.

"Pops, no!" I jumped off my stool and hurried after him. "Pops, it's okay, really." I caught his arm and tried to stop him. For an old man, and a thin one at that, he was surprisingly strong. Or maybe I was just weak. He practically dragged me all the way across the lot. "He can't help it if he's a snake, let him go back to the rock he slithered out from under."

Wicked, apparently overhearing me, stopped and spun around. Sensing that he might do something, I instinctively looked around for Tanner, spotting him angrily heading our way. I returned my gaze to Wicked, still clutching Pops' arm to my breast.

"Some other time, bitch. When your men aren't around to protect you."

What did he mean by that? By the time Tanner reached us, Wicked and his club had disappeared into the crowd.

"Jesus Christ, Pops, what did you think you were going to do?" Tanner snarled, before snapping his gaze on me. "And what the hell did you say to Wicked for him to threaten you like that?"

"Don't go blaming cutie-"

"I didn't say anything to him!" I said heatedly, releasing Pops' arm. It sounded like he was blaming me. "And if I did, what's wrong with that?" I wasn't about to cower in the face of his anger. Once I'd reached adulthood I'd sworn I'd never let another person tell me what to do or make me feel as though I'd done something wrong when I hadn't. His comment, and the anger behind it, reminded me too much of the tone my last foster dad had used on me. "You're not my dad." I knew it was a mistake the second the words left my mouth.

Pops snorted, but wisely remained quiet. More than one of Tanner's club members caught themselves from laughing at the last second, but not before their amusement was heard. A sharp look from Tanner quieted down the low murmurs simmering through the group. "No, but I'll be the one getting you out of trouble."

"I didn't ask you to, and don't worry, I won't. I've been doing just fine on my own, and I don't need anyone to take care of me." I was so mad I was trembling. "I may be renting a room in your house, but that's as far as it goes." He and I both knew that was a lie.

I could see that he was struggling to remain in control. A tic in his strong jaw twitched, revealing that he was clenching his teeth. His black eyes held no warmth, they were as cold and black as coal. I felt the urge to apologize for my dad comment, but I had a feeling that wouldn't make a difference.

"Why don't we all calm down and go back to the bar for a drink?" someone suggested, cutting through the tension in the air.

"I think cutie and I will go home." I glanced at Pops with surprise, wondering at the reason behind his remark.

It had been a long day, and then there was the stress of this incidence. Was he alright? I examined him closely, noticing that his color seemed a little off. Had he had anything to eat since breakfast? My sudden anger disappeared, overtaken by my concern for him. Tanner and I exchanged a brief glance, and I knew that he was worried, too.

"I think that's a good idea," Tanner said after a while. His gaze was still on me though. "You and I will talk later."

Translation—he'd talk, and I'd listen.

Chapter 16

R^{uby}

Ruby

I bent and picked up a shell that was half-buried in the sand. Most of the time they were broken pieces, but this one was perfect, ridged on the outside and smooth as silk on the inside. I brushed the sand off and slipped it into my pocket with the other two. I had no idea what I was going to do with them, but it seemed important that I keep them. This was my first walk on the beach ever, and I was enjoying everything about it.

After Pops and I had made it home I'd made a spaghetti dinner. He ate like a bird, but at least he'd eaten. He'd said it was good, too, and I had to admit that I agreed. Luckily for me, spaghetti was a fairly easy dish, and though I made it different every time, it somehow always came out good. I wondered how many days a week I could serve it for dinner before Pops and Tanner began complaining.

That thought made me smile. They'd learn soon enough that I wasn't much of a cook. Tomorrow I'd try my hand at a little housework, maybe change the beds and do some laundry. It occurred to me that I may have to explain to Pops why I was doing all that, considering he thought that I was just renting a room. Maybe Tanner could come up with an idea to pacify Pops. He hadn't come home yet, so we hadn't had that 'talk' he'd mentioned earlier in the day. But he was right, we did need to talk. I needed to set him straight on a few things. Mainly, that I was an adult and that he couldn't tell me what to do.

I had a feeling that he wasn't going to like that.

I was on my way back to the house, walking along the edge of the warm water, digging my toes into the sand. The surface of the ocean resembled black glass, and the moon reflecting off the water made it all seem so magical. The calm and peace surrounding me soothed my soul, or, at the very least, my nerves. It was an upgrade to the silence and loneliness of bedding down in the back of my car. I may have grown used to it, but it didn't mean that I liked it.

When I reached the house I noticed that a light had been turned on inside. Pops must have gone in to bed. When I'd left he'd been sitting in a chair smoking, but I could see that the chair was empty now. I knew it was getting late and thought about turning in myself, but the sound of the surf was so soothing that I opted for one of the loungers. I stared out at the dark water, marveling at the reality that two nights before I'd been settling down to sleep at a rest stop.

After a while I heard the sliding door open and close, indicating that Pops was probably coming back out for another smoke. He smoked too much. I was thankful that I'd never taken up the bad habit.

"Out for another smoke?"

"I don't smoke."

Tanner! I turned toward him, seeing him clearly thanks to the solar patio lights. He looked beat, but that didn't take away from his bad boy sexiness. I smiled as he sat down in the chair slightly opposite me. "Who's been running their hands through your hair?" I teased, accepting the beer he handed out to me. "Thanks."

He took a long swallow of his beer. "The same woman who ran her hands through it last night," he finally answered.

I sensed that he was telling the truth. He had no reason to lie or to make something like that up. We were nothing to each other. Still, his comment bothered me, and I didn't know why. Maybe because deep down, I was attracted to him. To cover up for it, I laughed softly. "So, where is she? You don't bring them home with you?"

"Never. We take care of business in the alley behind the bar and go our separate ways."

Was he serious? "That's kind of sad, Tanner." I took a drink, trying not to visualize the things he might have done with that woman in the ally. What kind of woman let a man do that to her anyway? And then I recalled our out of this world hot moment on Main Street that day. We'd been behind a bar, in plain sight, where anyone could have seen us.

"Says one loner to another," he snorted.

"Are you a loner?" I wouldn't have thought that he was. He had Pops and his brothers. But there were different kinds of lonely.

He shrugged. "I like my life the way it is," he said firmly. "I like variety in my women, my freedom, hanging with my brothers. What about you?"

"I'm not a loner because I want to be," I admitted. "I have no family. No friends. Never had a boyfriend."

"You seem to have hit it off with Jimmy."

"He's nice, and sweet, but not what I want."

"Just someone to have a fun time with?"

I nodded before realizing that he probably couldn't see it. "Yeah. I might let him have my cherry," I teased, not really meaning it. I liked Jimmy, but I couldn't see it going any further than friendship. Besides, he'd be gone soon.

The silence that followed seemed to last a long time, until it became strangely awkward. The breeze off the water caressed over us, making me aware of Tanner's manly scent of leather, smoke, and musk. It tantalized my senses and turned me on.

After a while Tanner asked, "Are you a virgin?"

"It's probably the only thing I have of value." I'd said it without thinking, realizing the truth behind the words. It was almost as sad as Tanner having sex with a woman in the ally.

"Fuck," he said low. "I didn't see that coming."

"Why? Because I'm on the road and live out of my car?" I couldn't explain it, but suddenly I was angry. "You think I'm a whore?"

"Whoa there! I never said that, and I certainly didn't think it."

I immediately settled down. "We need to talk about this, uh, arrangement, or whatever it is, Tanner. Pops thinks I'm renting a room. He's going to think it odd that I'm cooking meals, cleaning house, and following him around like a little puppy. What do I say when he starts asking? He's not stupid, and he knows his sister was looking to hire someone to stay with him."

"I talked to my aunt. She's happy with how things worked out. But you're right, he's going to ask sooner or later."

"Yeah, and he's going to expect rent sooner or later, too. He thinks I'm going to be out working every day."

"Shit." It grew quiet again. "He won't expect you to turn over rent because this is my house, so that's not a problem. But you're right about working, and it would defeat the purpose if you were to get a job."

"So what do we do?"

"Let me think about it."

"Well, while you're thinking about it, I think I'll go for a swim." I didn't wait for him to say anything else, didn't expect him to have any objections to my going.

I walked to the water's edge, which was far enough away from the patio lights so that I was cloaked in darkness. I hesitated briefly before slipping out of my shorts and then lifting my tee over my head. My bra and thong covered as much skin as a bikini would have. And besides, Tanner couldn't see me. I reached up and removed the clip from my hair, shaking my head until it was free and hanging to my waist.

"Don't go too far out!" Tanner hollered. "I don't want to have to come in and rescue your ass!"

"Jerk!" I hadn't intended to, anyway. I'd never swam in the ocean, but I was aware of the dangers out there. I knew predators fed at night, and I wasn't about to put myself in a position to become shark bait. The water was cool, and I stopped when it reached my waist.

Then I sank down up to my neck, digging my toes into the sandy bottom. It was so dark and quiet out there that I felt a moment of fear. An occasional seagull broke the silence, and then another and another.

I swam back and forth a little bit, the equivalent of the pool I'd used at the Y, until I'd reached ten laps. It was invigorating and worked out the stress of the afternoon. I'd been worried about Pops, too. His color hadn't looked good before we'd left Main Street, but once we were home and he lay down until dinner, he'd looked better. I'd asked him if he felt alright, and he'd responded, "About as good as any other day." He'd also sworn me to secrecy about his taking a nap, and even though he'd been teasing, there'd been an equal amount of seriousness to his request.

"Time to come in!" Tanner called from the beach.

I glanced toward shore to see his dark form at the water's edge. "When I'm done!" I hollered back. More and more seagulls began to arrive, seeming to focus on one spot further out.

"Now, Ruby!" His tone was sharp and impatient. "Unless you plan on donating one of your pretty limbs to the shark out there."

What? I made several panicked twirls, looking for said shark, but all I saw were the seagulls diving toward the water. I stood up and shivered violently as my imagination began to spin out of control and I began to replay all of the *Jaws* movies I'd seen as a teenager. Then something brushed my leg and I squealed like a pig, making toward the beach as fast as I could. Running in water, I soon learned, wasn't easy.

I hadn't even hesitated to expose myself to Tanner. I ran up to him, out of breath, only stopping when I reached him. "Did... you see... a shark?" I gasped out, glancing back at the water.

"I don't have to see a shark to know it's there, Trouble. You see those gulls?" I looked back towards the spot where the gulls were still circling. "They're diving for food. The same thing drawing them pulls in the sharks, especially if there's blood."

"Oh," I said, feeling my heartbeat slowly calm. "You scared the crap out of me."

He laughed softly. "I had to do something to get you out of the water." Something in his tone drew my gaze slowly to his. "I wanted to see you in your birthday suit," he admitted with a big, wolfish grin.

I stared at Tanner for a minute, wondering if I should be outraged by his admission, embarrassed, or if I should just go with the flow. He was staring down at me, but really, how much could he see? I laughed. "Well, too bad for you, I'm wearing my underwear."

He surprised me by reaching forward and slipping a finger beneath the strap to my bra. Just that small, intimate touch caused me to shiver with awareness. I hoped that he didn't think that it was a reaction to his nearness, but that the cool ocean breeze had made me cold because I was wet.

"Might as well be naked," Tanner murmured in a low tone. "The little bits of nothing you have on are transparent." He began to run his finger back and forth under the strap.

I glanced down and caught my breath. He was right! Though we were standing beyond the patio lights, there was enough moonlight to make up the difference. I'd always been a little self-conscious about the size of my breasts. They were big, and I could never quite seem to find a bra that held them all in. Such was the case now. My bra was overflowing with an abundance of flesh that strained the lacy cups with my every breath. My nipples were hard, poking through the sheer material like hard little kernels of corn.

Glancing back up at Tanner and seeing the raw look of *something*, I wasn't sure what, on his face, calmed any worries that I had that he may find them lacking. I grinned, all but thrusting my girls out so he could get a better look. His finger stilled as our gazes met in the semi-darkness. All of a sudden I wanted him to take me into his arms and kiss me.

I wanted him.

He shook his head with regret. "I knew that you were going to be trouble," he murmured as if to himself.

"I'm totally innocent," I grinned, waiting expectantly for the kiss that I knew was coming. "Why do you think that I'm trouble?"

"Oh, you're trouble," Tanner insisted, holding my gaze. "I have rules, and with you around and living under my roof it's going to be hard keeping them."

"What rules?" I was really curious. "Because you don't strike me as the kind of man who lives by rules." Without warning he ran the tip of his finger down my chest and between my breasts. A sliver of a moan escaped, flying away with the breeze. "You strike me as the kind of man who just takes what he wants."

His laugh was low and seductive. "If I did that I'd already have you under me." *Ohmygod, he didn't just say that!* "I'd be buried so deep inside you that you wouldn't know where I ended and you began."

Ohmygod! Was it possible to have an orgasm from just words?

"Wow." It was all I could think to say. I was momentarily rendered stupid, because all I could picture in my mind was the image his words brought to life. My body liked the thought, too, because I felt a coil of intense heat swirling around in my core, just simmering to be released.

"But that's not going to happen," he stated, dashing my hopes. "I have a one-fuck rule per woman, and you're not the type for casual sex."

Oh yes I was, just give me a try! I swore to myself. "Oh? And you know that how?"

"You still have your cherry, for Christ's sake. That tells me all I need to know."

"And if I didn't have my cherry?"

"Then I'd probably fuck you at least once."

At least once. I saw red as instant anger filled me, flushing out any desire that I'd felt for him. What a jerk! *Fuck me at least once?* I pulled away from him with a hiss. "You're an ass, Tanner. Don't flatter yourself. What makes you think I want to fuck you? Huh? Did it even occur to you that there might be a woman out there who isn't enamored with your hot self? Just because you ride around town in leather and give off that sexy, bad boy vibe you are *not* God's gift to women! I was going to let you kiss me, but even that's off the table now! You-you jerk!"

I put my hands against his chest and gave him a shove that made him step back a couple of feet. Then I stomped past him to where my clothes were, snatched them up, and walked as fast as I could toward the sliding glass door. I knew as I walked into the light that he could clearly see my naked backside, and didn't give a damn.

All I could do was pray that Pops wasn't around to see me as I stormed to my room.

Chapter 17

Tanner

  I watched Ruby stomp away, letting my gaze drop down her killer body when she reached the patio. She was going to let me kiss her? Hell, I'd probably have taken her up on that, but then I knew me, and one kiss wouldn't have been enough. Seeing her practically naked and wet, Christ, my dick was in full fuck mode. I didn't know if I believed her about being a virgin. There was only one way to find out the truth, but I would never know. I didn't do virgins, no matter how appealing they were.

Ruby was more than appealing.

I wanted her.

Bad.

I reached down and gave my dick a hard rub, visualizing her hand there, which led to me imagining her mouth replacing her hand. Shit! Shelly had given me another blowjob at the bar earlier, but it had been less satisfying than the night before. I hadn't really been into her, and it had taken me a long time to come. The trick had been to think about Ruby, and all the filthy things I wanted to do to her tight little body, and I'd finally come like a fucking geyser.

Now that I knew she was a virgin, fucking her was definitely off the table.

Trouble.

I headed toward the house, realizing that I'd forgotten to tell her about the solution I'd come up with for her not going to work every day. Something Pops would buy. Her bedroom door was shut, so I knocked a couple of times but didn't get an answer. She couldn't have fallen asleep that fast, so I opened the door, only to hear the shower turning off in her connecting bathroom. The room was still dark, she must have gone straight to the shower. I sat down on the foot of her bed and waited.

I didn't have long to wait. The bathroom door opened and I almost swallowed my tongue. My dick, still semi-hard from seeing her outside, rose to the occasion in record time. Like a hungry beast the fucker pushed against my jeans, wanting out, wanting in her cunt. I closed my eyes and groaned, trying to make the image of her stunning nudity evaporate into neutral ground. But it was too late. Ruby's beautiful curves, the image of her shaved, plump pussy would be forever stamped in my memory.

She caught her breath and stood there, obviously having seen me. I opened my eyes, mesmerized by how the light in the bathroom bathed her in an angelic hue. She was fucking perfection. Built like a woman, with softly rounded curves, her tits the perfect size for my large hands. Her long hair hung in wet strands to her waist, touching her innocent body. I took a deep breath, but it did nothing to calm my racing heart. Blood ran through my veins like hot lava.

How in the hell was I going to ignore her? No woman stood there like she was, as naked as the day she'd been born, looking so alluring and inviting, and didn't want to get fucked. Ruby may not have known it, but she was asking for it, hell, she was giving me permission to claim her. She may have been innocent, but she knew what she wanted, and she was ready to become a woman.

I couldn't do it. I refused to take her cherry, to ruin her for the right man. Her tits rose and fell with her accelerated breathing. I could sense her arousal. Hell, I could smell it. But there was also fear there. Good. She needed to be afraid. An innocent didn't stand there naked in front of a man she knew wanted her and not get burned. I wouldn't take her, but I could teach her that there was more to sex then putting my dick inside her body.

It didn't take me long to reach her. The closer I got, the wider her eyes grew, and then her pretty lips parted and I could hear her breathing. I expected her to take a step back, but she stood unafraid and almost challenging. Inside I grinned, but on the outside I was a hungry animal. I'd forgotten why I'd originally come to her room, staring into her confused, yet excited, eyes.

"Did you want something?" The softness of her voice was like a caress down the length of my dick.

My nostrils flared, taking in the scent of her arousal. "Yeah," I said in a barely contained tone. I wrapped one hand around the back of her neck and jerked her against me. "You." Her mouth opened as I lowered my lips to hers and I cut off whatever she'd been about to say.

I tongue-fucked her mouth for lack of a better description. Ruby opened to me instantly, accepting my tongue against hers, moaning as I thrust against hers. I groaned when her tiny hands glided up my arms to my biceps, clenching her nails into the muscle, before continuing up to wind around my neck. With a grunt I picked her up and she automatically wrapped her legs around my waist. I took a second to grind my dick against her lower belly before turning and walking back to the bed.

We didn't break our kiss as I lowered her down, following her there and covering her with my body. I was lying between her thighs, my dick right where it needed to be. Ruby moaned loudly and arched her hips into it, encouraging, demanding more. I gave her a few more pumps, surprised to find that I was close to losing control. Her sweetness, fresh and clean, surrounded me, sucking me into her spell.

"Tanner-" she said the second I released her mouth.

"What, honey?" My hand traveled down her body, shaping her luscious tits, outlining the curve of her waist, and further down her belly and below. I ran my open palm over her plump pussy lips.

"Wh-what are you do-doing?" she gasped.

"Just touching you," I growled against her neck, turning to give her a nibble. Her sex was hot as hell, and soaking wet. My finger swiped through her slit, gathering the slick cream there.

Ruby jumped wildly when I hit her clit. "Oh, my God, Tanner! Please don't stop!"

I knew that she was remembering the orgasm I'd given her earlier that day, and now I understood why it had been so intense for her. I wasn't stupid enough to think that it had been her first, but a hunch told me that it may have been her first by a man. And now I had her naked and willing beneath me, and I was going to show her a whole new world of erotic experience.

I flicked her clit several times, dipped my finger into the wetness gathered at the beginning of her pussy and brought the digit up between our faces. Ruby's eyes rounded wildly, her pupils dilated. If I could smell her arousal on my finger I knew that she could, too. I slowly put my finger against her parted mouth. "Taste," I rasped, slipping my finger inside. She sucked hard, I felt the feeling all the way down to my dick, and I pulled my finger free and slammed my mouth down on hers again. She opened beneath my attack, and I thrust my tongue inside to taste her essence.

Fuck! I needed more. I slipped my finger inside her pussy, feeling her hips move against my thrusts. Her whimpers encouraged me to add another finger. Once they were inside her I curled them into a hook and tortured her G-spot until she was squirming and twisting wildly beneath me, gasping for her every breath. I began to kiss my way down her body, starting with the sweet length of her neck, over the curve of her graceful shoulder, and back to the pulse point at her throat.

I made my way down her chest to the first tit, licking a slow path to the nipple. I took the berry into my mouth and sucked hard, feeling a gush of liquid heat coat my fingers working in and out of her body. Ruby whimpered, and then hissed when I took her nipple between my teeth.

"Aaaahhh!" she cried out, her hands coming up to clench into my hair to hold me tightly against her. "Tanner!"

I grinned around the tasty nipple in my mouth before releasing it and moving on to her other luscious tit. I licked at her nipple like a cat licking up cream, before taking the tip into my mouth and suckling. Her nails raked my scalp, turning my dick into cement. I wanted to remove my fingers and replace them by invading her warmth and pounding her into a hard climax, but I realized the danger of losing control and continued to taste the delights her body had to offer. When my kisses took me to the top of her pelvis, it was the first time Ruby tried to pull my head away, and I knew then that she'd never let a man go down on her.

If anything was going to make me lose control it was that knowledge. She was so innocent, yet a woman in every way. I began to grind my dick into the bed as I locked my mouth over her mound. She moaned and reared up, the action allowing my tongue the chance to sink easily inside heaven. Smooth, tasty cream coated my tongue, and I lapped it up hungrily, groaning deeply as I was enveloped in a heady scent of her sex and eagerness.

"Tanner, oh, God! What are you doing to me?" Her rushed tone revealed that she was panting her way to a hard release.

With my tongue buried inside her as far as it would reach, I looked up to see her lovely tits quivering with their hard, wet nipples. Her hands were fisted in the covers beneath us, her hips moving against my tongue the same way I knew she would be moving had it been my dick. My nose bumped against her engorged clit, causing Ruby to twitch and moan every time. Her breathing turned harsher, I grabbed her hips and pulled her tight against my face, feeling her insides swell and clench around my tongue.

"Tanner!" her cry revealed her surprise as she peaked and then exploded into sweet release. "I'm, I'm, coming...!"

The warmth and thickness of her cream coated my tongue, and I sucked as much of it as I could into my mouth. I wanted all of her virginal essence, and I was a greedy bastard. Her body jerked and quivered as she tried to escape my mouth, but I easily held her pussy right where I wanted it. I ate her out until I was satisfied that I'd gotten it all. When I pulled away I took a last, lingering sweep over her sensitive clit.

She pulled my hair roughly. "Tanner, I . . . please, I can't take any more."

Jesus, my dick was leaking, I could feel it, and it was so hard it hurt. I climbed up her body and settled it right up against her swollen, wet mound. "You are an innocent," I said softly, slightly in awe. "Because this is just foreplay." Her eyes snapped open and met mine. "First I make you come, then you make me come, and then we fuck our brains out." I rubbed my throbbing dick against her.

"We both know that's not going to happen," Ruby surprised me by saying. "Because you don't want my cherry."

Fuck. That damned cherry. In that moment, something else occurred to me. If she came that fucking hard from just the feel of my tongue, she'd set the sheets on fire if it were my dick claiming her. It was almost worth saying to hell with it and breaking my rule. But I didn't need that kind of trouble. As tempting as Ruby was, I needed to keep my head and stick to the rules. My throbbing dick reminded me that he needed attention.

"Want me to return the favor?"

Fuck, I hadn't expected that. "Thanks for the offer but no, honey." I didn't want to leave her. I needed relief, and she felt so soft and smelled nice, and I liked being against her curves. Naked would have even been better.

"Oh, that's right, you have a woman who can take care of that."

I thought she might be joking, but there was nothing in her voice to indicate that she was teasing. In fact, her tone sounded bitter, and there was a look in her eyes that I couldn't read. When her eyes turned bright I rolled off her. Fuck. I'd made a mistake. I didn't want to see her tears, didn't want to know what she was feeling. I had to do something quick to wipe that hurt look from her face.

I didn't want her to care.

The problem was, one emotion would wipe out the other. I decided to wipe out caring.

"Yeah, there's always one around at the bar willing to give me a blowjob." I was a prick, acting as if what I'd just done hadn't affected me, when it had. "Besides, you know the score. I just wanted to show you that there's other ways of feeling good without fucking."

"You know what, Tanner?" She was leaning up on her elbows, thrusting those magnificent tits out unintentionally. I couldn't help salivating, remembering how sweet her cream had tasted. "Don't do me anymore favors and don't offer me anymore experiences. I didn't ask you to come in here, and from here on out you either stay out of my room or I'll sleep in my car."

She was serious as shit, and I couldn't blame her. It was on the tip of my tongue to remind Ruby that this was my house, but I knew there was a deeper meaning behind her statement. Besides, I knew that she'd back up her threat by doing just that, and I didn't want her sleeping in her car. I'd honor her request to a point, because it was the right thing to do.

Chapter 18

R^{uby}

"I got friends coming over."

I paused from loading the dishwasher and met Pops' eyes. I didn't care if he had friends coming over, it was his house, but the way he'd said it sounded like a warning. I immediately thought about Tork, Jimmy, and the others, but wasn't sure why he would warn me about them. "That's nice," I finally said with a smile. I was secretly glad that he didn't want to go to Main Street again. We'd gone three days in a row, and I figured I'd seen everything at least twice.

At first I'd looked forward to going. I'd planned on entering some of the events to possibly earn some easy money, but watching the first wet t-shirt contest had quickly squashed my hopes, while smashing my confidence. The women had been busty, loud, and acted slightly trashy, rubbing their hands over their wet chests to bring attention to the size and shape of their breasts, their nipples poking through the thin material of their crop tops. It soon became apparent that I didn't have what it would take to win—guts—and I wasn't about to get up on stage and make a fool of myself.

"You think you can whip us up something for lunch?" He was sitting at the table, coffee cup in hand, an unusual sight considering that he went outside to smoke directly after breakfast most mornings.

"Sure. I might need to go shopping, though. What did you have in mind?" I turned to finish loading the washer.

"Hell, I don't know cutie. Something hearty, they're big boys."

That wasn't much help. "How many are coming?"

I turned in time to see Pops shrug. "Not sure. About five, I guess."

I had no idea what I was going to fix, but my biggest problem was that I didn't have any money, and I wasn't about to ask Pops for any. That left me with one option—hunt Tanner down. I hadn't seen him much since the night he'd rocked my world. He seemed to be gone a lot, and I wondered if it was because I was there and he wanted to avoid me. That kind of hurt.

"I'll come up with something," I finally said, turning back to face him. It was nice that he had friends coming over.

Pops got up and headed for the patio door. "Don't forget the beer, cutie. Better get a couple of cases."

"I will." It was on the tip of my tongue to ask Pops if he knew where I could find Tanner, but if he asked why I'd have to come up with a story, and I didn't want to lie to him.

Once he was outside I went to my room for my shoes and my empty purse. I had my keys and driver's license in there, along with some change, but that was about all. I headed outside to my car, wondering what I could possibly fix Pops and his friends for lunch. I'd had it easy the last few days since we'd spent most of the time on Main Street with Tork and his club. They'd always treated us to any food and drinks, so I'd just had to come up with ideas for dinner.

My first stop to find Tanner would be After Hours, since I'd learned that Tanner owned the bar and that was where his club held their morning meetings. A wave of relief crashed through me as I neared the building and saw the motorcycles parked out front. I pulled into the lot and parked my car, sitting there for a minute. As I worked up the courage to go inside, I counted the motorcycles. There were twelve of them.

Taking a deep breath, I opened my door and made my way to the bar's front door. I was surprised to find it unlocked, considering that the bar didn't open until one, as the sign on the door read. I stepped inside and immediately came to a halt when twelve big, sexy men ceased talking and all swung my way. The silence was unnerving, as were their serious expressions.

"Come on in, darlin', we don't bite," one of them said.

"Much!" another added.

Their laughter brought a smile to my face and set me at ease. As I walked closer to them my gaze landed on Tanner, who was the only one that didn't have a welcoming look on his face. He leaned back in his chair and crossed his arms, clearly not happy to see me.

"Want a donut, babe?"

I looked at the man who'd offered and grinned. He had white powder at the corner of his mouth. Other than that he appeared just as big and tough as the others. "No, thank you." I returned my gaze to Tanner. "I'm sorry for interrupting your meeting, but I need to talk to you."

"Is Pops okay?"

It hadn't occurred to me that my presence would make him worry about Pops, but it made sense. "Yes, Pops is okay," I quickly assured him.

"So what do you need to talk to me about?"

I made eye contact with several of his brothers, returning their smiles. They were an ominous group of men. All big, muscular, and handsome as hell. "So, uh, the criterion for belonging to your club is that you have to be big and sexy?" I joked.

Only one man didn't join in the laughter with his friends, and I noticed for the first time that his face was scarred. I felt a moment of regret, meeting his hard, unyielding gaze. Looking beyond the scars, I realized that he was probably the most handsome one there, but it was clear that he didn't think so. He seemed angry and bitter, a bear with his paw in a trap. Our gazes locked, and I refused to feel sorry for him.

"I'm waiting," Tanner said with a smirk.

No way was I going to ask him for money in front of his men. I released a frustrated breath. "Can we go somewhere private?"

"No," he snapped in a firm tone.

I hadn't been expecting that. And why was he so mad? My gaze moved around the group, seeing the change in their demeanors as they stared at their leader, as if trying to figure him out. More than one looked at him with surprise in their eyes.

"Never known you to turn down a pretty woman," one finally said as he reached for another donut.

"She's not here to give me a blowjob," Tanner responded crudely.

I refused to be embarrassed or outraged by his bold comment. Instead, I decided to fight fire with fire. "How do you know?" I glanced at the man who'd made the comment and gave him a wink. "Maybe I came here to finish what we started the other night?" I couldn't believe the words that were falling out of my mouth.

As raunchy comments and laughter erupted at the table, Tanner scooted back his chair with an angry motion and jumped to his feet. I stood my ground when he came around the table, grabbed me around the upper arm, and pulled me behind him as he stomped toward the back of the bar. I barely kept up with him, but I managed. Without knocking, he opened a door, yanked me inside, and released me. I heard the door slam behind me, and when I turned he was standing with his arms crossed and a scowl on his face.

"Now what was so important that you had to come down here and interrupt a meeting?"

"Why are you so mad at me?" I rubbed where his hand as been wrapped around my arm. I wondered if his anger had been triggered because I hadn't reciprocated the other night, or because I'd demanded that he stay out of my room.

He released a deep breath. "I'm not angry with you. We're dealing with some shit right now and I don't need any distractions."

"Well I'm sorry, but don't take your bad mood out on me. Maybe you need a couple more blowjobs to relieve the stress," I said without thinking, crossing my arms. I could tell that my comment angered him.

He released a harsh breath. "Yeah, that's exactly what I need. Now why are you here?"

I took a deep breath and just put it out there. "Pops has some friends coming over and he wants me to fix them lunch. I need some money and I didn't want to ask him."

Now Tanner looked just annoyed. "Get whatever the hell you need. I'll pay you back."

I felt the heat of embarrassment climb up my neck and settle into my cheeks. I lowered my eyes and sucked the corner of my bottom lip into my mouth, too embarrassed to admit that I was broke.

"Wait," he said. "You don't have any money?"

I couldn't look at him, mortified that he'd guessed my secret. I just shook my head, wishing the floor would open up and swallow me. I'd never cared about my lack of money more than I did just then.

"Fuck!" The sharpness of his tone caused me to jump, and then he released a long breath. "Ruby." I ignored him. "Honey, look at me." His endearment warmed me on the inside, and I slowly raised my gaze to his. "Why the fuck didn't you say something before?"

"Because I'm used to being broke, it's nothing new for me, Tanner. I know how to get by without money."

He just stared at me, and then he was reaching for something in his pocket. It was a money clip. He peeled off some money and held it out to me.

"Here." He took my hand and crammed the money into my palm. "When it's gone I'll give you more. And just so you know, I had a conversation with Pops. I told him that the job you thought you had fell through and that I'm paying you to do some cooking and cleaning until you can find another one."

"He fell for that?" It seemed a little too convenient to me.

Tanner shrugged. "You were already in the house, so it was easy, besides, he likes you."

"And you don't," I said bravely, and with a small smile.

I could tell that he was fighting a smile. "You're a distraction I don't need."

"I'm sorry, I don't mean to be. What can I do to not be a distraction?"

He growled. "Put a paper bag over your head and wear a potato sack." I just stared at him, slightly confused. He released an aggravated snort. "Jesus, you're naive," he'd said it disgustedly. "You're too damned appealing for your own good."

I let a slow grin move over my face, and then Tanner was the one with confusion on his. He narrowed his eyes at me, as if trying to figure out what was going on. "I knew what you meant," I confessed. "I just wanted to hear you put it into words."

He shook his head and glanced at the floor. "Trouble," I heard him murmur beneath his breath. Then he seemed to pull himself together. "What else?"

"What do I feed five men that go with two cases of beer?"

He didn't even have to think about it. "Roast beef sandwiches. Anything else?"

I shook my head. "Nope. I guess I'll get out of your hair." I moved toward him but he didn't get out of my way, so I was forced to stop and meet his eyes. "Do you have anything else?"

"Yeah," he growled, reaching for my shoulders. "Since you're here..." Suddenly I was flush against Tanner's hard length and he was slamming his mouth down on mine.

Wildfire erupted through my system the instant his firm, demanding mouth locked onto mine. It wasn't fair that he only had to kiss me to turn my bones to jelly. I heard a moan, and then realized that it was mine. My arms came up of their own accord, sliding around his thick neck and holding on. His following groan was all the encouragement I needed to open my mouth and invite his tongue inside.

Suddenly we were consuming each other in a clash of teeth and lips and tongue. Animal sounds erupted around us. I quivered against Tanner, feeling the solid bar of his cock against my lower belly. He was grinding and I was arching, neither of us getting what we really wanted, but I knew that he wouldn't end the torture because I was a virgin. I would have to rectify that soon, because I wanted Tanner, even if it was only a taste. I could live with a one-shot deal because I wouldn't be there for long.

My fingers moved through his hair and my nails scraped his scalp. He growled again, swinging me around and pushing me up against the door. His hands roamed over my body, over my clothes, having no trouble finding my erogenous zones. Jesus, I was going to go up in flames! I was attuned to everything about Tanner—his thick, powerful thighs straining against mine; his powerful arms caging me against the door as he stole my breath.

Without warning, he pulled away. Our eyes met. We were both panting. Then Tanner hit the door with a fist. I jumped because it was close to my head. "Fuck it!" he said harshly. "You're going to have to go."

My eyes grew round with alarm. Was he telling me to leave, as in leave town? "I don't understand." He'd need to explain it to me. It was hard to concentrate with my body thrumming with arousal.

"No, you wouldn't," he said with a twist to his lips. "You're so fucking innocent."

He made it sound like a crime, and I was tired of him throwing my lack of experience in my face. "You know, just because I haven't had sex doesn't mean that I'm stupid."

"No, but that's what makes you so appealing."

"Well then, maybe you should just fuck me so I'm not so innocent anymore."

Amusement flirted across his hard features. "Not going to happen."

I pressed my mouth, trying to think of a comeback that would wipe that grin right off his face. Knowing that I was playing with fire, I said, "Then I'll just go find someone who will!" I gave his chest a shove. He stumbled back with surprise. Before he could recover I swung around, opened the door, and rushed through it.

I didn't stop. I walked right past his club, ignoring the surprise and knowing smirks on their faces and hit the bar door open. I didn't expect Tanner to come after me. He didn't strike me as the kind of man who'd run after a woman. No, the women ran after him. I climbed into my car, started it, and peeled out of the lot, determined not to let Tanner ruin my day.

Chapter 19

T anner
      Trouble. That's all I could think of when I thought about Ruby. She was nothing but trouble. Cute, curvy, funny, and sexy as hell. When she'd first walked into the bar in those ragged little jean shorts and that crop top that revealed too fucking much skin I'd wanted to strangle her. The image of her naked curves, looking so soft and inviting on the bed the other night, was forever embedded in my mind and a constant distraction, to the point that it had interfered with my usual evening extracurricular activities.

Three beautiful women had offered to meet me in the back alley the last three nights, and I hadn't been able to work up enough interest to make it worth my while. My body was used to relief at the end of the day and it was building up. Having Ruby around wasn't helping. I wanted her, wanted to fuck through that cherry and claim her as mine. But old habits were hard to break. Better to stick with mindless fucks with strangers and the blowjobs out back then get involved with an innocent like her, even as her last comment about finding someone else to fuck her came back to torture me. My first thought went to Jimmy.

Would she give herself to him just to end her innocence? They'd been spending time together and he was closer to Ruby's age. I didn't like the thought of Jimmy's hands on her body, his mouth on hers, and especially his dick in her tight pussy. I'd never been jealous over a woman a day in my life, but I was aware that I was coming damned close to the feeling with Ruby.

And I had no right.

It pissed me the fuck off that I couldn't get her out of my head and focus on just getting through Bike Week. The Kings had been wrecking havoc whenever they could, petty stuff that the cops didn't have time to get involved with. Stirring up trouble between clubs, playing them against each other, was their worst offense, because hard-core MCs didn't take that shit lightly. They were more apt to go after the Kings once they figured out what they were doing. Wicked and his boys were more of a gang than an actual motorcycle club, they just happened to ride bikes.

Their stupidity made them dangerous. Their inexperience was going to be their downfall. The Kings had come to fruition a few years back, and almost overnight. All of a sudden word on the street that there was a new MC in Sanford was going around, and it was run by a punk that went by the name of Wicked. They thought they were tough stuff, and every one of them had been in jail at least once, but for minor shit like stealing and vandalism. They wanted to play with the big boys, but they were so far off the mark it wasn't funny.

That didn't make them any less dangerous, though. They were just wild enough to turn to some serious shit if the opportunity presented itself. So far their threats had been all bark, but it was just a matter of time before they crossed the line. I only hoped that it wasn't in our town. So far we'd been able to keep them under control when we crossed paths, but who knew what they were getting away with when we didn't have eyes on them?

Like now. Mark and Skipper were assigned the task of keeping eyes on the Kings once they located them. They were a small club and usually ran together. Other than the first day, they hadn't shown back up on Main Street, so I'd called Gabe and told him to keep his eyes open for the Kings in case they showed up there at the Cabbage Patch. He and Sully were spending most of the day there to keep trouble down to a minimum.

My phone rang, and I glanced down to see that it was Gabe. "Yeah?"

"No sign of the Kings yet, we just finished walking the campgrounds."

"Shit. I want to know where those fuckers are." Sid and Heath were riding the streets and they haven't seen them either. I released a frustrated breath. "If it wasn't Bike Week I wouldn't give a fuck."

"Well, we've spread the word, and if anyone sees them they'll call. All we can do, brother." I heard a commotion in the background, and before I could ask Gabe said, "Gotta go!"

There was no telling what was happening, but I trusted Gabe and Sully to take care of it before it got out of hand. Hell, I trusted all my brothers. We had each other's backs, just like when we'd been in the military. We'd all gone through boot camp together on Parris Island and ended our careers in special ops. Those had been some hellish, fucked-up years and had taught us the value of having control over our lives. So instead of coming home and finding jobs we had come together as a club and went into our own businesses.

I saw movement across the street in front of Boot Hill. A couple of bikers had exited the bar and were obviously drunk. Fuck! They were Kings. As they stumbled their way through the crowd, they knocked a woman to the ground. She looked like a tough chick, dressed in biker gear and sporting a Mohawk. Before she could get to her feet the man she was with punched the first King in the face, knocking him on his ass. His drunken brother went to help him, but by then the woman had gotten to her feet and had thrown a punch of her own.

I shook my head as chaos broke out. Most of the crowd rushed to get out of the way before stopping to watch. Two against two seemed fair enough, except that one was a woman. She was tough, but really no match for a man. I was about to cross the street to break it up when Pete and Mike, followed close behind by Mark and Skipper, showed up to do it for me. I watched Pete take a hit to the jaw by the woman. She was a holy terror and didn't let up on him. A snort escaped me, he was doing everything in his power not to use force against her, keeping her at arms length to prevent her from doing more damage.

It didn't take my brothers long to get the situation under control, and once the woman and her man realized that they were there to help, they stepped away and let them take over. The Kings were barely able to stand on their feet, so Mark and Pete each lifted one with a hand to the back of their denim cuts. I took out my phone and crossed the street. The crowd was breaking up as people lost interest.

Skipper had also taken out his phone, and I knew that he was going to call the cops. "I got it!" I shouted to him, just as the operator picked up.

"Daytona Beach Police Department. How may I help you?"

I recognized her voice from all the times I'd had to call in the past. That and the fact that she frequented the bar on the weekends. "Hey, Reba, can you put me through to Deputy Callahan?"

"Well, hey there yourself, handsome!" I could hear the smile in her voice. "You got a pick-up for him?"

I smiled. "Yeah, a couple of Kings need a room for the night. Drunk and disorderly."

"Where's your location?"

"Boot Hill Saloon."

"I'll get him the message."

"Thanks." I ended the call before she sucked me into one of the long-winded conversations she was known for.

"W-we did-dinn't throw the first pun-punch," one of the Kings slurred. I gauged him to be around twenty-two. He looked like he'd spent the night in an alley somewhere, dirty and greasy, and I had to wonder where he'd got the money to get drunk. His friend, who didn't look much better, glared at me through a curtain of stringy red hair.

"You're right, you didn't. But I saw you knock a woman to the ground, that's battery. You're lucky she didn't hang around to press charges."

That seemed to sober him up a little bit. "Cunt g-got in my-my way," he mumbled with indifference.

Pete gave him a rough shake. "Watch your mouth, skumbag."

I met his gaze. "Take them inside and wait for the cops to get here."

"Come on, pretty-boy." Mark jerked the guy around that he was holding and pushed him none too gently toward the door. As they walked through the threshold, the drunk tripped and stumbled to his knees, but Mark had him back up on his feet within seconds.

"Yo-you kn-know whoI am?" the drunk that Pete was holding asked.

"Yeah. You're a punk in a wannabe outlaw biker club that's going nowhere. Your club is a joke." I watched with amusement as his face turned bright red and he clenched his fists, which were bleeding. I grinned in the face of his rage. I expected him to spit in my face, and when he reared back and puckered his mouth I stepped out of the way of an impressive loogie.

Pete snorted. "Good move, man."

The drunk got even more pissed because he'd missed. "Fuuuck y-you asshole! My br-brother wil-l come for us an then he-he'll come for you!"

I ignored him, mainly because I didn't care. I gave Pete a chin nod toward the door, and he dragged the Kings member inside.

"Gonna grab a bite," Mike said, also heading inside.

That reminded me that Pops was expecting friends. I wondered how that was going. "Gonna head home. Pops invited friends over, and I want to make sure shit's okay."

I didn't like the knowing smirk that came over Skipper's face. "Sure. Because we all know Pops has been known to have wild parties at your place when you're gone."

My brows shot up. "You questioning my motives, brother?"

Skipper shrugged. "Come on, man, if I had a sweet young thing at home I'd find an excuse, too."

She was sweet, but I wasn't about to tell Skipper that, or that I'd already had a taste and wanted the whole damned package. I snorted, gave him the bird, and headed down to where my bike was parked, his laughter following me. He was guessing. He wanted me to deny that I was attracted to her, which would only be an admission in his warped way of thinking. There was nothing going on between me and Ruby.

And there wouldn't be, either.

Chapter 20

R^{uby}

Whew! It was hot outside, even with the ocean breeze coming off of the water. Thank God for air-conditioning. I carried the last of the grocery bags into the kitchen and filled a glass with ice-cold water from the fridge. I drank the whole thing down, and then went to the sliding glass door to look for Pops. He was in his usual chair, cigarette smoke swirling up around his head as he puffed his life away.

I was worried about him. He'd had a coughing spell earlier that had almost put him on his butt. He hadn't been able to catch his breath and I'd been a minute away from calling 911 when he'd finally got it under control. After that, he'd gone in to lay down for a bit. Fifteen minutes later I checked in on him, watching carefully until I saw his chest moving and knew that he was still alive. He was sick. I knew it. And I was pretty certain that it was serious.

I slid the door open enough to call out, "I'm home, Pops. When are your friends coming?"

"Anytime now, cutie. Did ya get the beer?"

I smiled. "Do you want one?"

"Yeah, I could do with one, it's hot as hell out here."

I couldn't argue with that, thankful that at least he was sitting out of the sun beneath the huge umbrella connected to the tabletop.

"Bring us all one, darlin'!"

I jumped at the gruff unexpected voice, my eyes rounding with surprise at the six men rounding the corner of the house and walking towards Pops. They were bikers, of course, all of them showing signs of being at least fifty years old or more. The only difference between them and Pops was that they looked healthy and carried themselves like much younger men. Their cuts looked ancient, well-worn leather, and were covered in faded patches, and for the first time I realized that Pops had one on, too.

As they got closer their smiles turned into winks, and then they were all welcoming Pops, dwarfing over his thin frame as they exchanged man-hugs and then sat down. I shut the door and went back to the kitchen to get their beers. There was a tray sitting on the counter. I was pretty sure that it was meant as a decoration, but I used it to carry the drinks out to them.

"This here is cutie," Pops said when I reached them. "She's family."

His comment made me feel warm inside, and I didn't correct him. "Hi." I handed the first beer to Pops. I smiled and made eye-contact with each man as I held the tray out to him. They in turn introduced themselves. "I hope this beer is okay. It didn't occur to me until I got to the store that I didn't know what to buy. So I asked the grocer to help me."

"It's good, cutie," Pops laughed, "but why didn't you call me?"

"I don't have a phone," I explained, receiving incredulous looks from all of them.

"Well, we're gonna half to do somethin' about that, darlin'," said the man sitting closest to Pops. "Too fuckin' dangerous these days for a woman to be on the road without one." Several of the others murmured agreement.

"Tanner will take care of it," Pops said.

"She his woman?" another man questioned. I think his name was Lifer.

Pops seemed to think about it, and I didn't answer because he hadn't been talking to me. "Not sure what their relationship is," he finally admitted. "Don't think he's tapped her yet."

Tapped me? What the hell was that? They were talking as if I wasn't there.

"Why not? What the fuck is wrong with him?" Lifer asked indignantly. He popped the top of his beer and brought it to his lips.

"Yeah, he gay or somethin'?" another asked, Shorty, I think. His comment drew laughter from all of them, and I realized that he'd been joking. "He better claim her before someone else does."

Well, I knew what 'claim' meant, which helped me to figure out what 'tapped' meant. In spite of their gruff and slightly crude banter, I found myself smiling. "You boys hungry?" I got in during a lull in the conversation. A chorus of 'starved' rang out, and I turned to go back inside. Thank goodness I'd decided to buy three pounds of roast beef at the deli.

As I neared the door my steps faltered upon noticing Tanner on the other side, watching us. I felt my heart rate pick up, and the flutter in my belly signaled another response to him. A warm flush spread through me as his gaze dropped with lazy interest down my body. I remembered our steamy kiss at the bar, feeling a pleasant buzz in my lady bits, followed by wetness. Damn it! That wasn't good. At least a woman's arousal wasn't as visible as a man with a hard-on.

My nipples betrayed me by pebbling under his intense stare.

Damn!

Why was he home this time of day? I plastered a smile on my face and Tanner opened the door when I reached it. I should have been angry with him for the way he'd acted back at his bar, but the truth was that I wasn't a grudge holder.

Besides, I wanted him too much.

"Hi. I didn't expect to see you here."

"I live here." There was a smile in his eyes as I squeezed past him into the house.

"Well, you're hardly home," I made the mistake of saying. I walked to the fridge to get the roast beef.

"You noticed? Does that mean you've missed me?"

I put the meat onto the counter next to the sub rolls. "Why would I miss you? I just saw you a couple of hours ago." Again the steamy kiss invaded my thoughts. I felt my cheeks grow hot, and I went back to the fridge for the mustard, praying that he didn't mention it. "I'm making sandwiches, would you like one?" I raised my gaze to his.

"I'll help you." He ignored my question, reached for the bag of rolls, and opened it up.

I expelled a nervous laugh. "You don't have to, it's my job," I reminded him. "Pops' friends are here."

"So I saw. They're part of the War Dogs MC, Pops' old club."

"Kind of like your club."

He nodded, spreading mustard on both sides of the roll before handing it to me. "Yeah. Only back in the day they were one percenters." Our gazes met, and I knew that he could see the confusion in mine. "Hardcore, baby. Everything they did was against the law. Every single one of them has done prison time. What you see out there is what's left of the original members."

I looked at Tanner with shock. "Pops has been in prison?"

He nodded, handing me another roll. I loaded it with slices of roast beef before cutting each sub roll in half. "You have a problem with that?"

I quickly shook my head. "No, I, I think it's... sad," I said slowly.

He stopped what he was doing and gave me a searching look. "Why?"

I thought about it for a minute. "Sad that he was away from his family. It must have been hard for everyone. After my grandma died I had no one." I hesitated. "No one who cared how I was being treated in the foster homes I'd been put in." I hadn't meant to say it out loud, but it was too late to take back the words now.

"I'm sorry. That must have been tough."

"Yeah," I said softly, realizing the truth and suddenly feeling emotional. My emotion was not so much because of how I'd been treated in those homes, but from knowing that no one had really loved me. I couldn't recall any hugs or tender moments, except from Billy, and those had creeped me out. I inhaled deeply and took the last sub roll from Tanner, giving him a shaky smile.

"So, -uh, are those men outside still one percenters?" I went to the fridge for the Swiss cheese, large sweet onion, lettuce, and tomato I'd bought. The subs took up the whole tray. "Do you have another tray?"

"The cupboard next to the stove. And yes, they'll always be one percenters as long as they wear those cuts." Taking in the age of the men, I shot Tanner a surprised look. "Doesn't mean they're still involved in illegal shit. Members can actually retire. Pops hasn't been an active member in years. He only puts his colors on when they get together."

"Oh." I liked to think that I understood, but I didn't, not really. The whole thing seemed complicated. I put down the paring knife and went to the sink to wash the smell of onions off my hands. "Do you mind helping me?" I asked him when I swung back around. There were two trays, one with the subs and one with the extras they could add to their sandwiches if they wanted.

He picked up a tray without answering and headed to the door. I followed close behind, watching the sexy way Tanner filled out his jeans as he walked in front of me to the table. Thoughts of filling my hands with that firm flesh set my blood on fire. I bet that he was firm all over.

"Damn, that looks good, cutie!"

I smiled at Pops, noticing how drained he looked. The heat couldn't have been good for him. "It's hot out here. You want to come inside where it's cool to eat?"

"That sounds like a good idea!" one of the men agreed. He was a large man, and not in a muscular way. The heat had to be uncomfortable for him.

"No, no! We don't want to be pampered, darlin'," Lifer said.

I kept my eyes on Pops. "I'm good, cutie."

"So, how ya been, boy?" one of the others asked.

Boy? I met Tanner's eyes with amusement, raising a brow. He knew exactly what I was thinking, giving me a wink before responding. "Good, Jack. And you?"

"We're all good." He seemed to be answering for the group. "Enjoying retirement. Going on charity runs, same old shit. Came down for Bike Week."

"Figured that," Tanner grinned.

"Yeah, we're camped out at Crackleberry."

"See you still got your club." The man whose name I recalled was Coffee nodded towards Tanner's cut. "How's that working for ya?"

I got the impression that there was a little animosity between Coffee and Tanner. Coffee's expression had turned hard and almost disgusted. I glanced back and forth between them, wondering what I'd missed. The glint in his eyes seemed almost threatening, yet it didn't seem to faze Tanner at all.

"It's working. Helping to keep crime down, got a good relationship with the local police."

That seemed like a dig. Then I recalled what Tanner had said about one percenters. It made sense if there were bad feelings between two people on opposite ends of the law. I glanced around at the others. Lifer and Shorty were shaking their heads with disgust, looking toward the ground. Doberman, Crusty, and Jack just looked on quietly, their expressions not giving their feelings away. Pops was staring out at the water as if something had caught his attention.

I couldn't stand the sudden tension and asked in a cheery tone, "Anyone need another beer?" I hoped so. That seemed to break the awkward moment up. I received a couple of nods, and grabbed Tanner's hand. "Come help me." I wondered what he was thinking as I pulled him along. Once we were inside and the door was closed I released his hand. "Whew! For a minute there I thought World War Two was going to break out."

I wasn't expecting Tanner's throaty laugh, and I shot him a questioning glance as I opened the fridge door. "What?"

"You mean World War Three." God, he was handsome when he smiled. "You had nothing to worry about. It's kind of a thing between me and Coffee every time he comes here."

"It didn't look like a thing to me." I began yanking cans of beer out of the fridge and setting them onto the counter.

"You were worried about me?"

"What? No! To tell you the truth, I was worried about me. I have a date with Jimmy tonight, and-" I let out a small cry when all of a sudden Tanner was there and boxing me in between his arms. "You move fast!" I laughed nervously. The fridge door was still open and my backside was suddenly up against the cold.

"Apparently not fast enough," he grumbled, leaning in close and baring his teeth. "When the fuck were you going to tell me you had a date tonight?"

My brows shot up. What was this all about? "Now, I'm telling you now." And then I kicked myself for being in that position. I worked for Tanner, or someone in the family that I didn't know yet, and he didn't own me. I could come and go as I pleased. Jimmy had been bugging me about going to the Cabbage Patch with him, and I'd finally given in. Tanner had no right to question me or to expect anything from me. "I told you that I was going to find someone to give my virginity to."

Oh, my God, that did it. When would I ever learn to think before speaking? Tanner was livid. I could feel the anger coming off him in waves, singing me with its heat. His eyes were live coals, holding mine captive in a smoldering look that went all the way to my soul. I was suddenly feeling a heck of a lot more than the cold coming from the fridge. I shivered when he invaded my personal space even more.

"So, is that the fucking plan?" he grated down into my face. "He's going to fuck you?"

I couldn't back down now. "Y-yes," I stuttered slightly, feeling anything but brave. "Jimmy's a nice guy. We have a good time together."

"Is that all you want? A good time?" he asked between his teeth.

"Well, it's a start. Jimmy likes me and, well, someone has to take my cherry." I winced, using his word, and I couldn't believe the shit coming out of my mouth. I had no intention of sleeping with Jimmy. I liked him as a friend. Tanner didn't even like me, yet I couldn't stop myself from wanting him. Everything about him made me hot and wet, like now. "Why do you even care?" I whispered up at him, wishing that he wasn't so damned strong and in control. Why wasn't I appealing enough for him to just grab me and say to hell with it?

His nostrils flared. "I don't."

And just like that he was gone. He stormed away, and then I heard the front door slam closed behind him. I winced as it shook throughout the house, and took a deep breath, just managing to hold the tears back. I had to get out of there. I couldn't take much more of being around Tanner and making a fool of myself. He'd made his feelings perfectly clear, he didn't want me.

He didn't care.

Chapter 21

Tanner

Son of a bitch, I was pissed. I'd done this. I'd pushed Ruby into the bed of another man. In fact, she and Jimmy could be getting all hot and sweaty right now, fucking their brains out. I was in a foul mood, and just thinking about it made me want to fucking destroy something. I raced down the highway in full throttle, feeling the wind hammer against me hard enough to sting, loving the familiar rumble of my bike as the powerful machine vibrated through me, giving me the high I was looking for. There was nothing that worked better to clear my mind than the freedom of speeding down the open road.

That and the release of a good, hard fuck.

That thought put Ruby's pretty face right there in the forefront of my mind. I clenched my jaw, determined to ignore everything about her, determined to fight the raw need to claim her and be done with it. My gut warned me that fucking her once wouldn't be enough. The image of her lying naked and spread out on my bed, her luscious curves stealing my control, the sight of her plump, wet pussy...Jesus, I was torturing myself.

And giving myself a fucking hard-on.

I roared against the wind, feeling my heartbeat pick up speed as the adrenaline rushed through my system. It'd been a while since I'd gone for a good, hard ride, and I realized that I had missed it. Once Bike Week was over and shit calmed down I was going to suggest to my brothers that we take a road trip. Maybe head out west to California and ride through Death Valley. Sid and Mark would probably want to bring their women with us, but that was fine. Lonnie and Judith had gone on runs with us before, they each had their own bikes and were good with keeping up.

I was forced to slow down when my exit came up. It was past one in the morning, yet the town was still awake with the influx of visiting bikers. Bike Week was one giant party, and every bar parking lot I drove past was jam packed with bikes and very few cars. Loud music, especially the deep sound of base, filtered out onto the street from inside the bars. Businesses would be closing up soon, and then the hotel parking lots would fill up.

I came to a light and slowed to a stop.

"Nice bike!"

I looked over to my right. A car had pulled up next to me, loaded with women decked out for a night out. I wondered how many of them were already drunk. The ones sitting in the middle and on the passenger side of the car in the back seat had crowded closer to the girls sitting on the driver's side so they could look out the window. It was hard to tell how old they were. I decided not to encourage them by keeping my response short and sweet.

"Thanks." I turned back to face the light.

"Give me a ride?"

I grinned and faced them again. All five of them were smiling and giggling, so it was hard to tell which girl had asked.

"Please? I've never been on a motorcycle before."

It was the girl sitting in the back directly behind the driver, and she was looking at me with big, pleading eyes. She was cute, but way too young for me. "No sissy bar."

"That's okay," she gave me a wink. "I can hold on to you."

The fact that she knew what a sissy bar was told me that she was probably lying about never having been on a bike. I contemplated her comment for a minute. The invitation on her face revealed her eagerness. I wondered what else she was eager for. My dick was still half-hard, and it had been a damn long time since I'd sunk it inside a nice, warm cunt. Lately all I settled for were blowjobs and rubbing one off in the shower once in a while.

In the end I decided against it. She and her friends looked like trouble I didn't need. Besides, I wasn't horny for her, and something told me that she wouldn't satisfy me. No. Right now the only pussy that could do that for me was Ruby's.

My bike shot forward as soon as the light turned green. I was heading home, but at the last minute I decided to stop at the bar. The parking lot was still full and I knew some of my brothers were there. I pulled into my reserved spot up against the building, backing into it next to Ace's, William's, and Heath's bikes. These days Sid and Mark went home early to be with their women. The rest of my brothers were riding the streets.

Before I even opened the door I could hear loud music, laughter, and the pounding of fists on the tables. The place was jumping with activity, and all eyes were focused toward the bar, where it appeared that an impromptu wet t-shirt contest was going on. There were five women on top of the bar, dressed in various styles of short shorts, stilettos, and tees, the kind that when wet left nothing to the imagination. The men sitting on the stools beneath them were drooling and shouting crude comments, but the women seemed to be eating up the attention.

I spied Ace behind the bar. He must have been helping Mike with the drinks. William and Heath were sitting at the end of the bar. I made my way through the dance floor, acknowledging a few customers who caught my attention.

"Hey, brother," Heath greeted in a loud tone.

I gave them both a chin lift. "Has it been like this all night?" I asked.

"Just about," said William. "We've been taking turns behind the bar. Dotty called in sick."

Dotty was Sam's partner. They'd been together a couple of years but still lived separately. "What prompted the wet t-shirt contest?"

146

Both men laughed. "Who cares?" Heath responded, ogling the redhead strutting her stuff directly above him. She was right up his alley with her long red hair and long legs.

"Not really a contest." I glanced at William for further explanation. "Their men challenged them to do it." My gaze followed the direction of his nod.

It didn't surprise me to see a table of bikers, and an MC at that. They looked big and mean, the exhilaration on their faces looking out of place as they hooped and hollered at their women. Their cuts revealed patches that looked like the real deal, but it was dark and I was too far away to make them out. "What MC?"

Heath answered. "Dark Menace."

A one percent club, but they were good guys. Their president, Stone, was a fair man. I didn't see him. Not surprising. He was good and married and extremely possessive of his beautiful wife. He'd never have allowed her to expose herself in public. "Any trouble tonight?"

"The usual."

Ace walked over and joined us. "Hey, man. Need a drink?"

"Whiskey," I replied.

"Whoa, the strong stuff." He turned to get it.

"You still pissed about something?"

I glared at Heath. I'd called him earlier and told him that I was going for a ride to let off steam, and not to expect me until late *if* I decided to stop in. I wished that he hadn't reminded me. I took the whiskey Ace handed me and shot it back with one swallow. The slow burn to the pit of my stomach was just what I needed. I handed the glass back to him. "Another one."

Heath was shaking his head. "Must be a woman." I didn't say anything, just stared at him and his cocky grin. Besides, if I commented he'd use it against me, and then I'd have to wipe that smirk off his face with a fist to the jaw. "I recognize the signs."

I snorted. "You don't know shit, brother." Ace returned and I grabbed the glass out of his hands, downing that one, too.

His brows rose high into twin arches on his forehead. "Really?" He paused significantly. "Your bad mood doesn't have anything to do with that little girl sitting over there in the corner?"

What? My gaze shifted about the room before finally narrowing on Ruby and Jimmy, who were sitting cozily in a corner booth. I clenched my teeth until my jaw ached, wishing that I hadn't stopped in. I quickly averted my gaze before my brothers jumped on it for staying on Ruby for so long. "She's nothing but trouble," I growled.

"Why don't you just fuck her and be done with it?" Ace asked. It was good thing he was on the other side of the bar or I would have reached for him.

"It's the perfect situation, brother." William decided to put in his two cents worth. "She's living right under the same roof. No back allies. Plus, she won't be around for long, so you don't have to worry about attachments."

"She's got a sweet ass. Watched her and Jimmy dancing earlier. I'd tap that in a second."

Heath's comment only fueled the fire. They were trying to get a rise out of me, but I wouldn't give them that satisfaction. I watched Ruby until I began to feel like a fucking stalker. She didn't belong here. Her innocence stood out, drawing more than one eye of interest. She had on some kind of clinging top that emphasized her perfect tits, and hung off her graceful shoulders. She'd pulled her hair up into a messy yet stylish bun, the kind my fingers itched to run through and undo. I wanted to run my mouth up the exposed column of her smooth neck, and suck the succulent flesh until I left my mark.

Fuck, my dick was getting hard again.

I wanted to fucking claim her.

I wanted to ruin her for other men.

THE SENTINELS

I was about a second away from going over there and snatching her away from Jimmy when she glanced over and met my eyes. A seductive little smile turned the corners of her glossy mouth up, the brightness of her eyes inviting, and then her tongue came out to run over that sexy bottom lip. Whether or not she knew what she was doing didn't matter. It was the end result that counted.

Fuck it.

Before the night was over, she was going to be mine.

Chapter 22

R uby

"Thank you for a nice evening, Jimmy. I really had a good time."

We'd taken my car so that I wouldn't have to sit on the back of his bike in a short skirt. I'd never been on a motorcycle before, and I wasn't sure that I wanted to give it a try. He'd been okay with it, grumbling a little about having to ride in a cage.

"My pleasure, beautiful lady." He'd come around the car and opened my door for me. "Thanks for finally going to the Cabbage Patch with me."

I'd laughed softly. We hadn't stayed long. It had been loud and a little wild, and when a fight had broken out, Jimmy, realizing my discomfort, had suggested that we leave. "I'm certainly getting an education this week on biker bars and etiquette. I didn't realize bikers had their own culture."

"It's complex," he agreed, nodding. "You know, we're leaving tomorrow." Suddenly I found myself backed up against my car. I gasped at the sudden movement. "Fuck, I'm gonna miss you, Ruby."

Before I knew it Jimmy was kissing me. I'd been wondering if he was going to make a pass at me before he left. We'd skirted around it all week with little touches that seemed a tad more intimate than I'd been comfortable with, like when he'd brushed the strand of hair behind my ear, or had reached down and taken my hand. I'd wanted to tell him then that I just wanted to be friends. I should have, because now I was facing the possibility of hurting him.

His kiss was nice, warm and tender, but didn't spark any arousal in me. Maybe he was trying to be considerate and didn't want to frighten me by starting out too enthusiastically. But one thing I knew, the longer I let it go on, the harder it was going to be to let him down gently. I didn't want him to think that I was leading him on.

Without warning, he was leaning against me, crushing me against my car, and the feel of his hard-on was like a bucket of ice water thrown over my head. That and the bright light of the motorcycle that was turning into the drive. All of a sudden we were in the spotlight.

Damn! Tanner had come home. I'd hoped to avoid him all together. I put my hands against Jimmy's chest and gently pushed him back, sucking in air. "Jimmy-" God, I wanted to get inside the house and to my room before Tanner reached us.

He leaned his forehead against mine, his breathing ragged from our kiss. "I know," he surprised me by saying. "You just want to be friends, and I'm okay with that."

He hadn't kissed me like he just wanted to be friends, but I was relieved that he'd said what I was feeling first. "Thank you. I don't know how we're going to remain friends once I leave here, though," I smiled.

He stepped further away and reached deep inside his front pocket. "Here." I took the folded paper he held out to me. "This is how you can reach me if you ever need me, or just want to talk. Whatever." His hands dropped to my shoulders. "Keep in touch, baby."

"I promise. Maybe one day I'll make it to California."

"That would be nice." He released a deep breath. "Guess I better go. At least get a few hours sleep before we head out." I nodded. "You take care, okay?"

"I will, you too." He walked to his bike, slipped on his helmet, mounted, and then gave me a wave before starting up. The noise was deafening but he saw me reciprocate, and then I saw Tanner exit the garage.

"Nice. You kiss all your men goodbye like that?" He walked right past me. "Or just the ones you fuck."

I winced, wondering if his foul mood was caused because of the alcohol I could smell on him, or for some other reason. There'd been nothing wrong with giving Jimmy a kiss goodbye. I turned to follow Tanner inside. "He's leaving tomorrow. Besides, I like Jimmy."

"So you said earlier," he reminded me gruffly.

We entered the kitchen and he flipped on the light. He opened a cupboard door, reached for a bottle of bourbon. I watched him uncap the bottle and raise it to his lips. "Don't you think you've drank enough tonight?" I asked, watching him gulp down a huge swallow. "I can smell alcohol all over you."

Tanner slammed the bottle down on the counter and turned his angry eyes on me. I knew I'd crossed the line by questioning him, but it was too late to take back the words now. All I could do was brace myself for the fallout. I held myself firm when he walked up to me. But then he grabbed me by the shoulders and jerked me closer against him.

"What else do you smell on me?" he grated at me through clenched teeth.

I inhaled, unsure of what I was looking for. He was so angry, his hands biting into my flesh. I caught my breath, held captive by the smoldering look in his eyes. And then it hit me, the strong fragrance of a woman's perfume. It was all over his shirt, much more prevalent than the alcohol. And was that lipstick on his neck? I was overwhelmed with a sudden rage. Without thinking, I slapped Tanner across the face.

"I hate you!" I said in a husky tone, swinging around and going to my room. I felt thoroughly rejected that he'd gone to another woman and was flaunting it in my face. I reminded myself that I really didn't have that right, that he wasn't mine, and that he'd gone out of his way to make it clear to me what he expected in a woman. I couldn't blame him for that. So why was I reacting this way? Why did it feel as if I'd lost something important?

And thinking of Tanner with another woman left me feeling numb inside.

By the time I jumped into the shower, tears were falling down my cheeks. I couldn't remember a time in my life that rejection had hurt so much, and I'd had plenty of experience with it. Right then I made up my mind to leave. I'd tell Tanner in the morning and give him—or his aunt, who I had yet to meet—two weeks to find a replacement. Hopefully I'd earned enough money to at least make it to the next town. So far, there'd been no discussion about wages, but anything was better than nothing.

I would miss Pops. I'd grown fond of him since I'd been there. He was like the granddad I'd never had. I'd miss Tanner, too, for completely different reasons. I would always wonder how things could have been between us.

The kisses alone had practically melted my panties. The trouble was he'd wormed his way into my heart.

• • • •

TANNER

I wasn't drunk, contrary to what Ruby thought. As I'd been about to leave the bar, Shelly had shown up and wrapped herself around me before I could stop her. After slathering sloppy kisses on me she'd spilled her drink on me, and then made it worse by spraying that shit she called perfume. Her untimely appearance had prevented me from catching up with Ruby and Jimmy after they'd left the bar. Finally, William had come to the rescue and taken the drunken woman away from me.

"Don't let her drive," I said, meeting his gaze. His response was a simple chin nod.

Jimmy and Ruby were gone by the time I got out to the parking lot.

Now there I was in my kitchen, wet and stinking to high heaven of booze and perfume, angry and aroused. I'd let Ruby believe the worst, but I was the one paying the price. I was a fucking fool. I put the bourbon back and went to my room for a shower. Maybe it would calm my frustration and cool my arousal. I left my clothes on the floor in a pile and stepped beneath the hot water.

I shampooed and lathered up and then stood beneath the spray, letting it pelt down on my back. As I watched the suds go down the drain my hand went to my stiff dick. I closed my eyes and gave it a couple of pulls, visualizing Ruby's soft hands wrapped around me instead of my own. It didn't take much to recall every delicious inch of her splayed out on her bed, naked and needy, her sweet pussy wet and inviting. *Christ!* I was just torturing myself.

I needed another drink, even if I already knew that it wouldn't stop me from wanting her. I wrapped a towel around my waist and went to the kitchen, still dripping wet, the unwanted image of her and Jimmy kissing in my head. It had looked pretty hot, he'd had her up against her car, grinding his mouth against her while their lower bodies had been flush. I'd nearly wrecked my bike when my light had landed on them.

I opened the fridge and leaned in, peering inside for something to nibble on, having decided to pass on another drink. The sound of a soft gasp behind me made me twist my neck to see that Ruby had just entered the kitchen. A quick survey of her delightful form revealed that she'd just got out of the shower, too. I straightened, shut the door, and faced her.

Maybe I'd nibble on her.

"I see we had the same idea." She indicated our wet bodies wrapped in towels. "Are you hungry, too?" she asked with a small, nervous smile.

One thing I liked about Ruby was that she didn't hold on to her anger.

I let my gaze rake over her, inhaled the clean, sweet scent of her. Her long hair was wet and clinging to her bare shoulders and down her back. The towel was tucked in between her tits, exposing plenty of creamy flesh. It barely covered her shapely ass. My dick was standing at attention again.

"Yeah, I'm hungry," I heard myself say, my tone hoarse with arousal. "And this is the only warning you're going to get from me. If you don't turn around and go back to your bedroom and lock yourself in, I'm going to kiss, and lick, and nibble on every part of you before I fuck you so long and hard you'll feel me for a week."

I watched Ruby's expression change with every word I uttered. Her expressive eyes grew large, and her pretty mouth dropped open. And then she slowly pulled herself together, and what I saw in her eyes was acceptance of the inevitable. She wasn't just accepting something she had no control over. She was giving in to something that was stronger than either of us. Anticipation danced in her eyes.

"Do it," I said gruffly. "If you have any qualms about what I'm going to do to you, leave."

She stood there stubbornly, a challenge if I ever saw one. And just to make sure that I had no doubts, she said softly, "Maybe I want you to do those things to me."

"It won't be slow."

"I don't want slow."

"I won't be tender."

"I don't want tender."

"Then what the fuck do you want?" I snarled, barely holding on.

She tilted that stubborn little chin of hers and said, "I want you, Tanner. And all that implies." My dick was hard enough to pound concrete. "I'm not afraid of you, Tanner." She took a step closer to me. "I want your mouth on me." She took another step. "I want your hands on me." And another. "I want your cock inside my pussy."

That was the straw that broke the camel's back, her husky words and that erotic image. I sucked in my breath at her use of the word 'cock,' and her explicit description of where she wanted it. The visual that her words brought forth was enough to make a weaker man come on the spot. But that man wasn't me, and I knew the first time I came it was going to be inside her wet body. She stopped just inches from me, and I grabbed her to me and slammed my mouth down on hers, groaning as if I were an animal in pain.

I fucked her mouth, drank the sweetness within, and swallowed her whimpers of pleasure. I was going to fucking claim every inch of her. And when I was done, I was going to start all over again.

Chapter 23

R^{uby} I felt tears build behind my eyes, but I refused to release them. I didn't want Tanner to misinterpret them. His kiss consumed me, his mouth masterful against mine, demanding everything, and I was willing. So willing. I curled my hands around his neck to hold on, afraid that this would end like all the other times had. I wanted him with an intensity that frightened me. Our mouths still locked, he picked me up and I instinctively wrapped my legs around him.

He transferred his hands to my butt, and the next thing I knew we were walking down the hallway toward our rooms. He took me into his, making sure that the door was shut behind us. Without breaking stride he took us to the bed and lowered me, following me down to cover my body with his. I moaned in pleasure when his hand went to my breast and squeezed.

"Spread your legs, baby," he demanded in between kisses.

I did as he asked and he settled his legs between mine, his terry-covered cock at the juncture of my legs. His kisses were hard and fierce, causing me to become wet where I wanted his cock. I bowed my hips against him, feeling the strength of his erection as it throbbed against my pelvis. He grabbed my wrists and pinned them above my head to the bed, holding me captive, while his other hand moved to where I had the towel tucked between my breasts. With a deft twist of his wrist he pulled the tuck loose and opened my towel until I was exposed fully to his scorching gaze.

I whimpered, glancing down to see my quivering breasts and my hard nipples pointing directly up at him. With a growl Tanner attacked them, nipping, licking, sucking them into his mouth before rolling my nipples between his teeth. The exquisite pain was almost more than I could bear, but within seconds it was replaced with a pleasure I'd never known, shooting right down to my throbbing clit.

I thought I'd die of pleasure when his hand smoothed down my body in the direction of my thrumming sex.

"Keep your hands here," he said firmly, before releasing my wrist.

"But I-"

"Do it, baby."

I wanted to touch him, too. It wasn't fair that I was totally exposed to him, his eyes and hands, while I couldn't touch him or see what the towel was covering. "So unfair," I sighed, doing as he asked.

I felt his smile around my nipple. "You'll have plenty of time to touch me later."

He released my nipple and began kissing his way down my body, his hands remaining on my breasts as he massaged them. My breath caught when he neared my pussy because I knew how exquisite Tanner would make me feel. I was twisting and straining beneath him, silently demanding him to put his mouth there.

"You're soaked," he rasped, his warm breath right above my mound. I jolted when his finger slipped inside me and hooked, hitting the sweet spot just inside. "Is all this sweet cream for me?"

I was panting. "Yes!" I replied, rewarded when he added another finger. "Oh, God!" I arched toward the delight his fingers were giving me. "It feels so good!"

I heard his gravely chuckle right before I felt his tongue lick me. When he took my clit into his mouth and sucked hard, my eyes rolled back in my head. I released a small cry as my body convulsed. Tanner's husky laugh vibrated over me like an electrical charge, causing a rippling effect throughout my nerves.

"Jesus, you taste good," he grunted, burying his tongue as deep as he could. His hands left my breasts and slid down my body, wrapping around my thighs and pulling me sharply against his mouth. His tongue went deeper as he ground his mouth against my pussy, his nose bumping my sensitive clit.

I felt my orgasm build, like a freight train running out of control. Tanner was ruthless, and between his tongue and fingers I was losing control. My hips rose and fell in tempo with the thrust of his tongue. I was panting hard, and I'd long ago lowered my arms to clench my hands into the bedding beneath me.

"Tanner," I whimpered helplessly, about to explode.

"Come on, baby, put some cream on my tongue." He went right back to tonguing my clit, his fingers thrusting in and out of my body.

"Tanner!" I yelled out, convulsing wildly as I climaxed hard. "Oh, God! Oh, God!" I was lost in a storm, cresting on a wave before I finally crashed on the other side, completely out of control and lost in the orgasmic cloud that surrounded my thrashing body.

I was still twitching when Tanner climbed up my body. Somewhere along the way he'd lost his towel. His skin was hot and hard, and I marveled at the size of his cock as it nestled against me. He kissed me, thrusting his tongue against mine and giving me a taste of myself. It was erotic and sent another, smaller rush of liquid between my legs. I moaned deeply, losing my hands in his hair and tugging roughly. He didn't seem to mind.

After what seemed like forever Tanner pulled his lips from mine, his breath choppy, nostrils flaring and eyes smoldering coals. "You still have your cherry, baby?

I tensed, worried that he would quit once I told him the truth. But I couldn't trick him into fucking me. "Yes," I breathed softly.

He closed his eyes, and said with obvious relief in his voice, "Thank fuck."

I was confused. "But I thought-"

He cut me off with another kiss, this one rough and feral. "You're mine, Ruby. I want to take your virginity, I want my dick to be the first one you feel sliding into your tight body."

"Yes, Tanner. I want that, too." I'd wanted it since the moment I had first looked into his eyes on the side of the highway.

I felt his lower body thrusting against me. His cock was a thick, hot bar against my pelvis, and I quivered with the knowledge that it would soon be inside me, making me his. His hand moved between our bodies, taking hold of his cock. I couldn't see what Tanner was doing but I could feel him brushing the head of his dick up and down my still pulsing slit.

"It's going to hurt the first time." I just stared into his eyes, trusting him. "You want me to go slow or rip the Band-Aid off quick?"

I grinned. I could see in his eyes that he was barely holding on to his control, yet he was willing to let me decide. "Band-Aid." I needed him inside me.

He lined up the head of his cock at my entrance. I felt a moment of fear and tensed slightly, then forced myself to relax. Tanner's expression was raw. He slammed his mouth down on mine and thrust forward, tearing through my hymen and going deep, until I felt his balls up against my ass. I bowed sharply at the initial sting and burn of his cock entering my body, but it wasn't as bad as I'd thought it would be once the initial pain subsided. He stilled, as if giving my body enough time to adjust to his size. I felt something hot and wet inside.

"You okay?"

"More than okay," I said hoarsely. I bumped up against him, smiling. "Are we done?" I teased, already knowing the answer.

He gave me a wolfish grin. "Not by a long shot, baby." He pulled his hips back until just the head of his cock remained inside, and then he thrust back in, groaning low.

I waited for more pain, but other than a little burning my body adjusted to Tanner's cock as if it were made for him. He was big, even my inexperience told me that, but the smooth glide of his hard shaft against my inner walls seemed to be scratching an itch that I'd never known I had. I ran my hands down his backside, marveling at the defined muscles of his back as he pistoned in and out of me. How taut his butt was, how thick and powerful the backs of his thighs were. Sweat was dripping off his brow and onto me as he worked up his speed.

"Jesus, you're tight," he grumbled, but it didn't sound like a complaint. "So fucking tight, honey." He hooked his arm beneath my leg, lifting it up and over his hip. The action caused him to go even deeper inside me, and we both sounded out our pleasure. He began to pound into me faster and harder.

"Oh, God, Tanner!" I felt myself moving up the bed with every thrust. They were powerful, and his grunt followed every one. "I never thought it would feel this good." I reached up and nipped his chin, my hands still roaming over his body and discovering every plain and valley. He was hard all over.

"I'm not going to hold out much longer, honey." He was breathing hard, his muscles glistening with sweat. "Put some fucking cum on my dick. Come on, baby." His mouth latched on to a nipple, sucking hard. I cried out, arching high, clenching my hands into the bedding. I felt the pull of his mouth all the way to my clit, the buzzing of it almost too much to bear. I was going to climax hard.

"Tanner!"

"Fuck!" His movements turned choppy, and then he stilled, turning to stone, his cock buried deep inside. "Aaaaggghh!" he grunted, pulling out of me and coming hard. I could feel the hot ropes of semen spray against my lower belly and thighs with every spasm of his body. "Sweet Jesus," he groaned out through his choppy breaths, "I almost forgot to pull out in time!"

A second of panic raced through me, but I tapped it down because he had pulled out in time. Now his hand was rubbing his seed over my belly and down my thighs, causing me to shiver at the erotic act. The scent of sex was strong in the air as he slowly collapsed against me. With his head against my breast I brought my arms around him, struggling to catch my own breath.

I had a feeling that it wouldn't be the only time I saw Tanner out of control.

"That was, that was-"

"Intense," Tanner suggested in a tired voice.

I laughed. "That, too. But I was going to say awesome."

He snorted beneath me. Neither one of us made an attempt to move. I didn't know about Tanner, but I was thoroughly exhausted, as if I'd just had a workout. Plus it was late, or early morning, depending on how you looked at it. As our breathing calmed, I let the silence of our surroundings lull me into a semi-conscious state of relaxation.

I was vaguely aware when Tanner rolled off me. The next thing I knew he was pulling a sheet up over us and turning me onto my side. We fell asleep spooning.

Chapter 24

Tanner

It was morning when I opened my eyes. Damn, I'd slept good with Ruby curled up next to me. Surprising, considering that I was used to having my bed to myself. I couldn't remember the last time I'd woken up with a woman in my arms. It had been a fucking long time. Way before Pops had moved in with me, and that had been at least seven years ago.

There was a digital clock on the nightstand that revealed that it was close to seven, still early considering how late it had been when we'd fallen asleep. Ruby had dropped off practically right after I'd fucked her. I smiled to myself. It hadn't taken me long before I'd wanted to fuck her a second time, but her angelic expression and light snoring had won out, and I'd left her alone.

That didn't mean that I was going to leave her sweet ass alone this morning. Being tucked up against her had intensified my morning wood. I alleviated some of the discomfort by stretching and forcing my dick against the soft curve of her bottom. I groaned low, creating another problem when my dick slipped between the cracks of her ass. I couldn't help myself. I thrust several times, clenching my teeth at how good it felt.

Ruby moaned and began to come around. She moved slowly, arching her curvy butt against me and groaning. I slipped an arm over her and rolled her onto her back, kissing the side of her neck. Her skin was like silk, warm and lightly scented with something fresh and tantalizing, reminding me of her innocence. Even with her lack of experience she'd been so fucking receptive the night before, and her actions had matched those of a more experienced woman. Pushing through her virginity had proven, though, that she had indeed been an innocent.

I kissed my way down to the curve of where her shoulder began and lost control, sinking my teeth into her. The need to leave my mark suddenly overwhelmed me, and I remembered smearing my seed into her skin after coming all over her thighs and belly. I'd almost fucking come inside her, without protection. I never fucked without covering up, that's how far gone I'd been with the excitement of finally claiming her.

That mistake couldn't happen again. Since she'd been a virgin, I doubted that she was on birth control. She moaned long and deep, the sound revealing her pleasure at the way I was rousing her from sleep.

"You're a nice change to wake up to in the morning," I growled against her fragrant skin. I licked over the area I'd nipped before moving down her chest to the top of her tits. I pulled back so I could view their perfection better. Twin mounds topped with tasty little dusty nipples, just begging for my mouth. I met Ruby's eyes. "Nicest tits I've seen in a long while." I licked one, watching her reaction. Her mouth opened as she sucked in a breath. I licked the other one several laps before taking the tip into my mouth and tugging on it hard.

"Tanner!" she cried softly, arching her back so that she was thrusting that tempting morsel in offering.

"Am I hurting you?" I knew better.

"No," she gasped with a delicate shiver.

"Want me to continue?" I ran my whiskered chin lightly over the quivering flesh surrounding her nipple until goose bumps rose over it.

"Yes, please, Tanner." Her hands fell to my head.

I smiled around her nipple and moved to kiss between her tits. Then I continued down her body, stopping at the top of her pelvis, the scent of my cum making my dick jerk. I stared down at her plump, pink pussy, inhaling Ruby's arousal, taking in the glistening slickness coating the slit. Jesus, she made me fucking hungry. The taste I'd had of her earlier had only been the appetizer. I'd taken her innocence, but that was only the beginning. I was going to ruin her for other men.

I kissed her pussy. "Are you sore?" I ran the tip of my finger through her slit.

"Oh, God!" She began trembling. "No, not sore."

I raised my head to meet her lazy lidded gaze. "Then I didn't do my job." I gave her a toothy grin, and then flipped her over. "Nice ass, baby." She shivered as my breath moved over her. "I'm going to own this." I knew it was too soon to claim her ass, Christ, she'd been a virgin a few hours before. But her lack of experience wasn't going to stop me from exploring the voluptuous moons.

I ran my open mouth over her flesh, once in a while giving her a little nip. She jerked each time, as if expecting it to hurt, and then relaxed with a whimper. I kept her on the edge because it kept me on the edge. Spreading the cheeks of her ass, I kissed my way down to the tiny star that would eventually take my dick. Ruby twitched wildly when my tongue touched her there.

"Easy, baby. Does what I'm doing bother you?" I waited, ready to move away if it did. Some people were into anal and some weren't, but the only way to find out which one you were was to experiment.

"Not exactly." Her tone revealed that she hadn't made up her mind yet.

"You tell me when to stop, yeah?" She nodded. "I need to hear you say the words, Ruby." I wanted no misunderstandings.

"Yes, I'll tell you when to stop."

Good. It would be hard as hell to stop, because she had a scrumptious ass, but I'd find the strength. I may have been a selfish bastard when it came to my needs, but I would never have forced something on a woman who didn't want it. I looked back at her tiny hole, my dick nearly punching a fucking hole in the bed at the thought of taking her there. He'd have to wait. Right now I had to show Ruby that pleasure could be found in many different ways.

She was lying flat against the bed. "On your knees, baby," I said as I put my hands on her hips and pulled her up. She complied without question as I moved directly behind her. I reached forward and ran my finger through her saturated slit. "Fuck, baby, you're soaked." I played with her clit, feeling the shudders travel through her body. Her breathing picked up as I explored further by sinking a finger inside her.

'Oh, God!" she whimpered, jerking.

I knew I had her the second she began to move her hips in sync with the thrusting of my finger. Gathering her thick cream with my finger I trailed it up to her anus and teased the opening, but didn't breach it. Ruby was panting out of control now, her hips moving against air as I removed my finger. I grinned. "Touch yourself," I demanded lightly. "Make yourself come."

She knew what to do. Her fingers replaced mine while I began to focus on her ass. Several times I gathered up more of her juices, wanting to make sure her hole was good and lubricated for what I was about to do. I could tell when Ruby's breathing turned louder and faster that she was getting ready to come. I timed it just right, slipping my finger past the tiny pucker into her dark passage. Ruby sucked in her breath, obviously not expecting that, but then she was crying out her release as her body began to convulse around her fingers.

"Tan-ner!" she cried in a choppy, breathless voice.

I wrapped my arm around Ruby and held her while she rode out her orgasm, at the same time fucking her ass with my finger. Jesus, she was tight. I pulled my finger away and wiped it on the bed. My dick was so fucking hard. I ran my hands over her smooth ass, before slipping one around to her sopping pussy. She was ultra sensitive, jerking away from my hand when I touched her little clit.

"Where you going, baby?" I teased into her ear as she began to collapse upon the bed. I held her in place, and pulled her up on her knees again so that her back was flush with my abs and chest, her ass flush against my dripping dick.

"Oh, my God, you have a mirror?" she rushed out, looking at our reflection in front of her.

The way the mirror was mounted made it appear as if it were the headboard to the bed. It had been left by the prior owners of the house, who'd used the room as a den. Because of the location of the windows the only place to put the bed had been against the wall with the mirror. I'd always intended to take that mirror down, but now I was glad that I hadn't gotten around to it.

I laughed at her shocked expression. She was flushed from having just come, her hair a wild mess and hanging down over her swollen tits, rock hard nipples peeking through. Her little pussy was swollen, too, and slick with her cum. I intended to add to it. I gave her time to look her fill. Hell, I was doing the same thing. I thrust my aching dick between her luscious thighs, right over her pussy, so that it was visible in the mirror.

She caught her breath. I hissed at the erotic sight and began to thrust slow and steady between her thighs. My dick was dripping pre-cum onto the bed at her knees. I brought my arms around her upper body, taking her tits into my hands and thumbing her nipples. "Look at that pretty, little pussy teasing my dick," I whispered in her ear, making sure I rubbed against her clit when I thrust. I tugged on the lobe of her ear before putting my mouth over her ear again. "Look at these beautiful tits, they barely fit in my palms."

"Tanner-" She was trembling, her voice weak.

"I'm going to fuck you so good, baby." Her reaction was a big shudder against me. "Do you want that, Ruby? Do you want my dick inside you?"

"You know I do," she replied. "Fuck me, Tanner. *Please.*"

Now I was the one shuddering, the sound of her plea getting to me on all levels. I took my dick into my hands and quickly covered it with the condom that I'd placed beneath my pillow when I'd gone to the bathroom at sometime during the night. I'd wanted to be ready the next time we fucked.

"Spread your legs," I ordered, giving my dick a couple of pumps. And then suddenly it hit me—my one-fuck rule. I froze, reconsidering what I was doing, knowing only that I'd never wanted a woman as much as I wanted Ruby right then. And now that I'd had her, I wanted more. I knew she was different from all the others, but did I want to complicate my life by letting this become more than it was?

What the fuck was I doing?

Did it really matter if I fucked her again?

Yeah, it would break my one-fuck rule. But in that moment I didn't give a shit. I wanted her. My dick wanted her. I ran my gaze over her naked, flushed curves. Fuck, she was beautiful. And then I raised my gaze to the mirror, meeting the worry reflected in her glazed eyes, and knew that I had to have her again. She'd spread her legs like I'd asked, and was waiting patiently. I lined up my dick to her pussy and thrust up, entering her with one plunge. We both sounded out our pleasure.

I began to fuck Ruby hard and fast. My arm was around her chest, holding her against me while I pounded into her willing body from behind. Every time I entered her she let out a little breathless grunt. We kept our eyes on each other, watching the scene play out until we collapsed against each other as release surged through our bodies. Only then did Ruby close her eyes and lean her head back against my chest, her convulsions controlling her movements.

I wasn't doing much better. I came inside her hard, grunting out my release and filling the condom with my seed, wishing there was nothing between us. What made it fucking perfect was the feel of her body clenching around my dick, as if trying to hold me inside while she was draining my balls. My heart was fucking going to pound right out of my chest, I'd come so hard, and when I was able to draw a halfway normal breath I pulled us down to the bed.

Just as we were settling, I heard my phone.

Chapter 25

R^{uby}
    When I woke for the second time that morning Tanner was gone. I vaguely remembered hearing him talking to someone on the phone, but I hadn't let it pull me out of the orgasmic stupor that I'd been in. I stretched with a loud moan, feeling aches that I'd never felt before, a pleasant reminder of Tanner's hands and mouth on my body and the intensity of his claiming of me. My hand traveled down to my pussy and explored it tentatively to discover that that was where most of the soreness was centered. It brought a stupid smile to my lips.

He'd been demanding and thorough.

I wondered what he was feeling right now. He'd been so determined to ignore our attraction, what had pushed him over? Had seeing me and Jimmy kissing been the deciding factor? Something told me that Tanner did things his own way, at his own speed, and that he didn't buckle under pressure. He struck me as being a man in control at all times. Well, most of the time. I felt myself turning warm when I relived those intimate moments between us.

The clock revealed that it was after nine and I jumped out of bed, reaching for, what? I hadn't been wearing clothes when Tanner had brought me to his room. I spied the towel hanging on the foot of the bed and snatched it up, wrapping it around me so I could walk across the hall to my room. I'd never slept in this late, and I'd missed fixing Pops' breakfast.

I opened the door. All seemed quiet, so I crept across the hallway and into my room. I quickly brushed my teeth and washed my face before throwing on a pair of shorts and a tank. I padded down the hall toward the kitchen, braiding my hair as I went. Knowing Pops' routine, I went straight to the patio door and peered out to see him sitting in his chair, cigarette smoke swirling above his head. I opened the door.

"Good morning," I said, walking toward him. He was facing the water and turned his head slightly to give me a smile, the cigarette hanging out of the corner of his mouth. "Have you had any breakfast?" I asked, moving around him.

"Naw. I don't need breakfast, cutie." He took the cigarette out of his mouth, giving me a sly grin. "Been eatin' it just to make you happy," he admitted.

I laughed. "I know that, but at least you're eating. Breakfast is the most important meal of the day." Wasn't it? I seemed to recall several foster mothers having told me that when I'd tried to skip it.

"Late night?"

I knew that was his way of saying that he'd noticed that I'd slept in. I nodded. "Yeah, Jimmy brought me home around one or two I think."

"Good kid. Tork and them left this morning."

"I know. Jimmy and I have agreed to keep in touch." I didn't know how we were going to do that when I didn't have a phone.

Pops nodded. "It's nice seeing old friends." I knew that he was including the bikers who'd come to lunch the day before. "When you get to be my age, that's about the only thing good that comes out of Bike Week."

I sat down on the edge of a lounger, recalling all the people that we'd come in contact with on Main Street that week, men that seemed to be more than just friends to Pops, more like brothers. Pops had explained that that was how bikers felt, especially if they were in the same club. They considered themselves brothers. There'd been a few women, too, who'd greeted Pops with obvious affection, women who'd been tanned and wrinkled, yet still beautiful, the kind you knew just from looking at them that they'd lived a hard life, and had played even harder.

"You're a lucky man, Pops. You have a lot of friends."

"Well, not as many as I used to have." He put his cigarette out in the sand. "I've lost a few over the years." There was a kind of melancholy to his tone.

I didn't know what to say to that. I assumed that he meant that they had passed on. Dying was part of life, and it was a given that we'd all go through it.

"A biker's life is a hard life, cutie, but it's exciting. Ain't nothin' more exciting than being part of something bigger than you, riding with the wind on your face, a good woman against your back." He paused and gave me a wink. "And on *her* back." He laughed at his own joke. "Free to live the way you want, fight for what you believe in..." He paused, getting lost in his thoughts as he stared out at the ocean. "Shit, I miss those fuckin' days."

"I guess you're not talking about, uh—" I wasn't sure how to say what I was thinking, ending up with, "regular people riding motorcycles."

Pops snorted. "Hell, no. There's all kinds of bikers, cutie. Some ride recreational, sometimes referred to as your weekend warriors. There's Good Samaritan clubs like the Sentinels who ride about town helping to keep it safe. And there's the bikers who belong in MCs that live, breathe, and die the biker life. Think about what you've seen down on Main Street this week."

He was right. After spending almost a week with him and his friends, I could almost see the difference Pops was talking about, although some were so subtle that it was hard to tell the bikers apart. It helped when MCs wore cuts identifying their clubs, but not all of them did. Pops had explained that that was so they weren't readily identifiable to the cops or rival clubs who were out looking for a fight.

"Aren't those hardcore clubs really just criminals?" I hoped I hadn't insulted him.

"Some might call them that," he chuckled, reaching for another cigarette.

Silence followed Pops' comment, and I figured that he wasn't going to say anymore on the subject. I rose to my feet. "How about brunch?" I smiled down at him.

"What the hell is that?" he grumbled around lighting his smoke.

"It's not breakfast or lunch, but a meal in between. I could make us a salad."

He glared up at me as if I'd offered him poison. "I don't eat rabbit food, cutie."

"Well, then, what would you like?"

"How 'bout a nice, thick steak?"

"For brunch?" I asked incredulously. The look on his weathered face revealed that he was kidding with me. "I'll see what I can come up with." Never had truer words been spoken, because I had no idea what I was going to fix him.

I turned and walked toward the door. There was left over spaghetti, but really, how many times could I get away with serving him that? Roast beef sandwiches were out, because his friends had wolfed all of them down the day before, and eggs were out because he'd had that for breakfast every morning. I opened the fridge and looked at my options. I wouldn't know what they were if they jumped up and slapped me in the face. Then I went to the pantry and stared at the contents.

"Ruby!"

Pops never called me by my name!

"Ruby! Call my boy!"

Something was wrong! I could hear the panic in his voice. I rushed to the door and my heart stopped when I saw what I saw going on outside. Pops was on his feet and surrounded by four men, one of which I remembered seeing the first day down at the Main Street Station. The same one who'd threatened me. He was talking to Pops with an expression that revealed that he was pissed about something, and was pushing him around. I couldn't believe it! Anger engulfed me that a grown man was acting that way, picking on an old man!

I didn't even think about it, I just reacted. Pops was spewing his own words, but when I saw him take a swing and miss and almost end up on the ground, I knew that I had to do something. I couldn't call Tanner because I didn't know his number. Shit, I didn't even know if there was a phone in the house. I pulled the sliding glass door open and rushed out, having no idea what I was going to do.

"He'll think twice about puttin' my brother in jail again, old man," I heard the man that Pops was facing snarl. "The Kings don't take shit from no one! You got that? You tell that fucker to mind his own business, or next time we'll do some real damage."

Next time. Part of me was relieved. It sounded like he was just threatening Pops verbally. Maybe it would all be okay and they would just leave. And then Pops took another shot, clipping the man's chin this time. My stomach dropped as doom set in, and I sucked in my breath when the younger man drew back his arm and punched Pops right in the face. He went flying backwards to the ground.

"Pops!" I cried out, afraid for him.

"Well, well, well. Look what we have here, brothers." The man who'd hit Pops stood over him, placing a booted foot on his chest to hold him down. His eyes were on me, smiling with something sinister in them.

"Leave him alone, you bully!" I screamed, running toward them. My heart was pounding with fear, but I didn't let it stop me from throwing myself at the man and knocking him away from Pops. I caught him by surprise, the force of my palms against his chest causing a grunt to leave his chest. "The police are on their way!" I lied.

I turned back to Pops, seeing the pain in his gaze as he tried to get to his feet, blood dripping out of his nose. He was so furious that he was shaking, his face ruddy-looking, pain and anger warring in his hard eyes. I started to reach out to help him to his feet, but halted at the stubborn look on his face. I felt so bad for him, recognizing the fight in him, but also the weakness of his body. He must have realized it, too, but a man's pride was a strong force to reckon with.

"Remember me, girlie?" A band of steel circled my waist, hauling me up against the hard body of the man I'd pushed away from Pops.

"Leave her alone, Wicked!" Pops grumbled, getting unsteadily to his feet. "Your beef's with Tanner."

"But she's so cute," one of Wicked's friends stated in a laughing tone. "I bet she's more important to Tanner than you, old man!" Everyone but Pops and I laughed at that comment.

"Take your hands off me," I demanded, pulling against Wicked's arm. I dug my nails into his flesh, but all he did was grunt and tighten his arm around me, cutting off my air.

"I don't have my hands on you *yet*," Wicked gritted in my ear.

Frustration led me to reach behind me and claw at Wicked's face. This time he reacted with more force, angrily spinning me around and slapping me. Feeling the sting on my cheek didn't take away from the satisfaction of seeing the red scratch marks that my nails had left down his cheeks. They were already beading up with blood.

"Fucking, bitch!" He slapped me a second time. The only reason I remained on my feet was the hurtful hand that he had wrapped around my arm.

"You little prick!" Pops hollered, going for Wicked. Two of Wicked's friends grabbed him back before he could reach us.

They were being needlessly rough with him. I saw his face contort with pain. "What kind of men picks on the elderly and women?" I hissed, struggling to get free. "Do you pick on small children, too? That make you feel big and tough? Picking on the weak!" I taunted, finally pulling my arm free. "I bet all the MCs out there are afraid of you!" I couldn't seem to stop my run away mouth, which often got the best of me. "Your mamas must be real proud of you boys."

"You have a smart ass mouth on you, girlie," Wicked grated, taking a threatening step toward me.

He wasn't a big man, not like Tanner and his friends, but he still struck a chord of fear in me. I didn't like the look in his narrowed eyes, and the way his hands had clenched into tight fists warned me that I might be on the receiving end of something more than a slap. He'd already proved that he wasn't opposed to hurting a woman. Hell, he'd already slapped me twice, and if it made him feel like a man to attack someone who was old enough to be his grandfather, I was certain that he wouldn't stop with a couple of slaps.

I turned to run, where I had no clue, because I wasn't about to leave Pops out there alone to face them. That's when my gaze fell on the barbeque grill and the long utensils hanging off one of the sides. I made a beeline in that direction and managed to unhook a couple of them. I swung back around, holding the fork-like utensil and spatula out in front of me as if I were wielding samurai swords.

"I suggest that you all leave before the police get here!" Why was Wicked still walking toward me? Didn't he see my weapons? My eyes rounded and I backed up. "Don't make it worse than it already is," I said, hoping that he'd see reason.

He laughed, and just as he reached out for me the sound of motorcycles racing down the street in front of the house could be heard. I immediately thought of Tanner. Everyone halted what they were doing and looked toward the direction of the sound as it continued to move closer, and then stopped. Within seconds, three bikers raced around the corner of the house, removing their helmets and tossing them to the ground at the same time. It was Tanner and two of his brothers, and their ferocious appearances revealed that they'd been expecting trouble and were ready for action.

I don't know what made me do it, but I took the opportunity to slap Wicked across his face with the spatula. It made a sounding smack, and he swung back to me with disbelief in his wild eyes, right before it quickly turned into fury. With a vicious growl he lunged at me, while his friends took on Tanner and his brothers. I let out a scream when I felt Wicked's hand in the back of my hair, and dropped the utensils to reach for the hand yanking my hair out. Before any damage was done Pops was there, pulling him away from me.

Grunts followed, and I spun back around to see Wicked pummeling Pops. My eyes widened, and fear for Pops replaced my flight instinct as I threw myself at Wicked. I jumped onto his back and wrapped my arms around his neck, pulling with all my might. Pops managed to get in a couple of punches of his own, but all too soon Wicked was in control again and doing damage. Everything happened so fast after that. He pulled me over his head and slammed me to the ground, gave Pops a punch that knocked him to the ground out cold, and pivoted back to me all within seconds.

He came at me like a rocket, his lips drawn back over his teeth in a snarl. I crab walked backwards as fast as I could go, my heart pounding with fright as I stared up at him with rounded eyes. He reached down and caught the material of my tee over my chest and started to pull me up, bringing his fist back at the same time. With a sick feeling in my belly I knew that he was going to punch me in the face. I let out a squeal as his fist came forward, and squeezed my eyes shut.

The hit didn't land. Wicked was there one second and gone the next. I snapped my eyes open to see that Tanner had brought Wicked to the ground and was pounding him mercilessly. My gaze flew to Pops. He was still out. I crawled over to him, hearing the sound of sirens in the distance. Someone, maybe a neighbor, had called the cops, thank God, and they were on their way. I stared down at Pops, taking his hand in mine and softly calling his name.

"Pops." He didn't look good. Wicked had done a number on him, and there was no telling what damage his fists had done to Pops' body. I felt tears cloud my eyes. "Pops wake up," I encouraged. The sirens stopped, and soon police were running into the back yard. "Someone call an ambulance!" I cried out.

Tanner dragged a beaten and bleeding Wicked over to where his brothers were containing the other subdued Kings, tossing Wicked to the ground. He glanced up at one of the cops. "Take this piece of trash away." He glanced back at me, and seeing that I was on the ground with Pops, headed our way.

"We've got an ambulance coming!" one of the cops yelled in our direction before turning to help his partners with the Kings.

I glanced up at Tanner when he reached us, seeing the worry in his eyes and the tightness of his jaw. "Tanner," I sobbed, reaching up to wipe my tears. "I'm so sorry." I don't know why I was apologizing. "I don't have a phone. I couldn't call anyone."

He dropped to his haunches, his gaze running over Pops. "Pops." His tone was firm as he picked up a thin wrist and checked for a pulse. He took a deep breath, and then met my eyes. "He has a pulse," he said. I watched his eyes zero in onto something on my face. He reached forward and brushed his hand against my cheek. "You okay, honey?"

I nodded. "I am now."

Chapter 26

Tanner

I'd gotten there too fucking late. Someone had phoned the police about a disturbance at my house. The cops had called me, knowing that I would be able to get there faster than them if I was at my bar. No one had expected to arrive there to find the fucking Kings attacking Pops and Ruby. Pops had come to when the paramedics arrived and in spite of all of us insisting that he go to the hospital, he had stubbornly refused. They'd checked him over, wrapped his ribs, then cleaned up the blood and treated his cuts.

I should have taken Wicked's threat to Ruby more seriously. Having his drunk, younger brother thrown in jail had pushed him to retaliate. The fact that he and some of his brothers were sitting in jail right now didn't satisfy the anger that was boiling inside me. I'd underestimated Wicked, believing that he was more of a punk and gang leader full of talk and no action. That's all he'd been in the past, other than getting into trouble over some petty shit.

He'd proven me wrong, and crossed the line by putting his hands on Pops and Ruby. Hell, he'd crossed the line by coming to my house. When I'd first run onto the scene and seen Wicked I'd wanted to kill him. No one messed with my family and got away with it. I didn't realize just how angry I was until I saw Ruby's face and knew that she'd been hurt. I'd practically flown across the yard to get him away from her. Sid and Pete had taken care of the other Kings, and by the time the cops had arrived they'd just had to cuff them and take them away.

I decided then to assign Sid and Mark to watch over Ruby and Pops at the house when I couldn't be there, at least until the end of Bike Week. Just in case. Wicked may have been in jail, but he could still order brothers on the outside to do some damage. Having Sid and Mark at the house would make Lonnie and Judith happy. They already thought what we did was dangerous, and didn't like their men out on the roads late at night. Hell, what we did *was* dangerous, and we'd been involved with a lot of situations like the one we'd handled today, but we didn't bring that shit home. They knew what we were about, we were dedicated to keeping our town safe, and sometimes had to use lethal force.

Sid and Mark were okay with hanging out at my place for a couple of days, but Pops had argued with me about it, until I explained that they were there more to protect Ruby than him. Although, seeing the way she'd jumped on Wicked's back to protect Pops brought a smile to my face, and showed me that she wasn't afraid to fight. She'd been fierce and unafraid, not like the women I was used to who thought that being weak and helpless was what a man wanted. The only place I wanted a woman to be submissive was in the bedroom, and only because I wanted her to feel what I was doing to her.

"Where'd you go, brother?" Gabe asked.

I snapped back to the present and couldn't help the grin that spread across my face. "Thinking about the sight of Ruby climbing onto Wicked's back."

Pete let out a snicker. "Yeah, that was a sight to see. You have a scrappy woman."

That wiped the smile right off my face. "She's not my woman." I tried to wipe away the memory of Ruby in my bed, of us fucking while we watched our reflections in the mirror. It had been hot. But just because I'd caved and claimed her didn't mean that we were an item.

"She went at Wicked like a tiger protecting her cub," Sid added, picking up his coffee.

I had to agree with him. We were all at Tom's Diner getting breakfast. Some of us, Skipper, Heath, Ace, and William were winding down after having spent the last five hours on the streets.

Gabe, Mike, Sully, and I had done the first five hours. Rod and Pete had the night off. We worked in shifts and mainly stuck to where we knew the trouble spots were. Sometimes the night was quiet, but most of the time there was at least an incident or two to remind us of why we did what we did.

"I'll bet she's a tigress in bed."

I was sure that my grin said it all. Knowing laughter followed. Hell, we were brothers and shared everything, especially when it came to our conquests. It wasn't unusual for two of us to be getting a blowjob behind the bar at the same time, with different women, of course. A couple of my brothers liked to share their women. Threesomes didn't interest me. When I had a woman I wanted her all to myself. I was selfish that way.

"You going home after here?"

I gave Ace's question some thought. My dick wanted to go home. He was thinking of Ruby and her tight little pussy. Every time she came up in conversation I got a boner. Christ, half the night I'd spent riding around town hard as fucking stone. It hadn't come as a surprise when I'd stopped to take a piss and discovered a wet spot of pre-cum in my jeans where my dick had been rubbing against it. That had been a first. I'd shaken my head with disbelief and a snort and zipped up.

"You can't get her out of your mind, can you?"

The amusement in Gabe's tone pulled me from my thoughts. Jesus that was twice in one meeting that I'd not been fully present. I was thankful then for the three waitresses that Tom employed who were walking over with our breakfasts. Twelve plates stacked with pancakes, bacon, sausage, and scrambled eggs. They'd have to come back with the grits.

"Man, that looks good, sweetheart," Sully said, giving his waitress a wink.

"You boys still growing?" Sunny joked, setting down the four plates that she had stacked up on her arm. Once the plates were down, they began refilling our cups.

"Best meal of the day," William said, already digging into his eggs.

"Heard about the trouble at your place yesterday." The other two waitresses walked off, but Sunny stuck around, resting her hand at the back of my chair while she looked down at me. "Pops okay?"

I nodded. "Bruised a little, but he's good."

"Too fucking mean to let a few punches keep him down," Ace said around a mouthful.

Sunny's eyes grew big, taking in his comment before swinging her gaze back to me. "What about that little girl I sent over there, Ruby?"

"She's good, too," I said, trying not to grin and give myself away. Sunny was observant and not afraid to speak her mind. If she thought there was an inkling of interest on my part she'd be on me like a barracuda.

"Good. I'm glad to hear it. Let me know if you need anything else." She turned to leave. "And you take care of that little girl!" she ordered as she walked off, passing the other waitresses as they were on the way back with our grits.

"Speak of the devil, look who just walked in," Skipper commented right before shoving a forkful of eggs into his mouth. Every one of us looked in the direction of the door.

Pops and Ruby, followed by Mark and Sid, had just entered the diner. I knew it wasn't a coincidence, since I'd told Mark and Sid that's where we'd be this morning. Pops looked like he'd been worked over, which he had, and was walking a little stiffly. Ruby's pretty face sported a bruise and a small cut, probably caused from one of the rings Wicked had been wearing. I felt my jaw lock with a sudden rush of anger, wishing I'd had a chance to do more damage to him before the cops had arrived.

In spite of what she'd been through the day before, she was fucking beautiful, and there was a smile on her face that made her eyes glitter like jewels. I liked how she'd done her long hair. It was braided in a loose, sexy kind of style and hanging down the front, bringing my gaze right to the tit it was resting against. Was that a nipple? I narrowed my eyes. Holy fuck, I could see right through the white off the shoulder blouse she was wearing.

I was infused with instant fucking lust, and my dick jerked with renewed arousal. The woman was going to be the death of me. One taste of her and I was suddenly addicted, craving more. *Needing it.* Hell, if we'd been alone I'd have had her on top of a table, her pretty legs spread, and be buried inside her so deep she wouldn't be able to sit down after I was done pounding into her. That sudden image brought a groan up my throat, loud enough for Gabe's head to snap my way.

"You okay, brother?" he smiled with a knowing look in his fucking eyes. "Boy, she's fucking got it going on."

He was looking for a reaction, but he didn't need to remind me that Ruby was hot. The ripped jeans she was wearing were skin tight and emphasized her mouth-watering curves. I stuffed a forkful of pancake into my mouth, giving Gabe a slight nod without making a big deal out of it.

"Thought we'd join you brothers for breakfast." Sid pulled out a chair at the next table. "The girls will be here soon." He sat down, Mark did the same.

"Hey, Pops. How you doing this morning?" Sully asked with genuine concern in his voice.

"Heard you had a run in with those little fuckers the Kings." William had never been one to mince words.

"Glad to see you're okay, darlin'." That comment had obviously been meant for Ruby. Our gazes met, but it was Gabe who pulled an empty chair from a nearby table over to our table, placing it between him and William. "Come have a seat."

"Here, Pops." Ace grabbed his plate and cup and rose to his feet, moving to sit at Sid and Mark's table.

I turned worried eyes on Pops as he sat down in the chair Ace had vacated for him. "You okay, Pops?" In his day Pops had been a force to be reckoned with, fast and fierce. He'd come home many times looking beat to hell, but I'd always known that the other guy had looked worse. In his prime Pops had been big and tough, but smoking, drinking, and years of fighting and partying had left him a shadow of himself. He looked a hell of a lot older than he was.

"I'm good." He glanced around the table, meeting the quiet eyes of some of my brothers. "You should see the other guy." Laughter broke out and ended with his hacking.

"What about you, darlin'?" Gabe looked down at Ruby. "Who did this to your pretty face?" One of the waitresses had left a pot of coffee and some extra cups in the center of the table. He reached for one and filled it.

She smiled, accepting the cup of coffee he handed out to her. "Thank you," she said, accepting it from him. "Some slime ball named Wicked."

"Yeah, he is a slime ball. And he's right where he needs to be, sitting in jail."

She gave Gabe a smile, those pretty lips of hers puckering as she took a cautious sip of her coffee. My gaze focused there for a minute until I heard the tinkle of bells that alerted that someone was coming into the diner. It was Lonnie and Judith, bright smiles spreading across their faces when they saw Mark and Sid. It was clear that my brothers had women who really cared for them, and the fierce, possessive expressions on my brothers' faces revealed that the feeling was mutual. The women walked directly to them, good mornings were exchanged, a few heated kisses, and then the women settled down on vacant chairs.

A waitress came over to take their orders, and I watched Ruby, watched her mouth form the words when she ordered a bowl of oatmeal. Oatmeal? Christ, that's what babies ate. Did she really like that shit, or...I didn't like where my thoughts had suddenly gone. Was she broke? I wouldn't put it past her to have spent the money I'd given her the other day on Pops and his friends and hadn't kept any for herself. Fuck. It occurred to me that we'd never got around to discussing money, and while I thought about it, I needed to get her a phone, too.

"Bring a bowl of fruit, too," I added, drawing the waitresses' eye before she left to fill the orders. "For the lady." I indicated Ruby. "I'll pick up the tab for everyone this morning." I purposely included my brothers and their women. If Ruby was broke, as I suspected, I didn't want her feeling embarrassed that I'd guessed her secret.

Her soft smile hit me right in my heart. Our gazes clung for a minute, hers saying more than I was comfortable with. Jesus, I'd taken her virginity. I'd been immediately reminded of that when I'd glanced down at my sheets and noticed her blood staining them. I'd yanked them off and tossed them into the wash, but something told me that the blood would still be there, a permanent stain I'd have to live with for the rest of my life.

I made a decision right then and there. As soon as she was done eating I was going to take her for a ride. I didn't know where, all I knew was that we needed to talk some things out.

Chapter 27

R^{uby}

I'd never been on a motorcycle before. I couldn't believe that I was sitting on the back of Tanner's bike, my arms wrapped around his torso, my hands against his hard, defined abs. I resisted the urge to run my palms over them, wondering what he'd do if I slipped my hands beneath his tee so I could touch his bare skin. It was probably not a good idea. We were flying down the highway, at least it seemed like we were, and then Tanner exited off and we were flying down a rural road.

Shortly afterwards he slowed down and turned onto a narrow dirt road that seemed to be leading nowhere. Trees lined the side of the road, and we didn't pass a single house. Finally we came to a clearing, and I knew immediately that it was used as a meeting spot for partying. The ground was covered with tire marks. There was some trash, mostly beer cans and bottles, and a lot of cigarette butts. A burned-out spot on the ground marked the place where a bonfire had been lit. A little further in was a small lake.

It was hotter than hell, and Tanner stopped his bike beneath a shady tree. His hand dropped to my thigh, and he gave it a squeeze. "Off, honey."

I wasn't sure that I could. "My legs feel like rubber," I laughed, awkwardly bringing one leg over the back tire. I had to grab Tanner for support, laughing softly at my gracelessness. He turned toward me. Our faces were close and I waited for a second, hoping he'd kiss me. I licked my lips with anticipation.

He reached forward and removed my helmet, which was really his. He'd had to ride without one. With a groan, he tossed it to the ground and then closed the distance between us. I felt his hand at the back of my head where he clutched a handful of hair. "Been thinking of this since the last time we kissed." He dragged my face closer and then his mouth came down hard on mine. In a flash we'd been set ablaze, losing control, and going at each other's mouths with sounds of mutual pleasure.

My belly did a flip-flop. I felt Tanner's kiss all the way to my core. My toes curled in my shoes. I opened my mouth to him, and our tongues thrust and danced around each other. The flavor of something sweet and slightly bitter exploded on my taste buds, and I realized that it was the syrup he'd poured onto his pancakes. As he ground his mouth over mine I sucked on his tongue, receiving a deep groan from him.

Tanner pulled away, and the next thing I knew he was lifting me and placing me on his seat in front of him. He arranged my legs over his so that I was straddling his powerful thighs, and our sexes were flush. We were both breathing heavily, and I thought that he was going to kiss me again, but he only leaned forward and placed his forehead against mine.

"I knew the minute I saw you, all wet and looking like a drowned rat on the side of the road that you were going to be trouble."

"Why do you keep saying that?" My heart was pounding out of control.

"Because you are." When he pulled back I was surprised to see his eyes were hard, his expression grim. "I fought against fucking you, but now that I've had a taste I want you even more."

I giggled. "To top it off you took my cherry," I teased, making light of it. He stiffened, clearly not in the mood, and then I realized that he was having a hard time with his desire for me. "It's okay, Tanner. I know about your rule." God, what was I saying? "I'm a big girl, and I won't be here long. I'm okay with, uh, us being fuck buddies." I winced at that, because it was crap I was spewing. I wanted him, yes, and I wanted for there to be more between us, but I had to let him off the hook, convince him that all there was between us was casual sex.

"You seem to know what you want."

Why did he sound so bitter? I shrugged. "I'm a free spirit." Jeeze, that made me sound like some kind of flower child left over from the sixties. "Life is too short to get serious over the, um, little things. It's all about the here and now, and, uh, living in the moment."

He captured my eyes with shards of anger reflected in his. "You believe that shit you're saying, or is that your way of downplaying what's going on?"

I exhaled noisily. "No downplaying. Losing my virginity was bound to happen sometime. I'm glad it was you, but that doesn't mean I want to, uh, get into a serious relationship with you." I paused, looking for the right words. "Because I have to tell you, Tanner, that if you want a serious, um, relationship between us, I'm going to have to, uh, find someone else to give me what I need. Sexually," I threw in for good measure.

His brows shot up at that, the slightest curve to his lips. "Is that so?"

I nodded. "Yep." I continued to nod, dying a little inside because I didn't mean a word I was saying, but I felt that he needed the words. And I was determined to avoid his words of rejection any way that I could. Lying seemed like a good idea.

"So are you saying that I can make you the acceptation to my one-fuck rule and you'll be okay with that?" He sounded skeptical. "That I can fuck you as many times as I want?"

I was beginning to feel like a bobble head. "Yep. Sounds good to me." I swallowed hard. "That is, if you want to, uh, fuck me again."

He threw his head back and laughed, the full throaty sound going straight to my clit. "Funny, I brought you out here to have this same talk with you." His words crushed me. "Hurting you is the last thing I want to do. I'm not sorry that I took your innocence, but I don't want you to think that it meant more to me than it did."

I swallowed down my hurt, because showing it would reveal that it had meant something more to me. "Don't worry, Tanner. I'd never think that. I'm aware of how you think of women." He frowned, and I wondered why. I'd only spoken the truth. "You don't have a monopoly on just wanting to fuck for the fun of it." I forced a smile. "You can be my teacher. Prepare me for the next man."

That seemed to get a reaction out of him, surprising us both. He put his hands on my shoulders and jerked me close. "Then let's begin with lesson number two," he ground out, making me wonder where his sudden anger had come from.

Hadn't I said what he'd wanted to hear? I'd just given him carte blanche over me. The next thing I knew his mouth was on mine with a roughness I'd not been expecting. Tanner was angry, the hands clutching my shoulders squeezing me painfully hard. I whimpered, and something must have got through to him because his hands loosened. His mouth turned soft, coaxing, our tongues colliding with sensual heat.

I wrapped my arms around Tanner's neck. He dropped a hand to my breast, giving it a squeeze, before losing control and pulling my blouse down and exposing it. He tugged on my nipple until it was a hard bud and I was arching further into him, moaning. The kiss ended abruptly, and then he was taking my breast into his mouth and suckling it. I threw my head back and closed my eyes as bolts of pleasure zapped through my body.

"Yes!" I encouraged in a husky plea, taking his head and holding him against me. I knew that I was wet, I could feel my panties dampen with excitement. Tanner pulled the other side of my blouse down and lavished attention to that breast, too. He couldn't seem to get enough, kissing, sucking, biting, leaving a sting of pain behind that morphed into little sparks of pleasure. "God, yes!" I cried, my eyes rolling back in my head.

I felt his hard cock against the apex of my thighs. We rocked against each other, frustratingly aware that we had too many clothes between us. Once Tanner finished loving my breasts he nudged me off his lap, and I found myself standing next to his bike on shaking legs.

"Get those jeans off now," he snapped, dismounting his bike.

I watched his hands undo his pants as I was slipping mine down my legs.

"Those, too," he indicated my underwear. "Unless you want me to rip them off you."

His words sent a little chill down my spine. I could hear the heavy arousal in his voice. My gaze was riveted to watching him remove his own jeans, not surprised that he wasn't wearing underwear. His cock sprang free, full and long, the slit in the mushroom shaped head leaking pre-cum. I caught my breath. Tanner heard me, our eyes locking. He reached out, his hand curling around the back of my neck and jerking me against him.

"Feel that?" he growled, grinding his cock into my belly. "Feel what you do to me?"

I knew that he wasn't expecting a response, not a verbal one, anyway. I reached up to kiss him, taking his hard flesh into my hand and exploring it. His groan vibrated against my lips, and he thrust his hips, encouraging me to keep touching him. I ran my hand up and down his massive girth, my fingers not even meeting up, feeling a shudder move through him.

"Am I doing it right?" I whispered against his lips.

"Hell, yes, baby," he hissed, thrusting so hard that the head of his shaft slammed against me, leaving behind a trail of pre-cum.

Suddenly, the need to taste him slammed into me so hard that I could barely breathe. "Can I kiss it?"

He made a hissing sound, instantly pushing me down to my knees. His magnificent cock was right there, in my face. I could smell the muskiness of his pre-cum, and stuck out my tongue to taste the pearly white substance. It wasn't unpleasant at all, and before I lost my nerve I closed my mouth over him and slid down his length as far as I could go. Tanner's thighs quivered beneath my palms, and I raised my eyes to his.

"If you could see how fucking beautiful you are right now, with your pretty mouth wrapped around my dick, cum glistening on your lip . . ."

His expression made me think of a fierce warrior, raw and hard, his nostrils flaring with lust. He dropped a hand in my hair and thrust deeper into my mouth before pulling out and then doing it again. I moaned, running my tongue along his cock, exploring the ridges and veins that made up the muscle of steel and velvet.

I eagerly ran my mouth up and down Tanner's cock, using my hand on the part of him that didn't fit in my mouth. Below that were his testicles, big and heavy, hanging where my chin bumped against them with his thrusts. When his breathing picked up, turning harsher, I sensed that he was getting ready to orgasm. He was pushing his cock deeper and deeper into my mouth, until it hit the back of my throat. I swallowed instinctively, and that's when Tanner released a low groan and pulled away.

"No!" He pulled me to my feet. "Maybe next time I'll let you swallow my cum, but this time I want to be inside your pussy." He turned me sharply toward his bike and the next thing I knew I was laying over the seat with my ass in the air. "So pretty," he growled, running his hand over my bottom. "Are you ready for me, honey?" He reached between my legs and ran a finger through my slit.

I let out a startled cry and bucked forward. His laughter followed, and then I felt him line up the head of his cock to my opening. "I know you're clean. I am, too. Tell me you're on some kind of birth control."

A chuckle escaped me. "A little late for this conversation, don't you think?"

"Baby," he ran the tip of his cock through my slit, torturing my clit until I was a quivering mess.

God, I wanted him inside me, I wanted to feel him with nothing between us, flesh on flesh. Was it wrong to want something that would feel so wicked, and so good? The feel of him running his cock up and down my slit was messing with my decision to choose right from wrong. A quick calculation in my head revealed that it was a safe time of the month for me.

"Baby?" Tanner growled low, dipping the head of his cock past the hood protecting my clit and onto my clit. "You want my dick bare?"

Ohmygod! The head of his cock was making little circles around my clit, teasing me past endurance. I couldn't think clearly when he was giving me so much pleasure. I trembled wildly, whimpering. "Yes!" I arched my butt out further. I couldn't wait to have him inside me. And then he was there, in a single thrust he penetrated my body and nothing else mattered. The man I wanted was fucking me, the man I thought I was falling for, and he was right. I was a fool for thinking none of this mattered.

"Feels...so...good!" I murmured jerkily, meeting his thrusts.

Tanner grunted every time he pounded forward. "Not going to last long, baby. You've got a sweet, tight pussy." His thrusts turned harder. "Come with me." All at once his hand was at my clit, and he was merciless, flicking and pinching it. "Put some cum on my dick, baby," he demanded.

He leaned over my back and nibbled at my shoulder and neck, thrusting faster, harder, and grunting, the hands at my hips bruising as he jerked me back onto his cock. Every time he bottomed out I felt his balls slap against the back of my thighs, heavy with cum. I was going to come undone. I welcomed the sweet rush surging through my blood, the fire scorching my veins. "Tanner!" As my orgasm exploded outward, my body shuddered against his.

He didn't stop shoving into me, or even slow down, but fucked through my orgasm, adding longevity to the intensity. I was panting, quivering, gasping, and whimpering, totally at his mercy. And he showed none. He was chasing his own release and his harsh breathing, the speed and roughness of his thrusts, revealed he was climbing high.

"I'm going to put so much cum inside your tight little cunt that you'll be leaking for a week, and then I'm going to fuck your ass and put some there, too." He grew taut and held his position for just a second, grunting, and then sinking against me as his orgasm claimed him. "Aaagggghhhh!" he groaned, the force of his release rocking his body against me. "Feel that, baby?" He ejaculated deep inside me, filling my body with his seed.

God, yes! I was amazed that I did. His fingers were clutching my hips hard enough that I knew there'd be bruises, but I didn't care. The rapture that consumed me was worth a few bruises. As Tanner's movements slowed down he buckled against me, and I held my breath, hoping that his bike was strong enough to hold both of our weight.

His warm breath was against my shoulder, and as he gained control I felt his lips rub along my shoulder. Gradually he moved, straightening. His cock slid out of me, causing us both to groan. He helped me stand straight, his arms keeping me flush against him while his hands palmed my breasts. I caught my breath at the sharp tingle that traveled from my nipple to my core, rolling my head back onto his shoulder.

"Was I too rough?" Tanner inquired against my ear, his warm breath giving me a pleasant tingle.

I shook my head. "I like it rough." I did. I loved it when he lost control and possessed me with rough caresses, love bites that stung a little, and the fullness I felt from his powerful pounding cock. I loved when he came inside me.

"Careful what you wish for, honey," he said low.

"Why, have you been holding back?" I couldn't contain my smile, he was already growing hard against my butt.

"Maybe a little," he confessed, kissing the side of my neck.

I arched my neck to the side so he had better access. "Do you hold out with your, uh, other women?"

"They aren't innocents like you." He began to suck at my skin, his hands playing with my breasts and nipples.

I frowned. "Are they hookers?"

He laughed softly. "No, they're experienced."

I thought about that. "Do you like experienced women, Tanner?"

"Right now I like innocent little virgins." He flipped me around. "Why are we talking about this?" His eyes narrowed on me.

I shrugged. "I'm just curious." I smiled at his wary expression. "Maybe I should sleep around to gain more experience. I wouldn't want you missing out." I was joking, but the look in Tanner's eyes revealed that he didn't appreciate my comment. Was he jealous? I quickly brushed the thought away, thinking about our earlier conversation. "Wouldn't you like me to become more experienced?"

"Any experience you get will come from me."

Well, this was getting interesting. "Oh, so does that mean we're exclusive?"

I could see that I'd backed him into a corner, and he wasn't happy. I didn't understand why, unless he was jealous over the thought of me being with another man. After all, he couldn't have his cake and eat it, too. If he wanted to keep our relationship casual, that meant we could sleep with other people, right? Not that I would, but he didn't need to know that.

All of a sudden his hands were covering my naked butt and he was pulling me up sharply against his loins. He lifted me and I wrapped my legs around his waist. I sighed, nearly coming undone by the savage expression on his face as he lowered me onto his stiff shaft. "It just means that we're fucking," he growled up against my lips, not making a commitment. He started walking, kissing me as he went.

"Where are we going?" I asked the second he let me up for air.

"It's damned hot, and I want to fuck you in the lake."

My eyes grew big. "What about alligators?" I began to look around nervously as we neared the water. It wasn't a very big lake. The crescent moon shaped shoreline leading up to the water was wide and clear, surrounded by a carpet of green prickly-looking grass. As we reached the water I was surprised to see how clear it was.

A deep, throaty laugh escaped Tanner as he took the first step into the water. "The only thing that's going to bite you in this lake is me."

I didn't care after that, because he fucked me into oblivion.

Chapter 28

Tanner

It was the last day of Bike Week and it was Ace's turn to host the annual cookout. It'd been something Pops had started after he retired from War Dogs as a way to make contact with old friends and brothers who'd come to town for Bike Week. The club had decided to keep it going. The Sentinels had friends from all over, other chapters that had started up in different states, and if any of them had come down for Bike Week they knew that they were welcome. Sometimes the cookout was the only chance we had to see them while they were in town.

Ace didn't have a place on the beach, but he did have a lake on his property, which was located off a long, dead-end road that you'd swear was taking you out to a marshy swamp. His place was surrounded by cypress and moss-draped oaks that were hundreds of years old, and it wasn't unusual to see deer, wild hogs, or other wildlife making their homes there. The old cracker-style home had a wide shade porch along the front, and sat on shell and lime pilings. He'd inherited the place from his grandparents.

It was early, but already people were showing up. Some would stop in long enough to say hi and leave, others would stay the whole damned day until well into the evening hours. It didn't fucking matter, we kept it simple with hotdogs, burgers, and beer until the last biker left, which was usually when the last of the beer was gone. In the morning a clean-up crew would be out to take care of any messes.

Lawn chairs littered the ground. Ace had opened up his home to anyone needing to escape the stifling heat. Some would take their chances in the lake to cool off until they were chased out by the alligators. Most found the nearest tree to duck behind and take a piss, but there were women present, too, and that didn't work for them. I was standing at one of four grills, flipping burgers, acknowledging who I could, but mostly keeping my gaze on Ruby. She was sitting beneath a shady oak with Lonnie, Judith, and a few other women who'd joined them.

She fit right in. I could tell that she made friends easily. She wasn't shy about talking to anyone, and when she laughed with abandon, like she was doing now, the melody made something possessive come alive in my gut because I wanted it to be mine and mine alone. I didn't want to share it, or her. When our eyes met across the lawn, her laugh settled down into a sensual, knowing smile that teased the animal in me.

I was fucking hot, and it wasn't from the fire beneath the burgers. It was clear that I couldn't look at Ruby without wanting her. Every movement, every laugh, every glance from her expressive eyes got me on some primitive level that demanded that I claim her. It was infuriating because I couldn't concentrate on what I needed to. Christ. I was the president of the Sentinels. We had a damned good club, and truthfully, any one of my brothers could run it as good as, if not better than, me. We didn't vote on shit like other clubs did, we just took care of what we had to. As the president I made suggestions and handled the paperwork involved with the club holdings, but that was all. If one of my brothers didn't agree with something, they spoke up and we worked it out another way.

Just because we weren't one-percenters didn't mean that we didn't have to deal with trouble once in a while. We did whatever was required to keep our town safe, even if it meant crossing the line. Killing was always a last resort, but we didn't hesitate if it meant protecting those we loved.

"Tanner! Tanner!"

I heard the familiar squeal well over the sound of everything else, and glanced up to see Olive Cartwright running toward me. What the fuck was she doing here? I hadn't seen her in five years, not since the night I'd ended our five year relationship. She'd been my last serious girlfriend, and the reason for my one-fuck only rule.

My gaze fell down her slender body, taking in the tight leather pants and lace-up vest that she was wearing. A lot of flesh was peeking between the laces, and her tits were nearly bouncing out of her top. Her platinum hair was loose and arranged into a style that made it appear as if she'd just crawled out of bed. She was as beautiful as ever, and she had a smile on her face that sent warning signals through me.

How she was running in those stiletto boots was a mystery, and I could tell by her momentum that she was going to jump me. I stepped away from the grill to avoid an accident just as she launched herself against me. I grunted and stumbled back at the impact, my arms automatically going around her as she jumped up and wrapped her legs around my waist just like she'd always done before.

What the fuck?

"I've missed you, baby!" she cried, grabbing the side of my face and planting her lips on mine. It was anything but a hello kiss, more like the kiss of lovers who were seeing each other after spending time apart. Hell, we had been lovers, and I guessed five years apart counted as time, but my feelings for her had died a long fucking time ago.

I jerked back with a scowl, taking her by the arms and pushing her away. As she was forced to drop her legs to the ground I wiped the grease from my mouth left from her lipstick. "What the hell are you doing here?" I growled, not exactly happy at seeing her. I glanced to where Ruby had been sitting. She was gone. Good, maybe she hadn't witnessed what had happened.

A familiar pout played on her red mouth. Nothing had changed. "Aren't you glad to see me?"

"Not really," I said honestly. I'd learned too late into our relationship that Olive had been a user, and she hadn't been opposed to using her sexuality to get what she wanted.

"Ouch! Not very welcoming," she pouted playfully. "I remembered a time when you couldn't keep your hands off of me."

Seriously? She was going to pretend that things hadn't ended ugly between us? She ran her hands up my abs and chest with a familiar ease that pissed me off. I took her by the wrists and pulled her hands off of me. "What the fuck do you want?"

She laughed. "I just wanted to say hi, that's all. I looked for you all week, but we must have just missed each other. Then I heard about this cookout and I knew you'd be here."

I was surprised that she hadn't just shown up at my house, but she knew that she wouldn't have received a warm welcome there. "You found me." I went back to flipping burgers and began putting them onto a plate when I noticed that they were done. "Now what?" I set the spatula down and gave her my full attention, crossing my arms so she couldn't wiggle her way against me again.

"Are you still angry at me for the way things ended?" There was a cooler at our feet, and she bent and helped herself to a beer. "I would have thought that after all this time..." She gave a shrug as though she hadn't broken the one rule that you didn't break in an exclusive relationship—cheating.

I'd kicked her ass to the curb.

"I didn't give you much of a choice, as I recall." I wasn't going to let her turn it into something it hadn't been. Our five year relationship had been good, most of it, anyway. We'd both made mistakes, and like a lot of relationships we'd grown lazy and comfortable with each other. But it was when I'd walked in on her and another man in bed that I'd realized saying goodbye had been long overdue. I hadn't even been all that upset. She, on the other hand, had been furious that I'd tossed her ass out.

"Yes." She handed me the beer. "Would you please?" She wagged her long, red-tipped nails in my face. I popped the top and handed it back to her. "You were particularly brutal that night. I know I hurt you."

I snorted. "You have to care for someone for them to hurt you, Olive. Walking in on you and your lover pissed me off because it was my fucking bed. But then I thought of all the time I'd spent on a relationship that was going nowhere. In a way you gave me insight into what I really wanted in life."

"And what was that?"

"That I didn't want a relationship." So why did Ruby's face flash before my eyes? I brushed it aside.

"So, you haven't replaced me?" One of her finely plucked brows arched, her brown eyes gleaming with interest.

I laughed. "Hell, yes, I've replaced you with a new woman in my bed every chance I get." I may have been stretching the truth, considering that we usually didn't make it to my bed. I never brought them home. "Are you still with . . . ?" I'd never got his name, but I'd often wondered if she'd hooked up with the man I'd caught her with.

She shook her head, giggling. "No. I haven't seen him in two years. We never got together, though. He was already married." She took a drink of her beer. "So, why don't we get together while I'm in town?" She ran the tip of her finger down the length of my jaw. "For old time's sake? We could start with dinner and see where that takes us."

If she'd shown up a week ago, before I'd fallen into the electric blue eyes of Trouble, I may have been tempted. The sex between me and Olive had been good. But I'd had my share of meaningless sex, and I could get that anytime I wanted. Sex with Ruby was different, and seemed to fill a void in me that I hadn't recognized I'd had.

Before I realized what Olive was doing, her finger had moved down my body and was now running up and down my zipper. Jesus, she didn't give up! I reached down and wrapped my hand around her thin wrist. "Let's keep this G-rated, okay?"

I glanced around, searching for Ruby. Where the hell had she gone? I saw Pops sitting with the same War Dogs that had shown up for lunch the other day, and a few old friends from other MCs. My brothers were scattered. I estimated that there were around a hundred people there so far. There were several identifying scents in the air—the familiar smell of charcoal and lighter fluid, cooked food, cigarettes, and weed, all mingled together.

"It's hard when it's been so long."

What? I glanced down at Olive, trying to remember what we'd been talking about. I noticed William and Heath motioning for me to go over to them. Something was up, I could tell by their expressions. "Look, Heath and William need me for something."

"But-"

I took off before she could say anything else. By the time I reached William and Heath, Sully had joined them. "What's up?" I asked.

"When did she get back?" Heath indicated Olive with a not so subtle nod in her direction.

"I don't know, but something tells me she's got an agenda."

"Christ, man, she's still hot," William added, lighting a cigarette. "Still can't believe you let a piece like that get away." He shook his head with disgust.

"Look, is this why you brothers motioned me over, to talk about my ex?" I snapped with irritation. Sometimes my brothers were as bad as snoopy old ladies.

"Naw, brother, we figured you needed saving," Heath laughed. "Olive looked like she was about to eat you up."

"When the day comes I need rescuing from a woman, just put me out of my misery and shoot me," I snapped back.

"She looks hungry," Heath observed.

That was Olive. During our time together she'd been hungry for a lot of things. She'd never been satisfied with what I'd given her, and I'd busted my ass trying to keep her satisfied. Back then I'd let my dick run my life, but not anymore, and never again.

"You want me to run interference for you?" Heath had a shit-eating grin on his face that revealed that he was just a little too eager. "Or if you want I can keep Ruby out of the way." He wagged his thick brows, his expression animated with enthusiasm.

He looked like he'd enjoy that even more, and I didn't want him anywhere near Ruby. "Stay away from Ruby," I growled.

Heath laughed. "That leaves Olive."

"You claiming Ruby?" William wanted to know, crushing his cigarette butt beneath his boot. "Because you know the rules of the club when it concerns women, brother. If she's not spoken for, anyone has a shot at her."

"Since when?" I demanded. We had no such rules. The only reason I'd made a big deal out of Ruby opening her mouth that day in the bar and letting everyone know that she wasn't claimed was to keep her safe. There'd been several members from other clubs there that did have that specific rule with regards to women. To them, an unclaimed woman was free game, and they wouldn't understand the word no.

William was testing me, trying to get a rise out of me. He and I both knew that he was all talk, the humor in his eyes spoke the truth. I was about to tell him to go for it when I saw Ruby step out of the house carrying a glass of water. Derek, a member from the Black Diamonds, was sided up too fucking closely to her. I knew Derek. He was a good guy, but he was a charmer when it came to women, and good at it. Ruby was laughing at something he'd said as they made their way back to where Lonnie, Judith, and the others were sitting.

"Looks like someone already beat me to it," William joked.

Not likely, I thought to myself. But when I saw Derek sit down in Ruby's chair and pull her down onto his lap, I thought I was going to lose it. She didn't even make an attempt to get off, either. She got good and settled, laughing at something he'd said. I felt my blood pressure go up. I had the urge to go over there and yank her off his lap, to show everyone that she was mine. But she wasn't mine, and I had to keep reminding myself of that fact. We were fuck buddies, but that was all. It didn't mean that she couldn't have male friends.

I'd warned Ruby to stay close to Lonnie and Judith when I wasn't around so that she'd be safe, and I'd asked the girls to keep her out of trouble. Everyone knew that they were Mark and Sid's women. There wouldn't be any advances made towards them, there was a strict rule about that among bikers, and the girls were wearing their "property of" cuts. I was hoping that since Ruby was with Lonnie and Judith that it would be assumed she was with someone in the Sentinels, too.

Her sitting on Derek's lap pretty much screamed out that she was free and available.

Swearing beneath my breath, I headed over to them. Ruby glanced up as I was walking, and our eyes met. There was a teasing glimmer in her pretty blues, and her subtle smile sent an invitation straight down to my dick. She was playing with fire, and she knew it.

Chapter 29

R^{uby}

Oh, shit! Tanner looked mad and determined, but it didn't stop the little smile from developing on my face. What did he expect? When I'd glanced over and caught that bleached-blonde, long-legged, leather-clad bimbo with her legs wrapped around his waist, kissing him, I'd been hurt. Then I'd reminded myself that we weren't in an exclusive relationship, or even a relationship for that matter, and that two could play at that game. So when I'd literally run into Derek in the kitchen while there getting a glass of water, I'd eaten up his good looks and southern charm.

I hadn't intended to end up on Derek's lap, he'd caught me unaware with that move, but I hadn't made any attempt to get off, either. He wasn't being disrespectful. His hands weren't traveling. One was behind my back holding a beer, his other was across my knees, and I was sitting sideways across his thighs. It was all very innocent.

The fact that Lonnie and Judith knew Derek set my mind at ease that it was safe to be friendly with him. The other women who'd joined us were old ladies of some of the bikers present. They'd been helpful in giving me a crash course about MC culture from a woman's perspective. The more I listened to their stories the more comfortable I felt around them. I got the sense that they were mostly good people who'd received a bad reputation from the few corrupt MCs that

were out there.

"Oh! Oh! Tanner's on his way over and he doesn't look happy." Judith reached over and patted me on the knee. I reluctantly pulled my gaze from his. "You might want to escape while you have the chance, honey."

I laughed. "Why should he be angry at me? I haven't done anything wrong."

"Oh, honey—" I glanced at Candice, a serious biker chick in full-body leather, boots, spiked purple hair, and piercings, and as sweet as apple pie. "You're sittin' on another man's lap. Bikers I know would kill over that."

Surely she was kidding. I turned to look at Derek. He just grinned and shrugged. "Not me, sweetheart. I'm too young to die. I'm a lover, not a fighter." He winked good-naturedly.

He didn't seem to be worried over the clenched jaw and narrowed eyes on Tanner's face that was for sure. Before I had the chance to look back at the too-sexy biker that was stalking our way, I felt a hand take one of mine and then I was being pulled off Derek's lap.

Tanner didn't say anything. I didn't say anything. It was obvious that he had an agenda, and I would know soon enough what it was. I shot a grin back to the girls and let him pull me toward the house and the door that I'd just exited from a few minutes before. He was walking so fast that I had a hard time keeping up. He pushed through the door, and didn't stop until we were in the bathroom with the door shut and locked behind us.

I tried to suppress a giggle, not fully comprehending what was going on. "What are you doing?"

He growled like an angry bear and pushed me up against the door that he'd just locked, caging me in between his powerful arms. "New rules." He ground the words out between his teeth, lowering his face closer to mine.

A mixture of smoke and sweat and something that was manly and all him, assailed my senses all at once. Arousal thrummed through me in response to his nearness, and suddenly I wanted him to lean in all the way and kiss me, run his big hands over my body, and just claim me. I was on fire inside, weak-kneed with anticipation, remembering with stark clarity the pleasure he could bring me. I knew that Tanner wanted me, a woman can tell that kind of thing, but I was confused at the anger underlining his actions.

New rules? What was he talking about?

"I-" That's as far as I got, and suddenly my wish was coming true. Tanner closed the distance between us and his mouth closed over mine.

In seconds we were hungry and out of control, consumed by that single contact. Shivers of desire raced through me as his tongue explored the recesses of my mouth with the firm pressure of his. What started out as a punishing kiss had turned sensual and exploring, his lips sucking and tugging on mine. I moaned beneath his fierce possession and let arousal intensify and blossom. I'd never been shy when I wanted something, and now that I knew how good sex felt, thanks to him, my hands moved to his belt buckle without conscious thought. Working blindly, I managed to get the snap undone.

Tanner grunted and tore his mouth from mine, zeroing in on the side of my neck where he proceeded to kiss and suck his way toward my ear. A thrill of excitement shot through me from my core to my clit, and I had to transfer my hands to his shoulders to keep from sinking to the floor in an unexpected bout of weakness. A sigh of delight escaped me when his hands moved to my waist and slid around and down to cup my bottom. He ground his hard cock against me and we both went a little mad. Lifting me, I instinctively wrapped my legs around him.

The sound of him pulling down his zipper seemed overloud in the small room, heard well above our uneven panting.

"This is going to be fast, baby."

I didn't care. I was so turned on that we could have been outside in plain sight and he could have taken me up against a tree. I knew that I was wet and ready for him, I could feel how soaked my panties were. I thanked God that I'd worn a sundress. It was already bunched up at my thighs and I could feel one of his hands against my sex as he worked his cock free. I had no doubts that Tanner had meant what he'd said about it being fast.

Fast wasn't all. Something was driving him. Before I knew it, he curled his hand around my panties and ripped them off my body. I gasped with surprise, and then gasped again when in the next instant his cock was buried deep inside me and I realized how close to orgasm I already was. The pleasure of that solid shaft sliding over my clit caused me to cry out softly. I threw my head back against the door at how satisfyingly full he made me feel, and clenched my hands into his biceps.

His powerful thrusts were without mercy, his movements slamming me back against the door. The impact of our bodies coming together caused grunts to fill the bathroom. I could only hope that the noise we made didn't go beyond the bathroom door. I could feel my body tightening around his cock, trying to hold him inside me. I clenched my muscles, enjoying his answering grunts.

"Come for me, honey," Tanner coaxed against my lips. He pulled out and took his cock in his hand, running the head up and down my slit, torturing my throbbing clit. I whimpered and jerked, so ready to come. We were both panting heavily and sweating in spite of the air conditioning. "Put some cum on my dick and I'll fill your cunt up with mine."

Ohmygod! "You're so filthy!" And I liked it. I shivered, wanting more.

"But you like it," he countered, sliding back inside me. "You're mine, Ruby. No one gets inside this pussy but me. No one gets to know how good you feel, how tight you are. No one gets to kiss this sweet mouth, or play with these big tits." He leaned down and covered one with his mouth, sucking my nipple through the material of my sundress. I watched, spellbound, as the thin cloth turned darker around his lips. "I see you with another man, I won't be happy. We clear?"

I wanted to remind Tanner that we'd agreed to be fuck buddies and that was all, so I was unsure of what he was talking about. All that mattered right then was what he was making me feel, and that I didn't want it to stop. Except that I did, because I knew an even greater pleasure would follow, the kind that gripped your body and rendered you completely helpless in ecstasy so intense that it had the power to paralyze you. I felt my orgasm climbing. My rapid breathing began to match Tanner's, and I realized that he right there with me.

"Are we clear?" he repeated.

"Yes!" I was concentrating on reaching the peak that would tip me over and nothing else. "I belong to you!" At that point I would have promised him anything. And besides, his fierce possessiveness kind of turned me on.

"Come for me." He ran his tongue along the seam of my lip, dipping inside briefly before grinding his mouth down on mine. At the same time I felt his finger move over my clit, flicking and pinching it until I lost control.

I began to quiver, and when my orgasm hit it turned my muscles to liquid and took my breath away. I jerked away from Tanner's mouth to suck in air. "Tanner-"

"Come with me, honey," he encouraged against my open, gasping mouth.

We shuddered against each other, riding out our mutual release to paradise and back. I couldn't hold back my cry, burying my face against him to try to drown it out. Suddenly his hands were cupping my butt and he was grinding against me. The friction was almost too much.

"Fuck, baby-" he groaned deeply, holding himself inside me as he filled my pussy with his seed, so much so that I felt it running down the inside of my thighs. And still Tanner pumped inside me, his large body shuddering.

I was sandwiched between Tanner and the bathroom door, slowing becoming aware of my surroundings. As my body calmed and my breathing slowed, I began to wonder if we'd been heard, had anyone missed us? Would anyone think it odd that we had disappeared at the same time? Was someone searching for us now? And how were we going to leave the bathroom without being seen? I recognized that I was beginning to panic, but I quickly squashed it down, realizing that we'd probably only been gone ten minutes, fifteen max. Not the lifetime that it had seemed.

"As much as I like this position..." The hands cupping my bottom squeezed a little.

Oh my God, I still had my legs wrapped around him. "Sorry," I said with mild embarrassment, reluctant to break the contact. I slowly lowered them until my feet were planted on the ground, and barely held back a moan when he pulled out of me and stepped back. Even soft Tanner was big, and like a cork once he'd pulled out of my body a river of cum came with it.

"Damn!" I swore when I saw my ruined panties on the floor. His gaze followed mine, and with a satisfied smirk he bent and scooped them up. Before I could say anything he slipped them into his pocket. I just stared at him and raised one brow as if to say, *really?*

He shrugged. "A souvenir."

"And what am I supposed to do about, um ..." I felt a rush of heat spread up my neck and knew that I'd probably turned red. The cocky grin he gave me while he was tucking in his deflated cock didn't help. It was as if he knew what I was trying to say, enjoying himself at my expense. I took a breath, opened my mouth, and then snapped it shut again. "What's so funny?" I finally asked, showing my frustration.

He laughed softly. "Knowing that you'll be walking around the rest of the day without panties beneath your dress is something to smile about." He paused and then added, "Knowing that you'll be wet and sticky with my cum leaking out of you is going to keep me fucking hard."

"Well, good. At least we'll both be uncomfortable."

He laughed outright at that. Then he surprised me by wrapping a hand around my neck and pulling me in for a kiss. This kiss was different from all the others. It was soft, coaxing, but just as arousing. It showed a softer part of Tanner that I hadn't seen before. Did he like me? Of course he liked me! I mean, we were having sex. You had to at least like the person you were having sex with, right? Well, maybe not, but this kiss, the sensual persuasion of his mouth, it left me yearning for something that I'd never contemplated having before.

He pulled back and stared into my eyes for a long time, and then someone pounded on the door, breaking the connection.

"Are you guys ever going to come out of there? How long does it take, anyway?"

My jaw dropped with surprise. Tanner took my hand. "Come on, let's go get something to eat." He opened the door and we came face to face with his brother, Gabe. "Apparently a lot longer than you, brother. I pity your women."

Gabe gave me a wink as Tanner yanked me past him and back into the kitchen. How long had Gabe been standing out there? I didn't have time to get embarrassed, but as we made our way outside to one of the grills I kept my eyes foreword, too chicken to meet anyone else's gaze.

I was sure that guilt was all over my face over what Tanner and I had just done inside.

Chapter 30

Tanner

Holy fuck! I realized that I'd screwed up by claiming Ruby, which just went to show that where she was concerned, I didn't act or think rationally. Hopefully she didn't realize the ramifications of what I'd said while I'd been fucking her. Or if she did, she'd hopefully chalked it up as just something that was said in the heat of the moment.

And hot it had been.

Christ. There wasn't another pussy out there that had satisfied me as much as hers did. She was tight and wet, and when I slid inside her she clenched around my dick, squeezing it good. The fact that I'd been the one to claim her cherry made me feel possessive as fuck, something I'd never felt with anyone else. Seeing her blood on my sheets had turned me the fuck on. I was seriously messed up, and my brothers knew it. It amused them to see that I'd let an innocent girl get under my skin.

Thank fuck they were smart enough not to let the ribbing get out of control. We were close brothers, but some personal shit was left where it belonged unless a brother asked for advice. When it came to shit about relationships, none of us were eager to step into something out of our zone of expertise. It would probably make a difference if more than just two of us were in serious relationships, but the truth was that most of my brothers, me included, liked spontaneous sex with whatever willing woman was on hand at the moment.

Wanting Ruby the way I did wasn't something I was comfortable with. I knew that I should distance myself from her before it got complicated. Yet here she was, sitting on my lap because I'd wanted the contact. Plus, it was fun seeing her squirm against my dick, which was directly beneath her delicious bottom, and hard as stone. I'd told her that I'd stay hard knowing that she wasn't wearing panties.

After a while it was a tossup as to which of us was being tortured more. I didn't hesitate to thrust up and grind my dick against her soft bottom as retaliation for the times that she wiggled until I nearly came.

Like she was doing now.

I groaned. "You keep that up and I'll finger you right here, in front of everyone," I threatened in a rough tone into her ear. I was rewarded by her shiver. "Unless that's your intention." I ran my tongue up the side of her neck. "Is that what you want, honey? You want my fingers inside you?"

"What?" The eyes she turned on me were large and round with shock, which did nothing to disguise the glaze of arousal.

I shrugged, grinning. "Look around you, honey. You think we're the only ones who grabbed a quick fuck somewhere private?" By the looks of the activity around us, some were still horny. And then there were those who didn't mind an audience while they were groping and exposing each other, or out-and-out screwing.

Like Killer and his old lady, for example. Subtlety didn't seem to be in their skill set. They were fucking up against a tree, a little ways beyond where everyone else had gathered. It didn't matter that they were still fully clothed. Their movements made what they were doing obvious. And the look on his old lady's flushed face spoke volumes.

"I can't believe people actually do that kind of thing in public," Ruby commented innocently. She must have spotted the couple, too. "Isn't that against the law?" She couldn't seem to draw her gaze away from them.

I threw back my head back and roared with laughter, drawing the interest of a few people who were close by. We were sitting in a kind of half-circle with several of my brothers, along with Lonnie and Judith, who were on Mark and Sid's laps. The crowd had thinned down considerably now that it was nearing evening. Ace and Skipper were manning the two grills that were still in operation.

"Well, isn't it?" Ruby demanded to know.

"Do you see any cops here?" Pete chuckled before taking a drink of his beer.

"That wasn't the question," she countered quickly, giving him a sharp look.

"Honey, do you really think they care?" I jerked my chin in the direction of Killer and his woman.

"Remember some of the things Lonnie and I told you, Ruby?" Judith's comment drew several frowns from my brothers. "Oh, relax," she said, shutting it down before they said something. "We didn't tell her any club business that had to do with the Sentinels, but she deserved to be told about the culture. We just pointed out some of the differences."

"Not all MCs are equal," Mark admonished lightly.

Judith turned to look at him. "I know that, babe. But some of the culture is the same. Like if a brother has an old lady, his brothers know that she's off limits, the way clubs protect their women and their families, how anything that happens in the club stays in the club, and the brothers deal with it. That's the kind of stuff we talked about."

Her explanation seemed to bring Mark's irritation down a few notches. He nodded and gave her a kiss.

"So am I off limits?"

The question caught all of us off guard. I stiffened uncomfortably, meeting the quiet looks of several of my brothers. Fuck, this was exactly what I hadn't wanted to happen. Before I could come up with an answer that might hurt Ruby or piss her off, Gabe said, "Hell yeah, baby, I'd say that you're definitely off limits...to the rest of us." His meaning was clear, since it was my lap that Ruby was sitting on.

I could feel Ruby's eyes boring into me but I avoided them, praying that she would just accept that answer and move on to something else. Across from us Lonnie and Judith and, fuck, even Sid and William, had knowing smirks on their faces.

"So does that mean I'm an old lady?"

I groaned inwardly, snapping my eyes toward Lonnie and Judith. "I thought you said you girls had given Ruby the rundown on MCs."

"We did," Judith said without hesitation.

Shit. That meant that Ruby wanted clarification about our relationship. I'd known that getting involved with her was a mistake. Virgins were too innocent to comprehend that sex didn't always mean that you were in a meaningful relationship. Fuck, change that. Some girls were born knowing the score, but not girls like Ruby, and I'd complicated the situation by telling her that no one else would have her. I should have fought my attraction and kept my dick in my pants, but it was too late now. I should have remembered that there was nothing shy about Ruby, in spite of her innocence.

"So I'm off limits, but I'm not an old lady," she said when the silence continued. "Kind of contradicts itself."

"Not really, darlin'. When a biker claims a woman as an old lady it's done in front of the whole club. The reason you're off limits right now is because you're sitting on Tanner's lap." That remark drew laughter. "Not sure what stage you're in."

I clenched my jaw, certain that Ruby already knew all that, compliments of Judith and Lonnie. I'm sure as my VP that Gabe thought he was taking care of the problem by offering up that inadequate explanation. I just wished that he'd shut up. Ruby was innocent, but she was far from stupid.

"You're a fuck buddy, sugar, and nothing else." *Oh, fuck!* Why hadn't anyone noticed Olive walking up on us? "That's all you'll be to Tanner, so don't expect the leather jacket that says 'property of'." She motioned to Lonnie and Judith, who were wearing cuts. She had the nerve to plop her ass down on William's lap. Of all the brothers she could have chosen she'd picked the one who'd always been a little enamored of her. "She's a little young for you, isn't she, baby?"

"Watch your mouth," I warned, not about to take her shit or let Ruby become a punching bag for her to bounce off of out of jealousy. I could feel the change in Ruby the second she become rigid on my lap. Having been told that she was just a fuck buddy had to have stung. But hadn't I basically said the same thing to her? All of a sudden I felt like a jerk. I had to give Ruby credit though, she was keeping her cool.

Olive pinned her scheming gaze on me, and I knew her well enough to know that she was going to start trouble. William was grinning from ear to ear, not about to toss her ass on the ground. He'd kept his distance and respected my relationship with Olive all those years ago, but enough time had gone by that if he wanted to act on it now, he could have her. Of course, knowing William, his infatuation would end the minute that he was done screwing her.

"Well, well, well, you're protective over your new toy," Olive observed in a bitchy tone. She gave Lonnie and Judith a quick glance-over and quickly dismissed them. "I don't see what's so special about you."

Her comment was directed at Ruby, who until then had been quiet and docile on my lap. I didn't realize that I was running my hand up and down her back until all eyes were on us. It was clear that they were expecting a response from Ruby. She broke eye contact with Olive and turned her face toward me, her mouth turning into an unconscious smile. There was something lazily seductive in her look.

Jesus. This girl was ruining me for anyone else. My dick punched up against her sweet ass.

She turned back to face the group, but her gaze met the obvious frostiness in Olive's sharp eyes. That Olive was jealous was clear, but it didn't affect me. I had zero feeling for her.

There was a trace of laughter in Ruby's voice when she finally said, "Maybe he likes how tight my pussy is."

Fuck. Me. Now.

In response to Olive's mouth-dropping expression the girls giggled and raucous laughter broke out among my brothers. I tried to contain myself, but I was so fucking proud of Ruby. No one had expected her to put Olive so thoroughly in her place. Murmurs followed the laughter once it died down, amusement stamped strongly on everyone's faces. Except for that of my ex. Olive was furious, staring daggers at me and Ruby.

With a huff she got up from William's lap. It was obvious that she was going to stomp off. She took a step and then came up short, scowling back at William. "Well, are you coming or not?"

William's surprised eyes shot back to mine, and then he raised his arms in a 'what am I gonna do' gesture and got to his feet to follow her, sporting a hard-on in his pants.

I tangled my hand in Ruby's hair and pulled her closer. "You know how much I want to fuck you right now?" I whispered into her ear. I licked a path up the side of her neck, absorbing her wild tremor.

"Are you going to take me up against that tree?" she teased in a husky tone.

I snorted. "Hell, no, honey. I'm going to take you right here in this chair." My hand had been resting on her bare knee, and I didn't hesitate to start walking my fingers up her bare thigh beneath her skirt.

"We got trouble!"

The fact that Mike was running toward me revealed that it was serious. Heath and Sully were right behind him. I yanked my hand from under Ruby's dress and nudged her to her feet. "Where?" My brothers and I jumped to our feet. Mark and Sid practically dumped their girls onto the ground.

"Two of our club properties, brother." He came to a panting stop, his eyes wild. "They terrorized the girls and destroyed property at the strip club, and set the tattoo shop on fire. The fire department is there now. A witness said they saw bikers with Kings' colors in the area, about the time the fire broke out. Someone from the strip club confirmed the Kings had been there, too."

"What the fuck?" Rod swore. "Are they crazy?"

Those were my sentiments exactly. I pinned my gaze on Gabe. "Call the station and see if Wicked's still in jail." I didn't think his club would make a serious move like that while their president was incarcerated.

I swung back to Ruby, taking in her frightened eyes. "Babe, find Pops and get home." I pulled her in for a quick kiss. "Don't leave there." I felt the adrenaline rushing through me thinking about what we might be facing, and I didn't have time to see if she followed through with my orders. I was already hurrying toward my bike with my brothers right beside me. "Anyone hurt?" I looked at Mike.

He shook his head. "No, thank fuck. The tattoo shop was closed today." Yeah, so they could attend the cookout. Ace and Skipper had apparently caught wind that there was trouble and had abandoned their grills, joining us at our bikes. We mounted our bikes, and once we were all there I began shouting orders.

"They haven't hit our personal businesses because they don't know what we own. Ace, this is your place. You stay here, brother. I want Mike and Skipper to hit the garage, make sure shit's locked down and the alarms set. Sully, Heath, you take the gym, get everyone out and have Roland close up early. Sid and Mark, take your women and head to my place." I didn't expect them to watch over Pops and Ruby while leaving their girls vulnerable.

"What about the rest of us?" Pete asked.

"You and William get to the tattoo shop and deal with the fire department. The rest of you come with me. We'll check out the damage at the strip club, make sure the girls are okay, and then we'll regroup to head out to find the fucking Kings."

Gabe was slipping his phone into his back pocket when our eyes met. "Wicked and his crew were bailed out earlier this afternoon, brother."

"Are you fucking kidding me?" I snarled. "The charges were trespassing and assault." There was always a possibility of getting bailed out, but with the Kings reputation I was surprised the motion for bond hadn't been turned down by the judge.

Gabe shrugged, mounting his own bike. "They found a crooked lawyer who found a crooked judge. Apparently one of his brothers comes from money."

I shook my head with disgust and kick started my ride.

It was going to be a long fucking night.

Chapter 31

Ruby

I was worried about Tanner, even though my instincts told me that he didn't need me to be. But the way that he and his brothers had rushed to their motorcycles and the unknown circumstances they were heading into frightened me. I had a feeling those men were formidable in any situation, and it had been clear by their reactions and lack of hesitation that they were to be feared if you were on the opposite side. I reluctantly thought back a few days to when they'd had to deal with the Kings, how fierce and rapid they'd been in handling it. I shivered thinking about what could have happened had they not shown up.

Finding Pops and trying to get him home had been a challenge. As worn out as he'd looked, his color had alarmed me. He'd probably been out in the heat too long, and knowing him he'd drank more than he'd eaten during the day. Beer and cigarettes seemed to be his main staple. But in spite of that he'd looked happy, a man in his element. I'd found him surrounded by his friends, laughing and catching up. When he'd glanced up and seen me and the look on my face, he'd known it was time to leave.

"Is it time to go, cutie?" His heavy sigh revealed how tired he was.

It made me wonder if he was feeling badly. He wasn't fighting me to stay there longer. I got the impression that the resigned look of disgust on his wrinkled face was aimed at himself, as if he'd found his lack of energy a weakness, one that he couldn't control because aging took its toll in the way that it saw fit. I imagined there'd been a time in Pops' life, when he'd been in his prime that he'd been able to go all day and nothing had stopped him.

"Yeah," I replied, smiling, making eye-contact with some of the rough-looking bikers that were standing around. The War Dogs and

I exchanged acknowledgements in the way of smiles and nods. Most of them were smoking, and not just cigarettes. I wasn't an expert, but I was pretty sure the strange smell that I picked up was pot. "I'm exhausted. Not used to this Florida heat." I didn't want anyone within hearing distance to think that leaving had anything to do with how tired Pops looked. He'd smiled gratefully up at me and slowly got to his feet.

He'd been ready to go home, but he'd been too proud to ask. Now there he was, in his usual beach chair, smoking and staring out at the water. I'd managed to get him to eat a decent dinner, trying my hand at making an omelet. Pops had scoffed that I was feeding him breakfast for dinner, but he'd eaten enough to satisfy me, and had even said that it was good. So far, my lack of culinary skills hadn't been questioned.

After I'd cleaned up the kitchen I'd gone in and taken a shower. Pops was still outside when I returned to the kitchen. I grabbed a couple of beers and decided to join him. The sun had disappeared behind some storm clouds, and there was a cool ocean breeze blowing in off the water. I saw Lonnie and Judith swimming while Mark and Sid kept watch. Mark had explained that they'd be staying at the house until Tanner returned home, for which I was glad. Knowing that they were around made me feel safer.

As I made my way toward Pops, muted voices and squealing drew my attention toward a family playing in the shallows. They had two little ones who were delightedly giggling as the surf chased them away from the water onto the sand. Their young parents stood watching with tolerant smiles on their faces, holding hands. I could almost feel the love between them, and something sad settled in my heart thinking that I hadn't had that growing up.

"Mind if I join you, Pops?" I held a beer down at him.

He glanced up, smiling around the cigarette dangling out of the corner of his mouth. "Sure thing, cutie."

I sank down into one of the loungers, twisted off the cap to my beer, and took a sip. "It's really nice here."

"Yeah. Brings peace."

I found his response telling. "You need peace, Pops?" I noticed the family moving further up the beach, walking along the water line.

"We all need peace in our lives," he replied, sinking his cigarette butt into the sand. "Especially when you've lived your whole life in turmoil." He kept staring straight ahead. "You might not think it, but this is the time of day I enjoy the most. When I'm alone with my memories."

That surprised me, because I'd always thought Pops was lonely. It hadn't occurred to me that he actually liked being alone. I wondered how he felt about Tanner's brothers and their girlfriends being there, or me, too, for that matter, until reminding myself that we were considered family.

"Don't get me wrong, cutie." He turned, holding my gaze. "I love it when I see my old friends, and I have a chance to spend time with them talking about the old days." He released a heavy breath. "These days I'm tired."

He sounded tired, and I had a feeling that there was a whole lot more attached to that one, telling word. I was sure that he knew he didn't look well, when he looked in the mirror and saw how thin and frail he was, and the unhealthy color of his skin.

"Have you been to a doctor, Pops?" I knew I had no right in asking him that, but in the days I'd been living there I'd grown attached to him. He'd become the grandfather I'd never known.

The silence grew so long that I'd given up that he was going to answer me. I sipped at my beer and looked out in the direction of the ocean. It was dark now, except for the soft glow of the

lighting near us. I could hear the surf crashing on the beach, hear Lonnie and Judith's murmured voices and laughter. The wind had picked up, too, and I instinctively knew that a storm was rolling in. I couldn't wait for it to arrive. I'd always loved storms.

"Don't need to go to a doctor to know I'm sick."

I snapped my head back to him. "Maybe they can help-"

"Naw!" He waved the comment away with a strong voice. "No help for a man like me. Besides—" He gave me a look of regret, "Time to pay for my sins."

"Yeah but you don't need to suffer," I said, feeling helpless.

A snort escaped him. "Cutie, I've made a lot of men suffer during my lifetime. The MC I was part of wasn't anything like the Sentinels, or a lot of other clubs around today. Believe it or not, back in my day we were true bad ass outlaws. We took what we wanted. Everything we did to get rich was illegal." He hesitated, as if he was not sure that he should go on. "We killed each other, killed a lot of others, too."

I caught my breath at his admission. Surely he was exaggerating. Wouldn't they all be in prison

if it were true?

"I know what you're thinkin'," Pops said, breaking into my thoughts. "We handled shit our own way. The law stayed away. Hell, most of the time they were scared of us. I'm not sayin' everyone avoided prison, but most of us did."

He hadn't said, but I wasn't about to question him about it. I digested what he said. "But the Sentinels aren't like that?" I knew what Lonnie and Judith had told me, but as old ladies to two of the members, wouldn't they have been careful of how much they divulged to me? Out of loyalty?

"They're not one percenters." I'd already known that. "But they could have been. They just chose to do things differently. They want to keep crime out and neighborhoods safe. The locals and cops appreciate their riding the streets at night. But when it comes to an attack on the club, they deal with it the club way."

Oh. I wondered what that meant for the Kings, but I was too afraid to ask. Maybe not knowing was better. "Have you heard from Tanner since we left the cookout?"

"Naw. Won't hear from him until he comes home." He gave me a speculative glance. "You like my boy, cutie?"

I'd been in the process of taking a drink when Pops' question caught me unaware. The beer went down the wrong hole and I went into a coughing fit. I could hear Pops chuckling as he got out of his chair, and the next thing I knew he was pounding me on the back. The fit lasted for a couple of minutes and left me dizzy.

"You okay?" I didn't miss the amusement in his tone. I nodded vigorously. He stopped and sat back down. "Is that a yes?" he snorted. "You could do worse, Tanner's a good man. And seeing you two together—well, you make a good lookin' couple." When it grew quiet I assumed that Pops was done. "Could make me some beautiful grandchildren."

Thank God I didn't have anything in my mouth at that time, because I would have been spraying it out everywhere. I prayed Pops wasn't expecting me to respond to any of that, because I wasn't sure how to. The thought of me and Tanner together was appealing. Just the thought of him made me warm and tingly inside, and made my lady bits buzz. Our quickie that afternoon had been thoroughly satisfying, yet I wanted more.

"Don't worry about my boy, cutie." He coughed a few times before continuing. "He knows what he's doing."

I was thankful when the first rain drops fell, thinking that it would keep Pops from lighting another cigarette. He smoked way too much, but deep down I felt that the damage had already been done, especially to his lungs. I kept my mouth shut, because to give him my opinion would definitely have been stepping over the line. Most smokers knew that smoking wasn't good for them.

It was sprinkling now. "I think it's time that we go in." I got to my feet and then picked up Pops' discarded beer bottles.

"Yep." He stood up, too. "Guess I'll go in and get my shower. Turn in early."

Good idea. I knew the day had exhausted him. We went inside. Pops continued to his room and I tossed the bottles into the trash before heading to mine. It was way too early for me to turn in, but I could get comfortable and watch some TV. I changed into a sleep tee, arranged the pillows on my bed, and got comfortable and flicked on the TV.

Chapter 32

Tanner

I turned off my bike and sat for a minute, my hands and clothes splattered in blood, violence still gripping my system. It had been a hellish night, a brutal one, but I was pretty sure that we were rid of the fucking Kings for good. We'd put a call out to our friends to be on the lookout for them, and when we'd finally caught up with them we'd beaten the living hell out of them. If they didn't heed our warning this time, next time we'd put them in the ground. With their attack on Pops and Ruby and the club property they'd destroyed, they were lucky that we hadn't already ended them. We didn't like killing, but sometimes there was no other option.

Thank fuck it had all gone down in the rural area where the Cabbage Patch was located. The Kings had been on their way home and had stopped for drinks, too cocky to even suspect that someone had seen them at both locations when shit had gone down and turned them in. That had given us the opportunity to make up some time to get close to them. We'd just missed them by minutes, but it hadn't taken long before their taillights had come into view. Our intention had been to force them off the road and then pound them into the ground, leaving them with a warning of what we'd do to them if they didn't stay out of Daytona.

The little fuckers had pulled their weapons on us, and then it was game on. We'd been forced to protect ourselves in the same way, wounding two of Wicked's brothers. Pete had been clipped, too, but it hadn't been bad enough to take him to the hospital. We could deal with flesh wounds, and hospitals were obligated to phone the police whenever someone came in with a gunshot wound. We'd left Wicked and his brothers bleeding and beaten on the side of the road.

The tattoo shop was gone, burnt to the ground. Insurance would cover the rebuilding of it. The strip club damage had been minimal in comparison, just a few broken chairs and mirrors. The Kings had focused on terrorizing the dancers and beating up Steve, one of the bouncers, leaving him unconscious and bleeding on the floor. He'd just been coming around when we'd arrived and had refused medical attention, letting one of the girls doctor him up. They knew better then to call the cops.

The Kings hadn't gone near the garage or the gym that we owned, probably because they were located in the center of town, too close to other businesses. It would have been hard getting in and out without witnesses. And though they had been seen in the area of the tattoo shop, we decided to keep that information to ourselves.

When it came to our club, we preferred not to involve the cops.

Fuck, I was still revved up inside. I needed to either consume a bottle of whiskey to calm that shit down, or fuck it out of my blood. I could have stopped at my bar, but hadn't wanted to answer any questions, had word of my appearance gotten out to the wrong people—namely, the cops. They weren't ignorant of the fact that we dealt our own way with club trouble. After all, we were still a motorcycle club and not a bunch of pussies that ran to the law every time we had a problem. I think they were secretly glad that we were around to help cut down on the crime in town just by being visible.

Plus, the club as a whole donated a lot of money to local charities.

I pulled my leg over my bike and dismounted, letting myself into the dark and quiet house. I'd phoned Sid earlier and explained what had gone down, telling him that he and Mark could go home. None of us liked doing babysitting duty, and thankfully trouble like what we'd had to take care of tonight didn't occur often.

My first instinct was to go to Ruby's room. I needed her. I needed to fuck her tight little body, but I wanted to clean up first. She was still learning about MCs, and I didn't want her to freak out at my appearance. With her in mind, I stripped, took a hot shower, and walked naked into her bedroom. I stood for a moment staring down at her form until my eyes adjusted to the dark.

I clenched my jaw as the sexy shape of her became visible, afraid for a moment that I'd lose control and hurt her. My dick had turned to stone, throbbing forward as if seeking her out. The lower half of her body was naked but for the tiny triangle of silk between her thighs. The tee she was wearing had bunched up around her waist, hiding her other treasures from me. Her long, silky hair beckoned for me to twist it around my hand.

I carefully dropped down onto the bed, covering Ruby with my body. With a sigh her legs opened as if she was making room for me, but I knew it was an unconscious movement. I lifted her shirt further up her body to expose her luscious tits, kissing them gently until I couldn't hold back any longer and I began lapping her nipples into tight little buds. I took a tit into my hand and held it captive against my sucking mouth. She began to squirm slightly against me, her little sighs revealing that she liked what I was doing.

My dick was right where it wanted to be but unable to slide into her pussy because of the thin layer of silk. It would have been so fucking easy to move aside that triangle, but before I did that I wanted a taste first. With that to look forward to, I continued lavishing attention on her tit until she gradually became aware that I was there and that she wasn't dreaming.

"Tanner-" she whimpered softly, sinking her fingers into my hair. "What-"

I schussed her by covering her lips with mine, kissing her full, succulent lips long and hard while I grabbed her wrists, bringing them above her head. She was fully awake now and gyrating beneath me with impatience. I ground my dick against her pussy with enough force that I was surprised that it didn't rip through her thong, thrusting my tongue into her sweet mouth like I wanted to shove my dick into her slick heat.

"Don't move those hands," I growled, releasing her wrists so that I could roam down her curves.

"Are you okay?" Ruby whispered in the darkness.

"I am now." I wasn't going to elaborate. I had more important things on my mind. I kissed my way back to her quivering tits, said goodbye to them with a trailing lick, and continued down her body, fighting the urge to just fuck her hard to relieve the turmoil inside me. But she was too tasty to pass up, and I wanted to feast before I conquered.

When I reached her pussy I pulled aside the material that was covering her mound and then gave her a firm lick from the bottom of her juicy slit up to her clit. Once there, I closed my mouth over the tight nub and gently worked it with my teeth. Ruby cried out, arching against my mouth, as if demanding more.

"Tanner!" she panted breathlessly. "I need more!"

Her need fueled my arousal, and she was already so fucking wet. The tantalizing smell between her legs drew me to cover her plump folds with my mouth. I buried my tongue in as deeply as I could, growling as I found extra slick nectar inside her body. As I greedily lapped it up Ruby whimpered and bowed her hips off the bed. I tongue-fucked her at a steady pace, determined to get her off before I gave in to my own needs, because when I finally sank between her legs I was going to fuck her hard and fast.

Until I came so fucking hard.

I felt her body responding in ways that revealed that her orgasm was approaching. Her breathing turned harsher, became faster. She'd lowered her hands to her tits and was squeezing them and plucking her nipples. I reached up and nudged her hands aside, taking control to push her over the top, caressing the enticing mounds, pinching her nipples just hard enough to make her suck in her breath. When her hands dropped to my head I sensed that she was just about there. I took her stiff clit into my mouth and sucked it hard.

"Oh, God!" She began to convulse. "Tanner!" she cried out, losing control. "Feels... so... good!" She twitched against my mouth.

I tongue-fucked her through her orgasm, determined to get every drop of her cream. I was dry humping the bed, my dick aching to be inside Ruby, so close to coming that I knew that once I got inside her I wasn't going to last long. Usually, after a confrontation like the one I'd had earlier with the Kings, I had the urge to fuck hard and fast the first available woman I could get my hands on. I didn't take the time for foreplay. I wanted the instant gratification that would quiet the unrest in my blood.

Ruby was different, and I was still trying to figure out if it was good different or bad different.

"Tanner..."

She was coming down, the tremors were lessoning. I could feel her relaxing against the bed, and I growled, moving up her body. I grabbed her wrists along the way. "I told you to keep your hands here," I said roughly, bringing them back above her head and slamming them down onto the bed. I ignored her gasp, meeting the quiet shock in her glazed eyes. Without warning I ripped the thong from her body, lined my dick up, and thrust foreword, penetrating her to the hilt. Sinking into her velvet heat felt so fucking good, the tightness pulling a groan from me. I took a minute to let her body to adjust to my rough possession, kissing her slightly parted lips.

The tight heat of her cunt and the way that it hugged my dick caused it to throb inside her. The slightest quiver ran through Ruby, signaling that she was still sensitive to the touch. I grinned against her soft lips, wondering why I was taking the time to notice those things when I never had with other women. I didn't want to examine the reasons, accepting that for some reason she meant more to me. Hell, my one-fuck rule had gone right out the window, and it was too late to change it now.

Besides, I didn't want to. I liked knowing that I'd been her first, that I was the only man who had tasted her. It made me feel possessive as fuck. I slowly pulled away from her mouth, dragging that swollen bottom lip with me and sucking it between my teeth. I released it to run my tongue along her upper lip before giving her a series of soft, gentle kisses.

"You're so fucking beautiful." She quivered and a husky sigh escaped her when I trailed my tongue along her neck. "So fucking responsive." I ran my tongue along the shell of her ear, hearing her breath catch. "Your pussy is the perfect sheath for my dick." She whimpered, trembling again. "I'm going to fuck you into tomorrow, honey. You're not going to be able to walk without feeling me between your legs." I grazed the length of her exposed neck with my teeth, reaching the sensitive area where her shoulder began, biting her gently.

"Tanner—" There was a touch of sweet desperation in her voice. "Please, fuck me, I need you!"

I grinned like a hungry wolf that had trapped its prey. I liked Ruby's desperation, I liked that she wanted my dick. I was slightly surprised that I wasn't already pounding into her. "You eager, baby?" I pulled out to the tip and slammed back inside her.

She let out a long, drawn out moan. "You're torturing me, Tanner." Her words came out in husky pants. "You won't let me touch you."

"Will touching me make you happy?"

"Yessss!"

I pulled out and then slammed back inside her again. "Then touch me, honey. I want to feel your hands on me. Bite me with those fucking nails."

Ruby didn't waste any time running her hands over my shoulders and down my arms, up my sides, then around to my back. She used her nails like tiny daggers to rake my back from the shoulders down, leaving a trail of fire that caused me to grunt and fuck her faster, harder. She clenched her hands into the flesh of my ass, gliding them down the backs of my thighs and back up again. Her touch was firm and revealed the height of arousal that was thrumming through her.

I couldn't take much more. Ruby's tight, wet pussy, the way that she was squeezing my dick as if trying to keep it inside, the soft mewling sounds that passed through her dewy lips, all threatened to end my control. I was fucking her without restraint, so hard that tiny grunts escaped from between her lips every time I slammed balls deep inside her pussy. The pressure building in my balls was going to fucking blow her off the bed when I finally released.

"Baby, fuck—" My hands were braced on the bed, and I was running my mouth over her tits. "I

fucking love your tits." I looked deep into her eyes. "Come with me." I reached between us and easily located the slick, swollen hardness of her little pulsing clit. I pressed down on it.

"Oh!" Ruby cried "God, yes!" she gasped, clenching her nails into my ass.

My balls tightened and I slipped my hands beneath her bottom. When the pressure released and I exploded, I ground down against her pelvis and held her tightly while spilling my seed into her. I roared out my release and came hard, harder than I could ever remember coming. I thought my fucking heart was going to pound out of my chest. I slammed my mouth down on hers, but within seconds I had to turn my head to suck in air.

Ruby was twisting beneath me, clenching her hands into the sheets and gasping for air. I could feel her body contracting around my dick as she came, giving my orgasm a reason to linger. She was so fucking tight, and she milked my dick until I was spent and my balls were empty. I sank against her, groaning, burying my face against the curve of her neck and shoulder while we both struggled to catch our breath.

Eventually our sweat dampened flesh cooled with the feel of the air-conditioning when it kicked on. Afraid of crushing Ruby, I rolled to the side when I could finally move, pulling her with me so that we remained connected. I settled her on top of me, my hands cupping her bottom in a possessive move. I liked the feel of my dick still inside her, holding my cum inside her.

"That was wild," she commented tiredly after a while.

"That was just the warm up, honey," I said, closing my eyes with relief. It was amazing how much a good fuck could take care of the stress of the night. I imagined my brothers were all in similar situations. Most of them had fuck-buddies that they could call on demand. "I'm going to spend the next few hours worshiping your tight little body. Unless you're not okay with that."

Her laughter caused her body to jerk, which caused my dick to slip out. We both groaned, immediately assailed with the wetness of cum that slipped out of Ruby's body. The strong scent of sex rose between us like an invisible cloud.

"I'm down with that," she replied softly, kissing my chest where her head rested. "You've turned me on to the pleasures of sex," she admitted. "If I'd known how good it felt, I would have given up my cherry a long time ago."

Her comment had the power to turn me instantly hard. She shouldn't have reminded me that I'd had that privilege. That knowledge made me realize why I felt so possessive over her. The thought of another man touching Ruby, or fucking her, sent a jealous rage through me. I knew that I'd have to get over that feeling or risk thoughts and emotions that I didn't want.

"Is sex like this for everyone, Tanner?"

Fuck no, but I had the feeling that she already knew that. Of course she had nothing to base it on, while I'd had a lot of sexual encounters to compare sex with Ruby to. If I told her the truth, I'd be setting myself up. Better to let her think that it was.

"I guess once I have more experience with men that I'll be able to answer that."

I gripped her by the hair and pulled her head back so I could meet her eyes. The innocence in her eyes forced me to loosen my grip. She couldn't know how her remark would affect me, didn't comprehend that I wouldn't take her casual comment about fucking other men well. All she knew was that we were fucking and that nothing would come from it.

And that was on me.

I thrust my renewed erection against the wetness between her thighs and locked my mouth onto hers. I was going to fuck her so good that thoughts of being with anyone else would be chased from her mind.

I was going to fucking claim her.

Until it was time to let her go.

Chapter 33

R^{uby} I was at the kitchen stove cooking breakfast when Pops'
hacking cough drew me to his bedroom. It sounded like he was
coughing up a lung, and my concern that he couldn't catch his breath
sent panic racing through me. His door was opened and I
approached it slowly in case he wasn't dressed.

"You okay, Pops?" I asked softly as his hacking lessened. I
remained behind the wall.

"I'm o-okay cu-cutie!" he coughed out.

I took a chance and peeked around the doorjamb to see him
sitting on the edge of the bed in a t-shirt and pair of sweats. "I'm
worried about you," I said when his eyes met mine. I took a step into
his room. "Have you been to a doctor?"

His laugh turned into a cough, and I waited patiently for him to
recover. His color looked really bad this morning, when a night of
rest should have left him looking rejuvenated.

"Don't worry 'bout me." His attempt at a smile failed. "Had this
cough for years," he confessed. "Though it's gotten worse the last few
months."

Since he'd avoided my question I guessed that he hadn't been to
a doctor. "So why don't you go get it checked out?"

The look in his eyes turned serious and slightly sad, as if he was
going to regret what he was about to say. I braced myself, sensing that
it wasn't going to be good.

"Been to a doctor. They can't fix what I have."

Oh. I swallowed the lump in my throat, not about to ask him
how much time he had left. "Does Tanner know?"

Pops shook his head. "I'm sure he suspects." He began to cough
again.

I didn't know what to say or do, never having had to deal with someone I cared for who was sick. My grandmother had been healthy until she'd had her stroke, and then things had happened fast after that—a brief stay in the hospital, another stroke, and then she was gone and I'd been put into foster care. I hadn't blamed my grandmother for that. I'd loved her, and looking back, I'd probably taken it for granted that she'd always be there until it had been too late.

I waited until there was a lull in his hacking and said, "Is there anything I can do?"

"Naw. Being here helps."

His wink made me grin. "Well, I'd better go check on breakfast." As I made my way back to the kitchen tears filled my eyes, but I quickly willed them away. Crying never solved anything, and it certainly wasn't going to help Pops. I was glad that my presence was a comfort to him.

I was surprised when I turned the corner and found Tanner at the stove, turning the sausage links over. He was a handsome sight in low riding jeans and barefoot, naked from the waist up. His hair was still mussed, and I couldn't help remembering that I'd had a hand in that. How many times had I held his head against me while he'd done delicious things to my body? A little shiver

ran through me. My body was still a little achy from all the times we'd had sex during the night. I'd left him sleeping in my bed.

"That's my job," I said, walking up behind Tanner. "Good morning."

He turned and glanced down at me, the spatula in his hand. "Morning," came his grumpy response, and I noticed that he hadn't put the 'good' in front of it. I also noticed his raw knuckles.

"Someone's cranky this morning," I smiled, reaching for the spatula. "I would have thought after last night that you'd be feeling, uh, quite relaxed and on top of the world." I started to nudge him out of the way, but he'd planted his feet and there was no moving him. Our gazes locked. "Why so grumpy?"

"Maybe because when I rolled over this morning there was no one there for me to plant my dick into."

My eyes got big and I was enveloped with instant heat. I was hotter than the fire beneath the fry pan. I couldn't pull my gaze from his, taking notice of the smoldering emotion that was simmering in the depths of his dark eyes. It was on the tip of my tongue to say something, but when I opened my mouth nothing would come. Tanner's gaze dropped to my mouth and someone moaned, I wasn't sure who. The next thing I knew he'd wrapped his hand around my neck and pulled me against him for a kiss.

This time I was certain that we both let out a sound of pleasure. The spatula made a clanking sound as it hit the floor, and I brought my hands up Tanner's naked torso and wound them around his neck. The action moved me closer against his body and he groaned, running his hands down my back and over my butt. He squeezed the mounds roughly before picking me up and sitting me on the counter.

Tanner's mouth was slightly aggressive, claiming mine in a series of hard, wet kisses that encouraged our tongues to engage in a battle that neither of us was going to win. He was devouring me, and like so many times during the night, I found my hands twisted in his hair, straining into him in an effort to meld our arousal. My nipples hardened against his chest, tingling with the needful lust controlling my actions and I was suddenly glad that all I had on was a sleep tee, giving Tanner easy access to my body.

After he'd thoroughly tasted my mouth, he growled. "Jesus, woman, I can't seem to get enough of you." Even now his hand was pulling my tee away from my neck, and then he was sucking and nipping the skin he'd exposed.

"Is that so bad?" I asked breathlessly, shivering beneath his sensual assault. When he snaked a hand beneath my tee and covered my breast, I bit down on my lip to keep from sounding out.

"I don't do this shit." His tone revealed his frustration and irritation. His hand cupped my breast while his thumb flicked over my nipple.

"That's right," I laughed softly, remembering his rule. He'd broken it many times with me. I wanted to believe that I was special in some way, but I knew better than to get my hopes up. "What happened to your one-fuck-rule?" I asked him anyway, knowing that I was leaving myself open for hurt.

I could tell that Tanner was losing control, letting the situation rule him. Both hands were beneath my tee now, massaging and squeezing my breasts until they were swollen and achy, but in a good way. With an impatient sound he pushed the material of my shirt up to my chest and then began to run his mouth over me, teasing, tasting, and licking my breasts. "Your situation is different," he finally mumbled, sucking a nipple into his mouth.

Different? I wondered what that meant. Right then all I could think about was what he was making me feel. I arched my back until my breasts were sticking out in a silent offering to him, and moaned sharply when he took a nipple between his teeth and tugged on it. The slight pain morphed into breath-stealing pleasure that splintered out in every direction. I was helpless against Tanner's expertise and growing knowledge of my body. He seemed to know exactly what I hungered for, and before long my body was responding with wetness between my legs.

"God, Tanner!" I gasped, digging my nails into his shoulders. I didn't want him to quit, the feeling racing through me was consuming. The warmth flowing through me was going to turn me into a puddle at his feet. I'd forgotten where we were. Nothing mattered but his mouth on me and the feeling of triumph when he stepped between my legs and pushed his erection against my buzzing sex.

"I could fuck you so easily right now," he rasped in a tone thick with arousal. "I should fuck you now. There shouldn't be anything between my dick and your pussy." His hands transferred to my hair, tugging my head back so that he could kiss his way up the side of my neck and over the line of my jaw before settling on my panting mouth.

"Excuse me, kids. I knocked, but no one answered," a deep voice laced with obvious humor said, dousing us with reality. "You sharing, brother?"

Tanner pulled away, bringing my shirt down as he stepped back. I thanked God that I was sitting on the counter with my backside against whoever had just entered the house. Tanner's gaze moved beyond us toward the direction of the patio door.

He grinned like a satisfied wolf. "As you can see, I was busy," he confirmed. "And in answer to your question, fuck, no. You know I don't share."

His possessiveness made me tingle all over. Aware of my position, of my hard nipples and the wetness between my thighs, I turned and glanced over my shoulder at Gabe. Damn! He wasn't alone, either. Ace and William were with him. I'd had a chance to get to know some of Tanner's brothers the day before at the cookout. I liked their easy-going comradeship, and it was clear that these men were close. "Hi."

"Hi, sweetheart." Gabe gave me a wink. "Wish I had someone like you at home to wake me up like that in the mornings," he joked. Both he and William had huge grins on their rugged faces, but Ace looked as solemn as ever. He gave the impression that nothing affected him and I found that kind of sad, more so than the scars that marred his otherwise attractive features.

I felt myself blush, and I faced Tanner again. "Um, could you please get me down?"

"I kind of like you right where you are," he murmured in a teasing tone, putting his hands on my waist. "But I think the sausages are burning." I caught my breath as he lowered me to the floor slowly, keeping me tight against him.

I felt the draft on the backs of my thighs and then my bottom before a whistle pierced the air and one of his brothers said, "Holy shit, man. Your woman's got a cute-as-fuck ass."

I quickly reached behind me to tug my shirt down, feeling a hot flush of embarrassment envelop me in the way of greedy flames. The look on Tanner's face suddenly turned grim, and I wondered if it was because his brothers had caught a glimpse of my butt or because one of them had referred to me as his woman. It made me think of what I'd asked him earlier, right before he'd kissed me, when I'd wondered why he'd broken his one-fuck-rule with me. But now wasn't the time to bring that up. I moved around him, bent for the spatula, and went to the stove.

Damn. The sausages had burned and were now stuck to the pan. "I'll have to make more," I said to no one in particular, putting the pan into the sink and running cold water into it.

"Don't worry about making me any breakfast," Pops grumbled as he entered the kitchen. "I don't feel so good this morning."

I swung back to look at him with concern. Our eyes met briefly before he looked away.

"You need to go see your doctor, Pops?" Tanner sounded just as concerned as I felt.

"Naw!" He waved away Tanner's worry. "Felt like shit before. It'll go away after my morning smoke." He was joking, but no one found it funny. After a few seconds Pops' smiling attempt at humor dropped. He pushed his way through the three large bikers and made his way outside.

"He's getting worse," Gabe remarked once the patio door was closed again.

"When's the last time he saw his doctor?" William asked.

Tanner released a deep sigh. "It's been too long," he admitted reluctantly. "Just can't get him to take his health seriously." He ran a hand through his already disheveled hair.

"He said they can't fix what's wrong with him." I wasn't sure if I should say anything, but Pops hadn't asked me not to, and Tanner was his son, after all. My comment drew eight sets of eyes to me, and the silence that followed spoke volumes. I realized too late that I'd only made it worse by saying what I had. "I'm . . . I'm sorry."

"Fuck, brother." Ace's gaze went to Tanner. William and Gabe murmured something under their breaths, too, but I couldn't make out what they were saying.

Tanner's eyes remained on me. "He told you that?" I nodded. "Christ." His gaze dropped to the floor, and I watched as a muscle twitched in his locked jaw.

It did something to me to see such a big and powerful man appear as defeated as he did at that moment. "I'm sorry, Tanner. I shouldn't have said anything. It wasn't my place."

"No, honey. That's on Pops, not you," he said in a firm tone. "Anyone hear from Pete this morning?"

Gabe's tone held a tinge of humor. "He's good," he snorted. "Sore. Managed to sweet talk his neighbor into taking care of him all night."

"I'm sure she took care of more than just his booboo." Snorts followed William's remark. "Said he'd be at the meeting this morning."

"What happened to Pete?" I asked before I could stop myself. It got quiet while the guys exchanged looks with each other that conveyed some kind of silent message that only they understood. I laughed softly. "Wrong question?"

Tanner's dark, slightly amused eyes captured mine. "Let's just say we had a little run in with the bastards who destroyed our property last night, and we had to convince them to stay out of our town."

"Oh." I was kind of surprised that he'd admitted as much. My gaze fell to his busted up knuckles, and for the first time I noticed the bruise on Gabe's jaw and William's split lip. Ace looked untouched, and then I remembered that he'd remained at his house when the rest had taken off. "The same bastards who came to the house that day?"

Tanner nodded, amusement flickering in his eyes. "Yeah, those bastards."

"You want us to go on to the bar and wait for you there?" Ace asked, clearly growing impatient.

"Give me five minutes."

I watched Tanner leave the room and then turned my attention back to the three men, who had yet to move from their positions near the patio door. "Would anyone like some coffee?" I didn't think that Tanner would mind my making the offer. It didn't matter anyway, because they declined. I turned back to the stove to clean up the mess and put away the eggs that I'd taken out for breakfast. I was scrubbing the burn marks off the frying pan when Tanner came up behind me, scaring the shit out of me.

"Here." I jumped with a squeal and spun around. He'd placed a phone and some money on the counter beside me. "I should have given you a phone a long time ago. I've programmed any numbers you'll need into it. Keep it with you wherever you go. The money is for any groceries we may need."

"We don't need anything right now."

"Then use it on yourself." His eyes turned serious, and the amount of time that went by as he continued to study my face was slightly alarming. I had the feeling that the emotion running through Tanner wasn't something that he was comfortable with, or even knew how to deal with. "You see anyone with a Kings cut on, you call."

I nodded, his concern warming me inside. He took a tentative step toward me, then thought better of it and pulled back. I wanted to believe that he'd been about to kiss me, but for some reason had changed his mind. Tanner seemed determined to keep some measure of distance between us, especially in the presence of people that he knew. The rejection hurt. It always had.

The sudden tears filling my eyes pissed me off, and I turned back to the sink before I humiliated myself. A few seconds later I heard the patio door shut quietly behind them as they left.

Chapter 34

Tanner

I'd wanted to kiss Ruby before I left the house, but instead I'd ended up hurting her. It hadn't been hard to miss. I'd seen the unshed tears in her eyes before she'd turned away from me and straightened her shoulders. I'd seen the looks of reprimand in the eyes of my brothers as they shook their heads with disappointment and stepped outside ahead of me. I knew what they'd been thinking, but had thanked fuck that they'd wisely kept it to themselves.

It had been all I could do not to order my brothers outside so I could finish what Ruby and I had started earlier. Christ, she'd been so damned sexy in that short tee, with her miles of silky hair clipped up and exposing the graceful curve of her neck. Knowing that she was naked underneath that thin shirt was going to feed my fantasies all fucking day.

I wondered how she'd feel if I showed up later for an afternoon quickie.

With a low groan I reached for my mug. Hell, most of us were on our third or fourth cups of coffee. We were all moving a little sluggishly, none of us having had more than a few short hours of sleep. I'd spent most of my time devouring Ruby's tight little body, and I knew that it hadn't been much different for some of my brothers. The violent confrontation with the Kings had spiked our adrenaline levels and, just as it had been during combat, when the situation was over the need for some kind of release stayed in your blood.

That could be accomplished in different ways. For Ace, Rod, Skipper, and Mike that meant a strenuous workout at the gym until they were exhausted. Gabe, Sid, and I liked to work through shit by fucking. Heath and Sully drank. A little bit of all three calmed down Pete, Mark, and William. I took a sip of my lukewarm coffee, making

243

eye contact with my brothers over the rim of my mug. Bruises, black eyes, and split lips stared back at me. Knowing that we'd left Wicked and his brothers in a lot worse shape on the side of the road had been a small price to pay for the damage they'd done. We'd also wrecked their bikes. With a little luck they were still walking their asses home.

"The way I see it, the Kings did us a service burning down the tattoo shop." All eyes shifted to Skipper. He shrugged, looking smug, as if the whole thing had been his idea. "Insurance will pay for the renovation costs that we were going to do. Sure we have to build from the fucking ground up, but now we can build it exactly the way we want it."

"Good point. Since Ruddy is your cousin you want to handle shit then?" The MC owned the business. Ruddy ran it and was one of the artists. He'd gone through a divorce recently and had lost his sugar-mama. She'd tossed his ass and what few possessions he'd owned out the door and changed the locks. He'd come to us with the idea to turn the top half of the tattoo shop into an apartment for him since it wasn't being used, which would take care of his living situation and earn the MC a cut in the rent.

"Sure, hand it over."

I slid the folder across the table. "Everything is in there. Insurance papers, property title and survey, business licenses. Even though we know it was arson, the fire department is conducting an investigation. I expect to hear from them by the end of the day."

Skipper nodded, tapping his fingers over the folder. "Once you do I'll call a company to clear the lot. What about Ruddy and Sissy? Hate to lose a couple of good artists because they have no place to work."

"Even if we find them a place, we'd still have to order tattoo guns and ink, other shit," Heath pointed out. "That will take some time."

"Ruddy and Sissy have made us a ton of money. I'd say they're both due for a paid vacation. By the time they get back, the new shit should be here."

"I like it, William." There were several nods of agreement from some of my brothers. "That just leaves finding them a temporary place to set up." I thought about the room I had in the back, but it wasn't big enough.

"The empty room you have in the-"

I cut Pete off. "Just thought about it, it's too small."

"What about the strip club?" My gaze swung to Pete. "The girls don't need that big of a changing room. Hell, they don't wear clothes. We can move them into Sam's office, and Sam can do his paperwork and shit in the corner booth."

"Sam's gonna love that," Gabe snorted.

Pete shrugged. "It's temporary, and he works for us."

"The girl's won't be too happy either," I added, "but we write their paychecks." A few chuckles went around the table. "Pete, cut down on activity for the next few days, take care of that leg. I'd like you to take over the strip club. Your presence there will give the girls peace of mind, give them time to get over the shit the Kings did to them." He nodded as I spoke. "You can oversee the orders Sam will need to put in for the new chairs and mirrors."

"What about neighborhood watch tonight, any changes there?" Mike wanted to know. He was leaning back in his chair, arms crossed, an unlit cigar clamped between his teeth.

I glanced down at the schedule in front of me. "The only guys who are off tonight are Heath and Mark. Oh, and Pete." I sat back and linked my hands behind my head. "I think that about covers it. How are you brothers going to spend the rest of your day?"

"I gotta get to the gun range," Rod responded. "Looking into turning part of it into an archery range." He shrugged. "I've had a few inquiries from hunters who travel up north a couple of times a year and want to keep their skills honed. Got another client who has two sons that want to get into competition."

"I just had a visual of cowboys and Indians fighting it out," Heath joked with a snort, scooting back his chair to get up. "I'm gonna hit the gym and then go home and take a nap." Snorts of laughter followed his comment.

"A nap? Your age is beginning to show, brother," William grinned.

Heath gave him the finger. As we began to get to our feet the door opened and Deputy Callahan walked in. Fuck. I knew immediately why he was there, and the fact that he was in uniform revealed that he was on the clock and that this wasn't a friendly visit. He'd been around a long time and was a good guy. He didn't necessarily go by the book, but he wasn't a crooked cop, either. He was the one we usually dealt with when there was an issue.

"Hey, Walter! How's it going, man?" Gabe was the one who greeted him first. "Haven't seen you for a while."

Walter shook his head. "Yeah, it's been nice not having to deal with shit," he grinned, but I noticed that it didn't quite reach his eyes. "Glad Bike Week is over."

We agreed with him. "You're not here about Bike Week," I said, getting right to the point. "And this isn't a social visit."

Walter took a big breath and released it, scanning the group of us. "Afraid not."

"Is this about the Kings and what went down?"

He looked at me with surprise. "As a matter of fact, it is. You wouldn't happen to know anything about it, would you?"

I played dumb. "Well, since it happened at my house it would be odd if -"

A brisk head shake stopped me from going any further. "Not talking about that incident."

"Then what are you talking about?" Ace asked without emotion.

Walter focused his brown eyes on the usually quiet Ace. "Last night. You boys didn't know? Some of the Kings got their asses whipped down in the Cabbage Patch area."

"No. Were they hurt bad?" Gabe asked with mock concern.

"Bad enough," said Walter. "Two of them ended up in the hospital with gunshot wounds." All of a sudden he was narrowing his gaze. "Where'd you get that split lip, Gabe?"

Gabe's face lit up into a grin. "Rough sex."

Walter's gaze began scanning over the rest of us. "Huh. Bruises, black eyes, split lips—" His gaze dropped. "Busted knuckles." He almost looked disappointed. "All of this from rough sex, too?" He rested his gaze on me.

"Did someone implicate us?" I crossed my arms. I was pretty certain that it hadn't been any of the Kings, because they liked to think of themselves as a hard-core club. It had to have been someone who was at the Cabbage Patch, someone riding through who didn't know us. The only reason Walter knew anything about the fight was because of the two Kings in the hospital.

He shook his head. "No, but a witness mentioned seeing some of the Sentinels around at about the same time."

"Huh." I rubbed my chin. "We did stop in there." I knew that admitting that we'd been there would have the desired effect. Guilty people didn't usually confess that they were in the same area at the time a crime went down.

"And you didn't see them?"

I shook my head. "Nope. They weren't there." It was the truth, they hadn't been at the bar when we'd stopped in.

He released a heavy breath. "I suppose if I checked your weapons they'd be clean as a whistle."

He knew we all had concealed weapons permits, but he'd never find the guns in question. Once we used a gun in an altercation we got rid of it permanently. There were perks to living near the beach.

As if on cue, every one of my brothers made a move to remove their weapons.

Walter quickly shook his hand to stop them. "That isn't necessary." He looked back at me.

"Have you talked to Wicked?"

"You know they aren't talking."

"Then what's the issue, man?" Skipper grumbled, heading toward the door. "If there are clubs out there shooting each other up, seems to me that makes your job a helluva lot easier." He opened the door and was gone.

"Makes sense to me." Rod headed for the door as well. "I got shit to do."

Walter finally turned back to me. I could see that he was torn. The man knew that we were the good guys, but he still had a job to do. If it hadn't been him questioning us, someone else from the department would have eventually shown up. Walter was more or less assigned to us, and we liked doing business with just one cop. We used each other.

"Anything else?" I asked, watching my brothers as they left one by one.

"No, I guess that's all." His gaze fell to my hands. "You didn't get those busted knuckles from rough sex, too, did you?"

I laughed heartily, putting my hand on Walter's shoulder and leading him toward the door. "Hell, no, man. I'd never hit a woman. This was done the other day at my house. Remember? When I was defending Pops from some of the Kings."

"Seems those Kings get around," he mumbled to himself.

"Yeah. Let's just hope we've seen the last of them." I was pretty sure that we had.

Chapter 35

R^{uby} Lonnie, Judith, and I were sitting at a small table close to the dance floor and even closer to the bar. We'd made plans for a girls' night out. Actually they'd had to talk me into going. Not because I didn't want to, I loved dancing and having a good time, but I'd been afraid to leave Pops alone. So they'd compromised by picking me up at ten, closer to his bedtime. Now we were at a club called The Grinders, a fairly new club according to the girls. The place was hopping, and it soon became apparent that some of the couples on the dance floor were incorporating the name of the place into some of their moves.

"So spill—what's going on between you and Tanner?" The expression on Judith's face was as animated as the emotion in her tone. Both women were dressed to kill, and I couldn't help but be surprised that Sid and Mark were okay with them going out without them.

I'd been waiting for that question. When I'd sat on Tanner's lap at the cookout, both girls had looked at us with curiosity in their eyes, and I'd known then that they couldn't wait to get me alone to ask questions. We just hadn't had a chance to talk since then. I picked up my drink, not sure how to answer. I felt that Tanner and I were in some kind of relationship, yet he distanced himself when other people were around.

"Come on," Lonnie giggled. "We know you're stalling." She reached for her drink, which already had a ring of her bright red lipstick around the rim. The smiles on the women's faces didn't waver, and I had a feeling that they were willing to wait for as long as it took for me to answer.

"Yeah, and we know there's something going on, so don't try and downplay it. We have eyes," Judith added, dousing any ideas I may have had to do just that.

I finally decided to be honest with them, giving a light shrug. "I'm really not sure what you'd call it." It was the truth.

"Are you having sex?" Lonnie came right out and asked the question that I'd been dreading.

"Wow." I laughed, and leaned back in my chair. "Get right to the point, why don't you."

"Look, girl, we know those men. You think Judith and I didn't have trouble with our men when we first got together? They're tight, more than brothers, if that's possible, since they served in the military together. They're set in their ways, especially when it comes to women."

"I hadn't noticed." I was thinking about Tanner's one-fuck rule. He certainly hadn't applied that to me.

"You're thinking about Tanner's one-fuck rule, aren't you?"

My eyes widened with surprise. How did Judith know about that? "Are you a mind reader or something?"

She shook her head, laughing. "Mark told me about it. He said that Tanner's had that rule for years and doesn't deviate from it no matter what. So if you've had sex more than once, you're halfway there."

"Halfway there?" I suspected that she meant we were on our way to a serious relationship, but I didn't agree with her. "What happens if we've had sex for, like, half a dozen times?"

Their eyes grew big and bright at that. "Then there'll be a wedding!" Lonnie giggled, obviously joking. She leaned across the table as if she didn't want anyone else to hear her. "Have you and Tanner had sex that many times?"

I finished my chocolate martini first. "I refuse to answer on the grounds that it may incriminate me."

Both threw back their heads and laughed like crazy lunatics and I had to wonder if some of it wasn't caused by the amount of alcohol they'd consumed. They were a couple of drinks ahead of me.

"Oh, my God!" Lonnie pulled herself together first. "This is great! Another Sentinel down, another old lady for us!" She was yelling.

I knew she was joking, yet it made me feel a little sad inside, because I knew it wasn't like that at all. I knew the truth. I was just a fuck buddy. And while my feelings for Tanner were growing, I had the feeling that he was content to keep our relationship strictly physical. If one could call what we had a relationship. He'd told me that I was different, but he hadn't clarified what that meant.

I realized that they'd both stopped grinning and were now staring at me with sober expressions. I forced a smile back onto my face when I recognized the slight sorrow reflected in their eyes.

Lonnie reached across the table and put her hand over mine. "We're sorry for assuming, Ruby. We know that anyone who gets through the tough shell Tanner surrounds himself in has her work cut out for her."

"Thanks to his ex," Lonnie added in. "You saw the bitch at the cookout." Her disgust was evident, and then she shrugged. "Not really sure where I was going with that. Tanner broke it off with her long before we came on the scene. Sid doesn't talk about it, no one does. But I think she's the one who turned Tanner away from relationships."

"And Tanner ended their relationship?"

She nodded. "Yeah," she hesitated, as if trying to decide whether or not to continue with her line of thought. "Apparently he walked in on her and another man." That was all she said. That was all she needed to say.

"Hey, come on, ladies, we're supposed to be dancing and having a good time tonight. Not trying to analyze relationships."

"I'm with Judith," I smiled, raising my empty glass. "Looks like I need another martini." I scooted my chair back and rose to my feet. There was no telling when the waitress would make her way back to our table. "I'm going to the bar to get another one." I glanced down at their drinks. It looked like they could use another round, too. "What about you two? Want anything while I'm there?"

Lonnie shook her head, but Judith said, "We'll wait for the waitress to come around. I'm going to dance right now."

"Me too!" Getting to their feet, they laughed their way to the dance floor.

I was still smiling at their contagious enthusiasm when I reached the bar. It was circular and located dead center in the room. Stools circled around it, and a huge glass rack hung from the ceiling directly over it, low enough for the bartenders to be able to reach the glasses. Their alcohol stock was obviously stored below the counter, and there were four sinks evenly spaced apart for convenience. It was quite chic and modern.

"What can I get ya?"

I met the smiling eyes of the bartender. "May I see a menu?" I didn't want to order another martini if it was too expensive. I felt guilty using the money Tanner had given me, even though I could probably justify it as my first paycheck. I accepted the menu and quickly sought out martinis. I almost had a heart attack when I saw the price of a chocolate martini, and just managed not to give myself away by exclaiming loudly over the twenty dollar price tag. Holy shit! I planted a smile on my face as I scanned over the menu, and then handed it back to the bartender.

"Think I'll have the Long Island Iced Tea." I had no idea what it was, but the price was much lower. The bartender smiled, and within seconds he set a tall, narrow glass in front of me. I took a sip before leaving the bar. A little strong, but it wasn't bad. I turned to head back to the table, scanning the crowd when my gaze landed on someone who was standing across the room that I'd hoped to never see again.

When our eyes met I came to a dead stop and froze. *Billy?* A chill literally ran through me, and my heart stopped for a moment. No way, it couldn't be! He was barely recognizable and far removed from the boy I'd last seen. He was a man now. He'd bulked up, which made him as dangerous as he looked. The smirk on his face spoke volumes, reminding me why I'd pretended to be happy to see him the last time he'd found me—self-preservation caused you to do things you wouldn't normally do. The same intuition that had made him creepy to me then warned me now that he was someone to be cautious of.

How had he found me?

I shook my head, looking at him incredulously, and then someone bumped into me, breaking the connection. I automatically held my glass away from my body as some of the liquid splashed onto the floor. I turned slightly and made eye-contact with the man who'd bumped into me, half-

listening to his drunken apology. I smiled, and when he realized that I wasn't pissed he grinned back before disappearing into the crowd. I swung my eyes back to where Billy had been standing.

He was gone now, another man standing in his place.

My gaze quickly moved around the general vicinity of where he'd been, wondering if I'd really seen him or if I'd just imagined him. The man standing there now wasn't looking at me, his gaze was searching through the room, obviously looking for someone. Had I imagined Billy then? I took a breath and relaxed a little, convincing myself that my mind had been playing tricks on me. It was easy to blame it on the two martinis I'd consumed earlier, and the fact that other than the occasional beer, I really wasn't a drinker. I would sometimes go to a bar, suck on a beer for the night, and dance, but that was usually all.

Tonight I'd decided to splurge, and I had to admit that it felt good. I'd splurged earlier in the day, too, spending money on new clothes. The little black halter-style dress and the stilettos I was wearing had been the first inedible things I'd purchased in two years. I was thankful to have found them on the discount rack. The shoes fit perfectly, but the dress could have been a size bigger. I'd styled my hair in a soft side bun, and the only makeup I'd taken the time to put on was a rosy lip gloss and smoky eye.

I made my way back to our table, surprised to see that Judith and Lonnie were still gone. I searched to find them on the dance floor, throwing their bodies around to "I Gotta Feeling" by the Black Eyed Peas. I sat down and took another sip of my drink, and then found myself moving to the music. The girls saw me back at the table and motioned for me to join them on the dance floor, but I declined, lifting my drink to show them that I was enjoying it. I sucked a few more swallows down, content to dance in my chair, until something by Drake began to blast through the room.

I couldn't stop myself from jumping up and going to the dance floor. Like everyone else, I threw myself into it, laughing and singing along, losing all my inhibitions. I threw my arms up in the air and began twisting my body, bumping and grinding my way through the crowd of dancers who were doing the same thing. At some point Lonnie, Judith, and I made our way to one another.

"I love Drake!" Lonnie exclaimed loudly. "'Hotline Bling' is one of my favorites!"

"Did you get another chocolate martini?" Judith asked over the noise.

I shook my head, laughing for no reason. "No, I switched to iced tea!" I closed my eyes and continued to gyrate, but when a wave of dizziness washed over me I was forced to open them again to regain my balance. I laughed again at my own expense.

"Iced tea?" They exchanged amused glances. "Do you mean Long Island Iced Tea?" Lonnie questioned with a smile.

I thought about it for a second. "Yeah, that sounds right." I twirled around. "Why?" I tried to focus my eyes on them.

"A Long Island Iced Tea is all alcohol!" Judith explained. "Drink it slow!"

I giggled, thinking about the half glass I'd already chugged down. "Too late!" My eyes grew big when suddenly I saw Sid and Mark move into position behind their women. The girls spun around, but were too late to avoid the arms that closed around them. The two couples began grinding all over each other and moving away.

Drake turned into something by Lady Gaga. I kept dancing, letting the words and music flow through my blood, turning me hot. I felt rivulets of sweat run between my breasts and gather above my lip as the glow of the disco lights above bathed everyone in red, then blue, then yellow. Usually I didn't like the blinking colors of the disco lights, they often gave me a headache, but the one above us now sent shooting rays of soft color down upon us.

"Didn't it occur to you to tell someone where you were going tonight?"

I started violently at the deep rumble in my ear, and before I was able to turn around two powerful arms wrapped around me and pulled me against a hard body. I turned my head enough to see that I was in Tanner's arms. I smiled in the face of his anger and started to dance against him.

"Don't be mad, Tanner. I didn't think it would matter if I went out for a while."

"Yeah?" I felt his lips move against my skin, shivering. "I come home to Pops snoring in his room, and there's no sign of you? You don't think I got fucking worried?" He gave me a punishing bite beneath my ear. "I don't mind you going out with the girls, but next time let me know, you hear me?"

"I hear you, Tanner."

I smiled at the rough possessiveness in his raspy tone, suspecting that he wasn't as angry as he was letting on. We were moving in sync to the music, our two bodies melding into one. Tanner kept me tight against him, and I released a dreamy sigh, pretending that I was dancing with a man who wanted me. Oh, Tanner wanted me, but not all of me. I was finding it harder and harder to keep my feelings separate from the physical needs of my body.

As I writhed sensuously against his hard muscles, my bottom tucked into the hollow of his hips, right up against his hardening cock, I brought my arms up and behind me to wrap them around his neck. His arms unlocked from around my waist. He settled his hands against my waist and slowly glided up my body to my breasts. My breath caught when he cupped them and plucked at the nipples, unconcerned that we were in the middle of a crowded room.

"Tanner!" I ground my bottom against his cock.

"I should punish you for worrying me tonight." He growled the words against my ear before raking his teeth against the side of my neck.

"Like spank me?" I teased.

He grunted. "Don't tempt me."

I giggled, knowing that part of my bravado was due to the alcohol I'd consumed. "Have you ever spanked a woman? I hear it can be quite a turn on." I hesitated for affect. "For both parties."

He grumbled. "Don't change the subject. We were talking about your lack of self-preservation."

Without understanding why, I laughed. "How did you find me?"

"Lonnie and Judith had the common sense to let their men know where they were going."

I contemplated that for a second. "But you're not my man, Tanner." I wanted him to be my man, but he was the one with the relationship hang-ups. "So I really don't owe you anything. I'm an adult. I don't need your permission to go out. I may work for you, but I'm allowed time on my own." He flipped me around but kept me anchored tightly against him. I leaned back enough to meet his eyes, smiling in the face of his irritation. "Say it isn't so," I challenged.

A muscle leapt in his hard jaw. "You live under my roof, I know where you are at all time. Yes, you're allowed time on your own, but be smart about it." I noticed that he had avoided the real issue. I smiled. "What are you smiling about?"

"You're a coward, Tanner." I saw instantly that he had not liked that one bit. The storm in his eyes churned dark and unpredictable, and I felt him stiffen slightly against me. However, I noticed that nothing deflated the hard bar of arousal throbbing against me. "You know what I mean," I said, moving against him. "It has nothing to do with your willingness to face a fight, so let's not confuse the issue."

"Suppose you tell me so there won't be any confusion," he insisted firmly.

I shook my head. "Nope. You have to figure it out yourself. It won't mean anything if I have to tell you."

I toyed with the hair that was hanging behind his ear, running my fingers through it and giving it a tug. Tanner turned his head and I trailed the tip of my finger over his strong jaw, down to his chin, and then up to his impossibly sensual mouth. It wasn't fair for a man to have such a beautiful mouth. I smoothed over his bottom lip, licking my own when I remembered what he tasted like. I had totally forgotten what we'd been talking about. "Will you kiss me, Tanner?" All of a sudden I needed his mouth on me like I needed air to breathe.

We were drowning in the loudness of the music and the people surrounding us, but I had no doubt that he'd heard me. As he began to slowly lower his head closer, my lips parted in anticipation. A pleasant tingling moved over me, causing other responses in my body. When his mouth finally closed over mine I melted against him. It was unlike any kiss he'd given me before—soft, tender, long, and sweet, exposing emotions that he was so damned determined not to have. And while he coaxed my mouth open for his searching tongue, I knew that I was already lost.

Things weren't going to end well for me.

Chapter 36

Tanner

Nothing had ever felt as fucking right as the woman in my arms did right then. Everything about Ruby, her softness, her sensual scent, her sexiness, let my dick know that we liked her and wanted to keep her. Christ, I wasn't too happy about that. I couldn't stay away from her, and when we weren't together she wouldn't leave my thoughts. Sometimes I felt like a school boy crushing on his first serious crush. I knew that I should stay away from her, but as long as she was under my roof and available that wasn't going to happen.

I was so screwed.

Even now I wanted to take her out back, find a dark spot somewhere, and fuck her. My dick had turned hard as stone the second I'd seen her on the dance floor, shimmying her tight little body in the sexy little dress she was wearing, showing just enough enticing skin to make my mouth water. It was a good thing she'd been alone, because if I'd found her gyrating her hot curves against another man it wouldn't have ended well. I realized that I felt possessive as fuck over her. I didn't want another man around her as long as she was mine.

She was mine.

By the time I pulled my mouth off of hers, my hand had found its way into her soft hair and the other one was clenching one cheek of her delectable ass. My dick ached and my balls were tight and full, and it was a miracle that I didn't come in my pants like a school boy. I was torturing myself by keeping Ruby so close, but she was so damned cute and desirable. She held nothing back when she gave herself to me, meeting my sexual demands without hesitation and exhibiting a level of skill that belied her innocence. I couldn't get over the fact that I'd been her first, and deep down in my gut I wanted to be her only.

As that knowledge settled in my mind it did something primal to me. I'd claimed Ruby, but I wanted to fucking own her, body and soul. Christ. I needed to clear my head, which was hard to do when you had a beautiful, curvy woman returning your kiss with unrestrained ardor. I tasted the alcohol in her warm mouth, the subtle remnants of something tasty, and wondered if she was just a little bit tipsy. As I wound my kiss down I took her luscious bottom lip between my teeth and tugged gently.

Her blissful sigh was for my ears only. At some point we'd stopped moving to the music, and were now just standing still, oblivious to the others around us. When her eyes opened to mine, the haze of smoky arousal I saw reflected there caused my dick to jump. My hand was still clenching the cheek of her ass and I gave it a squeeze, pulling her tighter against me so I could grind my dick into her. I wanted inside her so badly at that moment.

A small, seductive smile curved her swollen lips upward. "Are you going to take me home and fuck me?" she asked softly.

"You better believe it," I growled down at her. "I'm going to fucking put my scent on you so that every man you come in contact with will know who you belong to just by smelling you."

She laughed. "What's going to stop them from having me once I'm gone?"

It was a fair question, but the thought of Ruby with another man turned me into a fucking beast. I knew that when she was gone it would be over, that she would go on with her life while I went back to mine. It was a depressing thought that I refused to analyze.

"Or will I be out of sight, out of mind?" she asked a little sadly.

"Never, honey. You're not the kind of woman that will be easy to forget." I clenched my jaw from saying more.

"You, too," she said so low that I could have imagined it. Fuck, were those tears in her eyes? "I think maybe that I should leave soon." Her comment surprised me. "It will just get harder, the longer I wait."

I couldn't argue with that. I wondered if she was expecting me to ask her to stay, or if she was looking for a sign that I didn't want her to go. I reminded myself that I liked my life just the way it was. But there was no denying that I was going to miss the hell out of her. Until she left, I was going to fuck her every chance that I got, fuck her out of my system. I knew that made me a prick, but getting over her would be easier that way. Maybe it would make it easier for her, too.

All I knew at this very second was that I needed to be inside her. I took her hand and began pulling her off the dance floor.

"Where are we going?" Ruby asked breathlessly as I forced her to keep up with me.

"Somewhere I can fuck you," I answered bluntly. A few heads turned our way, hearing my words. I didn't give a shit. I'd never been in the place, I had no idea where the restrooms were located, but that didn't matter anyway, because I didn't want Ruby in a tiny square room surrounded by noise. When she came, I wanted to hear her.

I hit the entrance door with the palm of my hand and continued through, stepping out into the darkness and further away from the noise. I rounded the building and headed toward my bike, where it was parked with Sid's and Mark's. Thank fuck there were no parking lot lights close by. It wouldn't have mattered anyway, I wanted Ruby that badly. By the time we reached my bike, I pulled her into my arms and kissed her roughly.

As I ravished her mouth I cupped and squeezed her tit, my other hand on her ass. I fucking loved the fullness of both, and I wasn't gentle. I was too far gone to make love to Ruby, I just wanted to fuck her. Besides, her moans revealed that she liked what I was doing. Her little body was squirming against me, her tongue darting against mine as I explored her mouth. My dick was throbbing with a life of its own, demanding to be let out so that it could get into her tight, little pussy.

"You want this, baby?" I rasped against her wet, swollen mouth. "You want my dick inside you?"

"God, yes!" she cried, her hands running over my body. She made an impatient sound before I felt her hands work their way beneath my t-shirt and cut. Once there, she was like a little wildcat, raking her nails over my abs and chest, torturing my nipples. "I need you!" she whispered desperately.

I pushed her up against my bike, content to kiss and touch her while she returned the favor. "Fuck, yes!" I growled when she lifted my shirt and placed her mouth against me. The heat of her open kisses, the sting of her teeth against a nipple, almost made me come in my pants. And that wouldn't do.

Before I put us out of our misery and fucked her senseless, I needed to do one thing. I pulled her halter top down and exposed her luscious tits. There was no lighting, but I didn't need it, I remembered how beautiful and perfect they were. I cupped the full globes in my hands and raked my thumbs over her nipples until Ruby was whimpering, and then I leaned forward and covered them with my mouth. I loved them both equally, using tongue and teeth to ramp up her arousal.

She was a fucking goddess.

I tugged hard on a nipple, the tasty treat pulling a groan from me. "Baby, I need you now." I didn't give her time to respond. I whipped her around and pushed the top half of her body over the seat of my bike. Her skirt was short, nearly exposing her ass to me, but it wasn't enough. I pushed it up over the shapely moons so I could smooth my hands over them. "Jesus, where are your panties?"

Her light giggle sounded around us. "I'm wearing a thong," she confessed.

I'd already found the thin strip of silk tucked between the crack of her ass. I pulled it forward and kept going until it snapped against her flesh. Ruby moaned loudly at the feel of the little piece of material that covered her mound being pulled tight between her pussy lips. Grinning, I tugged again.

"Oh, God, Tanner!" she quivered wildly. "I need you inside me."

That sounded like a good idea. I tugged the thong away and reached between her legs until I found her dripping cunt. I ran a finger over the slit, burrowing inside to her burgeoning clit. Jesus, it was hard as a pebble and as big as a pea. She was so fucking wet, and I was about to come. I unzipped my jeans and pulled out my dick, lining the head up to her pussy. I eased the head in and then shot my hips forward, bottoming out in one, deep plunge.

"Tanner!" she groaned. "Oh, God! So good!"

I grunted, pulling out to the head before pushing back inside. "Jesus, you're tight, baby, and so fucking hot." I could hear her heavy breathing even though she was bent over my bike and her head was toward the ground. "I'll never get enough of your pussy." My dick was tingling from being squeezed so tightly by her pussy.

She began to push back against me when I thrust forward. I could already feel my balls draw tight, signaling that I was close, but I wasn't about to come before Ruby came first. I wanted to hear her come undone, wanted to feel the contractions of her pussy around my dick when she lost control. Without breaking rhythm, I reached between our bodies and zeroed in on her pulsing clit.

I leaned over and put my mouth near her ear. "You want me to come, honey?" I took her ear into my mouth and sucked on it, feeling her shiver beneath me. "You want my cum inside you?" I whispered into her ear. Her whimpers and moans were my answer. I smiled, putting my lips against the side of her neck and licking her. "Come for me, Ruby. I want to feel your cream soaking my dick." I fingered her clit, satisfied by her erratic breathing.

I began to pound into her faster, harder, the need to come too strong to resist any longer. My balls were about to explode, they were so fucking tight. I pinched Ruby's clit, hearing her little cry, and then pressed down on it hard. "Come for me now, baby!" I demanded hoarsely, feeling my balls let go. I sank my teeth gently into the crease of her neck and shoulder, and that's when she screamed out her release, her body jerking uncontrollably beneath mine.

I followed close behind her, gripping her hips and pulling her sharply against the cradle of my loins, spilling my seed inside her. We came at the same time, and it was fucking heaven and hell

at once. I couldn't remember ever coming as hard, but it was the fault of her tight, clenching little body that was holding my dick captive. Jesus! I was going to have a fucking heart attack, my heart was pounding so hard. The intensity couldn't be healthy.

Ruby's moans gradually slowed, as did my grunts. Every time my dick ejaculated more cum inside her I lost a second of control. When the only thing I could hear was our heavy breathing I knew that it was time to step back and let Ruby move. I hated like fuck disconnecting from her. Her jerk and whimper told me that she hated it, too. I quickly tucked my dick away and did up my pants before helping her to stand straight.

"Lean against my bike," I said, realizing that she was as limp as a noodle. I grinned.

"You wear me out," she admitted with a slight laugh.

"You ready to go home?"

"Judith and Lonnie-"

"Baby, this is how all their girls' nights out end. Sid and Mark eventually track them down, dance with them a little, and then take them home and fuck their brains out. They know you're with me, so they won't worry if you leave without telling them."

"But my tab and money..."

I yanked out my cell, punched out a text to Sid, and then returned it to my pocket. "All taken care of." I gave her a kiss because I couldn't help myself. "Let's go."

We mounted my bike, I made sure her arms were locked tightly around me, and then I took off. Every once in a while I reached back and put my hand on Ruby's naked thigh to keep her close against my backside. Her little dress had ridden all the way up, exposing all of her thighs and legs. I could almost imagine the heat of them against the back of mine, but nothing disguised the heat of her pussy against my backside.

I grinned, remembering that her cunt was naked, and probably leaking.

And I planned on fucking her again.

We were about halfway home when I started to get the feeling that we were being followed, and closely. Every turn we made, whoever it was they stayed right on our tail. I purposely went down side roads that had no traffic and still didn't lose them. It wasn't until we had to stop at the first red light that I was able to see that it was a big, red truck that was following us, a fairly new model. I couldn't see the driver though, because of the darkly tinted windows. He had his fog lights on, and the one on the driver's side was shining directly into my side-view mirror. I made sure that the driver knew that I was irritated by staring at him in the mirror. He was so fucking close to the back of my bike that I could feel the heat coming off the grille of the truck.

The next light that we stopped at, the same thing happened. The driver pulled up threateningly close behind me and I began to get concerned for Ruby. I felt her stiffen behind me, and I turned to see her nervously looking back behind us. I walked my bike up a little to put some distance between us and the truck, but the fucker did the same damned thing. Son of a bitch! I turned the key and kicked down the kick stand.

"I'll be right back, baby." I carefully dismounted and walked to the driver's side of the truck. The tinted window rolled halfway down so that I was only able to see the upper half of his face. "What the fuck are you doing? You're practically up my ass. Now back off!"

He threw his hands up. "Sorry, man. I didn't realize I was doing anything wrong. I'm lost."

I had nothing to say to that. If I'd been in a better mood I would have asked him where he wanted to go and then given him directions. I stomped back to my bike.

"Short trip."

"Give me that smart mouth." I gave her a quick kiss and then mounted my bike. Since the light had already turned green, once I started my bike again we shot off down the road. The next time I checked my mirror the bastard in the truck was still behind us, but further back. We made the rest of the trip home without any other problems.

I held my hand back to help Ruby dismount. Once she was on her feet I slipped an arm around her waist and pulled her against me. Eyes locked, I slid a hand up the inside of her thigh. "I want you in my room."

She licked her bottom lip. "Okay."

I'd gone high enough up her thigh to flick a finger over her mound. It was still swollen and, fuck, slick with our combined cum. My dick jerked. "Go get in the shower, I'll be in after I put my bike away."

She shivered wildly when my finger parted her slit and ran up and down her labia. I grinned, because so far she hadn't made a move to go inside. She was purring like a satisfied kitten. I watched the lazy look in her eyes widen with surprise when I buried my finger inside her past the knuckle.

She moaned and lay her head down on my shoulder. "You have magical fingers," she murmured low.

A rough laugh rumbled in my chest. She began to move her hips in tune with my thrusting finger. I hadn't intended to make her come again, but Ruby was so fucking responsive, and the little sounds that she made, the little puffs of warm air against my throat, turned me on. I added two more fingers, almost bringing her to her toes. With my thumb on her clit I managed to get her off within minutes.

Her soft cry of release was muffled against my neck. I kept a firm arm around her waist as she convulsed against my fingers. Warm cream ran down my hand, and I inhaled deeply the scent of her arousal. My dick was ready for round two but I wanted Ruby in my bed. As her shudders weakened, I pulled out.

"Go, baby."

With a weak smile she turned and headed for the house.

Chapter 37

R^{uby}

It was nice waking up the next morning with Tanner still in the bed beside me. Actually, he was half under me, as I'd somehow ended up with an arm over his chest and a leg between his two muscular thighs, resting slightly over his cock, which was growing harder by the second. Morning wood. I smiled. The man never seemed flaccid in my presence, and I couldn't say that I didn't like it. My effect on him made me feel confident in my waning innocence. Tanner was a highly sexual man.

Opening my eyes to his sleeping face kept the smile on mine. It was the only time I'd seen him so relaxed and at peace. He was so fucking hot, even in sleep, his strong-boned features half-covered by his mussed hair, hair that I'd had my fingers in most of the night, tugging on it while in the throes of sexual bliss. Sex between us was intense, all consuming, and exhaustingly satisfying. The man's stamina, though I had nothing to compare it with, was, in my book, incredible. Something told me that he would have put most men to shame.

I didn't want to think about leaving, but I knew that if I didn't soon I would just be setting myself up for more hurt. I already hurt inside, reluctantly accepting that Tanner didn't want a relationship with me. The words he'd uttered about claiming me and belonging to him while we'd been fucking had been said in the heat of the moment, and I hadn't taken them to heart once the orgasmic bliss had diminished. Yet I couldn't get over the knowledge that Judith and Lonnie had said they'd had the same obstacles with Sid and Mark in the beginning, and they'd beat down their resistance. I wanted to believe the same thing would happen with me and Tanner because I knew that he'd ruined me for other men.

Besides, I loved him.

Yeah, I'd gone there.

Shaking off the sadness of the reality that nothing serious was going to happen between us, I leaned up and kissed Tanner's scruffy chin. When he didn't respond I scooted up further to reach the corner of his mouth, and then I began to rain a series of short kisses over his closed mouth until he responded with a lazy smile. Once I knew that he was rousing I started to kiss my way down his magnificent body, marveling at how rock-solid and well-built he was. And right then he was mine.

All mine.

I ran my lips down his neck to the crease where his shoulder began, giving a little nip there before moving down his chest and attacking his nipples. I licked and sucked the solid nubs, being rewarded by a low groan. With growing confidence, I kissed my way down his defined abs to his belly button, finally reaching his loins. Oh my, he had a beautifully long and thick cock, a powerful tool for giving pleasure. The knob-shaped head was smooth, shiny, and slightly bigger than the rest of his cock, the slit filled with a creamy white substance that lured me in for a taste.

As soon as my tongue lapped up that pearly liquid Tanner's hips left the bed and his hands reached for me. "Come here," he growled in a rough voice.

I resisted. "No, Tanner, I want to taste you."

"Oh, shit!" he groaned weekly, letting his hands drop to the side of the bed. The tautness in which he held himself caused me to chuckle.

"Relax, big boy," I said with humor, giving the tip of his cock another firm lick." This won't hurt you, I promise."

"I'm not afraid of you hurting me, baby," he admitted huskily. "I'm not sure I'll survive your mouth on my dick."

A wicked laugh escaped me. "Well, let's, shall we?" The power I wielded over Tanner at that moment was intoxicating. I stared at his throbbing cock, thinking about all the erotic romance

novels I'd red. I'd never done this before, but really, how difficult could it be? I wrapped my fingers around the base and lowered my mouth down over him. He immediately bowed up tight, and I saw his hands twisting in the sheets.

I ran my mouth up and down several times, licking under the head and exploring the enticing ridges before pulling off. "You like that?"

"Fuck, yes!" he hissed.

I closed my mouth over his length again, enjoying the taste of pre-cum that was pouring out of the slit. Several times I wiggled my tongue into it to get more. "Yum," I breathed, just before I began to lick his shaft like a Popsicle. The entire time Tanner was trembling, his solid thighs quivering, and he was panting heavily. "I like the taste of you." I gave attention to the two huge testicles at the root of his cock.

His hands dropped to my head, fingers twisting into my hair as he groaned like a man in pain. "Don't let me hurt you," I said with concern. "I've never done this before."

"Baby you could never hurt me. It just feels so fucking good."

It hit me then that Tanner must have been experiencing the same pleasure that I felt when he ate me out. This time, when I lowered my mouth over him he took control of my movements, pushing me down as far as he could. When his head hit the back of my throat I swallowed instinctively, hearing his groan.

"Jesus! For an innocent, you fucking know what you're doing." I couldn't speak because his cock was in my mouth and his hand was holding me there as he began to pump in and out. It didn't take long before I picked up on what he wanted. He was literally fucking my mouth. As he thrust, I instinctively wrapped my hand around the portion that I couldn't fit inside my mouth and pumped.

"Jesus Christ," he swore. "You're killing me."

With pleasure, I hoped. I controlled the urge to smile and moved up and down his hot shaft, moaning my pleasure, because I was enjoying it, too. Tanner's breathing turned louder, harsher, and I sucked hard, hoping to push him over the edge. I took his balls into my hand and rolled them around, squeezing them gently, marveling at the heaviness of them.

"Ruby-" he groaned, his thrusting picking up speed. "Baby, I'm going to...fuck, if you don't want me to come in your mouth, get off me now!"

I held tight, taking as much of his cock as I could into my mouth, swallowing hungrily when he jammed the head at the back of my throat. I continued to pump my hand at the bottom, sucking hard. Tanner's hand clenched in my hair, his body turned solid, and I felt his cock swell even more. And then he was erupting in my mouth, shooting ribbons of warm, salty cum down my throat.

I swallowed as fast as I could, moaning in response to his groans, and let his powerful release run its course. When his cock stopped shooting cum and slowly grew soft, I pulled away and began to lick his shaft clean. Tanner continued to pant above me, his chest rising and falling hard, and twitched at my administrations. I couldn't help the wide smile from spreading over my face, I felt as if I'd accomplished something significant. It was silly, I knew. It was, after all, just a blowjob. Gradually, the hand in my hair loosened and fell to the bed.

"Come here, woman." When I didn't move right away a heavy hand dropped to my shoulder, and I crawled up to lay in the curve of his body. "I'm keeping you," he rasped, smiling weakly. I knew they were just words.

"Good morning," I said softly.

"Yes, it is."

I laughed softly, totally content, wondering what came next. His arm wrapped around me to pull me close, and a big hand massaged my ass. I realized that I could easily have fallen back to sleep. Listening to Tanner's steady breathing and calm heartbeats, I was halfway there when his cell rang. He made a frustrated sound and we both moved so he could reach for it.

"Yeah?" He listened for a minute. "What time is it?" More silence. "Yeah, that sounds good. Call the others and we'll meet here." He glanced down at me with lazy humor. "For some reason I'm having a hard time getting out of bed this morning." He disconnected and put his phone back on the nightstand.

"Are you blaming me for your laziness?"

He laughed, clarifying, "No, for my exhaustion."

"Oh." I felt myself blushing.

"That was Gabe. One morning a week we hold our meeting here and have breakfast with Pops. They'll be here within the hour."

"Breakfast in the way of donuts?" I teased, recalling what they'd been eating the morning I'd gone to the bar. "I don't know how you boys keep your shapes so fit."

"What did I tell you about calling us boys?" All of a sudden Tanner rolled and I was beneath him. "We work off the extra calories in inspired ways." I giggled, wondering what those were. "I'm about to get inspired now," he teased, lowering his head to kiss me.

I reached up to meet him halfway. It was a long kiss, no tongue, just a sensual moving of our lips against each other. It was just as stimulating in a kind of slow and lazy way. Arousal thrummed through my blood, and I instinctively spread my legs to make room for him. His cock was hard, but he wasn't making any move to fuck me. When the kiss was over we stared into each other's eyes for a minute, keeping our thoughts to ourselves.

"I'll be leaving soon."God, I didn't know why I'd said that, especially at a time like this. The bright glimmer of contentment in Tanner's dark eyes faded instantly, turning his eyes hard. I could have kicked myself for reminding him that this thing between us was temporary. But maybe he needed reminding, since it was what *he* wanted.

He gave me a brief kiss and rolled away. "I need a shower before my brothers get here."

I sucked down my disappointment. "I'll make some coffee." I tried but couldn't keep my eyes off Tanner's impressive form as he left the bed. His cock jutted out from his body, bobbing with a life of its own. Why hadn't he fucked me? I'd sensed that he'd been about to. I left the bed, too, and his gaze shot to me.

The intensity of the thorough look he gave my body caused my breath to catch. Lust flashed in his eyes, and then he seemed to pull himself together. He turned and entered his bathroom. I released a breath that I hadn't known I'd been holding, and walked across the hallway to my room. By the time I got there tears were rolling down my face, and I couldn't explain why. I mindlessly got a quick shower and dressed before going to the kitchen.

I realized while making the first pot of coffee that one pot was not going to do if all of Tanner's brothers showed up. Luckily, I found a tall picnic jug for cold or hot liquids. I cleaned it out and began filling it with pots of hot coffee. I was just taking out a stack of Styrofoam cups when Pops came by.

"Morning, cutie."

I turned and gave him a smile. "Good morning." It took effort to keep the grin on my face when I noticed his condition. It appeared that he'd come straight from the shower. His long, thin hair was wet and hanging loose. He'd put on a t-shirt that clung to his bony frame and a pair of shorts. It was the first time I'd seen Pops in shorts, and the thinness of his legs was appalling. His pallor was even worse than it had been the day before, and the look in his eyes revealed just how sick he was. He was shaking, too. It saddened me that I could be watching a man die right before my eyes.

"The boys coming this morning?" His tired gaze moved over the jug and cups.

"Yep," I answered in a cheery tone. "They're gonna have breakfast with you."

"Yeah. I like when they all come for breakfast. We keep it simple, cutie. None of those fancy eggs you make me eat. They'll bring donuts and we'll eat outside."

"You like my eggs," I said defensively. "And there's nothing fancy about them." I poured the fourth pot of coffee into the jug, filling it.

"Here, I'll take them cups out. Goin' out for some fresh air."

I laughed. "Is that what you're calling it now?"

He gave me a wink, grabbed the stack of cups from me, and headed out. I went to the door and watched him for a minute, catching my breath when I saw him stumble slightly. He seemed unbalanced. Watching him, I knew that I needed to leave soon. I couldn't stay there and watch him die. Just before I stepped away, five of the guys came around the corner of the house and approached Pops.

I turned back to get the jug of coffee just as Tanner came into the kitchen.

"That the coffee?" I nodded. He held his hands out and I turned it over to him.

I met the quiet contemplation in his eyes. "I'll keep it coming."

"Thank you, honey."

God, sometimes we acted so much like a normal couple, until we weren't. I grabbed the new pot of coffee and made my way outside. I noticed that Sid, Mark, Heath, and Pete weren't there yet. Pops was smoking as usual, the ever present plume of smoke whirling above his head. Mike was sitting on the ground, as all the other chairs and loungers were taken. As they noticed me approaching, it grew quiet and all eyes were on me.

Someone let out a wolf whistle. I sensed the men's eyes on me, curious, and maybe slightly lusty, but not disrespectful. I imagined that they had questions in their heads regarding what was going on between Tanner and me. I plastered a smile on my face, set the coffee pot down, and straightened. "Good morning, boys."

"Oh, boy," William mumbled, pinning his gaze on me. I returned his smile, which kind of looked like a dirty sneer.

"Sweet!" This came from Skipper. "Can't beat the view out here, that's for sure." He looked way, too happy to be sitting outside in this kind of heat.

"Lookin' damned pretty this morning, sweetheart," Gabe grinned, getting a sharp look from Tanner. "The prez sure is one lucky man."

I began to get suspicious of their comments, but said anyway, "Thank you, but the sun must be in all your eyes." I didn't have any makeup on, my hair was pulled back into a messy ponytail, and I had on raggedy denim shorts and a faded, slightly holey tank that was an old favorite.

"It's not the sun, darlin.'" In spite of the death glare being directed on him, Gabe ignored Tanner's growing anger and gave me a playful wink when he caught my eye.

Something was going on, and apparently at my expense, but I wasn't going to give them more ammunition by asking. I turned my gaze on Mike. "Would you like a chair?"

"Mike can get his own damned chair," Tanner snapped, drawing my gaze. "Get a donut before you get your ass back inside." My eyes grew round at the way he was talking to me. I was clearly missing something, and was clearly being dismissed.

I glared at him. It hadn't been that long since we'd been happily rolling around in bed. "What is your problem?" I demanded, slapping my hands on my hips. "And why are you taking out your bad mood on me?"

"Oh, damn, that just made it worse," said Mike. He grinned when Tanner turned his glare on him. "What?" he asked innocently.

With a sound that said that he'd had enough, Tanner swung his sharp gaze back to me. "Maybe you should change before you come out next time," he snarled. "Unless you get a kick out of exposing yourself to my brothers."

My brows shot up at his comment. What? I instantly glanced down, and then twisted to look behind me, but didn't see anything for cause for alarm. Then I began to feel around incase I'd forgotten to zip up or something. Someone groaned as I ran my hands over my clothes. I looked back at Tanner because I honestly didn't know what he was talking about.

"Your tit's on display," he said crudely with a tight mouth.

I glanced back down and groaned. That was an inaccurate statement, and I quickly plucked the material away from my breast, feeling an inferno of embarrassment sweep over me. "It's a nipple!" I clarified, aiming my remark at him. It wouldn't have even been noticeable if not for the fact that it was hard and peeking right through one of the holes in my shirt.

"That's worse," he stated shortly.

"How is that worse?" I asked, scowling at him. When it remained quiet I glanced around at the men present. I almost laughed at the speed at which they averted their eyes. Everyone except for Pops, who was just sat there grinning, and Ace, who never showed any emotion, anyway. "Ugh!" I threw up my hands in irritation and stomped back toward the house.

"Get a donut!" Tanner called after me.

"Go to hell!" I swore without turning back. Honestly! You would have thought that I'd done it on purpose or something. Did he think that I liked showing my nipple to all of his brothers? And why was he so angry about it? It's not as if I were his girlfriend. I shut the patio door so forcefully that the glass shook.

Chapter 38

T anner
    Jesus H Christ! I watched Ruby stomp back to the house, the sweet little crescent-shaped bottom half exposed and bouncing with every step. It was bad enough that she'd come out here with her nipple hard and poking through her shirt, giving my brothers a peek at something that was mine. Now she was giving them a show of her delectable ass and what a handful it was.

"Why you so upset, brother? It's not like we haven't seen a woman's nipple before," Gabe remarked with humor.

"Maybe it's that particular woman's nipple that he doesn't want us to see," Mike offered, grinning. "You know how it is when you get all territorial about a woman you're screwing."

"And a pretty little nipple it was, too," said Skipper.

Pops gaffed loudly, getting in on it. "You been screwing cutie, boy?" He seemed a little too happy over that prospect.

"Enough!" I finally snapped, grabbing everyone's attention. They quieted down, but it was clear from their expressions that they still found the situation funny. Ace was the only one who hadn't engaged, but there was the slightest quirk to his mouth. I wasn't in the mood for this crap. "Can we get back to the meeting now?"

Pops worked his way out of his chair. "Start without me, gotta go take a piss."

No one said anything because he didn't usually take part in our meetings. Once a week he was included because we had breakfast there, but that was about all. If he happened to voice his opinion we listened, but it was rare that he did. He was tired, and I noticed that he'd been getting weaker and thinner by the day. I released a heavy breath after he disappeared inside the house.

"Brother-"

I held my hand up, stopping Gabe from saying more. "It won't help anything. He won't go to the doctor and I have to respect his wishes, even if you and I and everyone else know that his days are numbered."

Gabe nodded his understanding. My brothers knew that when the time came it was going to be hard for all of us. I was about to take up where we'd left off discussing the changes at the strip club when a muted scream cut through the air, sending a chill through my body.

"What the fuck-"

We all jumped to our feet and ran toward the house.

• • • •

RUBY

I was grumbling beneath my breath all the way down the hallway to my room, unable to make up my mind if I was embarrassed or just plain angry over Tanner's unwarranted treatment of me. He'd acted like a possessive, jealous boyfriend, and I was tired of trying to figure him out. He couldn't seem to make up his mind, blowing hot one minute and cold the next. Well, I was going to make it easy for him by leaving as soon as possible. He'd been clear from the beginning that he didn't want a relationship, yet he'd broken his one-fuck rule for me. I still didn't have an answer as to why.

I yanked off my tee and tossed it toward the bathroom, deciding that after what had happened today I would just throw it away. I reached for another tank and pulled it on, and then walked to where the other one was on the floor. I snatched it up so that I could toss it into the trash can. As I neared the bathroom door I was able to see inside the room by the mirror over the vanity. And the reflection that I found staring back at me took my breath away.

I froze instantly, too shocked by what I was seeing to even breathe. The man I'd seen at the club the night before, and now knew without a doubt was Billy, was half-hiding behind the door. Just as I wondered if he could see me where I stood, he realized that I could see him, too. As he pulled the door open and bolted around it I let out a screech and turned to run. He caught me by the hair before I reached the door, jerking me back against him.

"Billy-" With dread I realized that it was too late to pretend that I was glad to see him.

"So you did recognize me last night," he said against my ear. "I was beginning to think that you were lost to me forever. Do you know how long I've been looking for you?"

Yeah, I did. As long as I'd been hiding from him. "You've changed, Billy," I said, hoping to feed his ego a little and get some leverage. "You're not a boy anymore, but, uh, a handsome man. I wasn't sure that it was you last night. I . . . I tried looking for you afterwards."

"Was that before or after you let that biker scum fuck you over the seat of his motorcycle?" he whispered angrily into my ear, pulling my hair until I hissed in pain. "Or after he kissed you after bitching at me for following so close?" *Ohmygod!* He'd been the one following us! "You're a little liar!" he accused between his teeth. "But I'm willing to forgive you this one last time."

I shivered in fear, my panic growing. If I could keep him talking long enough, maybe someone would come inside and help me. "How-how did you find me?"

"You mean after you just deserted me the last time?" He jerked me sharply, and I was sure the hand in my hair was going to rip it out at the roots. Tears smarted in my eyes as he twisted even more. "It was a fluke, really. There was news footage on TV about Daytona Beach Bike Week, and guess who showed up on it? The rest was easy."

I didn't see how, but I wasn't going to argue with him about it. "Billy-" I reached back for the hand that was gripping my hair. "You frightened me the last time. I didn't mean to hurt you, I swear." I thought about his parents. Their foster home had been one of the few that I'd felt welcomed in, but his weirdness had forced me to leave. "Your parents-"

He laughed, and it was an evil sound that made me shiver. "Poor mom and dad, they had a little accident. As their only son I inherited everything. Who would have thought those two stingy penny pinchers would have so much money in the bank." He jerked me closer and ground down into my face, "I have enough money to take care of us now. We can go anywhere we want."

He was sicker than I'd thought.

The way he'd said that they'd had a little accident sent warning signals through me. Looking back, I'd missed the signs that Billy had been unstable, and was most likely mentally ill. I'd been young at the time and had brushed off his unusual behavior as him just being a weird teenager who was trying to find his way. I'd often found him watching and following me. And when he'd hunted me down after I'd left his home I'd begun to suspect that maybe he saw me as more than just a foster sister. Now I was kicking myself for overlooking what had been right in front of my eyes.

"Time to go."

I heard the telltale sound that indicated someone had opened the patio door. Billy was pulling me down the hallway as if nothing was wrong. We stepped out into the kitchen area just as Pops was walking through toward the living room. He halted with surprise when his gaze fell on us. I saw his eyes move from me to the hand that was wrapped around my arm, before narrowing on my eyes. I knew there was fear on my face, because I'd never been so frightened in my life, and Pops was smart. He figured out something was wrong right away.

"What the fuck is going on?" he scowled. "Who the hell are you?" His scowl fell on Billy.

"Pops-" Even I heard the stark fear in my tone. I was about to tell him to run, he was still close enough to the door that he could make it. Maybe I could hold Billy back long enough for Pops to call for help.

"He a friend of yours?" Pops asked, still frowning.

I shook my head. "No, Pops run!"

I should have known that a man like Pops would never run. Instead of turning around and heading back to the patio door he charged toward us with a roar. I grabbed Billy by the arm to hopefully give Pops some leverage, but Billy was too strong for me. He shook me off like a pesky gnat and faced the older man with a look on his face that terrified me. I screamed as loudly as I could. Billy was big, and I knew one hit from him could probably kill Pops. I grabbed for Billy, just as he picked up Pops' frail body and body slammed him onto the floor. The sharp *oomph* that escaped from Pops revealed that his lungs had emptied of air at the jarring impact.

"Billy, no!" I screamed again, when he went to repeat what he'd just done. Pops was barely moving, and he was moaning in pain. "Billy!" I pounded my fists against him, tears falling down my cheeks, but he acted as if he didn't even feel it. He picked up Pops again and was body slamming him for a second time when the patio door flew open and Tanner and his brothers rushed inside. The rage on Tanner's face as he quickly assessed the situation caused me to step away, because I knew that he was going to go at Billy no holds barred.

I was vaguely aware that Ace had come to my side, pulling me behind him as if to protect me. Gabe and Hawk bent to Pops' still, broken body to see if they could do anything for him. They exchanged sorrowful looks with each other before glancing up at the others standing close by. In unison they slowly shook their heads. Pops was gone. No! I wailed behind Ace, my heart broken for the craggy old man I'd grown to love. Ace turned and took me into his arms, letting me sob against him. Tanner's brothers stood by the door in tense silence, their jaws locked in grief.

I watched Tanner beat into Billy without mercy, landing punch after punch into Billy's face and upper torso until his knuckles were broken and bleeding, and sweat was running down his face. The hate and violence I was seeing had transformed Tanner into a killing machine. Billy hadn't stood a chance against the experienced, older biker. By the time Tanner had finished with him, he resembled a piece of raw meat. I was shocked to see that he was still conscious.

"Oh, Billy," I sobbed shaking my head with regret while blaming myself for him being at the house in the first place. If I'd known how truly sick he'd been maybe his parents could have gotten him help and Pops would still be alive. Another sob escaped me as I looked towards Pops lifeless form.

Tanner's head snapped in my direction, while he still had a hand gripped on Billy's torn and bloody shirt. "You know this piece of shit?" he snarled in disbelief, his lips pulled tight over his teeth. I hardly recognized his face, it was so twisted. "He's the same fucker who followed us last night."

I shook my head, too distraught to comment, too afraid of the look in his eyes. My gaze darted to his brothers, who all held the same look of growing condemnation. That was when it occurred to me what they were all thinking. Calling Billy by his name had made it obvious that I knew him, and now they were thinking the worst.

I didn't want Tanner believing that I'd been a willing participant in this. "Tanner-"

"She's mine," Billy said between torn and bloody lips, recognizing the situation that I'd suddenly found myself in and purposely adding fuel to the fire. I shuddered when I saw that some of his teeth were missing.

"You brought this scum here?" Tanner's question was more of an accusation. The hate I saw in his black, blaming eyes tore my heart in half.

"No!" I cried out desperately, reaching up to wipe my eyes. "I-"

Billy's laugh was filled with madness, the look in his eyes filling me with dread. He was set to ruin me. "We lived to-together," he said, making it sound as if we'd been together as a couple. I shook my head vigorously, willing Tanner to see the truth. "She told-she told me where you'd be l-last night so I could follow you home."

"No!" I screamed, turning wild, tearful eyes on Tanner. "You know that's not true! I was a virgin-" My eyes flew back to Billy. "Billy, don't do this. Please! Tell them you're lying!" He was going to ruin the best thing that had ever happened to me. But more than that, he was going to destroy Tanner in the process. "Don't!" I pleaded before returning my eyes to Tanner. "Tanner-I've been running from him-"

Tanner just stared at me, and I saw something die in his eyes. Fresh tears rolled down my cheeks when I realized that he'd already made up his mind and that I was dead to him. He believed what Billy was telling him. "I didn't know he was here. I would have never done anything to hurt you...Pops...you have to believe me, *please*, let me explain."

"I don't have to let you do anything." The words were so cold, so final, spoken without emotion. I sobbed, watching him push Billy to the floor and then swing my way. "I knew from the beginning that you were bad news."

Without warning, he wrapped his hand around my throat and jerked me away from Ace, pushing me back until I hit the wall with a jarring thud. I opened my mouth to suck in air, feeling his fingers tighten. My hands came up to his, trying to loosen his brutal hold. "Please, Tanner-" I sobbed brokenly.

He punched the wall next to my head so violently that he left a hole."No!" His expression was wild, and I'd never felt so much loathing directed at me before. He was so enraged that he was trembling. The hard glitter in his eyes captured mine as I tried to blink away the tears. "Do you know how much I want to hurt you right now?" he growled in a low savage tone. "It makes me sick."

I wept silently, while inside I was screaming.

"Brother."

Tanner ignored the caution in Ace's voice, bringing his face down close to mine. "You want to know why I broke my one-fuck-only rule for you? Because I knew you were leaving eventually. That's the *only* reason I fucked you more than once." His words destroyed me. I sensed movement with his other hand but couldn't move, I could barely breathe. "You gave up your virginity for nothing," he hissed with barely restrained control. Before I knew it he was tossing money into my face. "You have ten fucking minutes to get your shit and get out of my house. After that, I won't be responsible for my actions."

"Brother!" This time the harsh warning came from Gabe. "Don't do anything you'll regret."

"Please let me explain," I croaked, fighting a wave of dizziness. Before it sucked me completely under, Tanner had the presence of mind to ease up his hold on my neck. "Please..." I wasn't beyond begging.

"I'm done with you." He turned and walked to where Pops' motionless body was lying.

I was determined to get the words out, even if they didn't make a difference. I put a hand up to my aching throat, swallowing with difficulty. "It's not what you think! I was running from Billy! He lived in the last foster home I was in!"

On his haunches next to Pops, Tanner took his bony hand into his. I could see the tic in his clenched jaw as he stared down at his dad, who looked as if he were just sleeping. I lost it when I saw a tear roll down his cheek. He glanced up to where his brothers hadn't moved. "Feed that scum to the alligators."

"Noooooo!" Billy groaned, hearing what they had planned for him. He tried to move, but couldn't.

Mike and Skipper moved toward Billy. Tanner glanced back at me, hate and sorrow in his eyes. I hadn't moved from the wall. He made eye contact with Ace and jerked his head toward me in silent communication. Ace took me gently by the arm. I made a last ditch attempt to get Tanner to listen to me, digging in my heels when Ace tried to pull me away.

"I know you blame me for this. I know you hate me. I was wrong for not telling you about Billy. But I never thought for a minute that he'd find me again. I didn't know how mentally ill he was. I'm sorry for that. I'm sorry for everything." A sob escaped me as I realized that I was about to bare my soul to him. "But I'm not sorry for loving you."

Tanner didn't move, didn't acknowledge me in any way. I could have been speaking to a block of ice he was so cold and unfeeling. Through blurry eyes I looked toward his brothers, and the only one who'd meet my gaze was Gabe. "I loved Pops, too," I whispered brokenly.

I let Ace guide me from the room, hearing someone say that they'd call in a clean-up crew. It wouldn't take me long to gather my meager belongings and leave, if only I wasn't blinded by the tears that wouldn't stop flowing from my eyes. I felt sick inside. My heart hurt. Ace stood watching as I tossed my things into my bag and made my way back to the kitchen. My eyes fell to the money that Tanner had thrown on me and was now strewn on the floor, but I ignored it. Tanner was nowhere around, and neither was Pops.

Ace followed me all the way to the front door. "I can find my way from here," I said in a small voice. I felt drained, and I no longer had the energy to care about anything.

"Are you okay to drive?" he asked. I smiled weakly at the concern in his voice but just nodded, taking a step. A hand on my arm stopped me. "Are you sure, sweetheart?" I clenched my jaw to keep from crying again. I nodded, unable to look at him.

I managed to make it to my car, toss my bag into the back, and get behind the wheel. I sat there in misery, letting the events of the last hour wash over me, and buried my face in my arms against the steering wheel. "I'm sorry, Pops! I'm so sorry!" I sobbed uncontrollably. I wasn't sure how long I'd been sitting there when someone tapped on the window beside me. I sat back reluctantly and looked up to see Ace standing there. How long had he been there?

He made a gesture for me to put the window down. I cranked it halfway, and then ran my hands over my wet cheeks. His expression revealed nothing, as usual, yet I wanted to believe that there was a smidgen of compassion in his eyes.

"You remember how to get to my place?"

That was the last thing I'd expected him to say. I thought about it for a second before giving him a nod. "Why?"

He handed me a key. "I want you to go there and wait for me."

"But why?"

"Tanner is hurting right now, hell, we all are. But he needs a few days to deal, and I don't want him regretting for the rest of his life something that he did in the heat of the moment."

I thought about what Ace, was saying but refused to give in to hope. "I think the best thing for me to do is just move on," I said weakly, not really wanting to.

He released a frustrated breath. "Go to my house," he insisted in a firm tone. "And don't make me have to hunt you down for my only house key."

I couldn't speak as emotion threatened to consume me again. I nodded and turned the key in the ignition. I backed up, noticing in my rearview mirror that Ace was still standing there, watching me, and making sure that I drove away.

Chapter 39

R^{uby}

I was numb. I couldn't think. I couldn't function. The pain of Pops dying would never go away, the pain caused by Tanner's words had settled like a cold, dark void inside me, surrounding my heart and anything else vital that I needed to survive. I felt cold all over, and I wondered if this was what dying felt like because everything that had mattered to me was gone. I hadn't had much, but it had been just enough. Enough to make life worth living.

I loved Tanner. He hated me. Those were the only two things I was certain of. I'd cried until there'd been no tears left to shed, until I was drained and sick to my stomach, my face swollen and blotchy. At least that's the face that had looked back at me in the review mirror when I'd first arrived at Ace's house. I was surprised that I'd managed to find it, considering that I couldn't remember driving there.

I couldn't bring myself to go inside Ace's house. It somehow felt wrong, and I didn't know how long I'd been sitting on his porch, just staring straight out in front of me at the yard. It looked a lot different than the first time I'd been there. Now it was clean and neat and quiet. Only one grill was visible, set up beneath the huge, moss-covered oak tree we'd all sat under on the day of the cookout. A variety of lawn chairs were folded up and were leaning against the tree.

What was I doing there? I should just leave. I could leave Ace's key somewhere where he could easily find it and just take off. But as soon as the thought entered my head I had to remind myself that my car was closer to being on empty than full or even halfway full, and I was broke. I wouldn't get very far, unless I could work up the nerve to ask for a small loan from Ace with the promise that once I got settled somewhere and found work, I'd repay him. And that's when I thought about Jimmy. I had his contact information. Maybe he could help me.

The sound of a motorcycle getting close to the house revealed that Ace was on his way. I watched as he slowed his bike and finally came to a stop. Kicking the stand down, he removed his helmet and dismounted. He took the stairs to the porch two at a time and then he was standing above me and looking down. I couldn't meet his eyes, keeping mine focused on his parked bike as if it would protect me.

He finally released a loud breath that revealed his annoyance. "You been out here this whole time?"

I sensed movement and glanced up to see him crossing his arms. "Yeah. I just couldn't bring myself to go inside." I handed him his key. He took it from me and leaned back against the rail. "Why are you being nice to me?"

"I'm not a nice man, Ruby." I winced, but didn't look away. "Tanner is my brother and I don't want to see him make a mistake that will ruin him."

"I don't understand," I said honestly.

"Right now he's angry. He feels betrayed and used and he isn't thinking clearly. He just lost his father and the woman he loves all in one day." The woman he loves? My confusion must have shown on my face because he continued. "Tanner loves you, he just doesn't know it yet. Or he does know it, and he's in denial." Ace paused, narrowing his eyes on mine as if he could see the truth there. "I need to know if what you said about loving him was the truth."

I felt a fresh wave of tears gather in my eyes, and I bit down on my bottom lip to keep from releasing them. I could only nod at first, vigorously. Then a sob escaped me, and I cried, "Yes! I love him more than anything. But I don't think any of that will matter, Ace. A man I knew came here and killed Pops. How do we get through that? How will Tanner ever forgive me?"

"So tell me why he should."

I shrugged, wiping my cheeks. "I wouldn't forgive me," I said softly. "Billy caused Pops' death."

"That's right, Billy caused Pops' death, not you. You're not responsible for the actions of others, Ruby."

"But he was here because of me."

"Did you invite him here?" I shook my head. "Was he here as your family?" I continued to shake my head. "As a friend?" Again, no. "A lover?"

"Never!" I said with feeling. "Tanner knows he was my first."

"And he thinks you used your innocence as a way to get close to him, to get him to drop his guard."

"Yeah, he made that clear." I couldn't help the slight bitterness in my tone. "Does he know that I'm here?"

"No." Ace straightened. "Give him time. In the meantime, make yourself to home." With that, Ace disappeared inside the house.

That had been four days ago. Ace had come and gone several times since then, never explaining himself other than to say that he'd be back. I felt more like an intruder in his house than a guest. We rarely spoke, didn't take meals together, we were just taking up the same space. I began to wonder how long I could keep up this hopeless existence, how long he would tolerate me. I supposed that it all boiled down to how much he loved Tanner.

Tanner. I hadn't heard anything from Ace about how he was doing. I didn't ask, afraid of what his answer would be. I imagined that he was drowning in grief, as I was, as we all were, because I'd known that Tanner's brothers had all loved Pops. None of the others had come by, and I was secretly thankful for that. I was left alone with my sorrow, and thoughts of what I could have possibly done differently.

Pops burial was later today at Daytona Memorial Park. Ace had been gone when I woke up, but he'd been thoughtful enough to leave a note with the details of the service. I wanted to go, but I was afraid of what kind of reception I'd get. Did they throw unwelcome people out of funerals? Maybe I could remain in the background somehow. I at least owed it to Pops to show him respect, and to tell him that I was sorry one last time before I left the area for good. But when I dug through my clothes I couldn't find anything suitable for a funeral.

Did it really matter if I showed up in jeans and the only black top that I owned? I decided that it didn't, especially if no one noticed that I was there. I got a shower and dressed in my best jeans and a black georgette blouse with cutouts, still not a hundred percent sure that I was doing the right thing. I arranged my hair in a soft bun and put on dark sunglasses, hoping that one small thing would give me enough of a disguise.

One thing I was sure of, my car wouldn't go unnoticed. I decided to skip the service and went straight to the cemetery. I parked in the last spot, as far away from the motorcycles as I could. I was amazed at how many were present. Thankfully, no one noticed my arrival, as they were all heading toward the gravesite. I'd purposely come late so that I could remain at the back.

I saw some familiar faces, people I'd met on Main Street, and later at Ace's house. When I spied Lonnie and Judith I dropped back, feeling like I was doing something wrong. I immediately searched for Mark and Sid, finding them a few feet behind the women. Mark looked directly at me when he turned his head to say something to Sid, and I quickly glanced away, hoping that he hadn't noticed me. God, I was going to be sick before it was all over.

Why had I ever thought this would be a good idea? And damn Ace for leaving the information behind. It was as if he'd done it on purpose, knowing that I couldn't stay away. I tried to slow my heart rate by taking several deep breaths, reminding myself that I was there for Pops. I had every right to say goodbye. Eventually we arrived at the open gravesite. Everyone began to spread out until they circled the plain, yet beautiful, mahogany casket placed atop the casket lowering device.

I kept my eyes lowered as a few words were spoken, under the illusion that if I didn't make eye contact with anyone that I wouldn't be recognized, and then the casket was slowly and carefully lowered into the ground. A river of tears flowed steadily down my cheeks, and my mouth was trembling uncontrollably as I watched the casket disappear from sight. That's when I glanced up to see Tanner standing with his arm over the shoulder of an older woman. She was weeping silently, and I had to assume that this was Marge, Pops' sister. Next to them were Tanner's brothers, and some of Pops' club members who'd come to lunch that day at the house.

A lot of people had shown up to show their respects. I watched as hugs were exchanged, as well as words of sympathy. Tanner's expression appeared drawn and set in stone, and yet he acknowledged every one with a head nod and one or two words. His aunt offered watery smiles and not much else. An elderly couple walked up to them and she threw herself into their arms, sobbing loudly. Words were exchanged and the couple walked off, taking Tanner's aunt with them.

I'm not sure what alerted Tanner that I was there, but all of a sudden he was looking in my direction. Even though he was wearing sunglasses I could feel the burn of his stare. I don't know how long we stood like that, just looking at one another, but I knew when his attention was drawn away by an approaching couple that it was time to leave. I realized as I turned and began to walk briskly away that I was saying goodbye to more than just Pops right then. I was glad that no one stopped to talk to me.

I went straight back to Ace's, packed my stuff, and loaded up my car. As soon as he got home I'd give him his key, thank him for his hospitality, and beg him for a loan. I had to get out of there. There was nothing holding me back now. I'd said my goodbyes, and it hurt too much to be in this town and not have Tanner. I was sitting on the porch when I heard the sound of his motorcycle. Only it wasn't Ace who pulled up in front of the porch.

I could barely breathe as Tanner turned off his bike, kicked down the stand, and sat there staring straight ahead. He hadn't worn his helmet, I could see the muscle working in his jaw, and his hair had that mussed look that I liked. For the first time I noticed that he wasn't wearing a suit. No, he was dressed like the bad ass that he was, showing the world that he was the president of the Sentinels. I'd been so grief-stricken at the cemetery and afraid of being noticed that I hadn't noticed what anyone had been wearing. Not that it had mattered.

I opened my mouth to speak, and then closed it. He must have followed me from the cemetery. The sound of another motorcycle revealed that Ace would soon be there. He pulled right up next to Tanner and shut down. Both men looked at each other.

"You fucking kidding me, brother?" Tanner began in a tone that intensified with each word. "You brought her here to your house?"

I couldn't tell if Tanner was angry over my being there with Ace, or over the fact that I was still in town.

I didn't want to cause trouble between them. "I'm leaving." They both ignored me.

"She's in my bed now," Ace said with a smirk. Then he shrugged. "You didn't want her."

What the hell was he doing? My eyes grew round with disbelief and I jumped to my feet, nearly knocking over the chair. "No I'm not!" I shouted, this time drawing both their gazes.

Ace dismounted his bike and began walking toward me. "You got a connecting bath in your room?" he asked smugly. I looked at Tanner's shocked gaze before snapping my gaze back to Ace. "My bedroom is the only room with a connecting bath, sweetheart," he went on to explain.

He'd given me his room? My gaze shot back to Tanner. "I didn't know! He-I-we're not sharing the bed, Tanner, I swear!" Why would Ace set me up in his bedroom?

"Yet," Ace put in purposefully. I glared at him, closing my hand with the need to punch the cocky look right off his face. What was he doing? He was only making it worse by taunting Tanner like that. He spun back to Tanner. "Why should you care where she's living or who she's fucking? You know I'd never make a move on one of your women until I was sure that you were done with her. And I clearly heard you tell her to get lost."

"You son-of-a-bitch!" Tanner swore, leaving his bike and flying toward Ace with a look of betrayal and rage on his flushed face. He tossed his sunglasses aside and threw himself at Ace, giving him a solid punch to his jaw.

I screamed. Ace stumbled several steps back, but managed to remain on his feet. He rubbed his jaw as the two men faced off. "Wait." He held a hand toward Tanner as if to hold him off. "Before you hit me again, brother, ask yourself why you're doing it." Tanner stopped short, heeding the subtle suggestion in Ace's slightly humorous tone. "Why does it matter if Ruby is in my bed or not?"

I wished he'd stop implying that, it only made Tanner bare his teeth and snarl like a mad dog. Yes, why did it matter? But as the silence grew, and it became obvious that he wasn't going to respond to Ace's question, I couldn't take it anymore. Before I burst out in tears and revealed how much his silence hurt, I was going to take off. Forget asking Ace for a loan, I'd go as far as my damned car would take me, and figure out what to do then.

Emotion choked me, and, clenching my teeth, I walked quietly toward them. I met Ace's serious eyes and handed him his key. "Thank you for your hospitality, Ace, and for being so kind." I sensed Tanner's eyes on me but refused to meet his gaze. I couldn't bear to see his cold hatred and rejection of me. Once Ace curled his hand around the key I'd dropped into it I turned to leave.

I got all the way down the steps and to my car when Tanner's hard voice cut across the distance. "Where the fuck do you think you're going?"

Was he serious? I didn't glance back, not even when I heard the front door of the house open and close. I paused at my car door with my hand on the handle and sucked in a deep breath to steady my nerves. "Away, Tanner. You wanted me to leave, so I'm doing it."

"You wait until I show up and just decide to leave?"

I closed my eyes because I knew by the sound of his voice that he was moving closer to me. "I packed up my stuff after I returned from—" I hesitated and then pulled myself together, "Pops' funeral. I was just waiting for Ace to return so I could give him his key and then thank him."

Sensing his nearness, I opened my eyes to see that I was caged in by two muscular arms on either side of me, his palms flat upon the surface of my car. I could feel the heat of his large body behind me. I wanted to lean back against him, and fought against it. Something came alive inside of me, a tiny shard of hope.

"You're not going anywhere *yet*."

I swallowed hard at his gruff voice that was so close to my ear. It didn't give anything away as to what Tanner may be feeling at the moment. A few seconds ago he'd been ready to pound on Ace, but why? I was anxious to know the answer to the question Ace had put to him right before I'd walked away. I wanted to believe that Tanner's reaction to the suggestion that I'd been sleeping with Ace was because he still wanted me.

But more importantly than anything else right then was telling him how sorry I was about Pops. I'd told him before, but I doubted he'd heard much of anything I'd had to say that day. "I'm so sorry about Pops, Tanner," I said softly. "So very sorry."

"I know, baby," he whispered into my ear, his tone full of sorrow and regret. "I'm sorry for the way things went down." I knew that he was talking about how he'd treated me. "I know that it wasn't your fault, but that day, I was blind with rage. All I could see was Pops' broken body, and then hearing that you knew the attacker-" He cut himself off.

"You believed the worst."

"Yes." After a long silence he added, "And I'll be sorry for that for the rest of my life, Ruby. You didn't deserve that, you were just as much a victim, you were just as torn up over Pops. And all I did was threaten you and tell you to get out."

I could only nod, too overcome with emotion right then. As soon as he'd called me "baby" the tears had begun to gather, clouding my eyes.

He released a heavy sigh. "God, I'm so fucking glad you didn't take off. When I looked up at the cemetery and saw you, I realized that I was given a chance to make things right with you. But then I got distracted, and by the time I looked up again you were pulling out of the parking lot."

"Ace told you where I was?"

He gave a sharp laugh. "No, Gabe told me where you were. Apparently everyone else knew." I smiled at that. "Baby . . ." All of a sudden he was nuzzling his nose against my neck. "Turn around."

He didn't have to ask me twice. I knew I looked a wreck, and a deep breath turned into a sob but I faced him anyway. He hadn't removed his arms so I was still caged in, and I leaned back against my car to put a little more distance between us. My gaze rose slowly to his.

His hand came up, and Tanner rubbed the back of his knuckles against my cheek. "So fucking beautiful," he whispered, as if to himself. "So sweet. You dug your way deep into my heart before I even knew that you'd breached the barriers." He turned his hand and ran his thumb over my bottom lip. "I need you, Ruby. I need you like I need air to breathe. If you had left Daytona I would have looked for you."

"What are you saying, Tanner?" I was too afraid to make any assumptions. "You want me to stay?"

"Hell, yes, honey. I want you to stay. With me. I love you, Ruby." I caught my breath, the crack in my heart mending. "I realized how much as soon as you left my house. I'd convinced myself that I'd broken my one-time-only fuck rule for you because you wouldn't be staying, but I was only fooling myself." He was halfway to lowering his face to mine and I thought, *yes, kiss me please,* but then he stopped and looked deep into my eyes. "Can you forgive me, Ruby? If you'll give me a chance to be in your life, I promise to spend the rest of mine proving how much I want and need you."

"Tanner-"

"Yes, baby?"

"Kiss me, please."

With a growl of need he closed the distance between us and slammed his mouth down on mine. I wrapped my arms around his neck, and his closed in around me until we were locked tightly together. We explored each other's mouths with unrestrained passion, tasting and nibbling, grinding our mouths together to the point of delicious pain. The kind of pain that awarded us immense pleasure while healing our broken souls.

Tanner's rough possession claimed my whole being and I gave him everything, willingly, showing him how much I loved him. He held nothing back. This strong, bad ass biker was exposing his emotions, and showing me that he could do love. I was in a state of bliss, in the safe arms of my man, knowing that there was no one else for me.

As he started to pull away I sucked on his tongue, bringing about another wild moment of wet kisses until we had to part in order to breathe. Overwhelmed, it was all we could do to lean into each other and gasp for air. In time I realized that Tanner was crushing me against my car, and I welcomed his weight against me.

"I love you."

He leaned back and captured my eyes. "I don't deserve you. But I'm a selfish bastard and I'm claiming you. Everyone will know that from this day forward, you belong to me."

His possessiveness wrapped around me like a warm cloak, making me feel safe and protected. Making me feel loved. I thought about his words. I had my own demands. "That works both ways, Tanner." I couldn't keep the expression on my face serious while he had a sexy, crooked smile on his.

"I don't want anyone else, honey. Only you. Are we good?"

I made him wait for my answer, watching the worry replace the hope in his dark eyes. "I suppose," I teased, trying not to smile, but failing miserably.

"You suppose?" he repeated with a raised brow. "Maybe I need to work more on convincing you." He lowered his face to within inches of mine. "And if this kiss doesn't work, I'll be forced to take you home, where I'll fuck you until you respond with a little more enthusiasm."

"That sounds like a threat."

He'd been about to kiss me when he jerked back at my words. "It is, Trouble. I've missed you. I'm looking forward to fucking you into submission, until neither of us can walk. Does that work for you?" he growled.

God, yes! I screamed to myself. My heart felt like it was about to burst, it was so full of love for this man. I gave him my answer in the way of pulling his head the rest of the way down and planting my lips onto his. I may have taken the initiative, but Tanner took control and kissed me back like a drowning man searching for sustenance.

THE SENTINELS

And when the earth-shattering, mind-blowing, all-consuming kiss was over, there were no doubts left on either side.

Epilogue

One year later
Tanner

Fuck, I was nervous, and it didn't help that I was dressed in a monkey suit, uncomfortable as hell, because I'd wanted to give my girl the dream wedding that she'd wanted. I'd known for a long time now that I'd do anything for Ruby, anything to keep that beautiful smile on her face and the sparkling light in her eyes. And here I was, standing at the altar with Gabe as my best man and the rest of my brothers taking up the first pew, Aunt Marge sitting in the midst of them.

As I reached up to loosen the constricting collar and tie around my throat for the umpteenth time, the most beautiful woman in the world walked through the double doors at the end of the aisle. Christ, she looked like an angel, all in white, her gown and long veil flowing around the gorgeous shape of her. It appeared that she was floating above the ground. The full skirt hid her baby bump, while the tight bodice pushed her tits up and over the top, making my mouth water. Jesus, how did I ever get to be so lucky?

My heart puffed up with pride because this woman was mine.

She was radiant, her smile never wavering and clearly seen through the lace of her veil. She was holding tight to Ace's arm. Much to everyone's surprise, she'd asked him to walk her down the aisle, and, shocker, he'd said yes. They'd developed a close relationship since the time she'd spent at his house, but I suspected that it had more to do with his making me see what was right before my eyes that had made him so special to Ruby. I didn't want to think about where I'd be today if he hadn't stopped her from leaving.

Yes, I did. I would have moved heaven and earth to find her.

As she glided closer, my heart swelled. I fucking loved this woman, and she was making dreams come true for me that I'd never even contemplated having. The fact that she was carrying my sons was the icing on the cake. I'd convinced myself that a wife and family weren't in the cards for me. Now I had both, and in three short months our boys would be here, and life would be complete.

As Ruby reached me I saw the tears glistening in her happy eyes. I reached forward automatically for her small hands, taking them in mine and squeezing lightly to let her know that everything was okay. With trembling lips she mouthed the words, 'I love you', and I said them back. And then together we turned toward the preacher to begin a new chapter in our lives.

The End

Thank you for reading my book! The Sentinels continues with ACE, due out late 2018.

ACE

A road side bombing left Ace disfigured and dead inside. He faces the world with silent bitterness and a damaged ego. Then a quiet beauty comes into his life, cracking the shell around his wounded heart and healing his soul.

Phantom Riders MC Trilogy

Phantom Riders MC - Book 1

Betrayal leaves Hawk, president of an outlaw motorcycle club distrustful and hating woman. Once he's satisfied his animal urges he casts them aside without a second thought. But then Audra shows up, threatening his club and way of life and Hawk has to decide to turn the sexy pint-sized package of trouble loose, or claim her for his own.

No Mercy - Book 2

Rock's the VP of Phantom Riders MC. Dangerous. Unpredictable. Ruthless. A killer who'll stop at nothing to keep what's his. Allie had given Rock her virginity, and then ran away when she got pregnant. Club trouble doesn't stop him from showing up at her door seven years later, demanding his son, and claiming her.

What He Wants - Book 3

Big John...club enforcer. He's big and scary and he sets his sights on Daisy the instant he locks eyes on the curvy beauty. Daisy...she's grown strong and independent since leaving an abusive marriage, but nothing prepares her for the hulking, sexy biker who wants to claim her!

Ruthless - Book 1

Blurb - Wildman forced Rebel to take Ginger's innocence in a sick and twisted initiation to prove his loyalty. He helps her escape, and she disappears soon after, helping herself to his money first. Four years later he tracks the innocent beauty down, but it isn't just his money that he's after. He wants Ginger for himself, and he'll go to any lengths to claim her.

Dangerous - Book 2

Jace is a nomad, an outlaw biker who likes to work alone. Fierce, dangerous, a killer when he needs to be. He calls no place home, and no woman owns his heart. Until *her*. Luna.

Furious - Book 3

Moody had it all once, and lost it in a heartbeat. Now he goes through life as a cold, heartless nomad. A man to avoid and be afraid of, uncaring that each day could be his last. He gives a fuck about nothing and no one, until an innocent woman appears out of nowhere, unafraid of his fury, challenging his demons, making him want to live again. Is he strong enough to let her into his heart?

Don't miss out!

Visit the website below and you can sign up to receive emails whenever Tory Richards publishes a new book. There's no charge and no obligation.

https://books2read.com/r/B-A-WTJ-PKUU

BOOKS 2 READ

Connecting independent readers to independent writers.

Did you love *The Sentinels*? Then you should read *Ace*[1] by Tory Richards!

[2]

The Sentinels continues with ACE.Standalone MC romances!A road side bombing left Ace disfigured and dead inside. He faces the world with silent bitterness and a damaged ego. Then a quiet beauty comes into his life cracking the shell around his wounded heart and healing his soul.

Read more at www.toryrichards.com.

1. https://books2read.com/u/mZPWZl

2. https://books2read.com/u/mZPWZl

Also by Tory Richards

Desert Rebels MC
Cole
Demon
LD

Nomad Outlaws Trilogy
Ruthless
Dangerous
Furious

Phantom Riders MC Trilogy
Phantom Riders MC - Hawk
No Mercy
What He Wants

The Evans Brothers Trilogy
A Perfect Fit
Surrender to Desire

Burning Hunger

Standalone
Up in Flames
Bishop's Angel
The Mating Ritual
Out of Control
Wicked Desire
Someone to Love Me
Wild Marauders MC
Big, Black and Beautiful
Carnal Hunger
Dark Menace MC - Stone
His Possession
No Escape
The Evans Brothers Trilogy
The Sentinels
Hands-On
Kiss Me!
Obsession
Wild Surrender
All the Right Moves
Hers to Claim
Nothing But Trouble
One Night Only
The Cowboy Way
Ace
The Alpha Wolf's Mate
A Soldier's Promise
Taken by the Outlaw

Watch for more at www.toryrichards.com.

About the Author

Tory Richards is a fun-loving grandma who writes smut with a plot. Born in 1955 in the small town of Milo, Maine, she's lived most of her life in Florida where she went to school, married and raised a daughter.

Penning stories by hand at ten, and then on manual typewriter at the age of thirteen, Tory was a closet writer until the encouragement of her family prompted her into submitting to a publisher. She's been published since 2005, and has since retired from Disney to focus on family, friends, traveling, and writing.

Read more at www.toryrichards.com.

Lightning Source UK Ltd.
Milton Keynes UK
UKHW040809271022
411151UK00001B/29